M000082087

Burning Bright

Burning Bright

JAY S. RUSSELL

ST. MARTIN'S PRESS
NEW YORK

ISBN 0-312-18545-6

First published in the UK by Robinson Publishing Ltd.

First U.S. Edition: May 1998

10 9 8 7 6 5 4 3 2 1

For Jane Stokes,
who gave me the dream

ONE

⌒

'This girl is buck naked.'

'Sir?'

I lowered the newspaper and glanced at the driver. He had big flecks of dandruff on the back of his collar. A healthy dollop of hair oil, too. I couldn't recall the last time I'd even seen hair oil. He sized me up by way of the rear-view.

'Here. In the paper. Right on – Jesus Christ! – page three. A naked broad, with enormous . . . hell, I don't think she's old enough to be a broad. "Sexy Sarah, 22," it says here. "Swansea Sizzler". What's that supposed to mean? And why should I care that she likes Mars bars? What is a Mars bar, anyway? Anything like a Milky Way?'

'First time in England, sir?' the driver asked. All I could see reflected in the mirror were his tiny brown eyes, but they looked awfully amused.

'Actually no,' I mumbled, turning my attention back to the photograph. No *way* she was 22. 'But it's, uh, been a while.'

'The Page Three Girls have been with us for some time now,' the driver said. 'A gift from Mr R. Murdoch. An institution, some might even say.'

'Like the Queen, you mean?'

'More like the Duchess of York, I should think. How long since your last visit across the pond, might I ask?'

I had to stop and think about that one. I knew it was sometime after my sitcom, *Salt & Pepper*, had been cancelled, but before my acting career sank to the very bottom of the toilet. It was at a point when I still *had* an acting career. At least, that *particular* acting career.

'Going on – oh, man – twenty-five years, I think. I can't remember, to tell you the truth. I'm pretty sure I liked it, though.'

'Ah, well,' the driver said, 'time does move slowly here. That's our blessing and our curse, we English. There are a lot more cars, a few less hopes. Mrs Thatcher, you know. It is still England, though. Some things never change.'

'*Everything* changes,' I told him. There must have been something in my tone of voice, because the driver half-turned to look at me over his snow-capped shoulder. I thought I saw him give a resentful nod of agreement before he turned back to study the road.

Everything changes.

I should know. I've had more ups and downs than a manic depressive elevator jockey. From child TV star to teenaged has-been. From the heights of Hollywood celebrity to the depths of anonymous ignominy. From glitzy nights in spanking new Jags to dull days in dented old Subarus. From the perfumed cleavage of Swansea Sizzlers to . . .

Oh, hell, you get the idea.

And for just over a year now I've been on a whiplash climb back from the pits to the peaks. One day I'm a bargain basement private investigator running skip traces and credit repos on overextended Chicanos in East LA, the next I'm the toast of the town, regaling Oprah and Dave and Larry King with my exploits as a latter-day St George, having slain the fiercest of movie-land dragons. Overnight, it seems, I went from having my HBO turned-off for not paying the bill to starring in my own network show.

Back on top: back on the tube.

As a result of having dispatched (with a lot of luck and more than a little help from some unusual friends) back to the pit from which he slithered the late-but-couldn't-be-late-enough Jack Rippen – multimedia mega-mogul and would-be demon lord of Los Angeles – I landed smack dab on my Florsheims. (Of course, technically I landed flat on my back, what with an extended hospital stay, but we're talking figuratively here, so what the hey. Oh, and I wear Bruno Maglis now. Damned if O.J.'s going to ruin perfectly good footwear for the rest of us.) Before I could even complete the circuit of talk shows – which I propose as a new Olympic event; it would be infinitely more relevant, not to mention gruelling, than any mere marathon or decathlon – I had inked the papers making me the main man in *Burning Bright*, a new detective series. I hadn't acted in twenty years – a fact which seemed to worry no one other than me; though of course, it is the Fox Network that I work for, the people who brought you *Herman's Head* – and I would have sworn on a stack of Gutenbergs and a whole cemetery's worth of my mother's graves that I'd never do it again.

But there you go: never believe a goddamn thing anyone tells you, especially actors. And make *sure* that their mother's really dead when they start swearing on her grave.

In any case, back before the cameras went I. Marty Burns starring as Marty Burns, PI. Mean streets. Man not himself mean. Walking alone. You know the genre. You can probably hum the theme music in your sleep.

The thing of it is, though, the real kick in the head: I'm pretty good.

All right, so De Niro isn't glancing nervously behind him and Gwyneth Paltrow isn't worried about losing the cover of *People* just yet, but I've watched the finished product and all things considered I'm not too bad. (I categorically dismiss the comment by the *LA Times* critic who wrote that my acting was 'as flaccid as the shrivelled organ of an elderly saltpeter salesman.' A typo, surely.)

My own thesping notwithstanding, *Burning Bright*'s been a hit. If not a Top-Ten, keys-to-Fort-Knox, have-your-way-with-my-daughter bonanza, the show is, at least, a hanging-in-there, buy-you-a-drink, have-you-met-my-divorced-sister sort of deal.

A Fox Network (but not *The X-Files* or *Simpsons*) kind of hit.

A renewed-for-another-season, praise-be-to-Allah kind of hit.

A we've-sold-the-overseas-rights-go-and-promote-it kind of hit.

A free trip to England, first-class all the way, which is more than good enough for me. That kind of hit.

So go figure.

'Everything changes,' I said again, shaking my head and leaning back into the limo's plush upholstery.

'If you say so, sir.'

I tossed the newspaper aside and stared out the window. Except for being on the wrong side of the road – another thing I had sort of forgotten about and was finding surprisingly unnerving even as a passenger – the landscape around Heathrow looked like the surrounding terrain of any big city airport: dull, flat and thick with traffic. I opened up the limo's mini-bar, tucked away in a corner, and browsed through the little bottles. While I'd never say I never drink, I rarely put down the hard stuff on plane trips, especially long ones. Most people go ga-ga over the booze in first-class – somehow ignoring the fact that, if you actually broke down the price of the ticket, each of those little glasses was setting you back something like a double sawbuck. Some just drink to relieve the boredom or to help them get to sleep. But even though I don't get airsick, something about drinking when flying makes me want to throw up.

Which is odd, because usually it's not drinking when not flying that makes me want to heave.

'No beer,' I said, with disappointment. Somewhere in the back of my head I had a fond memory of British beer.

'Oh yes, sir,' the driver said. 'On the shelf to your right. Above the glasses.'

I slid back a little compartment and sure enough, found a row of tall cans.

'I don't know any of these brands,' I said. 'And the cans are warm.' Another, not so fond Blighty beer memory was creeping up on me.

'They're supposed to be. It's bitter, sir. There should be a lager or two in the fridge, though. Perhaps more to your liking.'

Another root through the mini-bar turned up a semi-cold can of Stella Artois. The driver jealously glanced my way as I popped it open with that delightful 'chusshhhh!' which is equally lovely in any country.

'Pretty good,' I said, ignoring the glasses and taking a hefty swallow. 'British beer is as good as I remember.'

'It's Belgian,' the driver sighed. 'Brewed under licence.'

I glanced at the side of the can. 'Huh, so it is. But only since, uh, 1367 it says here. Still, I think I'm going to enjoy this little visit.'

'I'm sure you will, sir.'

Wrong, wrong, wrong.

The folks from the satellite channel who'd bought the UK rights to *Burning Bright* had me booked at the Savoy. The evening traffic in central London was murder, but I asked the driver to take the long way around and show me a few of the sights. We cruised up the expensive streets of Chelsea and Kensington and down the overrated shopping Mecca of Knightsbridge. I had a fame flashback as we drove past good old Harrods, an incident which I honestly hadn't thought about in years.

It was during my first visit to London when I was seventeen, hot with the success of *Salt & Pepper* and as obnoxious as a human being can possibly be. I'd been cajoled into a spur of the moment jaunt to Europe by my blonde bimbo du jour, a wannabe model whose IQ didn't come to three digits even if you threw in her prodigious chest size. She ditched me somewhere on Carnaby Street (this was when that name actually meant something) for a gravelly-voiced folk singer in a black turtleneck, and I somehow got hitched up with an Italian macrame tutor with a hard-on for hallucinogens and an ass like a heart. I think peyote may have figured in it somehow, but we ended up screwing like gophers on a king-sized bed in the Harrods display hall. Quite a crowd had gathered before the security guards came for us, and at the time it was the most applause I'd ever garnered for a performance in front of a live audience. I'm not completely clear on how we didn't end up in jail, but I think it involved sharing our stash with the security guards (ah, the sixties) and buying the bed. I know it never got delivered, not to me anyway, though to this day, tucked away somewhere in a box in the hall closet, I've got a rainbow macrame plant holder hand-woven by my mad Italian bella. I wonder where she is now?

We inched our way through the traffic towards the seat of government in Westminster. I actually made the driver pull over so I could gawk at Parliament like some camera-laden tourist from Bloomington. The sight of Big Ben and the winding Thames at sunset struck me with a sudden and overwhelming sense of unreality. The big clock tower and the gothic spires of the halls of Parliament, impressive as they are, seemed as absurd and inauthentic as Cinderella's Castle in Disneyland. I think maybe that's the legacy of a century of culture based around images from movies and television: we've seen everything from the Washington monument to the Taj Mahal so many times, in so many *fake* contexts, that even the real thing feels like just another prop or special visual effect. And one, you get the feeling, that Industrial Light & Magic could probably do better. Sad, really.

'Say,' I asked the driver, 'why is it called Big Ben, anyway?'

'I haven't the faintest bloody idea,' he said. 'It is rather big.'

'Hmmm,' I muttered. I know that the residents of any city are usually the worst informed about its history, but at least I could explain how Disneyland got its name.

The driver asked if I wanted to continue the tour, but I suddenly felt the jet-lag start to kick in and thought maybe I should hold out for a hipper tour guide. I told him to just head for the hotel. I was a little surprised that there was no one there to meet me – it doesn't take long before you come to expect star treatment everywhere you go, even when you're a lightly rebounding has-been like me – but a very nice suite indeed awaited me, with the obligatory basket of semi-rotten fruit and a bottle of lukewarm champagne. I tipped the bellboy, a tad over-generously judging from his reaction, kicked off my shoes and sprawled out on the bed.

There was a remote on the night table so I flipped on the television. For some reason, I could only tune in five channels, other than the hotel ones offering dirty movies and information about room service, and two of them had shows about gardening on. Two fat slobs were playing darts on another channel, while this oily guy in a tuxedo, with all the charm of a sideshow barker, kept screaming 'Game on!' and yelling out their scores as they tossed the darts. I couldn't find the satellite station I'd crossed the ocean to promote and reckoned that the television must be broken. I thought about dialling down to the front desk to ask them to bring up a working TV, but the darts action suddenly got exciting, with the really obese dude coming from behind against the merely-big-as-a-house guy. Even so, I fell fast asleep before I got to see who won.

Game off!

TWO

〜

The television woke me up the next morning. The hotel had one of those systems where the damn thing turns itself on to let you know there's a message waiting for you.

This is what I don't understand about technology. It used to be in hotels that you'd have a little light on the telephone that would flash to tell you there was a message. Or you'd stop by the reception desk on your way out and ask, 'Any messages?' And son-of-a-gun, a real live subservient lackey would actually tell you. Truth be known, I sort of miss the good old days when you'd get a snappy 'No, sir,' from a liveried clerk who knew you didn't have any messages and what's more weren't the type who was likely to *ever* have any messages waiting for you. He'd diligently check anyway – because people used to do their jobs well – and not only wouldn't there be an ounce of condescension in that 'No, sir,' but despite the clerk's knowledge of your unlikely message-receiving status, there'd be a hint, just in his tone or the cast of his gaze, to suggest that you really *should* ask again later, because, damn it, a message just might come in at any moment and you wouldn't want to miss it.

At least that's the way I remember things.

Now you get a blinking message on the blanking TV.

The kicker, of course, is that all that the TV screen tells you is: you have a message. You still have to call the goddamn front desk to find out what it is. And these days the clerks are never subservient, but are *always* condescending, even if there's a stack of messages waiting for you from the pope, the president and Jerry Seinfeld.

Christ, I feel like an old fart sometimes.

8 JAY S. RUSSELL

I glanced at the digital clock – also built into the TV. (Not to harp on a theme, here, or shit where I eat – heaven forbid – but it's clearly only a matter of time before you have to crap into the fucking tube, too.) I saw it was just after eight. Which made it I haven't got the slightest idea what time in Los Angeles, because I never could keep my time zones straight. All I knew was that I felt like I'd just come off a three-day bender. I travel about as well as an off-the-rack polyester suit. One of those three-piece jobbers.

My immediate goal was to shut off the still-blinking television. I looked around for the remote, but couldn't remember what I'd done with it. I felt around under the covers and thought I'd found it against my leg, but it was only my dick. I had to pee real bad.

I flailed at the buttons on the front of the set as I stumbled past on my way to the toilet, but only managed to change the station and turn up the volume. It was the adult movie channel and I stopped for a second at the sight of a set of flexing buttocks. I quickly recognized them as belonging to Sean Young (call it a talent) and frankly it was just too early in the morning for such things. I relieved myself in the deepest possible meaning of the word and splashed some water on my face, noting that the hot was a little slow – more like nonexistent – coming on. Still, it woke me up well enough and say what you will about the quality of television at the Savoy, their towels are delightfully fluffy.

I slipped into an equally extravagant Savoy bathrobe – with my satellite buddies picking up the tab, you just *know* that puppy was going back to America in my suitcase – and scanned the room-service menu to calculate just how expensive a breakfast I could manage to order. It's not like I wasn't making good – hell, obscene – money thanks to *Burning Bright*. Or that I get off on playing the star. (Well ...) It's just that I'd been down the celebrity road once before. I was a stupid kid at the time and I enjoyed the hell out of those *Salt & Pepper* days, but I never fully *appreciated* them. It all came so fast and I was so young that I took it for granted, assumed it was something that I deserved, and would last forever.

And then it all went away. Faded like a Coppertone tan.

I knew it could, probably *would*, happen that way again. Not because I'm plagued by self-doubt or worry or world-weary pessimism, but simply because, as everyone knows, that's show biz. Just ask Philip Michael Thomas or Larry Linville.

So this time, I wasn't about to let it all glide on past me. I planned to enjoy every luxurious, self-indulgent, greedy-to-the-depths-of-my-inflated-ego moment.

Which is how, at least at the Savoy Hotel in the heart of London, you can run up a thirty-dollar tab for what amounts to little more than a bacon and eggs and lukewarm coffee breakfast.

But, man alive, does it ever taste good.

I called down to the front desk for my message.

'Room number?' a prole of indeterminate gender asked.

'Can't you tell?' I said.

'Sorry?'

'Can't you tell what room I'm calling from without asking? Isn't it on your computer or switchboard or whatever?'

'Don't you know what your room number is?' s/he shot back.

'Yeah,' I said. I did know, of course, but I wasn't sure I wanted to let on.

'Then why won't you tell me?'

'Why should I tell you if you already know?'

'Because now I'm suspicious.'

'But . . .' I caught myself before this went on any further, recognizing a losing situation for what it was. If I *really* had a star's ego I'd have thrown a snit. It sort of pleased me to know that I hadn't reached the snitty stage just yet, and I forgave the clerk for blessing me with this tiny, but not insignificant ort of self-knowledge. I happily divulged the dark secret of my room number.

'You have a message from June Hanover of Star-TV. She'll be waiting for you in the hotel's main lounge at your leisure.'

I had no intention of saying thank you, but the desk jockey hung up on me before I even had a chance. I meant to ask what time the message came in, but wasn't about to risk another call. Instead, I grabbed a quick shower – definite hot water issues happening here – threw on a shirt and slacks, grabbed an only slightly wrinkled sports coat out of my garment bag and hustled on downstairs.

Hotel lobbies are great. I love 'em. There's a thrill and a romance to walking through one, even if you *aren't* a guest at the hotel, that you can't get anyplace else. Airport terminals come close, but they're too inelegant and they have too many cult crazies and Chinese nuns hawking flowers and salvation. I imagine train stations, round about 1930, must have had the same feel. It's a kind of liminality, a sense of other-worldliness. People act differently, walk differently in hotel lobbies. Just being there makes you feel a little bit special. It's a sense that's exaggerated when it's a swanky joint like the Savoy, but sometimes I can even get a whiff of it checking into a Motel 6 as long as it's got an ice machine. Maybe it's just me.

I sauntered my way through the ground floor plaza – strangers will actually still smile at you in a hotel lobby; maybe the real appeal of such places is that they're the last outposts of an otherwise lost civility – and strolled into the central lounge. A couple of dozen people, all in expensive suits, were scattered around the big room, sipping coffee, chewing croissants and reading the papers. I had no problem picking out June Hanover. She was sitting alone on a big, comfy looking divan. She wore a pale orange power suit and carried a briefcase emblazoned with a big red logo of the satellite company. She was also the only woman there.

It's not for nothing I star in a detective series.

She stood up as soon as she saw me, dropping a sheaf of papers on the floor in the process of extending her hand. 'Mr Burns! Good morning. I'm June Hanover. Oh, dear.'

She seemed torn between holding my gaze and gathering up her papers. I bent down and scooped them up for her.

'Oh, thank you, Mr Burns.'

'Please,' I smiled, 'it's Marty.'

'Marty,' she nodded and smiled back at me. She had crooked teeth and was ever-so-slightly cock-eyed, but otherwise fairly attractive in that underwhelming, middle-management, oops-is-that-a-glass-ceiling way. It was a little hard to form an accurate judgement what with the power suit, which was about as flattering on her as a manilla envelope. She had big, bright eyes, though, and I took an immediate liking to her.

I sat down on the couch, which wasn't as comfy as it looked – gotta keep 'em moving in a hotel lounge – and June plopped down beside me. 'I'm sorry to have kept you,' I said. 'If I'd realized you were here, I'd have been down earlier. How long have you been waiting?'

'Oh, only since about seven,' she said.

'Seven!' I glanced at my watch. It claimed that it was two o'clock. I had forgotten to reset it when the plane landed. I looked up and found a big clock on a far wall, saw that it was nearly ten. 'You've been sitting here for three hours?'

'That's my job,' she said. She looked at me with some slight suspicion. I suspect I wasn't acting the star I was supposed to be. I wanted to apologize some more, but was afraid she might start asking for ID if I played it any more humble. No point in taking chances after that call to the front desk.

'So what's the plan, June?' I asked.

'Well, whenever you're ready I'll escort you to the Star offices. There's no rush, though. Would you like to have some coffee first?'

I glanced at the snack menu on the table and saw that a cup of joe in the lounge went for two pounds. It was almost enough to tempt me into a cup or three, but I was still full from breakfast and I felt reasonably confident that there'd be plenty of other opportunities to piss away the network's money.

'Nah,' I said. 'Let's blow this taco stand.'

'Pardon?' June asked.

'Let's go to the office.'

'Brilliant!' she said. I thought it excessive praise, but followed her as she went to call for the limo.

The network's offices were located in a massive complex called Canary Wharf in the wilds of East London. The road signs on the way indicated that we were heading for the Isle of Dogs.

'So the offices are on an island?' I asked June.

'No,' she said.

'But it says Isle of Dogs.' I pointed out the window at another road sign.

'Yes, but it's not really an island. It just runs along a sort of bend in the river.'

'Huh,' I said, but I still didn't get it. 'So why Isle of Dogs? I mean the dog bit?'

She just pursed her lips and shrugged. 'I'm not sure. I never really thought about it.'

'No doggies?'

'No more so than any other part of London I shouldn't think,' she said.

'Too bad,' I said.

'Are you a dog lover then?'

'Not especially,' I told her. I saw she was looking at me sort of funny all of a sudden. 'Just sounded kind of cute,' I added. She nodded and forced a smile.

'Any idea why it's called Big Ben?' I tried.

'Sorry?'

'Big Ben. The . . . skip it,' I told her. She nodded again and I decided against asking any more questions.

Canary Wharf turned out to be anything but cute. A huge and fairly new looking office complex, it was dominated by a central, almost self-parodying phallic tower, built in the middle of what otherwise seemed to be an awfully run-down part of town. The limo dropped us off right in front of the big pee-pee. I gazed up toward the glans, then out across the water at an equally new looking hotel. It was all pretty in that utilitarian, corporate, man-am-I-glad-I-only-have-to-*work*-here kind of way. Architects are such pricks.

'It's not yellow,' I said.

'Sorry?' June asked. Why did she keep saying that?

'I thought it would be yellow, but it's not. Just the name, I guess. So why is it called Canary . . .'

I saw what I can only describe as a look of terror blossom on the poor woman's face and I bit off the end of the question.

'I like it,' I said, smiling. 'Isle of Dogs. Canary Wharf. Good British names.'

She smiled very nervously and gestured me into the building.

'Why a duck?' I muttered to myself as we went through the revolving doors. June made like she didn't hear me, but a little twitch in her cheek suggested that she had.

The Star offices and studios occupied three full floors of the skyscraper. I spent most of the morning strolling around, shaking hands and even signing a few autographs, though I got the feeling that the secretaries and such had been prompted to ask because none of them seemed too sure of exactly who I was. There was the usual artificial cheeriness and forced laughter at woefully unfunny repartee that always accompanies these things, but it's all part of the job. And as jobs go it sure beat hell out of chasing after the street scum and low-life of LA, which was what I'd been doing for the previous ten years.

Following a series of mercifully brief introductions to the high muckety-mucks of the operation – who love to be *photographed* with actors and celebrities, but would sooner surrender their share options than actually talk to you – we got down to the real business at hand. June Hanover walked me over to the station's PR operation, located at a conspicuous remove from the executive suites, where three broadly grinning young men were waiting for me. The PR flacks all looked to be in their late twenties and each had dark, slicked-back hair. They all had their jackets off, their sleeves rolled up and wore suspenders, though each set was a different colour: red, gold and mauve. *Mauve?* I wondered. Judging from the look of them, I suspected they kept some kind of chart so that no one clashed with either of the others' suspender colour on any given day.

(By the by I don't trust people who wear suspenders. I suppose they call them braces when you wear them with a suit, but calling a pig a chicken don't mean the rabbi eats pork. I don't even like them on farmers. There's something too *eighties* about them. It was a bad decade. I mean, the seventies weren't so terrific either, but nobody wears leisure suits anymore. Though someone recently told me that flares are now back. May God have mercy on our souls.)

They all introduced themselves to me, but I didn't catch a single name. It's not that I was being snooty or anything, but tacked up on one wall was an immense poster advertising the show. They must have put it together themselves because I'd never seen this particular still used in the States and had no idea where they got it from. It was a massive close-up of me winking at the camera, with the word 'Burning' down one side and 'Bright!' down the other. The channel's logo was superimposed over my chest like Superman's 'S'. But the close-up was so big that every pore on my face looked like an oily gopher hole and the gap between my front teeth was big enough for David Letterman to ride a moped through. It was the kind of hateful self-portrait you might expect from someone like Robert Crumb, but it was the last image you'd think would entice viewers to tune in and be entertained by an action show.

It was grotesque.

'Catches the eye, doesn't it?' Mr Red said. (I was reduced to distinguishing the three by suspender colour.)

'Like a pungi stick,' I said.

'We thought you'd like it,' Mauve nodded. He added a wink. I glanced back toward June, but she was nervously eyeing the poster, too. Probably afraid it'd ask her about Big Ben.

Mr Gold took charge: 'We have a few ideas we'd like to try out on you, Marty. Thought we might toss them about over a bit of lunch though.'

'Sounds good,' I said.

'I thought we might have an Indian. There's a lovely little place not far, or we can send out and have lunch right here. Whichever you prefer.'

I took another look at the poster and contemplated the idea of forcing down a curry with that picture of me looming overhead.

'Let's go out,' I said.

'Brill!' Red and Mauve said in unison.

Off we trooped.

Gold wasn't going to invite June along, but I insisted. I figured if she'd had to spend three hours sitting around a hotel lobby waiting for me from the crack of dawn, the least these greasy sports could do was spring for her lunch. Mauve sort of scowled when she said she'd love to join us, but Gold just smiled.

The limo was long gone, but a big black cab waited for us downstairs. Although it wasn't terribly far to the restaurant, within a couple of blocks of the office complex the neighbourhood took a conspicuous turn for the poorer. The clean-scrubbed white concrete of Canary Wharf gave way to faded brown brick tenements covered with graffiti scrawl. Actually, it reminded me a bit of the financial district in downtown LA where the big bank towers stand shoulder-to-shoulder with the homeless missions and soup kitchens. Which is more than you can say about the people who *work* inside those big office blocks.

The colour guard were greasing me up about what a wonderful show *Burning Bright* was and how thrilled they were to be working on it blah-blah-blah, but they'd all put their jackets on when we left the office, so I no longer had any means to tell them apart. I managed to re-establish Gold's identity when he paid the fare, and I took my own jacket off as soon we were shown to a table by the front window. Of course, the PR boys immediately followed my lead, revealing their true colours, and I chuckled at my ingenuity. June sat next to me and caught the chuckle. It earned me another odd look, but then she eyed up each of her colleagues and looked back at me with what I took to be a knowing gaze. I think she was on to my game.

The view of the street outside the window was a bit on the grim side, but the restaurant was bright and lively and spick and span. Smelled good, too, though the same bit of whiny music that seems to play in every Indian restaurant I've ever been in could be heard in the background. The dining room was long and narrow, with tables set about as close together as could be squeezed in. Almost all of them were occupied, mostly by power suit types of both genders who I took to be drones from Canary Wharf. The menu was immense and utterly confusing to me. I'd had Indian in LA a few times, but it's not one of your major southern California cuisines. Doesn't stand a chance against all those cheap Mexican and Thai joints. I had some kind of synaptic connection between 'vindaloo' and 'diarrhoea', but otherwise nothing looked too familiar to me.

'Shall we order a little of everything and share?' June suggested. I quickly nodded agreement and closed the menu, relieved that I wouldn't have to try to pronounce any of the names of the dishes.

'The food here is wonderful,' Red said. 'It's the only place in this part of town that does South Indian along with the usual tandoori menu. It's become a little too popular since *FHM* wrote it up, but still it's the best around here.'

The waiter came for our drink order. The others all ordered Kingfisher, and though I had no idea what it was, I figured when in Bombay . . .

We made small talk over hors d'oeuvres – a whole range of scrumptious goobers – though the samosas threw me for a loop.

'Wasn't he the dictator of Nicaragua?' I asked, cautiously inspecting the little triangular pastry for booby-traps.

The three men exchanged glances, but June laughed out loud.

'Somoza,' she said. 'These are samosas. Different pronunciation. A bit tastier, too.'

She was right on about the yummy factor, but I still couldn't help feeling slightly counter-revolutionary eating them. As if The Clash wouldn't approve. The Kingfisher was A-OK, too. I definitely felt like I was warming to British beer, at least until I read the label on the bottle and saw that it was Indian.

Conversation over the food was limited to small talk. They asked me the usual LA questions – no, I never met O.J.; yes, nobody ever walks anyplace; sorry, I don't know if it's true about Uma Thurman and Matthew McConaughey – and I hauled out two or three of my current Hollywood anecdotes. The colour boys were a suitably appreciative audience, laughing and nodding or frowning and shaking their heads at the appropriate moments, but I could tell they were just waiting to get down to the post-prandial business at hand. I found myself directing most of my conversation and eye contact at June who was only distracted, and who could blame her, by the genuinely delicious food.

The owner of the place stopped by our table to accept our compliments on the meal, though Mauve suggested that one of the dishes, I think it was something jalfrezi, was perhaps a tad salty. The owner practically abased himself apologizing, which seemed to be the precise response that Mauve was fishing for. I got the feeling he was the sort of guy who always took advantage of a situation in which he held social superiority, so I decided to contradict him, telling the owner I particularly liked the dish, but the poor man seemed unsure whether to start thanking me or to continue apologizing to Mauve. Fortunately the waiter came to clear the dishes, providing him an escape route.

'So, Marty,' Gold said once the table was clear, 'We've got an idea.'

'Always a dangerous thing,' I said. June started to laugh, but turned it into a cough when Gold glared at her.

'What is it that you're most famous for?' Gold asked me with a patented PR this-is-gonna-kill-ya smirk.

'Ummm,' I pretended to think, 'bad thinning hair days?'

A suitably fawning guffaw from the peanut gallery.

'No, seriously. What one thing?' Gold prompted. I smiled and shrugged,

'Jack the Ripper!' Mauve barked.

'Right,' Gold said. I don't think Mauve was supposed to steal the thunder. 'You're the man who brought down bad old Jack Rippen. Marty Burns, ace detective, solves the case of Jack "The Ripper" Rippen.'

'Yesterday's news, isn't it, boys?' I smiled at June. 'And girl.'

'Hold on a minute,' Gold said, holding up a finger.

'This is great,' Red whispered. Mauve nodded. I glanced June's way and detected (ace-ly, of course) significantly less enthusiasm.

'And what crime is England most famous for?' Gold asked, leaning forward.

I was sorely tempted to say something about 200 years of cultural imperialism and the colonial subjugation of countless millions across the globe, but I suspected that this wasn't the answer Gold was looking for.

'Jack the Ripper?' I offered with a sigh.

'Yesss!' Gold hissed with a clap of his hands. His wad shot, Gold slumped back in his chair.

'Picture this,' Red said. 'Marty Burns, star of *Burning Bright*, has come to England, not just with a great new show, but to solve the century-old mystery of the Whitechapel murders. The man who brought Jack Rippen to justice reveals the identity of the *original* Jack the Ripper.'

'It's a publicity wet dream come true,' Mauve added with a nod.

That unleashed a whole series of unpleasant images in my head, but I did my best to ignore them. 'And, umm, how exactly am I supposed to figure out who the real Jack the Ripper is?'

Gold took charge again. 'It couldn't matter less, Marty. No one actually expects you to solve the mystery of Jack the Ripper. Bloody hell, there is no solution to it. But think of the publicity generated by the announcement that you *plan* to solve the case. The tabloids will eat it up. And with your background, even those poofs at the *Guardian* will run with it. We'll plant the story before the premiere of *Burning Bright* and play it as best we can for the two or three days after. It should net us some nice numbers for the debut and then we'll simply let it drop.'

'And what precisely would you want me to do?'

'Very little really,' Red said. 'We'll send you off to the East End. Get some video and pictures of you snooping around the various locales of the original Ripper killings. Maybe over to the British Library for a few shots of you perusing old books or papers or what have you. Then we'll just feed some red herrings to the tabloids about what you've found.'

'But I won't have found anything.'

'Marty, do you have any idea how many books have been written about the Whitechapel murders? Ripperology is a cottage industry. We'll just pull bits and pieces from different sources and create some slight variation on what's already been suggested.'

'The royals,' Mauve said. 'You can't go wrong blaming one of the royals.'

'Precisely,' Gold nodded. 'There's no shortage of conspiracy theories to choose from. Perhaps we can even offer something novel.'

'Maybe I'll even solve it,' I said.

A sudden tension descended as they couldn't decide if I meant it.

'Joke,' I said. More appreciative laughter.

'So what do you say, Marty?' Gold asked.

I had to admit that it wasn't a half-bad idea. Maybe these guys were more on the ball than I had given them credit for. It struck me as a sure-fire publicity gimmick, though I was a bit worried that everyone would see it for what it was.

'What do you think?' I asked June. The eyes of her three associates locked on her like lasers. She was very clearly aware of that fact.

'I like it, Marty,' she said. 'I think it will really create interest in you and the show. I think you might enjoy it as well.'

A big smile lit up Gold's face, though I had a sense that Mauve was disappointed, or maybe just surprised, by June's team spirit.

'But don't I need to actually know something about the case?' I asked.

'We've already put some items together for you,' Red said. 'A précis really, but with all the key names and dates. It shouldn't be any harder for you to remember than a script. And you'll only have to fool a few journalists. We'll keep any real Ripperologists far away.'

Ripperologists? Could that be for real? I let it pass. Along with the fact that I've never actually been very good at learning

my lines. It's not for nothing they call me Twenty-take Burns.
Still . . .

'Okay,' I said, conspicuously tendering my agreement to June
before looking back at Gold. 'Okay.'

'Terrific, Marty,' Gold said.

'Fandabadozy!' Mauve squealed. I was starting to wonder precisely
what his function in this little triumvirate was.

'Right,' I said, standing up. 'Any idea where the little Ripper's
room is in this joint?'

Gold pointed toward a stairway at the back of the restaurant. I'd
taken two steps up the narrow aisle when a thunderous crash came
from behind. I spun around amid shrieks and screams and saw that
the big plate glass window by our table had been smashed, and
shards of glass littered the scene.

Gold and Red were on their feet shaking glass off their clothes.
Mauve had slumped to the floor, blood pumping furiously out of
a gash in his forehead. I saw slivers of glass in June's hair, but she
was already at Mauve's side, pressing her napkin against his head to
staunch the flow of blood. Incredibly, none of the others appeared
to be injured.

I dashed to the front door in time to see a dark car screech around
the corner. There was no chance to catch the licence number and of
course I wouldn't know one English model from another even with
a good look.

Red and Gold were helping Mauve to his feet, leading him to
a chair away from the mess. I saw the restaurant owner on the
phone, presumably calling for the police and an ambulance, while
the waiters tried to calm the other customers. Or at least prevent
them from bolting before they paid their bills.

June was still standing by our table looking a little bit in shock.
Blood dripped down her forearm, but it was all Mauve's. I found a
clean napkin, dipped it in a pitcher of water and cleaned the blood
off her arm. She watched me do it, but still didn't move.

'Hold still,' I said somewhat extraneously as I gently picked bits
of glass out of her hair.

The owner had come over, a waiter trailing on either side, and
was inspecting the damage and apologizing as profusely as humanly
possible. He was actually pulling at his hair as he did so.

As if it was *his* fault.

It was only then I noticed the brick that sat smack dab in the middle
of our lunch table, atop the peshwari naan. Obviously, this was the
projectile which shattered the window. (Ace detective, remember?)

It was a filthy old thing, chipped and battered, but big as a loaf of rye bread. I knew better than to touch it before the cops arrived, but I didn't have to in order to read what had been scratched into each rectangular face:

ULTIMA THULE

THREE

The Star PR team set the publicity wheels in motion and two days later, far too early in the morning for decent folk, I found myself on a strange corner in London's East End, surrounded by a mob of yowling cameramen and photographers. Gold, whose real name was Mahr, had provided me with a brief outline of the details of the Jack the Ripper story as promised. He also sent along about a dozen books on the subject and I'd spent most of the previous day skimming through them. Apparently there were as many theories about the identity of Jack the Ripper and the circumstances of the Whitechapel murders as there were writers who thought they could make a buck out of it. And judging from the length of the various bibliographies in the books, there was obviously a fair buck to be made.

Mahr, or one of his minions – I still hadn't worked out Red and Mauve's actual names – had boiled it down pretty well in the précis, so I'd concentrated my efforts on committing that to memory. There were quite a few names and dates and I had trouble remembering which prostitute was killed where and when, but June Hanover helped me run through it enough times that I felt like I could vamp my way through the very tightly controlled media interviews. Originally, Mahr had assigned Red to be my babysitter or caretaker or however they saw it, but I asked that June be the one to look after me. Mahr quickly acceded to the request, but I saw him furtively eye June again as if to ask: why would you want *that*?

In fact, despite what Mahr was almost certainly thinking, I had not the slightest 'romantic' interest in June. She was attractive enough

in a slightly mousy way, but much as I was again enjoying the many
vain and excessive trappings of celebrity, playing the sexual predator
just wasn't on my agenda. I don't want to be misunderstood here: I
like feeding the weasel as much as the next guy, but I remember all
too well those crazy old days of Hollywood priapism and I think
they're best left in the past.

For one thing, I'm not as young as I used to be; the weasel still
likes to snack, but he doesn't have his old appetite. Or perhaps, his
diet has become a touch more refined.

For another, I was sort of involved with someone back in LA Rosa
Mendez and I – who had saved each others' lives in more ways than
one – were still lost somewhere in a long-term on again/off again
thing. As I'd flown out of Hollywood, the relationship switch had
once more been flipped to the 'off' position, but I wasn't quite ready
to have the electricity cut off for good just yet.

In any case, I asked for June to look after me, not because I wanted
to jump her bones, but because I sort of liked her. And I *didn't* much
like the other three stooges or the way they treated her.

(A perverse fount of honesty which gurgles away somewhere in
the vicinity of my pancreas, however, compels me to report that my
gleaming escutcheon of middle-aged moral principle is not without
stain: I did, while on a Hawaiian location shoot for the *Burning
Bright* Christmas special – it was a seriously hyped cross-over
episode reviving Tom Selleck's Magnum PI – weaken in sexual
resolve when faced with an offer from a young actress, whispers
of whose singular oral skills had reached even my generally clueless
ears. The whispers proved entirely accurate, but my guilt-inspired
reporting of this incident to Rosa – can you hear the honesty
bubbling? – led to the initial flipping of the relational off-switch.
All of which only proves that we grow not so much wiser with age,
as merely more aware of our own capacity for stupidity.)

As it turns out, the East End is chock-full of pubs and plaques
marking – celebrating, really – the various sites of the Ripper killings.
June told me that there are even folks who offer Jack the Ripper
walking tours of the neighbourhood and, sure enough, a small passel
of camera-clicking tourists, led by a stout-looking fellow in mutton
chops and Victorian period dress, stopped to check out my own little
media circus near Mitre Square, where poor Catherine Eddowes was
butchered. It was all harmless enough fun, I suppose, given that the
murders took place more than a hundred years ago, but something
about the gawking, giggly rubber-neckers made me uncomfortable.
I wondered if fifty or a hundred years hence, a similar group might

not be following the bloody trail of John Wayne Gacy or Ted Bundy or Henry Lee Lucas, led by some twenty-first century entrepreneur wearing mauve suspenders and a power tie. Somehow, that didn't strike me as quite such harmless fun.

We finished up with the last of the press just after one o'clock. I've been in The Business long enough to suffer publicity sessions with good grace, but I'd reached my limit for one day and having had to pose with (and, QED, *drink*) pints of beer at the various pubs for the photogs, I was feeling a bit tipsy and in need of something a little more solid to put in my stomach. Everyone else had taken off except for June and a chirpy Star photographer named King who was supposed to accompany me and record my 'investigation'.

'Lunch,' June said. 'Umm . . .'

'What?' I asked.

'Well, really this is the place for Indian food. Just about the best in town over on Brick Lane. But I don't know how you feel about it after what happened the other day.'

'There's Klein's,' King said with a wink.

'Oh dear,' June sighed.

'What's Klein's,' I asked, intrigued.

'Kosher,' King said. 'Been in business forever. Apparently they used to send out to Klein's for take-away when they were building the Tower.'

'That sounds all right by me,' I said. 'I could go for a knish.'

June looked puzzled, but the photographer laughed out loud. I soon found out why.

Klein's looks a little like Cantor's or Junior's or one of LA's other faux-kosher delis, but the resemblance quickly fades. Instead of middle-aged matrons cracking wise – *de rigueur* for any Los Angeles deli – the waiters are all slightly stooped, balding Jewish men in white lab coats. And I wouldn't call what they offer service so much as forbearance. After only three days in London, I had already come to realize that every lackey who serves you thinks that they therefore have leverage over you and thus don't have to be pleasant – apparently the full meaning of 'service economy' hasn't quite sunk in yet in England – but the staff at Klein's pushed this unique notion of anti-service to some theoretical limit.

I wanted a corned beef sandwich and a knish, but couldn't find either item on the menu.

'It's called salt beef here, mate,' King told me. June, whose picture should be in a Yiddish dictionary under 'shiksa', looked entirely confused.

When our waiter finally strolled over to take the order – race notwithstanding, he was a dead ringer for Lester Bowie in that white coat – I asked about a knish with my salt beef. He stared me down with a look that would have made Clint Eastwood blink, and eventually said, 'I'll bring something.' For some reason, raw intimidation I suspect, I thanked him as he sauntered off.

'Nice place,' I said to King. 'Thoughtful of you to suggest it.'

'It's an essential bit of East End atmosphere.'

'It seems just a mite out of place, don't you think?'

The waiter came by and tossed a plate of bread in the middle of the table without actually stopping. It was plain white bread, looking suspiciously like Wonder Bread, I thought, though I sort of doubted that Wonder Bread was kosher. No butter. King started to chew on a slice.

'Maybe now,' he said, 'but this whole area used to be Jewish. Been the centre of the rag trade for years. Dating back a century at least. The East End's always been the place for immigrants to live. They come here first and then get out quick as they've earned a bit of dosh. It's mostly Bengali now . . .'

'I thought it was Bangladeshi?' June said.

'Whatever,' King shrugged. 'I always forget. But Germans, Irish, Jews . . . they've all been through here, one time or another. A few have even stayed. There's a mosque just up Commercial Street across from the old Spitalfields Market that used to be a synagogue. It was a Huguenot church before that. Built on the site of a Druid altar, wouldn't surprise me. Of course, it's all bloody Muslim now. Except for one tiny synagogue back toward Liverpool Street.'

'How do you know the East End so well?' June asked.

'Born and raised, darling. East Ham, Bow, Stepney. Me mum still lives in Hackney,' he said, vaguely indicating a direction with a cock of his head. 'Right across from Martin Amis, no less.'

'A regular wide boy, eh?' she said.

'I worked for the *News of the World*, didn't I?'

'Wide boy?' I asked.

'A good lad,' King said and winked at me.

'It means don't trust him as far as you can throw London Bridge,' June said with a smile.

I glanced around the restaurant. 'I already figured that out,' I said.

The waiter brought out our orders. He actually stopped long enough to put the plates in front of us this time. The meat on my plate looked vaguely like corned beef, but it was a family resemblance at best. Like ordering Michael Jackson and getting Tito. An unknown side order was plunked down next to it.

'That is *not* a knish,' I said.

'Eat,' the waiter ordered, and walked off.

I made it for some variation on potato kugel and while it was a little bit heavy – I think they make anchors for ocean-liners from the same stuff – and most definitely *not* a knish, it wasn't half-bad. The salt beef was surprisingly edible as well. It wasn't as good as nice, lean corned beef, which is to say I wasn't ready to forget Nate and Al's in Beverly Hills just yet, but the taste was at least recognizable. The others seemed equally pleased with their lunches, though June looked a little bit troubled by the raisins in her noodle pudding. She packed it away pretty good regardless.

As the waiter brought me a coffee, and tea for June and King, I remembered something which had been bothering me since the incident at the Indian restaurant a couple of days before.

'What does "Ultima Thule" mean?' I asked June.

A glass smashed behind me. I looked over my shoulder at an old Jewish man sitting in the adjacent booth. He was a little blob of a person, about as perfectly round in shape as a human with arms and legs can possibly be, with curly grey hair and a bushy beard. He wore a tiny yarmulke and in front of him was a plate with nothing on it but one bright red frankfurter, as squat and round as the man himself. Ice cubes and the shards of a glass littered the table, a trickle of water running off the side. Our waiter ran over – I would never have dreamed he could move that fast – to clean up the mess. I had the feeling the old guy was the owner or maybe a rabbi or something. Whatever he was, he stared at me with fire in his eyes.

'Oops,' King said, looking over my shoulder. But he didn't wink at the rabbi.

'I don't know,' June said. But she was watching the old man, too.

'Huh?' I said.

'Ultima Thule. I never heard of it before.'

King just shrugged. But a voice from behind me answered.

'The End of All Things,' the little man said. He had a deceptively deep voice and one of those generically foreign accents, half Bela Lugosi, half Ricardo Montalban, that I couldn't peg. Definitely not British, probably eastern European.

'I beg your pardon?' I said, turning around. He was still staring daggers.

'Ultima Thule . . .' – thew-lee, he pronounced it – '. . . the end of all things.' We all stared at him, but apparently he had nothing more to add.

'Uh-huh,' I said. 'Well, thanks.'

The three of us exchanged a look and King muttered something vaguely profane under his breath.

'Check, please,' I said.

'Bill,' June told me. 'You ask for a bill, not a check.'

June got the *bill* and said she'd charge it to the company, which was fine by me. I generally tend to be a big tipper, especially when a network is picking up the tab, but in this case I argued passionately that we leave no more than two cents.

'I am *not* leaving a 2p tip,' June insisted.

'How much do *you* think that service was worth?'

She got a little flustered and King started to laugh, but finally she just told me to mind my business. As we got up to leave, I glanced back at the old man who was still tracking me. The little hot dog sat on his plate untouched, looking for all the world like a boiled dog's dick. I looked his way again as we walked out the door and saw that his eyes were glued to my back. I had to suppress a small shudder.

'Well, wasn't that special?' I said.

Outside the restaurant, June seemed a little reluctant to take her leave. 'Are you sure you're going to be all right?' she asked. 'Parts of this neighbourhood are very dodgy, you know.'

'I'll keep me eye on him, darling,' King said with a wink – whether aimed at June or me, I wasn't sure.

'I'll be fine,' I said. 'I'm just gonna have a wander around, really. Soak up some of the atmosphere. Find me a serial killer.'

She didn't look very reassured, but King hailed a passing black cab and ushered her in. As it pulled it away, she turned around in her seat to watch us out of the back window. I waved, King winked.

'Bloody hell,' King said, 'I thought mother hen'd never go.'

'You don't like her?'

'Ahh, she's all right, I suppose. A bit posh for these parts is all. She's not as bad as those tossers she works with.'

'Tossers?'

'Wankers! The lot of them. Bloody flacks. Who else'd work for an outfit like that?' he said. He winked again. It was getting annoying.

We started walking up Whitechapel High Street, though I had no particular destination in mind. I thought I might follow the little map of key Ripper sites that Mahr had given me, if only to fix the geography of the area in my mind. We'd rushed from one place to another for the morning PR sessions, and the various pubs and streets and alleys were just a blur to me. Mahr had made it quite clear that I didn't need to bother with any of it; that the pre-arranged photo ops were all that really mattered. But while I had no illusions about actually investigating the Whitechapel murders of a century past, I felt like I should take advantage of the chance to see a part of London I wouldn't otherwise visit. And like most Americans, I reckon, I'm a sucker for the romanticized myth of English history. Scratch the surface of the average American and you find the heart of an Anglophile underneath.

At least, so long the Brits pay to see our movies, sell us their oil, and do exactly what we tell them to in NATO.

King kept up something of a running monologue as we strolled the back streets of Whitechapel. He had an opinion – often more than one – on absolutely every subject and had no reluctance about sharing his every thought with me. After a while I sort of tuned him out, though I had to pay half a mind because he regularly wanted to stop to snap a few pictures. He didn't stop talking even with his finger on the shutter.

Whatever romantic notions and Victorian images I might have held about Whitechapel were quickly dispelled by our tour of the area. It was a grim, dilapidated part of town mainly comprising a mixture of tandoori and Balti restaurants and schlock clothing merchants. It reminded me of the garment district in downtown LA, except that the Asians who worked and ran the East End sweat shops were Indian and Pakistani instead of Korean and Chinese. Otherwise, deprivation looks about the same everywhere. Something to do with multinational capitalism, I suspect. Good thing I'm not political.

Heavy-duty poverty was the dominant mode of the neighbourhood, though in no sense was it as run-down or outwardly frightening as your average American slum. Muslim women wrapped from head to toe in black, and grey-bearded old men garbed in white (though of a distinctly different cut than the Klein's lab coat look) leisurely strolled to and fro. I didn't think I'd care to walk there alone at night, but at the same time I didn't feel as unwelcome or as much like an intruder as I might have in LA. We didn't receive so much as an untoward look as we wandered up and down the streets. There are not entirely dissimilar parts of Los Angeles where you wouldn't walk even with an armed escort.

As if on cue, a police car passed us on the opposite side of the street. 'Do the cops here really not carry guns?' I asked.

'Ahhh,' King said and he was off again. I should have known better. I quickly learned that not only do the cops not carry guns, but received a brief history of the London Metropolitan Police force beginning with Sir Robert Peel, along with a stinging editorial on the failings of the British justice system and the deficiencies of the current Home Secretary. King was embarking on a monologue about homosexuality among the judiciary when I interrupted him.

'So why's it called Big Ben?' I asked. Surely, the answer would be at hand.

King stopped dead in his tracks. He looked up and down the street as if a finger would appear and write the answer on a wall in fire.

'Bugger me,' he finally said. 'I don't know.'

'What about . . . wow!' I exclaimed as we turned a corner.

'Heh?'

'What is that?' I asked.

Two or three blocks away, the street we were on dead-ended in an absolutely astonishing looking building.

'Haven't you seen it before?' King asked. 'It's Christ Church, Spitalfields. One of few remaining glories of the old East End.'

'How could I have missed it?' I mused.

The church rose up out of the ground like an immense spike of white stone. It seemed as out of place, and dominated the streetscape like a single, first tooth in a toddler's mouth. The geometry of the building seemed vaguely impossible: the church was virtually all tower and steeple. Actually, the sight of it made me think of that last shot in *Planet of the Apes*, where Charlton Heston comes across the top half of the Statue of Liberty buried in the sand; the church seemed to just emerge from the street as if its bottom two-thirds had been cut off, or was somehow rooted in the underworld of the city.

The raw power of the architecture grew even more pronounced as we approached the front of the building. Looking up at the belfry, and above an arched portico supported by four large columns, the steeple gave me a feeling of dizzying, unnatural dimensions and I staggered. I heard King laugh, but I couldn't take my eyes off the tower. I walked off to one side, which reduced the reverse-vertigo, but the steeple was magnificent from all angles.

'Watch it!' a voice growled.

I looked back down and saw that I'd nearly stepped on the legs of a raggedy old wino who was sprawled on the floor near a stone stairway leading to a below-ground entrance.

'Sorry,' I muttered. I saw two or three other wino-types perched on the steps. They all scowled up at me.

'It's a rehab centre,' King said, grabbing me by the elbow. 'In the crypt. For alcoholics mostly. Homeless, too. It's the main use of the place these days.'

'You gotta be kidding me,' I said, looking up at the grandeur of the architecture again. I saw, though, that the side of the building was in a poorer state of disrepair than the front. The stonework was filthy and chipping. The building could do with a serious sandblasting, if the walls could take it.

'They were going to tear it all down at one time not so long ago,' King told me.

'No way!'

'Can you believe it? Back when I was a kid. Me and me pals used to play in the ruins of the churchyard. Had to sneak in under a fence. It was a creepy old place, what with the graves and statues all overgrown and wild. All kinds of stories about ghosts and spooks and such, too. The building was in a terrible state, though. They've done a lot of work on it since then. The windows were just barely boarded over in them days and we'd dare each other to go inside.'

'Did you ever do it?'

King shook his head. 'Too chicken,' he said and offered a wink. 'It was probably bloody dangerous, looking back, but we loved it.'

'I don't think I've ever seen a building quite like it,' I said, strolling back around to look at the front again. Looking up, I realized it was the first time I'd ever had such a sense of vertigo while standing *on the ground*.

'I'm not real big on all the heritage shite your chattering classes are always on about – Christ, half the people in this poxy country think it's still the nineteenth century . . .'

'Or wish it was,' I suggested.

'Maybe,' King nodded. 'All those bloody costume dramas on the BBC. But I'm glad they've saved this. They've given a big chunk of lottery money over to finishing the restoration, so I hear.'

I found myself nodding agreement. Just seeing the church definitely validated my decision to spend the afternoon touring the East End.

'Care for a pint?' King asked. He nodded at a pub across from Christ Church, where the Ripper victims once gathered to drink. Or so they say.

'Why not?' I said.

*   *   *

The pub was surprisingly crowded for the middle of the afternoon.

'Tourists,' King sniped. But I heard all British accents. One table
of young men gave us the hairy eyeball as we sat down. The three of
them were exceptionally loud and all had a cruel look about them.
They had cold laughs and, while I wasn't paying attention to them
as such, I could clearly hear the word 'nigger' sprinkled into their
conversation.

'Nice crowd,' I said.

King shrugged. 'It's the neighbourhood. What can you do?'

I took a shot at returning their dirty looks, but either mine wasn't
dirty enough or they simply didn't care. I didn't much like their talk,
but I supposed King was right: what can you do?

Three pints later – four for King, who derided me mercilessly for
drinking lager and drinking it slowly – I'd had enough. The beer
was fine, it was even cold, but King's one-man show was finally
getting to me. I didn't mind it at first when he told me what he knew
about the church and Nicholas Hawksmoor, the man who designed
it, and about the history of the neighbourhood, but somehow the
conversation turned to cricket, and King got it into his head that
we were not going to leave the pub until I understood the intricacies
of the game. I think I've accidently seen cricket once or twice on
ESPN during a late night channel surf, but King's explanations and
the accompanying diagrams drawn on the back of cocktail napkins
meant absolutely nothing to me. He must have realized it was a lost
cause, because he was just getting started on rugby when I told him
I had to get back to the hotel to receive a call from LA. There was
no such call, of course, but he had just ordered another pint and I
figured I should get while the getting was good. As I walked out the
door, I saw out of the corner of my eye that he'd already cornered
some other poor bastard for a lecture on god-knows-what.

There was nothing else on the agenda for the day so I *could* have
grabbed a cab back to the hotel, but with no plans for the evening
beyond another expensive room service dinner, I decided to wander
around a little more. I took a last admiring look at the church and
followed my nose down the narrow streets of Whitechapel in the
approximate direction where I remembered seeing an Underground
station.

As I walked around the neighbourhood, I found that at various
moments I would be surprised by glimpses of the Christ Church
steeple through gaps between the tenement buildings. It was amazing
how the old church dominated the horizon of the area once you knew

to look for it. This part of the East End had a strange feel: it was hard to get a grip on it based on the buildings, which were all fairly grotty, but self-evidently of very different ages. King had told me that much of the East End had been destroyed by *Luftwaffe* bombs in the Second World War and I suppose it's amazing that Christ Church itself survived intact. As far as King could recall, the church dated back to the early eighteenth century and apparently a few odd buildings in the area were even older.

As I casually wandered the back streets, however, I didn't see anything that looked all that much older than your average downtown LA storefront. Occasionally I'd come across a historic looking facade, but it would be sandwiched between much more recent, but incredibly shoddy looking, housing projects. All the locals seemed to be Asian and the pungent scents of home-cooked curries set my stomach juices to gurgling.

As I walked on, I realized that I was not headed where I thought I was. I had one of the Ripper maps that the PR boys had provided for me, but there seems to be a conscious and perverse effort in London to make the street names as difficult as possible to locate, and when I did spot a street sign I couldn't seem to figure out where it was on the map. At one point, I wandered down a footpath that cut through the middle of one of the housing projects – council estates was how King referred to them – and for the first time drew unfriendly glances from a group of teenaged Asian boys. I started walking a little faster and felt better when I saw that they didn't bother to follow me. If it had been LA, the happy youths would already have tossed my dismembered body parts into garbage cans, and be out selling my watch and shoes.

I came out of an alley onto a deserted cobblestone street – no visible street name, of course – and looked left and right, hoping to maybe catch a glimpse of the church tower and orient myself with that. The street was lined with three and four storey tenements, though, and I couldn't pick out any landmark above their heights. With a mental eeny-meeny-miny-mo I took a right, but within a couple of blocks started to doubt the choice, because the already grimy looking neighbourhood around Christ Church was taking on the appearance of a serious slum. It was still nothing in the order of East LA or Long Beach, but the streets were noticeably dirtier and for the first time I spotted graffiti on the walls. I didn't think much of it until I saw the first ULTIMA THULE scrawled in red that looked just a little too much like blood.

I wasn't exactly worried just yet – I'd been beaten up in much worse places than this over the years – but walking alone in a bad part of a strange city is not exactly a clever thing to do. And something about that ULTIMA THULE particularly unnerved me. The only people I'd seen on the street for the last few blocks were black-garbed Muslim women who never looked up, and gangs of Asian youths who conspicuously did; neither of whom it struck me as a good idea to approach for help.

As a slight, but distinct panic began to build inside me, the cobblestone street came to an end in a slightly wider, paved road with several small shops visible. This street, too, seemed awfully quiet for the time of day, but I breathed an audible sigh of relief at the sight of a small convenience store on the corner. I made a bee-line for it, determined to get a cold drink and directions to the subway.

A buzzer sounded as I walked in the door and a middle-aged Asian man with a Groucho Marx moustache and pudgy cheeks nodded at me. I smiled back and said 'How do', which seemed to throw him a bit. The long, narrow shop had only a single aisle, but was about as cluttered as could be with everything from candy bars to cans of soup. A magazine rack hung on one wall and few of the titles were in English. A stand in the middle of the store contained a bunch of battered looking videotape boxes depicting actors and actresses in brightly coloured saris and what I assumed was Hindi writing. I spotted a refrigerator in the back of the store next to a beaded curtain leading into a private area. I headed straight for the chugging cooler, figuring the proprietor was more likely to be helpful to a paying customer.

The fridge was mostly full of Coke and Diet Coke, none of which – surprise, surprise – was all that cold, but I eyed some bottles of Snapple, of all things, on the bottom rack. I knelt down to sort the various Snapples from the Fruitopias (ugghh! Snapple-wannabe) when I had the feeling of being watched. I peered up from a bottle of Passion Fruit Potion and saw two dark eyes measuring me up. They belonged to a gorgeous little girl, the owner's daughter I imagined, who looked to be about four years old. She had long, shiny hair and wore a very incongruous 'Good girls go to heaven; bad girls go to London' T-shirt that drooped down to below her knees. I smiled and waggled my fingers at her and she giggled back, but then got all shy and tried to hide behind the curtain.

I couldn't decide between the Mango Melanoma and Grapefruit Goitre (I may not have those flavours *exactly* right) and held the two bottles up to my little friend, asking her to choose. She seemed to take the responsibility very seriously and was carefully studying the two labels when the entry buzzer sounded. I didn't pay it any mind until I saw the little girl's gaze shift up from the bottles and over my shoulder. Her smile very quickly vanished and her eyes went wide with fear. I glanced back around toward the front of the store to see what she was looking at and felt something considerably colder than the Snapple settle in my stomach.

Two thuggish white kids were harassing the very scared-looking owner. One was a textbook skinhead: short and squat with a close-cropped pate and cauliflower ears. He was wearing black jeans, a black T-shirt and Frankenstein boots. The other was taller and thin, with long, scraggly hair and a wisp of a beard. He had on a too-big leather jacket and held something shiny in his hand. The skinhead was leaning over the counter and grabbed the owner by the collar. He slapped the Asian man back and forth across the face; not that hard, but loud enough that I could hear the sound of flesh on flesh. He was yelling at the little man, but I couldn't quite make out the words for his Cockney accent. The leather dude was jumpy, looking back and forth between the counter and the street. Neither of them had spotted me kneeling at the back of the store.

The skinhead was laughing uproariously as he cursed and slapped the owner: it sounded like he was calling him 'fucking Porky', which didn't make any sense to me at all. His partner was smiling, but said nothing. I saw him take a long look out at the street, then he walked around behind the counter.

He held a butterfly knife in his hand.

'Fuck, shit, fuck,' I whispered. Or something pithy like that.

There are moments in life when you just don't think, you act. Some of these moments are good and some bad:

You're cruising in your car, singing along with Bruce Springsteen on 'Two Hearts' and plough through a stop sign: bad.

You see an old lady at the supermarket check-out with just a loaf of bread so you let her get in front of you: good (until she tries to pay with a post-dated fourth-party cheque).

You're introduced to an intelligent and impressive young woman at a party and you're checking out her tits before you've looked her in the eye: well, you make the call.

I didn't think.

I stood up and took two running strides toward the front of the store, a savage, atavistic growl escaping from somewhere deep inside.

I threw the first bottle of Snapple as hard as I could.

I saw the bottle twirl end-over-end down the length of the store, the pink liquid almost glowing under the fluorescent light. (What's *in* that stuff?) I saw the two thugs turn to look my way, the vicious glee on their faces turning to surprise.

The bottle shattered as it caught the skinhead right across the bridge of the nose. A wave of pink stuff splashed across the front window of the shop as the skinhead lost his grip on the store owner and crumpled to the floor.

The thug in the leather jacket was already leaping over the counter as I let fly with the second bottle. The stuff inside was a brownish colour and didn't catch the fluorescence as impressively. The kid was halfway out the door when the bottle struck him in the middle of the back, propelling him on out into the street. I heard the glass break, but couldn't tell if it was the kid's body or the ground that caused it to shatter.

I ran down the aisle to the front of the store. I saw the owner down on his knees behind the counter, but he looked to be okay, just shaken up. The skinhead was writhing on the floor and moaning, his hands covering up the bloody mess of his face. Between his fingers, shards of glass poked out of his cheeks. I went outside, but the kid in the leather jacket was nowhere to be seen. I saw the smashed bottle on the sidewalk, but if it broke against him it couldn't have done too much damage. More's the pity.

I walked back in. The owner had composed himself. He'd come out from behind the counter and stood with a cricket bat raised over his head, ready to give the skinhead a good whack. He looked up at me and I saw the question in his eyes.

'Hey, go ahead, Chief,' I told him. 'Take your best shot. I won't tell.'

The little man raised the bat higher, but he couldn't deliver the blow. A woman, carrying the little girl in her arms, came running up from the back of the store crying and screaming in a language I didn't understand. The owner was crying, too, as he threw the cricket bat away and hugged his wife and child.

I looked down at the skinhead: there was blood and fruit juice everywhere. I saw his steel-toed boots. And up close I could see that there was writing imprinted on his black T-shirt, silver lettering that read: ULTIMA THULE.

I reared back and kicked him in the balls as hard as I could.

I think they must have heard the scream on Sunset Boulevard.

A flash went off behind me. King stood in the open doorway, camera in hand. The flash went off again and again and again.

'Brilliant,' King said, still clicking, a mile-wide smile on his face. 'Fucking. Brilliant.'

FOUR

〜

BURNS, BABY, BURNS!!! screamed the headline on the front page
of the newspaper with the naked honeys. I didn't mind the 72-point
type, but the third exclamation mark struck me as a tad excessive.
One of King's photographs of, I have to admit, a pretty cool-looking
me standing over the prone skinhead in the shop took up most of
the rest of the page. (Though, of course, it was not the snap of me
kicking the scumbag in the balls.) The other main item was a picture
of a minor member of the royal family who was rumoured to be
planning a sex change.

In fact, I made the front page of most of the next day's papers,
though I was below the fold on all the broadsheets except for *The
Times*. Only the *Guardian* didn't use King's photo, so he must have
made out like a bandit. Mahr and his PR boys didn't even have to
work up a sweat on the publicity end. The media lemmings were
crawling all over each other to jump off my cliff. The Ripper stuff
we'd toiled over the previous morning was all thrown away – no
great loss – in the light of my convenience store adventure. Mahr
summed it up best: 'What do we need with that PR bullshit when
we've got a *real* hero on our hands?'

I half-wanted to remind him that 'that PR bullshit' was his life,
but sleeping dogs and all that.

'Hero' seemed a little excessive, too, truth be known, but that was
the angle the papers played and the folks at the satellite company
were only too happy – orgasmic might be a more apt description –
to go along with it. The corporate execs who had previously shaken
my hand and disappeared were back in force. Mahr busily shunted

me from one grinning face to another, but none of them registered in my consciousness. Those executive types all look the same anyway, as bland and unremarkable – and for all their inflated salaries, about as bright – as cashiers at the supermarket check-out.

A full day of interviews and photo ops loomed and Mahr and his gang were already reworking the *Burning Bright* ad campaign to capitalize on my newfound notoriety. I'd spent the morning being shuttled from studio to studio so I could appear on the various breakfast TV shows. I've always hated crap like *Good Morning America* and *Today* with all that fake morning cheer – who the fuck even *wants* to be in a good mood at seven in the goddamn a.m. – and was unsurprised to learn that the British variations on the theme aren't any better. The first show I appeared on was hosted by a man and woman who weren't married but acted like they were, while the second starred a pair who *were* married, but acted like they weren't. Another show starred a virtual platoon of hosts, so marriage wasn't an option outside of Utah. They were just as nauseatingly jolly as the others while on-the-air, but sniped at each other like Israelis and Palestinians during the breaks.

Naturally, they all asked me about my brave adventure in the East End, but fortunately I'd been primed by the PR machine to quickly focus on the more important stuff, like showing clips from *Burning Bright*. I've never been too comfortable with live interviews, but I'd had to make similar media rounds when *Burning Bright* was first aired back at home, and I had my standard spiel for the show down pat. I'd memorized a summary description of what had gone down in the convenience store, too, and didn't need to stray from the script to answer any of the largely fawning questions.

None of them said anything about Ultima Thule.

I wasn't surprised, of course. Mahr's PR material talked up how I'd foiled an attempted robbery and that was how the morning papers told the story, too. The official statement from the police said much the same, congratulating me especially for my display of civic duty even though I was a foreigner. Something about cheeky Yanks. Or was it plucky?

I wasn't sure it was quite so simple, though.

The first cops to arrive on the scene – I'm too embarrassed for them to call them 'bobbies' – were a couple of beat patrol officers. They took statements and called for an ambulance for the skinhead, but the young female constable who took my statement was on the ball, and when King told her who I was she immediately radioed for someone higher up to come to the scene. She hadn't heard of

me – 'I hate detective stories,' she said, 'too bloody ridiculous' –
but having been informed as to my celebrity status, she adopted a
cautiously starstruck attitude. She even asked me to autograph her
citation pad, though she studied my name with poorly concealed
puzzlement.

Her boss was a tall, middle-aged geezer, hard-looking, with a Jay
Leno lantern jaw. Actually, like so much else that I experienced in
England, he struck me as particularly Pythonesque. I half expected
him to tell me his name was Sergeant There's-a-tiger-behind-you,
but he introduced himself as DCI Carling and pulled the street cop
off to one side to get the lowdown. He was all effusion and good
cheer as he walked back over to me, though he leaned so far into
my personal space that I feared he might take my eye out with that
chin. The lady constable, whose name was Walton, trailed a couple
of steps behind him.

'Well,' Carling said, 'rather an adventure you've had, Mr Burns.
Well done, indeed, sir.'

'Right place at the wrong time,' I shrugged. 'Or vice versa.'

'Yes,' he said and scratched an acre of chin. I wondered just
long it took him to shave every morning. 'I've just been reviewing
your account of the situation with PC Walton. It all seems rather
straightforward, sir, but I do have a bit of a question about what
you say you heard during the robbery.'

'What do you mean?' I asked.

Carling held out his hand and the officer handed him her little
note pad. 'You say,' he said without even glancing at her notes, 'that
the assailants grabbed hold of the shopkeeper and verbally abused
him, as well as physically assaulting him.'

'Yeah, that's right.'

'You also say that they referred to him as, pardon me, sir, a
"fucking porky".'

'That's what I thought I heard,' I said. 'He didn't look that fat to
me, so it didn't make any sense. But then the officer here explained
to me that they were probably calling him a "Paki". I never heard
of that before in the States, but I take it that's some kind of racial
insult here?'

'Sometimes,' Carling said and glanced unhappily at his officer. She
tried to avoid his gaze. 'Are you sure about what you heard, sir?'

Something was starting to smell here and it wasn't just the spilled
passion fruit juice. 'Like I say, I thought they called him a "porky",
but I was at the back of the store and I find some English accents
a little hard to understand. Ugly American and all that. But given

what the officer here said . . .' – Carling flashed Walton another grim look – 'it seems fair to assume that they called him a "Paki" and I just misunderstood.'

'But you heard them say "porky",' he prompted.

'Strictly speaking, yeah, I suppose I did.' I thought I could see where this was going.

'Then,' he said, leaning in even closer to me, 'could I ask that you report it precisely in that way when you make and sign your official statement.'

He had me leaning backward to avoid the arc of his jawline, but now I straightened up. 'What gives?' I asked.

'Sir?'

I flashed a look at the constable then turned my full-bore gaze onto Carling. Actually, my full-bore gaze has all the intensity of a dying penlight. 'What is this all about?'

'You're from Los Angeles, Mr Burns. Is that correct?'

'City of angels.'

'I've never been myself, but I take it that Los Angeles is a city of a certain racial . . . disharmony.'

'We've got an official riot season, if that's what you mean. But you have to book early.'

'Yes, sir, that is precisely what I mean. The thing of it is, we'd much prefer not to see anything similar take hold here.'

'Meaning?'

'Meaning that there are always tensions that boil away beneath the surface in a city as large and as diverse as London. Particularly in a neighbourhood such as this where one finds a certain . . . coming together of divergent cultural groups.'

I knew what the cop was getting at, but I didn't think I liked it. And I didn't feel like making it easy for him. 'Why don't you just say what you mean here, boss?'

Carling pursed his lips and looked at Walton, who was still studiously avoiding any and all eye contact. 'Why don't you see if PC Baxter needs any assistance?' Carling said to her. About as subtle as his chin.

'We have ongoing, long-term racial problems around here,' he said, once we were alone. 'There is regular, if low-level, harassment of the Asian community by the likes of the yob rubbish such as you encountered. This harassment tends to be followed, understandably I grant, by an equally angry response from the local Asian youths. We try to keep a lid on things to the extent possible, but publicity can and will only make matters worse. And you are almost certainly going to attract a great deal of publicity for this. Now, if this incident can be passed off as nothing more than a botched robbery, there will likely be few repercussions. But if there is any suggestion that the attack was racially motivated . . .'

'Which it was,' I interrupted.

'Well, we don't know that for sure, do we? And if you merely report what you *heard* the villains say, rather than someone else's suggestion as to what was said, then perhaps we can avoid greater nastiness in the days to come.'

The cop looked at me expectantly. I suppose what he said made sense, though there was something about it – okay, it was the manifest dishonesty – that I didn't like. Still, it was *his* patch of turf and who the hell was I to tell him what was right or how to maintain order in it?

'Ultima Thule,' I said.

His eyebrows scooted up and his big jaw drooped like a steamshovel. 'Sorry?'

'Ultima Thule,' I repeated. 'What does it mean?'

'Where have you come across that expression?'

I made a face and pointed at the skinhead who was only just being led away. You could still read the lettering under the blood on his T-shirt.

'Right,' Carling said.

'And I've seen it around. Most noticeably on a brick which got tossed through a restaurant window into the middle of my chicken dansak. But I've seen it around the neighbourhood, too. On some of the walls.'

'It's a slogan taken up by certain of the local hooligans. It's a reference to something like judgement day, as I understand. Rather apocalyptic sort of talk. Millennium and all that nonsense. And it's very much a part of what I was just telling you about. It's why your cooperation is so important. And would be so very much appreciated.'

He looked at me questioningly. I don't know: other than the chin, he seemed like an okay guy. As cops go, I mean.

'Porky it is,' I told him. 'B'deh-b' deh-b'deh, that's all folks.'

'Thank you, Mr Burns,' he said and started to walk away.

'Hey,' I yelled. He turned around. 'Do you guys *really* call these bastards "villains"? I mean, you aren't just yanking a Yank here, are you?'

'Please believe me, Mr Burns, villains is what they most assuredly are.'

I nodded and wanted to ask him something else, but Mahr and the press gang arrived and I didn't get the chance.

I did another live interview on the BBC's lunchtime television news before finally getting a break. Though I would have preferred June's company, Mahr had insisted on escorting me around town all day. Given that this had turned out to be a big deal I couldn't say no. Still, the guy proved to be a terrible fussbudget and was seriously getting on my nerves. He asked if I had any preferences regarding lunch, which was my cue to exit stage right.

'Listen,' I said. 'I could use an hour or two on my own. Just to clear my head, you know?'

'We have rather a busy schedule yet this afternoon,' he warned. He looked horror-struck.

'Yeah, that's cool,' I comforted. 'But I just want to, you know, take a walk. Relax for a while.'

Mahr didn't seem to know what to say. He clearly didn't care to let me out of his sight, but he didn't want to offend me either.

'When's the next gig?' I asked.

He whipped out a little electronic data-thingy. 'We have an interview for an *Observer* profile at two. That's back in Clerkenwell.'

'Okay,' I said, invoking star's prerogative, 'tell them I'll be there at . . .' – I glanced at my watch: it was nearly one – '. . . three.'

'But where will you be until then? There's not much to do in this part of town.' He sounded like my mother.

'I'll get a cab. I'm a big boy. Just want to have a stroll, grab something to eat. A slice, a dog. Whatever.'

'A slice? A dog?' he asked.

'Pizza? Hot dogs? You know?' He looked appalled. Obviously no outlets of Pink's in London. 'It doesn't matter. I just need a little space. It's a California thing. Ever done Est?'

That did the trick, God bless loopy old Werner Erhard. Mahr reluctantly agreed (not that he had any choice) and we made arrangements to meet up again in time for the newspaper interview. As I walked up the road – in fact, I didn't have the faintest idea where I was or which way I was going – I sensed Mahr watching me. I glanced back after about a half a block and sure enough he hadn't moved. He was still standing out in front of the BBC studio, tracking me. I turned around and waved at him, offering a little smile. He half-raised his arm and waved back, but his heart wasn't in it. He looked like he wanted to cry and I felt like a little kid setting off for his first day of school.

I didn't turn around again until I was sure that Mahr would be well out of sight.

Mahr was right about the neighbourhood: deadbeat city. I strolled for a while, enjoying the quiet, but there was nothing much there other than dull office buildings, most of which seemed to belong to the BBC, and my tummy began to rumble. I stumbled upon a Tube station and browsed the map. I saw that I wasn't too far from Kensington, which rang a positive bell in my memory, so I boarded the first train heading for Kensington High Street.

The London Underground is very neat. Unlike the nascent LA subway it actually goes everywhere, and unlike the even more immense New York system, it is reasonably pleasant to ride. In fact, with its cushioned seats, working doors and lights, and graffiti-free cars it doesn't fit the American definition of a subway at all. The maps are even easy to read; a sure sign of no involvement by anyone who's ever worked for a metropolitan transit authority in the United States.

Kensington itself didn't look at all familiar to me when I got out on the street, but it was the kind of place I was looking for: upscale shops and cafes and lots of likely places to eat. Most of them looked chi-chi, though, and I didn't want anything too fancy. Mahr had already told me that the network had a big congratulatory shindig planned for the evening, so I figured it was best to keep it light and easy.

I wandered into a relatively clean-looking lunch joint and ordered up a turkey sandwich and a Coke. I didn't pay much attention to what they'd given me until I sat down with it at a table and took a bite.

It was a turkey sandwich.

Literally.

Two paper-thin slices of turkey on buttered white bread. Nothing else.

And the Coke was warm.

Now, ill-travelled though I be, I *am* aware of the reputation for kvetching that Americans abroad have. I'm not normally one to complain, but this item was to American sandwiches what the London Tube is to the New York subway. But vicy-versa, if you know what I mean.

The gentleman behind the counter, who looked Greek, but spoke with some kind of Slavic accent, seemed genuinely puzzled by my complaint, not to mention unmoved: he had given me precisely what I had ordered and more importantly, already paid for. He

had the happy look of a man with the customer's money jingling
in his pocket. I began to explain to him the history and philosophy
of the sandwich – lettuce, tomato, cheese, mayonnaise; cucumber,
even, in some of the world's more exotic climes – but he wasn't
amused.

'Lettuce and tomato extra,' he snarled.

'Mayo?' I asked.

'Mayo extra!'

I hated to ask, but, 'Cheese?' I ventured.

'No cheese.'

I had to fork over another 40p for the extras and lay them on
myself, but an ice-filled, essentially clean glass for the soda was no
extra charge. I wanted to explain that I hadn't wanted butter on the
sandwich, either, but lost my nerve. I decided that next time I'd just
go to McDonald's where, I assumed, they didn't butter the sesame
seed buns before slapping on the special sauce.

I was about halfway through my sandwich, thumbing through a
tabloid paper that someone had left on the table when the man sat
down across from me. The cafe was small and there were no empty
tables, so I didn't think anything of it. Hell, I can be communal in an
emergency. I didn't even look at him, just folded the paper in half to
free up some table space.

It took about thirty seconds before I realized he was staring at
me.

There are lots of neat things about fame: money, adoration,
money, no waiting on line at restaurants, money. But there's always
a price.

When I was on the skids after my adolescent success had
become a memory, I used to scream with fury when I'd hear
an actor or celebrity mouth off about the trials and tribulations
of fame and the loss of privacy and all that jazz. Most of them
are mealy-mouthed liars. Unless you're an absolute megastar –
and there are only a handful of them at any one time – you
can be an actor and lead a basically normal life if that's what
you want.

But most *don't* want.

Since *Burning Bright* went on the air in the States, I sometimes
get recognized in the supermarket and hit up for the occasional
autograph, but it's not too bad. I can even put up with the odd
insult which gets hurled by some short-dicked pinhead showing off
for his friends. It's all part of the game.

Every so often, though, you run across a scary one.

The man across the table immediately had me thinking uh-oh city. It's in the eyes.

It was a little hard to figure, since *Burning Bright* hadn't even debuted yet, but between the Ripper ploy and the foiled robbery my mug had been all over the place for the past two days, so I couldn't be too surprised.

He wasn't big, but he had that Anthony-Perkins-is-his-own-mother intensity about him. It was the shaved head and eyebrows that gave me the initial scare. I immediately thought, 'skinhead,' but he was Asian– Indian, I reckoned – so the numbers didn't add up. He looked young, but the shaved head made it hard to tell; he might have been twenty, he might have been thirty-five.

The piercings were the other thing that got me. Modern primitive, my Aunt Fanny! A variety of ornaments dangled from and through his ears: a series of serpentine gold bands and thick wooden hoops. A gold stud pierced his left nostril and he had one of those stick-pin things pinching the corner of his right eyebrow. The kind that normal people can't look at without wincing and thinking, *what an asshole.*

I tried Plan A: a smile, a nod, a Mel Gibson wink and back to my lunch.

He just continued to stare. Damn that Mel Gibson.

Plan B: 'How you doing there? Nice to see you.'

He ran his tongue along his chapped lips. It was pierced with a Raisinette-sized gold sphere.

I glanced around at the surrounding tables, but the only one paying any attention was an elderly woman eating a baked potato. She was staring at the dude's eyebrow and wincing.

I tried another round of ignoring, but it was no-can-do. 'You got a problem, buddy?' I finally asked.

'You are Mr Martin Burns,' he said. His accent held a very slight Indian inflection, but the gizmo in his tongue gave him a serious lisp.

'That's right.'

'I have seen you this morning on the television and in the newspapers.'

'Been a busy day,' I said. His expression was utterly blank; I couldn't read him at all.

'What you did was a very good, a very brave thing,' he said.

I exhaled and relaxed a little. 'Thanks,' I said. 'I only did what seemed right at the time.'

'So why do you not do right now?' he asked.

I tensed up again. 'What do you mean?'

'You are on the television, on the radio. Why do you not speak of
the Thule? Why do you not use this opportunity to bring a message
of warning to all? You must do this thing.'

'I don't know what you mean,' I wheezed.

'Ultima Thule is The End of All Things, Mr Burns. I believe you
are aware of this. You know what they are, what they aspire to,
yet you are silent about their threat. You would so make yourself
accomplice to their horrors.'

'I don't know what you are talking about,' I said, but I felt the
buttered turkey trying to take flight in my stomach.

The bald Indian stood up now. He wore only a thin T-shirt that
stretched tight against his chest as he rose. I could see various
protuberances bulging through the cotton: he was pierced all over.

'Ultima Thule would destroy us all,' he shouted. 'You must not
be silent against their storm. You must rage with equal force. Such
opportunities may not come again.'

Everybody in the place was watching now. The man slammed
his hands down on the table, sending my soda glass crashing to
the floor.

'Death to Ultima Thule,' he screamed. Then he began to chant
in a language I didn't recognize.

The Slavic guy came running out from behind the counter, yelling
'Get out, get out!' He pushed at the crazy man and somewhat to
my surprise, had no trouble manhandling him out the door. The
Asian continued to rant and tried to get back in, but the owner
kept pushing him away. I saw him wave at a pair of cops strolling
across the street. The lunatic must have seen them, too, because he
immediately started to run in the opposite direction.

Everyone in the place was now staring at me.

'Heh-heh. I just wanted a sandwich,' I explained. 'No butter.'

Satisfied that the crazy man was gone, the owner came back into
the restaurant.

'You, Mr Cheese-head,' he said, pointing at me. 'Out.'

I still had half my sandwich on the plate and thought about
arguing, but I'd lost my appetite. And I didn't think an encounter
with the police over this would be the kind of publicity the network
wanted. I held up my hands and got up.

The turkey was dry anyway.

I hailed a cab to get back across town. Traffic was hellish and
the fare meter was clicking away like a fashion photographer's
camera as we inched through it, but I barely noticed. I had

plenty of time before I had to meet up with Mahr at the newspaper office.

And I was feeling just a little shook up.

I shouldn't have. Like I say, there are always crazies out there on the street and you sure as hell don't have to be a celebrity to meet up with one.

But there was something different about this guy.

If he'd just been a run-of-the-mill Vietnam/Gulf War/Honk-if-you-love-Jesus ex-vet with a steel plate in his head and a song in his heart I'd have just (nervously) laughed it off. But even though he went ballistic there at the end of our little impromptu confab, and even though he was done up like a New Age pincushion, his tirade about Ultima Thule worried me. I honestly didn't know what he was on about, but I was starting to wonder if maybe the cop, Carling, hadn't quite given me the whole lowdown on this Ultima Thule deal.

Perhaps a little investigation of my own would be in order after all.

In the end, I was late arriving at the offices of the *Observer*, but you should *always* make journalists wait. It actually keeps them from being even more snotty than they normally are. Mahr fidgeted a bit at first, but the interview went well so he was my blood-brother, best buddy again by the time it was over. We hopped another cab back to Canary Wharf. Mahr was all abuzz over the events of the past two days, clearly thrilled with the publicity coup of his life. I appreciated his enthusiasm, but the trouble with PR types is that they're so used to spewing bullshit that they never quite know when to shut it off. That's why they're *always* divorced. Or gay. Or both.

'You ever hear of Ultima Thule?' I asked him during a brief lull in his running monologue. I noticed that the cab driver, the darkest skinned black man I'd ever seen, shot a glance my way when I asked.

'No, no,' Mahr said, drumming his fingers on his thigh. 'Wait, yeah! It's one of those video games, yes? Nintendo 64. I'm sure I remember seeing an ad for it on the sci-fi channel. Tony Kaye. Brilliant.'

'I don't think so,' I mumbled.

'No? Well, I could be mistaken. Come to think of it, I believe it was Play Station not Nintendo. And I saw the ad at the cinema.'

He started talking publicity again, and I tuned out. I did note that the driver kept a close eye on me for the rest of the trip, though. As we were walking up the steps into the office building, I glanced back and thought I saw the man make an odd gesture at me as he pulled away. Even I know that in England you flip the bird with two fingers instead of one; that definitely wasn't the gesture. I was about to comment to Mahr about it, but he had already wandered into the lobby.

I still had one more PR obligation to fulfil before the day was through, but that would be at yet another BBC studio in the early evening. Mahr wanted me to submit to an additional photo session with the network's photographer, though I couldn't believe they could possibly need even one more picture of me at that point. Still, it goes with the territory. I told him I needed to use the little detective's room first and said I'd wander back to his office when I was ready.

After Mahr had walked off, I borrowed the phone from a nearby desk and asked to be connected to June Hanover.

'Oh hello, Marty,' she chirped. 'Where are you?'

'I'm here, in the building. Listen, June: you guys got a library here?'

'You're in the building?' she asked.

'I'm on the fifth floor somewhere. I managed to ditch Mahr for a little while.'

'I see,' she said, and lowered her voice. 'Ah yes, he's just walked in.'

'Can you meet me?'

'I suppose so. Where are you?'

'I . . . don't know. Wait.' The person whose phone I'd appropriated had returned to her desk. She was looking at me starry-eyed and not mad, so I reckoned she knew who I was. 'What's your name?' I asked her.

'Amanda. Jones.'

'I'm at Amanda Jones's desk,' I told June.

'Which one?' she asked.

'Huh? I don't know. How would I know?'

'Well, is it the thin Amanda or the fat Amanda?'

I took a good look. I was stumped. And a little afraid to guess wrong.

'Uhhhh . . .'

'The thin Amanda,' Amanda said. Not entirely happily.

'Thin Amanda,' nodding vigorously. 'Very thin Amanda. Could maybe use a few pounds, even.'

'Be right there,' June said. She was still laughing as she hung up.

Fortunately, thin Amanda was thick-skinned and readily assuaged by an autograph and a winning smile. Even more fortunate, June was a fast mover and we were on our way before I could suffer any further embarrassment.

'We share a library with a couple of newspapers,' June told me as we got on the elevator. 'It's all the same ownership a couple of corporate names up the ladder.'

'Isn't everything,' I said.

'Have you been enjoying the day?' she asked.

'Oh, man, publicity is something you endure not enjoy,' I said.

'I suppose,' she nodded. June was so soft-spoken and pleasant that I almost forgot that she was part of the PR team. I realized she may have taken offence.

'Still, it's what the makes the rest of the business possible,' I offered, relying on my actorly instincts for conviction.

She bought it.

The library wasn't quite like any I'd ever seen before. A series of glass and steel cubicles with a computer on every desk. It reminded me of the set of an early seventies sci-fi movie I'd co-starred in about computers taking over the world. Orson Welles was the voice of the computer. Sad.

'Where're the books?' I asked.

A friendly-looking little guy with curly black hair and a five o'clock shadow came over to greet us.

'Hello, Raphael,' June called.

'Hey, June, what's happening?' he said. I immediately picked up on his New York accent.

'Norteamericano!' I said, holding up my arms.

'Hey,' he said, 'you're whatchamacallit . . . Kid "Dy-no-mite".'

'You're off by about ten years,' I sighed. 'Not to mention two networks and a heap of skin tones.'

'Oh, yeah,' the librarian said, 'that's right.' He looked at me more carefully. 'Marty Burns, isn't it?'

I explained to Raphael who, I judged, had a major crush on June Hanover, that I was looking for information about Ultima Thule.

'It's some kind of far-right group, isn't it?' he asked. 'Like Combat 18 or something.'

'Raph knows everything and everyone,' June said. I wondered if the crush was reciprocal. I thought he was a little short for her myself.

'I don't know that other one, but yeah, apparently it's a skinhead group or something. But that's all I can seem to find out.'

'Not really a lot of skinhead action these days,' the librarian said.

'The ultra-right is more sophisticated than they used to be. They still use skinhead crews for muscle though.'

'Tell me about it.'

'Yeah, I heard what happened. Nice going. But like I say, the fascist and Nazi groups tend to be a little more subtle these days. Very cyber-literate. Still, let's see what we can find.'

Raphael led us over to a computer and booted-up some manner of search engine. I watched him type in 'Ultima Thule' and tapped my fingers along with his beat as we waited for results.

'This is a unified database of the major broadsheet papers. If there's been any mention of Ultima Thule in the last three years, it'll come up.'

The machine beeped at us and the librarian clicked his mouse a few times. A list of a half-dozen sources came up on the screen.

'Not much,' Raphael said. 'Want to take a look?'

'Please.'

He turned the screen my way and clicked on the first article. It was a short piece from the *Independent* from eighteen months earlier about several racist attacks in a town called Bradford. 'Up north,' June told me, reading over my shoulder. 'Big Asian community.' The article quoted a police spokesman as citing a new group called Ultima Thule as possibly responsible for the attacks, but gave no other details.

'Pretty thin,' I mumbled. 'Almost Amanda Jones.' June chuckled. I went on to the next article, but the next three on the list were just variations of the same story from different papers.

'Boring,' Raphael said.

The fifth article wasn't an article at all, but a crossword puzzle from *The Times*. 'Ultima Thule' was part of the clue for 23 across.

The sixth article was completely screwy. It was a travel feature from a Scottish paper about boat tours of some of the small islands that make up Orkney, in the far north of the country. It mentioned that Thule was a mythical place of power rumoured to have once existed among the islands, but didn't expound any further. No mention of skinheads or Nazis or any such.

'Huh,' I said. 'Not much help.' I glanced at Raphael. 'How is it that *you* knew what I was talking about?'

The librarian shrugged. 'I keep a lot of strange shit in my head,' he said. 'Did you know that Canada uses as much natural gas every year as would be used by two billion Pakistanis?'

'Is that true?' June asked. The librarian just shrugged again.

'Is there another database you could tap into?' I asked.

'Dozens. If you want . . .'

Just then Mahr walked in.

'There you are,' he said. 'Marty, we *have* to get you ready for the Beeb. Really, June, it's Desert Island Discs!'

He said it like a whole western town should freeze. June looked guilty, but Raphael was back clicking away at his mouse.

'Tick, tock,' Mahr said, tapping at his watch. I nodded at the librarian and headed for the door.

'Did you know that the volume of radium used to paint the faces of alarm clocks in the 1950s was sufficient to produce an atomic bomb three times the size of Hiroshima?' Raphael said without looking away from his screen.

'Really?' Mahr asked.

'You made that up,' I said.

The librarian broke out in a cheesy grin. 'I did,' he said. 'Later, bro'.'

I couldn't figure what the fuss was about, but everyone else was thrilled that I'd been asked to appear on this Desert Island Discs thing. It seemed to me that this was the kind of stupid gimmick show that every 40-watt radio station in America runs – what music would you take with you to a desert island and why – but apparently the programme has been running for decades on the BBC and has acquired the unassailable status of cultural icon.

I caught on that TV stars, especially Americans, were not the sort who were usually invited on, which was why Mahr and his gang were so orgasmic, but frankly music isn't that big a part of my life and I had a hard time making up a list I could remember, much less that I could tell stories about. I'd had to come up with it earlier in the day, too, and though Mahr kept pressing me to add classical pieces to the list I finally had to admit I didn't know any.

'Surely, you know *some*,' he insisted. I don't think I'd ever felt so *much* like a television actor.

'Ummm, not really,' I admitted. 'Well, there's dum-dum-dum-DUM! The Beethoven thing.'

'I think not,' Mahr sneered.

'I know that other one. What's-his-face: Taco Bell.'

Mahr looked at me with horror.

'You *know*. They use it in commercials all the time. Da-da-DA-da, da-da-DA-da, DUM-de-da-da, DUM-de-do-do . . .'

I'm not quite tone-deaf, but a singing career has never been in the cards for me. Even so, awareness shot across Mahr's depressed features.

'Pachelbel. The canon.'

'Yeah,' I shouted, 'Pachelbel. That's it.'

'I suppose if we're stuck, that will do. Can you tell a story with it?'

'Ummm,' I ummed. 'Actually, I hate the fucking thing.'

In the end, the closest I could come to classical was Gershwin's *Rhapsody in Blue*. Unless you want to count Ennio Morricone's theme from *The Good, The Bad and The Ugly*. Mahr didn't.

Mahr had been certain all day that the BBC would call to cancel after seeing the list of songs I'd submitted, and even as we rode to the studio for the taping, he kept nervously eyeing the cell-phone that was death-clutched in his hand, as if awaiting a call from the governor on execution night. As I looked over my list again and tried to think of stories to go with the pieces – *Mississippi Goddamn, Kicks, At Long Last Love, Rock and Roll High School* – I sort of sympathized with him. (Mahr had steadfastly refused to let me include a Barry White song; callous disrespect for the Walrus of Love, I say, but he wouldn't be swayed.) Who the hell listens to the radio these days anyway?

We arrived at the studio a little early and got shunted off to the VIP lounge – I'd hate to see where the BBC stack their *un*important people, must be like Dachau – where we were treated to bitter coffee and stale cakes. The host of Desert Island Discs briefly stuck her head in the door and waved, but was gone before I could even swallow my dry cookie crumbs. I wasn't paying attention to the live news feed that was piped in through tinny ceiling speakers until I heard the clunk of Mahr's telephone falling to the floor. I glanced up from my notes and saw him staring up at the speaker. I looked up, too.

There was nothing to see – well, actually, the BBC might paint their ceilings a little more often – but the reporter was good. A clear image formed in my mind very quickly. The miracle of radio.

There'd been a firebombing in East London. An Asian shopkeeper and his family – his wife and four children, aged two to twelve – had been killed.

It was, the reporter pointed out, the very same shop in which American television personality Marty Burns had broken up a robbery and assault just one day earlier. Police were looking into a possible connection.

I never did get to tell my *Rock and Roll High School* story. It involves a good deal of nudity and some highly gratuitous violence, so it's probably just as well.

FIVE

⤳

When the PR guys scream at you, you know you've hit a nerve.

Mahr was livid at our meeting the next morning. The other suspender boys were inconsolable. One just sat in his swivel chair, arms crossed over his chest, shaking his head back and forth like a petulant child; the other was actually pulling his curly hair out.

Even June looked upset.

'No, no, no, no,' Mahr shrieked. 'Absolutely, positively, absolutely not!'

'So what are you saying, exactly?' I tried.

He definitely wasn't in the mood.

Faced with the undeniable facts, the police had reluctantly characterized the previous day's convenience store arson and murders as racially motivated. That admission set a whole other set of events into motion, culminating in a series of street fights between Asian and white youths during the wee hours of the morning. Amid the inevitable calls for restraint by various mealy-mouthed politicians and community leaders, a protest march through the East End and past the burned-out shop had been announced by a coalition of various anti-racist groups for one day hence. I made the mistake of mentioning to Mahr that I wanted to attend.

'You can't, you can't, you can't,' he told me again.

'Oh yes, I can,' I replied, and made a mental note to add *Annie Get Your Gun* to my list if I got another shot at Desert Island Discs.

'Marty. You cannot be seen at this demonstration. We've already been swamped with questions about what really happened at that shop the other day.'

'So? I've got no problems with talking about it.'

'No? Okay, then tell me, Mr Burns: what did you think the assailants meant when they addressed the shopkeeper as a "fucking porky"?'

'How do you know about that?' I asked

'I'm good at my job,' Mahr said, and you know, I suddenly believed him. 'And so are the tabloid scum who'll have the same information.'

'It's what the cops wanted me to say,' I explained. 'They practically begged me.'

'*I* realize that. But the police may not be so happy to corroborate your version of events right now, and the public might not understand at all. Your appearance at this march can only raise more questions and create the kind of publicity that will do not do any of us any good. Least of all you.'

'I thought there was no such thing as bad publicity,' I said.

'Tell that to Prince Charles,' the hair-puller said.

'There's already been some backlash,' Mahr said and handed me a folded-back newspaper. 'We weren't going to show this to you, but perhaps it will give you some idea of what we could be in for, how the tabloids play the game here. If we don't position you just right, this sort of thing will be splashed on page one and not buried on page twenty-three.'

'Oh, Christ,' I said, recognizing the picture immediately. *Honey Pot*.

The paper ran a slightly fuzzy still culled from a movie I'd done at the rock-bottom, molten core of the journey-to-the-centre-of-the-earth nadir of my career. It was a deeply awful, soft-core porn/biker/drug flick called *Honey Pot*, in which I'd played a stoned and horny vice cop. I did it because I desperately needed the money – something to do with a bar tab, as I recall – but it was only a five-day shoot and the producer stiffed me in the end with a rubber cheque. There was an implied blow-job scene (it *was* only soft-core), but of course that was the still the tabloid had managed to find. You could see the back of a blonde's head floating over my lap and me with a look somewhere between rapture and I-smell-rotten-eggs on my face. The tabloid had slapped the caption 'OUR HERO?!?' over the still.

(In fact, *Honey Pot* has been an albatross around my neck for years mostly because it features, or so I'm told by those who know about such things, the last-ever screen appearance by the now legendary Ed Wood. The Wood cultists have thus clutched the wretched bit of celluloid to their pathetic bosom, dragging me along for the bumpy ride. Wood barely even registered in my consciousness at the time, and I fuzzily remember him only as a *Day of the Locust* sort of figure with a sot's BO and the saddest eyes I've ever seen.)

'Now in and of itself this is no big deal,' Mahr said. 'Given our target audience and the kind of show *Burning Bright* is, it maybe even brings in a few extra viewers. But that's not why the paper ran the photo.'

'I don't get it,' I said. 'This piece of shit is twenty years old and dull as dishwater to boot. Who could possibly care?'

'Time stands still in tabloid-land,' June said. 'Twenty years ago, twenty minutes ago . . . it doesn't matter. It all just blurs into one timeless ball of sleaze and celebrity. They only care that you've given them the opportunity to publish a provocative picture. Give them another chance and they'll do you even worse.'

'We've had a jolly good ride here, Marty,' Mahr said. 'We got far more publicity out of all this than we could have hoped for going in. You've got name recognition now and we can build on that in a positive way. By and large you're seen as a hero. We don't want to do anything to risk what we've developed.'

'And you think that my going to the march tomorrow will put that at risk.'

Mahr tapped my picture in the paper. 'I'm certain of it,' he said.

I glanced at June again. She nodded at me with determined earnestness.

'I don't know,' I said. 'I guess I'll have to think about it.

I stopped by the library to visit with my American buddy Raphael and see if I could cadge any more information from him, but he wasn't around. I sat down in front of one of the computers and tapped the keys a few times, thinking maybe I could sniff around a database or two on my own, but the damn thing started beeping at me so I beat a hasty retreat out of the room.

There was nothing on the agenda for me for the rest of the day. Mahr, playing the nervous nellie to the hilt, had cancelled a couple of minor PR events. He wanted to keep me away from any reporters until some of the brouhaha over the convenience store killings abated and my role in the affair had been forgotten. I didn't know if I agreed with him – I definitely didn't like it – but I couldn't argue with him. I've been in and around The Business long enough to know that the public is a fickle creature. They're like a feral cat that looks as cute as any domestic tabby, but can suddenly turn on you with shocking ferocity. I've seen it happen to actors and actresses who thought they were in control of the PR game, only to have the beast turn around and bite their asses off.

I'd been through a lot to get back to where I was and I didn't want to blow it on a too-hasty decision. Although I felt strongly about wanting to be a part of the demonstration in the East End, there was more than just me to think about these days. A lot of people depended on *Burning Bright* and had a stake in its success. It had been a while since I'd been in such a position. In the old days, when I was a kid, the fate of those around me, the cast, the crew, even the folks at the network, wasn't the sort of thing it would have occurred to me to think about. I'd booze and whore and snort what was offered without a moment's consideration of the consequences.

I wasn't a kid any more, though. Not even squinting in the dark. I'd told Mahr I'd think about what he said and that was exactly what I intended to do.

But before I could make any decision, there was something I felt I had to see.

I'd first stumbled upon the convenience store by chance, but now it was all too easy to find. The area was hip-deep in cops for blocks around. They looked tense, too; expectant. If not for the oddly disturbing fact that none of the police wore sidearms, I might have thought it was East LA rather than the East End of London.

The area in front of the burned out convenience store was completely cordoned off, with four officers standing fairly casual guard along the perimeter. The store itself was nothing more than a black hole in the ground floor of the heavily charred, three-storey building. All the glass had been blown out, along with the windows of the neighbouring stores on either side. I couldn't see inside the ruins from across the street, but just looking at the mess on the outside of the building it wasn't hard to imagine the fiery hell it must have been for the poor family trapped inside. I flashed on the face of that pretty little girl in the 'Bad Girls Go to London' T-shirt and felt a shudder go through me.

The sidewalk in front of the store was knee-deep in flowers. Scattered among the lilies and daffodils were various stuffed animals and small toys, which I found odd, but guessed were meant as a memorial to the children who had died. As I stood and watched, a woman clad in head-to-toe black with a little boy in tow was allowed through the cordon to add a small wreath of flowers to the pile. The boy delicately placed a single white rose beside a teddy bear and though I thought he couldn't possibly understand what he was doing, as they walked away I saw that he was crying.

One of the cops was steadily eyeing me now. Keeping to the other side of the street, I walked on past the scene of the crime. Just down the block I spotted a sidewalk display of flowers for sale and headed for the shop. I scooped up a bunch of sombre white flowers – the signs weren't in English so I'm not actually sure what they were – to add to the tributes.

The same cop watched me as I approached the convenience store, but I gestured slightly with the flowers, raising an eyebrow and he nodded at me to slip on through the police line. A narrow path had been left between the piles of flowers to provide access to where the front door had been and I walked right up to it. I looked inside and saw that the store had been thoroughly torched. A few blackened cans lay on the floor in puddles of brackish water, and I spotted the burned-out shell of the refrigerator from which I had grabbed that fateful bottle of Snapple, but virtually nothing else was even recognizable. You could still smell the char and ash and there was a trace of a thicker, sweeter smell like . . .

Burnt meat.

I slapped my hand over my mouth and took a hurried step back away from the door. I tried to recreate a picture of the inside of the store in my head; tried to recall if the shop had sold any fresh meat products.

I didn't think it had.

I felt my gorge start to rise and I had to turn away from the front of the shop. I suddenly realized that the flowers were still in my hand, though I was holding them so tightly that I had snapped most of the stems. I threw them down on top of the others, earning me a fresh look of suspicion from two of the cops.

That's when I saw him.

Standing across the street and up the block, from near the spot where I had initially scoped out the scene. His neatly shaved head was what first caught my eye, but when he turned slightly to his left the sun glinted off the spike that pierced his eyebrow.

It was the lunatic from the sandwich shop. The pincushion Asian dude who had started screaming at me about Ultima Thule.

'Hey,' I said as we caught each other's eye. Then I yelled it: 'Hey!'

He didn't move at first. Then he pressed his hands together in front of him in an almost prayerful way and nodded his head slightly.

He started to walk away.

'Hey!' I yelled again, never at a loss for words.

The cops had grown visibly tense and started walking toward me. One of them, a lady cop, was looking across the street at my bald friend, but she was talking into a microphone velcroed to the shoulder of her uniform. My stick-pin buddy was walking faster now in the opposite direction. I started to walk through the perimeter after him.

'Just a moment, sir,' the nearest cop said, holding up his palm.

I admit I sort of ignored him in my haste to follow the bald man. I ducked right under the cordon and took a step into the street. The cop grabbed me by the arm and spun me around.

'I said wait,' the cop hissed.

'That man . . .' I tried to explain.

Then I heard the unmistakable whirr-click-whirr-click of an automatic still camera. I glanced to my right and saw my buddy King snapping away while the cop held me tightly by the arm and his fellow officers closed in around me.

I glanced back across the street, but of course the bald man was history.

'I bloody love you, mate,' King smiled, still shooting. 'You're gonna earn me that Mercedes I've always wanted.'

It's so nice to be loved.

I didn't sleep well that night. I worked my way through the hotel room mini-bar and then ordered up a late, obscenely expensive, room-service snack – why does *everything* in England come with fries? Fish, okay. But lasagne? – but even that didn't make me feel any better. I flipped on the TV, was almost disappointed when I couldn't find any darts to watch. I looked again at the piece of paper which Mahr had faxed over just before ten o'clock.

It was a slightly blurry copy of the front page from the first edition of one of the morning tabloids featuring a big blow-up of my inamorato King's photograph of me being manhandled by the cop. I had the look that everyone in the grasp of the police has: guilty. Of what, I don't know, but there was definitely some shifty-eye action going on there. And King had managed to catch me with my mouth half-open, making me look not only guilty but stupid as well. I suppose I didn't blame him, everybody's got to eat. Of course, it doesn't have to be champagne and caviar in the back seat of a German luxury automobile.

After King had taken his fill of pictures, he'd intervened with the cops on my behalf. He's one of those guys who seems to know everyone, everywhere and they let me go on his say-so, especially after one of the cops recognized me from King's pictures in the paper the day before. They did suggest that I might want to keep my distance from the convenience store in the future. I tried to thank King for his help, but he cut me off with a mysterious, 'Don't thank me yet,' before scurrying off.

Now I understood why.

Predictably (and not unreasonably) Mahr hit the roof when I told him what happened. He actually started yelling at me until he remembered who I was and what he was doing. Even then, he just walked away. The fax with the next morning's front page wasn't even accompanied by a note, just one of those officious little 'with compliments' slips with Mahr's name printed on it. Turns out his first name was Nigel, which was the first I'd heard of it. It suited him, though.

I felt restless and took a walk down to the lobby. It was after midnight so the hotel bars and restaurants were shut and there wasn't a soul around. I wandered outside, but it was drizzling, and depressed though I was, a walk in the rain in the dark wasn't top of my list. I plopped down on a comfy chair in the lounge for a while, but got sick of the dodgy looks I garnered from the hotel staff. I figured sitting by myself in the Savoy lobby late at night probably didn't do my career image a whole lot of good either.

Sometimes I forget about that whole celebrity thing. Mantle of fame and all that.

Back in my room, I realized that I was just feeling sort of lonely. I thought about giving Rosa a call – even picked up the receiver – but decided that *that* was definitely not a conversation to be had given my present mood and a distance of six thousand miles.

Then I remembered that June had given me her home number. She'd scrawled it on the back of her business card. Just in case.

It was a little late to be calling, but I was feeling just pathetic enough – and able to exploit that modicum of star's prerogative I now possessed – to punch the number.

'Hello,' a very grumpy, very male voice answered.

'Ahhhh . . .' I improvised. 'Oops.'

And hung up.

I don't know what I expected. I had no reason to be surprised, certainly had no reason to have hung up. For all I knew, June was happily married with three kids (though I had noticed that she didn't wear a wedding ring). Or shacked up with the crew of a Turkish freighter. Or a women's basketball team. (Though the

male voice sort of cast doubt on the last supposition. Could have
been the coach, I suppose.)

It wasn't like I had any romantic designs on June. I just wanted
someone to talk to. I'd have written it on the board a hundred times
if I'd had one. And some chalk.

The phone rang about two minutes later.

'Marty? It's June Hanover.'

'Oh,' I said, 'hi there.'

'Hi. I'm sorry if I'm wrong, but . . . did you just call here?'

'Ummm,' I said. 'Yeah,' I added.

'It's okay,' June laughed. 'Really. I told Terry I thought maybe it
was you.'

'Terry?' I asked. It wasn't what I meant to say.

'Terry's a friend,' June said. Matter-of-factly.

'That's good,' I replied. 'Friends, I mean. They'll be there for you.
Of course, you have to be there for them, too.' What the hell was
I talking about?

'Are you all right, Marty? Is everything okay?'

'Oh. Yeah. Fine,' I said. 'I was . . . ah, I don't know, just looking
for someone to talk to. Hotel rooms do that to me sometimes. I
think it has something to do with those little bars of soap.'

She laughed. It sounded nice. 'I think it's the plastic stuff they
wrap the plastic cups in. I've never entirely understood that.'

'Or the paper wrapper they put around the toilet seat.'

'Oh no, I like that,' she said. 'It makes it feel cleaner to me,
somehow. A false sense of security, I'm sure. But then clutch onto
what you can, I always say.'

We both laughed, but it tapered off into a lengthy and uncomfortable lull. Then we both spoke at once.

'I don't . . .' she started.

'Have you . . .' I said.

'Go ahead,' she insisted.

'I got a fax from Mahr,' I said.

'Me too,' June sighed.

'Morning paper?'

'Yes, Marty. It's not good, but it's not that bad, either. You weren't
doing anything, so the publicity shouldn't hurt us too much.'

'*Too* much.'

She sighed again. 'I can't tell you that this is a good thing, Marty,
but it's done. Why did you go back there?'

'I just wanted to see it,' I said. 'I just felt like it was something I
had to do before I could decide what I should do tomorrow.'

'And have you decided?' June sounded like she was holding her breath.

'Are you asking as a dedicated employee of Star Television?'

A brief silence. Then: 'I'm not sure. I guess you should assume that I am. Though it's too late for me to call Mahr, if that helps.'

'Does anybody call him Nigel?'

'I don't think so. Why would they?'

'Point,' I said.

'You haven't answered my question,' June said.

'I know.'

I heard the murmur of another voice – Terry's, I imagine – but I couldn't make out the words. June said something back, but I couldn't quite make that out either.

'Sorry,' she said. 'Listen: it's your decision, obviously, but beyond the question of the PR for *Burning Bright*, I'm worried that you may not entirely understand the situation.'

'How do you mean?'

'These anti-racism events and marches happen all the time in London, and they aren't always what they appear to be. Given what's happened, I'm not doubting the good intentions behind this particular demonstration, but these things are often covers for something else.'

'I don't think I understand.'

'I know. And that's what worries me. British politics can be very peculiar. These marches and protests are sponsored by different groups for different reasons. You have the rump of the old far left: your CND and Socialist Worker types who protest anything and everything. You have groups who call themselves anti-racist, but who have their own agendas, like some of the fundamentalist Muslim groups. You have the deep greens and animal liberation extremists, and various other elements who try to use every even vaguely leftish rally to suck in supporters for their own causes. And then there are the people who truly are marching against racism.'

'You make them sound like an afterthought,' I said.

'It's just that sometimes I'm afraid they are.'

'So you don't think this rally tomorrow is legit?' I asked.

'I don't know, Marty. It may be exactly what it claims to be, it probably is. I just want you to consider that you may not understand the situation and might be letting yourself in for more than you bargained for. It would be easy for you to be . . . used in these circumstances.'

'You seem awfully clued up about this stuff,' I said.

There was a pause and yet another sigh.

'I used to be,' she said. 'When I was a student at South Bank University here in town I used to go along on all the anti-Nazi marches. This was back when the National Front was still a happening thing.'

'National Front?'

'They were a far-right . . . oh, it's too much to try to explain to you right now. Which is sort of my point. It's also too late. But I was very much into these things at the time.'

'That's pretty much the definition of being a student isn't it?'

'I suppose. At least it used to be.'

'So what happened?' I asked.

'I got disenchanted. And I graduated. And I took a job in the public relations department of one of the world's biggest, richest media companies.'

That led to a long silence.

'So what are you going to do, Marty?' June finally asked.

I didn't question her again about who she was asking that as. 'I'm going to go to sleep. You should, too. Kiss Terry for me. Goodnight, June.'

I hung up the phone before she could say anything else. Or before I could hear what she might have to say.

I had a very bad dream. It woke me up with a start at about four in the morning, but faded so fast I couldn't remember anything but a feeling.

The feeling was cold and dark, and though the room was warm, I was covered in sweat

It felt like death had come and kissed me in the night.

I fumbled around until I found a little bottle of Jack Daniels in the mini-bar. Ah, that distinctive shape.

It took about an hour – and a second helping of JD – but finally I fell back asleep.

SIX

~

The phone rang again early the next morning, but I couldn't be bothered to pick it up. I assumed it was Mahr, and I didn't want to find out for sure.

I guess I knew all along that I was going to go to the demonstration. I did think about what June had told me, but I've always been a have-to-see-it-for-myself kind of guy. Hell, I even went to see *Heaven's Gate*. In 70mm yet. Though June might be right about the Byzantine politics of her country and the event, in the end none of that really mattered to me. I knew I wanted to go simply to express my anger and sorrow over what had happened, and I figured that *some* of the other people would be there for that very same reason. If enough of us who felt that way made our presence known, then the rest of the fanatics and politicos and goofballs of all persuasions tagging along for the ride wouldn't make the slightest bit of difference.

At least that's how I explained it to June.

She was waiting for me in the lobby, you see. I had intended to get over to the rally site early, partly because I wasn't that sure of my way around town, but also in order to scope out the situation just in case the event smelled like something that I *didn't* want to be a part of. Once again, I had no idea how long she'd been sitting there, but found that I wasn't all that surprised to see her.

Or displeased.

'Better watch out,' I said by way of greeting. 'Keep hanging out here and the management are going to think you're working the joint.'

'Do I look like a prostitute?' June asked with a smile. She was wearing black denim jeans with a white DKNY sweatshirt and black Reeboks. Hardly the uniform of the day for a call-girl. Or an anti-racism marcher, come to think of it.

'No,' I said, sitting down beside her. 'But back in LA, in the Polo Lounge, you can identify the hookers by the fact that they don't look like hookers at all.'

'Sounds confusing.'

'Yeah, well, fortunately the network executives are easier to pick out.'

'Don't tell me: they're the ones whose lips move when they lie.'

'No, they all look like prostitutes. And you're far too young to be so cynical,' I said.

'I'm not that young.'

'Well, you're not that cynical, either. But you will be if you keep hanging out with me.' I waved at a waiter for a cup of coffee. June declined. 'It's very nice to see you and all, June, but, ummm, what are you doing here? Shouldn't you be at work? Or are you?'

'I called in sick. First sick day I've taken in over a year.'

'Sucker.'

'That's life on the corporate ladder. Especially if you don't happen to own your own pair of testicles.'

'What if you only have one?' I asked. She shrugged. 'Helluva way to make a living,' I muttered.

'We can't all star in our own television programmes, Marty,' she said. She still had a smile on her face, but there was a bit more incisor in it than before.

I'd been a nobody for so many years that more often than not I still think like one. In part, that's because I've been determined not to mutate back into the kind of snotty ego-beast all too common in The Business, and so much like I used to be when I was riding the crest as a teen star. But even with all the temptations and opportunities to play the haughty celebrity, temptations I admit to succumbing to on occasion, for the most part I just don't enjoy it. I like the money and the odd touch of adulation – who wouldn't? – but this time around I feel like I can see through more of it. Like knowing the secret behind a stage illusion – perhaps *the* stage illusion – and the thrill just ain't there.

And of course now I've seen other things, more amazing and secret things, that show up the shabby cups-and-ball magic of Hollywood and The Business for the pathetic little diversions that they are.

The trouble is, I still forget that everybody else doesn't know the secret, and most think that the disappearing rabbits of TV entertainment are miracles to behold.

'I'm sorry, June,' I said. 'Really. I didn't mean anything by that. Believe me when I say I know that you work twice as hard as I ever will on *Burning Bright*. And I wouldn't dis you.'

Some of that lupine quality dissipated from her smile. 'I believe you,' she said. 'Forget it.'

'So I suppose you plan to go to this rally with me.'

'Hey-hey,' she chanted, 'ho-ho. Racism has got to go.'

It drew a few glances from the thin-nosed, three-piece crowd in the Savoy lobby.

Ho-ho, indeed.

When it got ugly it got ugly *fast*.

We'd hopped on the Tube to the advertised starting point for the march near Brick Lane. I was about to hail a cab, but June pointed out that, thanks to the march, traffic through the East End was likely to be a disaster.

'And, Marty,' she added, 'I admit it has been a while since I've done this, but somehow taking a black cab to a protest rally doesn't feel quite the Johnny to me.'

I wasn't sure who or what Johnny was – but I took her point.

We grabbed the District Line train to Aldgate East, where many of the other folks got off with us. It was a mostly young, fairly scraggly crowd, but more diverse than I might have expected. There were an awful lot of preachy T-shirts to be seen – I saw one couple, the man's shirt declaring 'Animals Are Human Too' while his partner's read 'Humans Are Animals Too' – but mixed in were more than a few suits and ties. There did seem to be a preponderance of particularly filthy hippie types, many with dreadlocks and almost-as-mangy dogs in tow. I remarked on it to June.

'Crusties,' she said. Without much enthusiasm.

'Pardon?'

'They're called crusties. Hippies with attitude for the New Age.'

You could hear the horns honking before we even got up to street level and I saw that June was on the money about the traffic. The police had cordoned off various streets, though there were a couple of lanes of cars still allowed access to the main street through Whitechapel. Protesters were milling everywhere, ducking under and around the police lines, some of them, mostly crusties, taunting the cops as they went where they shouldn't. I saw quite a few officers on horseback loitering at the fringes, and the overall police presence was considerable, which I generally thought of as a good thing.

The march had been billed as 'No to Nazis' and all the official marshals wore white T-shirts emblazoned with a big, red 'NO!' They carried mobile phones and portable PAs and managed to direct the crowd up Brick Lane with slow, but steady success. It was all a bit chaotic, but the mood seemed jovial enough, especially given the incident which had sparked the rally. As we turned up Brick Lane, I saw that several of the Indian restaurants had set up little stalls on the sidewalk to sell snacks and drinks, and there were even a few street entertainers roaming the edges of the crowd, plonking on guitars and juggling. At one point the crowd let up a mighty cheer as the police chased a mime away.

There was one thing in particular which did strike me about the crowd: it was the visibility of people of colour.

In meaningful terms, LA may be as socially and economically stratified as anyplace on earth, but in surface ways at least, it *is* a deeply multi-ethnic community. In fact, whites are actually a numerical minority in Los Angeles, so you're hardly jarred by the sight of black and brown and yellow faces around you all the time.

But looking at the plethora of blacks and Asians in the crowd (though they still weren't the majority) I realized how few non-white faces I'd seen in London. Admittedly the lobby of the Savoy and the studios of Star-TV and the BBC aren't likely hotbeds of multi-culturalism, but the sudden presence of so many different faces suddenly made strange to me the homogeneity of what I'd encountered before.

What really bothered me, though, was how I hadn't even noticed it until that moment.

I couldn't say exactly when or how the march proper began, but suddenly we were all moving in a vaguely organized fashion up Brick Lane. June had managed to grab a xeroxed flier from one of the marshals and it outlined the planned route which went east from Brick Lane, past the site of the bombed-out convenience store, and then up to someplace called Bethnal Green, where a series of speeches and a non-denominational memorial service were scheduled to be delivered. We had drifted far enough up Brick Lane to be near the front of the march, the rainbow array of banners sporting the names of the supporting organizations no more than half a block ahead of us.

There was nothing at all remarkable about the march as it went along, except perhaps that it was so utterly unremarkable. June and I just followed along with the crowd, shooting the shit about nothing in particular. You could hear a few people chanting slogans from time to time, but it was all rather disorganized. Occasionally a kid would come tearing through the crowd screaming something incomprehensible at the top of his lungs, but it was no more out of place than someone chasing a Frisbee across your path in a park. Police were lined up all along the route and I saw more officers on horseback waiting down the side streets, but there wasn't even a hint of trouble.

Until it happened.

The buzz of the crowd went quiet, like a theatre audience when the lights dim, as we turned up the street leading to the burned-out store. The charred shell of the shop had just come into sight when the explosion went off.

It wasn't big or loud as these things go (or so I was later told). But it was big enough. Loud enough.

Suddenly there were flames at the front edge of the march. One of the banners, with the name of an anti-Nazi group, was on fire and a woman, her hair alight, was screaming. A second later there was another explosion.

Then a third.

Then a lot more screams.

Pockets of fire dotted the street and the semi-orderly march immediately degenerated into panic. I saw a line of police on horseback pour into the middle of the street – I don't know where the hell they came from – but one of the horses got spooked by the sight of a man on fire and bolted, pitching its rider right on through the plate-glass window of a fish and chip shop.

Several people were pointing up at a nearby roof and I saw a group of black-clad figures leaning out over the edge. One of them had a bottle in his hand. I saw him light it and chuck it into the crowd. Another explosion went off to our left and people started running.

Most of the mob tried to go back the way they had come, but the oncoming column of marchers, unaware of what was happening, continued pouring into the street from around the corner. We got jostled and shoved from all sides, and every few seconds another Molotov cocktail was hurled down from the rooftop, adding to the panic. I grabbed hold of June's arm, but had to let go as another mounted cop came charging right at us through the crowd.

'Cocksucker,' I yelled at the horse's ass.

I shouldn't have done it. Not because he heard me – no chance in that chaos – but because, just like that, I lost track of June.

It seemed impossible. She had been two feet away from me a second before. I screamed her name, but the street had become a roiling river of frightened bodies, as wild and dangerous as white-water rapids. People whirled about like slam dancers, bouncing off each other, off lampposts, off horses. The idea that the world had turned liquid was magnified as I saw people just fall and seemingly vanish, as if dragged beneath the surface of the crowd by an unseen predator circling below. A small girl went down right next to me as I hunted for June. I managed to haul her to her feet before anyone could step on her, but then she, too, was yanked from my grasp and carried away down the building tide of panic.

The explosions seemed to have stopped and a quick glance up revealed that the rooftop had been deserted, but that didn't quell the hysteria. Some people, wisely, had run into the nearest shops to get out of the street, but now I saw a group of crusties standing in a doorway hurling bottles and cans at the policemen on horseback. I saw another group of kids, either protesters or locals, smashing the windows of other shops and looting what they could grab – it wasn't much. Further up the street a line of police in riot gear had appeared and were trying to force the crowd away from a row of as yet untouched stores on the next street. I understood their motive, but with people still coming up from behind they were creating a potentially deadly squeeze. At first, those trapped in the street tried to give way, but maximum density was quickly reached until the folks being squashed had no choice but to push back at the police. This launched a whole series of skirmishes, and I even saw a mounted cop go down *with* his horse, crushing people beneath them as they fell.

I desperately wanted to find June, but there wasn't a hope in hell. I tried to climb atop a metal garbage bin to get a vantage point, but before I could even attempt to find my balance it was swept from under my feet. I landed hard, in a half-crouch, catching an unwitting foot to the side of the head in the process. I felt myself start to tip over when a hand reached out and yanked me up. It was enough to get me back to my feet and I never even saw whose hand it was, but I believe it may well have saved my life. If I'd fallen, I'd have been trampled for certain.

I had to get out of there.

The cops were still fighting with the protesters at what would otherwise have been the open end of the street. I thought about heading that way and trying to communicate, but the sight of batons connecting with crusty heads changed my mind. The other end of the street was all screaming, spitting, snarling mob. The sound of sirens came from all around and gasoline fumes and smoke filled the air. For the first and only time in my life I wished I were a Tengu who could sprout wings and fly, but wishing wasn't going to get me anywhere.

There was no place to go except through one of the stores. Many of the shopkeepers had hurriedly tried to close the steel gates and shutters in front of their properties to deny the looters, but for most of them it was already too late. The cops tried to establish a perimeter near the storefronts and though the looters kept coming, the ones the cops grabbed hold of were getting laid into with truncheons and batons. Having lived my life in Los Angeles, riot capital of the west, I've got no sympathy at all for the kind of scumbags who loot, but the London cops, I saw, could give the good old LAPD a run for its money when it came to inflicting a beating. I didn't want to get mistaken for a looter, but having been nearly trampled to death once on the street, I didn't see any alternative.

I raised my shoulders, stuck out my elbows and forced my way toward the closest store. The door had been barricaded, but someone had just smashed the window with a cinder block. Though the display had already been cleaned out, a gangly Asian youth was trying to pull a torn sari off a mannequin. I couldn't imagine why, but a riot isn't the place to look for rationality. He snarled at me when I leapt up into the window and I tensed for a fight. Instead, he just grabbed the whole mannequin and awkwardly tried to run with it under his arm. I watched him make it as far as the nearest mounted cop.

Careful of the jagged glass still wedged in the window frame, I hauled myself up into the display area without attracting the attention of any police. It afforded me a slighter better view of the street scene and I again scanned the street for sign of June, but with no success. All that could be seen was panic and pain.

I turned around and saw that the looters hadn't bothered with the place beyond the front window. Maybe it was because the store stocked nothing but saris, not that that had deterred the dude with the mannequin. The glass on the floor crunched as I walked up the aisle and I was so busy trying to step around it that I didn't see her until we were almost face to face.

She was a middle-aged, sari-clad (naturally) Asian woman with one of those red dots between her very angry eyes and a thick hunk of wood in her hands. She quickly raised it above her head,

'Whoa!' I yelled. 'Time out.'

She barked something at me, but it wasn't in English. I held my hands up and tried to look harmless.

'I'm not a looter,' I said. 'I don't mean any trouble. But it's murder out there. I just wanted to get off the street.'

She didn't lower the club – better yet, she didn't swing it – but she did narrow her eyes at me. She cocked her head to one side, then the other.

Then she said it.

'It is being hot enough for you?' she asked.

'Fucking hell,' I said. *Another* devoted fan of *Salt & Pepper*. Whoever thinks we don't live in a goddamn global village doesn't know Charlie Sheen from Shinola.

The woman finally lowered her weapon. I nodded my thanks and she smiled at me in that aw-shucks, fancy meeting a celebrity here, kind of way that you get used to after a while (albeit not usually in the midst of a street riot – or so I would have imagined). I half-thought she was about to offer me a cup of tea when another loud crash went up in the street. She cast a nervous look at the front window then gestured at me to follow her.

She led me behind the counter and into a back room. We had to wend our way through haphazardly stacked cardboard boxes until we reached the rear entrance. She shot back a series of deadbolts and hesitantly opened the door. It opened out into a narrow garbage-strewn alley behind the shop which, incredibly, was deserted.

She gestured me out the door and I nodded my thanks.

'You gonna be okay here by yourself?' I asked. But she had closed the door before I finished asking the question. I stood there staring at it as she slid the deadbolts back into place.

The alley wasn't even wide enough for a car, but it led to another which was. As near as I could tell, it was taking me away from the furore on the street so I followed it. I quickly found myself in a small, unpaved parking lot behind a low-rise block of flats. I was still near enough to the riot to hear the sirens and whistles and shouting, but there was no one on the street here. Looking up, I saw a few people on balconies staring back from where I'd fled, but no one even glanced down at me. I saw a phone booth and thought about calling someone for help, but who could I call? No cab was going to come anywhere near this part of town and there were plenty of cops here already, thank you very much. I briefly considered calling Mahr at the Star offices, but the mere thought sent a needle-prick through my pride. I figured my best bet was to hoof it to the nearest Tube station I could find and escape underground.

Under normal circumstances, though what the hell I would have been doing there under normal circumstances I don't know, it might have been a good plan.

On riot day in the East End of London, it wasn't half so clever.

As I wandered up the winding back-streets between the apartment buildings – a sign identified it as the Criswell Estate, which struck me as little grand for what amounted to a ghetto housing project; Criswell himself would never have predicted it – I grew increasingly uncomfortable. For one thing, the streets were eerily quiet, suggesting that word had quickly spread about the riot and those who knew better were staying inside.

Worse, the few faces I did see on the street were none too welcoming. I seemed to have wandered right out of the Asian neighbourhood and on into a serious white-trash slum. I saw a few swastika graffiti on the walls along with one or two 'THULE RULES'. At first, it surprised me that the white and Asian communities were in such close physical proximity – in LA somehow there seem to be unofficial demilitarized zones, called freeways, separating the various ethnic enclaves – but then it struck me that it was precisely that proximity which likely accounted for the high degree of tension. In any case, I took little comfort in suddenly finding myself among 'my own kind'.

I walked a little faster, but since I didn't know where I was going, it didn't help. The 'estate' seemed to go on and on, and though there were maps posted pointing out the names of the individual buildings, there was nothing to indicate how to get *off* the grounds. Surely, sooner or later I had to stumble across a main street, but when a couple of particularly unhappy looking youths began to follow me from a distance of about fifty yards, I decided that sooner would be much preferable to later.

I tried not to panic, but it was hard not to keep glancing over my shoulder. Especially since each time I did, another kid seemed to have joined the club that was trailing me at closer and closer range. I don't know if they were skinheads, exactly, but they clearly weren't selling lemonade. The count was up to five when I heard the distinct roar of streaming traffic just ahead. I figured if the worst came to the worst, I'd run out into the traffic and cause a scene. I gave up on nonchalant and broke into a jog, following the road as it curved around to the left past a taller apartment building. Sure enough, I came in sight of the edge of the estate and a traffic-clogged road that wound around the fringe.

The bad news was the ten-foot-high, barb-topped cyclone fence that stood between me and free London. I thought I knew how those old East Berliners must have felt in the days of the Wall.

The pack of young thugs – none of whom looked too childlike at that moment – formed a loose crescent around me, leaving me no place to go except back toward the fence. I briefly considered taking a shot at going over the top, but the sight of what looked undeniably like caked blood on the barbs shot that plan to hell. It was an open spot, well visible from the street, though the cars zipped by pretty fast. Somehow, this crew didn't seem too worried about being seen.

With kids – even if they're thugs – you can often bluff your way out of things. I'm not much of a fighter, but sometimes you find yourself in situations. When doing repo work in LA, you find yourself in neighbourhoods you don't want to be in, facing people who you'd rather not know. If you can get them talking, though they might be talking trash, you can often avoid an ugly incident or a hospital stay.

'So,' I said, 'any of you guys get satellite?'

I never even saw the guy who kicked me.

I sure felt it, though. He caught me square on the side of my right knee and I went down like a Hollywood hooker on Hugh Grant. The mouthful of dirt I tried to spit out suggested that this wasn't going to be a talking kind of situation. A steel toe to the temple provided the unspoken exclamation mark.

The blows came in a flurry. At first I tried to get back to my feet, but they were all over me. I don't know if they were pissed about the riot, unhappy with an outsider on their turf or just a bunch of sadistic creeps. At that point it didn't much matter. I curled up and covered myself the best I could and prayed it would be over fast.

When the flash went off I thought it was inside my head.

I thought: wheelchair.

I thought: permanent brain damage.

I thought: wait a minute, would I be thinking this if I had permanent brain damage?

So I looked up.

My assailants were sprawled on the ground around me, screeching with pain and holding their hands over their eyes. Their exposed skin looked burned and blistered and a couple had blood pouring out from their eye sockets. One, face down in the dirt, didn't move at all.

'Goddamn,' I breathed.

It took a few seconds before I saw the bald man standing there. It was Pin Cushion Dude.

He held his arms straight out in front of him in the classic shooter's stance. But clutched in his fingers wasn't a gun, but a small silver and emerald charm. It was the kind of chintzy-looking thing you'd expect to see on sale at three a.m. on the Home Shopping Channel. At that moment I'd have ordered half-a-dozen and not even waited for the cheap price.

'Perhaps now you will be listening to me,' he lisped.

Just call me Mr Ears.

SEVEN

My bald buddy set a hurried pace as he led the way around the confusing, all but identical streets and alleys of the housing estate. I felt a little bruised and winded from the assault, and there was an egg-shaped bump on my temple, but there were no breaks as far as I could tell, so I counted myself damned lucky. Another few minutes and things might not have turned out quite so well.

There were still very few people about, and though we drew hard looks from some of the pale-faced locals, no one approached us or made any kind of trouble. Then, we turned a corner and were suddenly strolling down a busy shopping street. Once again there were Asian faces along with white and I felt like I had popped out of the rabbit hole and back into the real world.

Baldy walked a little slower as we approached the familiar terrain of Whitechapel High Street. I could once again hear sirens blaring in the distance and at one point a speeding brigade of fire trucks whizzed by as we drew closer to the site of the march and riot. I started to get a little nervous when a group of crusties, all of them banged-up and several bleeding from cuts on their foreheads, ran out of an alley in front of us, but before we could get any closer to the action, my companion suddenly led us off in an entirely different direction.

The streets grew quieter again, though more uniformly Asian in complexion, as we trooped along in what I guessed was a roughly southerly direction. Baldy had a tendency to walk faster, until a gap had opened between us, before waiting for me to catch up at the corners. Thoroughly lost once again, and not a little bit tired,

I finally grabbed him by the arm before he could dash across another unfamiliar street.

'Whoa, doggies,' I said. 'Time out.'

He stopped, but fidgeted and looked anxious, like a dog straining at the leash. I went over and sat down on a small flight of stone steps that led up to a boarded-up tenement building. I took off my shoe and dumped out a little stone. Reluctantly, he followed me over, but didn't sit down himself, just bounced up and down like he had to pee real bad.

'Rest period,' I said.

'We do not have far to go,' he told me, pointing vaguely up the street.

'Yeah, well, let's talk about that, huh?'

He glanced down at me, but didn't say a word.

'First of all, thank you,' I said. He continued to look at me blankly. 'For back there, those fucking animals. You saved my ass from a major whomping.'

'I am very pleased about your ass, but no thank you is required. I merely act as instructed.'

'Instructed? By who? For what?'

He looked uncomfortable with the questions, but I got the feeling that he didn't want to insult me, either. It was sort of like dealing with the PR guys.

'I am only a servant, doing as I am bid,' he finally said. 'It is not my place to answer such questions.'

'So whose place is it? See, I generally like to know who's throwing the party before I accept an invitation.'

'It is not much farther,' he said, looking up the street again, his bladder apparently bursting.

'Okay,' I sighed. 'In for a penny . . .'

I stood up slowly, wincing as I massaged one of the nastier bruises on my shoulder. 'Can you . . . wait a minute,' I said. '*What* is your name?'

He stopped bouncing and looked very seriously at me. I think he was trying to decide if this was something he could reasonably divulge to me.

'Dasra,' he said, nodding. 'You may call me Dasra.'

'Dasra,' I said. 'Okay.'

He started marching up the street, already half a dozen paces ahead of me when I called out to him. He stopped and looked back at me.

'There's one other thing I just have to ask you, Dasra,' I said.

A wave of consternation washed over his face. 'That little hunk of metal you got stuck through the middle of your tongue. Doesn't that hurt?'

Dasra smiled at last and briefly flicked his studded tongue out at me.

'Like a son-of-a-bitch,' he lisped. And walked on up the street.

Good answer, I thought. And followed.

Dasra had again drawn a half-block in front of me, but this time I caught up with him in the middle of the street, in front of an Indian restaurant so dingy that it that practically begged for a board of health inspection. There was no name on the place that I could discern. A menu had been plastered in the front window, but it was so bleached out by the sun that I couldn't read a word on it. The neighbouring shops were boarded over and there was a paucity of foot-traffic on the street. Dasra pointed to the front door of the restaurant and nodded.

'Ahhh, I'm not really hungry,' I said.

Dasra's eyes widened and his shoulders sagged in a give-me-a-break-why-don't-you kind of way and he pointed again, this time pushing the restaurant door open in front of me.

'Right. Saag city here we come,' I said, and walked in.

The interior wasn't quite as awful as the front, but neither was Egon Ronay likely to visit anytime soon. Frankly, Howard Johnson might have had second thoughts.

The restaurant consisted of a single room, no more than twenty feet square, with a dozen or so small tables wedged in wherever space allowed. And where it didn't. A door in the rear opened into a tiny, cluttered kitchen in which two small Asian men screamed at each other – and occasionally at a bored looking waiter – in Hindi. Amazingly, every one of the tables was taken, and the customers seemed to be enjoying their food. To be honest, it smelled damn terrific.

The only other white person in the restaurant was a butch-looking woman of about thirty-five, sitting alone at a table just to the left of the front door. She had close-cropped, sunset-red hair and a face like a tree stump. I saw her eyes flick up briefly to take me in, but she never stopped shovelling forkfuls of what looked like rat-meat in shit sauce off her plate and into her big mouth. Whatever she was eating, it must have been spicy because her cheeks had gone as red as her hair and tears streamed down her face. After every two or three bites she'd take a swig of beer from a sweating bottle of Kingfisher, or a bite out of her naan bread, but she never stopped eating.

All of the other tables, except for one, were occupied by groups of tiny Asian men, chattering away like parakeets. A few looked up when I walked in, but they quickly turned back to their meals when they saw Dasra behind me. In the far right hand corner of the restaurant, sitting by herself, was a young Asian woman with flowing black hair. There was nothing on her table, but a white teapot and two flowery teacups. She lifted her cup in both hands, then extended it out toward me and bowed her head. I glanced over my shoulder at Dasra who offered a curt nod in response. I squeezed through the tables and chairs and sat down across from the woman.

'Good afternoon, Mr Burns,' she said. Her accent was 99 per cent BBC, with just the faintest trace of not-born-here mixed in. 'I'm pleased to see that you are looking well.'

'You shouldn't judge a book by its cover,' I said.

'How about a television programme?' she asked, smiling.

'Only by its commercials. My show's sponsored by Preparation H. So who are you?'

'My name is Uma Dharmamitra,' she told me and put out her hand.

Her skin was soft and warm, and I felt a trickle of electricity run up my arm as I shook her hand. Nice electricity. Like I didn't want to let go.

'Uma?' I asked.

She nodded.

'Do you know Oprah?' She shook her head and looked puzzled. Serves me right for using cast-off Letterman material. 'Skip it,' I added.

'Would you care for something to eat, Mr Burns? The food here is very good even if the decor is a trifle . . . inelegant. The rogan gosh is rather exquisite.'

'I'm not hungry,' I told her.

'Tea?' she asked, picking up the teapot.

'I know when in Rome and all, but tea isn't really my, um, cup of tea. I wouldn't say take a hike to a beer, though.'

Uma waggled a finger and almost before she lowered her hand the waiter was there, plunking a glass and a jumbo bottle of Kingfisher down in front of me. I pushed the glass aside and took a short swig from the bottle which proved to be on-the-mark, TV-beer frosty.

'Cold enough for you?' Uma asked. I couldn't tell from her

poker-face if she was jagging my wires or not, so I shot a patented
Marty Burns PI glare at her just to be safe.

No effect. Works every time.

'It's fine,' I said and took a healthier swig. 'Nice to know that
there's one working refrigerator in this country.'

'Actually, I prefer real beer, myself,' she said and took a delicate
sip of her tea. 'A matter of taste, I suppose.'

'Like butter on your turkey,' I sighed.

'Pardon?'

'Nothing,' I said. 'Nothing at all. So what's all this about then?
Your boy Dasra . . .'

'Who?' Uma asked.

My bald friend had joined some buddies at a table by the door.
He glanced up when I half-turned and aimed a thumb at him.

'Dasra. He saved my butt from a passel of thugs over in the
projects. Or whatever you call your slums here.'

'Dasra?' Uma said again.

'Hello?' I said. 'You know, Dasra? The stickpin kid? Curly-Joe
over there.'

'Dasra,' she repeated. She had caught his eye, and I saw him
smile as she said his name. I had a feeling they were sharing
an elaborate joke at my expense, but was damned if I got
the punchline. 'Yes, *Dasra* was able to assist you. I am very
pleased.'

'Why?'

'Why am I pleased? Perhaps I am just a devotee of quality
television.'

'I don't think so, somehow. You strike me as the Merchant-Ivory
type. Or Jane Campion, anyway. Why did Dasra, or whoever he is,
help me out back there? Why has he been following me? Who the
hell are you?'

'Let me ask you something, Mr Burns: how do you see the
world?'

That got me. I shook my head. 'Huh? What do you mean?'

'A simple question, I should have thought. How do you see the
world? What does it look like to you?'

'Fifty-seven channels and nothing on,' I sneered. What the hell
was this?

'I did not ask how the world looks to Mr Bruce Springsteen, much
as I enjoy his perspective. I asked how it looks to *you*.'

She was looking at me kind of goofy; half-knowing, half-expecting.
As if she was hip to the fact that my fly was open and I wasn't. I had

a strong feeling that, in fact, she knew a lot more about me than she could or should have.

'I've seen things,' I admitted, surprising myself. 'Strange things.'

'I believe that you have.'

'I've seen that there's more to the world than even a pretty close inspection reveals. The trick is in knowing where to look. Or having the right guide to show you the way.'

'And accepting what it is that you see? What you are shown?'

'That's the really hard part,' I agreed.

Uma refilled her teacup from the pot. Faithless bastard that I am, I'd all but forgotten about my poor beer. I apologized with a hefty swallow.

'Tell me, what have you seen since you have been in London?'

'I don't know; lots of old buildings, fat guys playing darts, riots in the streets . . .' I snorted a laugh. 'A lot like LA, really, but without the Mexican busboys.'

'Is that all you have seen?' Uma looked very serious.

'No,' I said softly. 'I've seen hate. And death. And a lot more pain than I bargained for. Hell of a vacation spot. Next time I'll head straight for the West Bank.'

'There is a great deal happening in this city, in this land right now. Forces are gathering. Dark forces. There is very much to be observed *if* you know where to look.'

'Or if someone shows you?'

'Exactly.'

'Of course, you do have to be able, and willing, to accept what you see, don't you?' I asked.

'I think you understand me, Mr Burns. And I think that you are destined to be a part of what is happening.'

'And just what might that be?'

'The end of all things.'

'Those seem to be the secret words,' I said. 'But I'm still waiting for the duck to drop.'

'Pardon?'

'Never mind. The end of all things, you say. Christ, I feel like George Burns.'

'So some would have it. What you saw today, for example, what you've . . . been through in your time here. That is just the merest taste of what others would bring to us all.'

'Sounds like a laugh fucking riot. You should pardon the expression.'

'I don't suggest for a moment that it is a handsome sight.'

'And this has to do with what happened in the convenience store the other day? The skinhead dude I clocked with the Snapple bottle?'

'That is just the visible edge of it. There are many others of his ilk. And others yet who are much worse. Because they are cleverer, less visible.'

Part of me wanted to ask exactly what we were really talking about here, but another, almost certainly smarter part bid me bite my tongue.

'It's quite a sight,' I nodded. 'But . . . what if I don't care to look any more? What if I'm just, you know, passing through? A stranger in these parts?'

Uma suddenly looked very hurt. She leaned back in her chair and pushed her teacup to one side. 'Then you should enjoy the sights. At least, the ones that you decide you can bear to see.'

I thought, very hard, about things for a minute. I shook my head.

'I think maybe that's what I'm going to do. It's not that I don't sympathize, but this just ain't my turf. Not my place. And . . .' I took a long look around the now very quiet restaurant, but thought about the charm that Dasra had used to ward off my attackers, '. . . no offence, but I've already had more than enough weird shit in my life. I don't think I can handle any more. At least, not right now. I mean, I really appreciate how Dasra saved my butt back there, but I have a feeling that whatever you folks are involved with is *seriously* weird shit.'

Uma nodded, but wouldn't meet my gaze. 'Dasra will see you out,' she said.

Then Dasra was there standing beside me, looking very grumpy indeed. I hadn't noticed that he'd walked over.

'No hard feelings,' I tried.

Uma finally looked up. 'Take care, Mr Burns,' was all she said.

I felt a little crummy as I rode back to the hotel. Dasra hadn't said a word to me as we walked out of the restaurant and he led me back toward a main street. Cops were still visible in force and lots of people were milling around, but it also seemed like a sense of order had been restored. You could practically smell the panic in the air before, but the scent had blown away. I managed to hail a cab and in the time it took for the big black car to pull over to the kerb, Dasra disappeared. I scanned the street for a sign of his shiny noggin, but there wasn't a trace.

I replayed in my mind the conversation with Uma Dharmamitra

as we inched our way through the rush hour traffic. She hadn't said anything specific, but I was sure that she was hinting that she knew something about events I've already been through. That she somehow knew of my experiences with . . .

The truth is, I still don't know what to call it.

I hate the word 'supernatural'. There's just something a little too Edgar Cayce, too *Kolchak: The Night Stalker*, too Stephen King about it.

It makes me feel stupid.

The problem is that I don't know what else to call . . . *it*. Because, really, there aren't words. I've seen creatures that aren't human. Worlds that exist – beyond? beside? within? – this one. I've beheld spirits of the dead and signs of life most definitely not as we know it, Jim.

And I don't want to see any more.

Because, mostly, it scares the bejesus out of me. The thing is that normal life is more than strange enough these days. It's hard enough nailing my lines and working with the network brass and still keeping off the sauce without worrying about all the nasty things that might want to bump me off – or hump me – in the night. Maybe I'm just a coward at heart, but perhaps most of us *choose* not to see certain things, as Uma suggested, because we'd rather not admit them into our lives. If we want weird, we've got Mulder and Scully. And if it costs us a bit of wonder to shield our gazes, it may be for the benefit of a little comfort and security.

Especially if the alternative is sticking a pin through your tongue.

If a part of me wondered what Uma and Dasra were up to, I'd have to live with the unquenched curiosity. I was sorry about everything that had happened – the arson, the deaths, the riot – but it was all well out of my control. I only had a few more days in London anyway and I was no more likely to solve the city's racial problems than I was to discover the identity of Jack the Ripper.

Some mysteries don't get solved.

I thoroughly cursed myself because somehow – profoundly thought-less self-absorption, that's how – I'd forgotten all about June Hanover until I saw her sitting in the lobby of the Savoy.

She looked a bit dishevelled, but not too much the worse for wear. Her dirty clothes clearly drew a few disapproving looks form the hotel staff, but she stared daggers right back at anyone who dared raise an eyebrow. She'd obviously washed her hands and face, but she was definitely loitering in bad hair day territory, and I could see where she'd missed a soot streak on the back of her neck. She came running up when she saw me and was about to hug me when her reserved English nature got the better of her. She grabbed me by the elbows and squeezed hard.

'Marty! Are you all right? I've been going crazy.'

'I'm fine. All things considered. Are *you* okay? What happened?'

'I don't know. One second you were there and the next it was all just . . . it was horrible. Marty, there were people on fire and getting trampled and . . . god, it was the most terrifying thing I've ever been through.'

'I know. I tried to find you in the crowd, but it was impossible. I got swept up and away by the flow and finally had to just get the hell out of there. I . . .'

I realized that in recounting the riot we were both talking at the top of our voices and attracting a crowd. I grabbed June by the hand and led her toward the elevators.

'Let's go up to my room,' I suggested.

An old blue-haired dame wearing big pearls, a little white hat and carrying a smelly Pomeranian in a sweater got on the elevator with us.

'Hey, pup,' I said, but the little bastard bared his teeth at me and growled.

'Ramsey hasn't had his pill,' his owner explained.

'Ahh,' I said, as if I understood. 'Isle of Dogs?'

'Excuse me?'

'Ramsey. Did you get him on the Isle of Dogs?'

'I should say not!'

'I thought that's where they came from,' I said, as the doors opened on my floor. June tried not to laugh. Ramsey snarled and yipped.

The TV in my room was blinking at me again to say there was a message waiting, but I just shut it off.

'Probably Mahr,' June said, a little guiltily.

'Fuck him *and* his goddamn suspenders. Want a drink?'

The mini-bar had been restocked – one of the daily wonders of hotel living – and I pulled out a beer for myself. June took an orange juice. I offered to pour one or two of those cute little bottles of Absolut in with it, but she shook her head. I kicked my shoes off and sprawled out on the divan. June curled up in a big easy chair.

'So what happened?' I asked. 'How'd you get out of that mess unscathed?'

'I'm not sure. I got knocked around when I lost sight of you, but I managed to stay on my feet. Just. Somehow I got pushed all the way across the street as the police were cordoning off one of the side roads. They let a few us through before they blocked it off. I tried to explain that you were still out there, but I couldn't get anyone to listen. It was madness.'

'I'm not surprised. You were lucky to get through there at all. The cops fucked up bad. They shouldn't have brought in the mounted units so fast. I saw someone go down under the horses.'

'They had the TV on in the lobby. They said two people got killed in the melee.'

'I believe it. It's a wonder it wasn't more. Did they catch those bastards who tossed the Molotov cocktails?'

'I don't know. It didn't say anything about that.'

'But you saw them, right?'

'I saw the explosion in the street, but I didn't see where it came from. I think I was too scared to look.'

'It was up on one of the rooftops,' I said. 'I don't know how the cops could have missed them. Fucking Nazi bastards.'

'I did warn you that you don't understand the situation here, the politics of London, the East End.'

'Hey, I'm not blaming you for anything, June. I'm the one who insisted on going, remember? I shouldn't have let you come, though. It's hardly your fault that there was a riot.'

'I feel responsible though.'

'That's just the PR in you talking. The little devil in mauve suspenders that sits on your shoulder and whispers bitter nothings in your ear.'

'Don't you have a devil like that?' June asked.

'Yeah,' I said, 'but mine wears RayBans and tells me I need an entourage.'

'So why don't you?'

'They wouldn't all fit in the back of my Porsche,' I smiled.

I got up and grabbed another beer. June took another orange juice and opted for a little vodka with it this time.

'Here's to the devils we know,' I toasted. June hoisted her glass in salute.

We sat there for a while, each of us contemplating our drink. After some serious soul-searching, I concluded that I needed pretzels with my beer. I scoured the mini-bar, and found a bag of something that

looked vaguely pretzel-esque. I tore open the bag and popped a
couple in my mouth. The smell hit me just as I was swallowing the
first taste.

'Whah ah veze?' I asked through a half-chewed mouthful. I
presented the bag to June

'Twiglets,' she said.

I read the label on the package: Twiglets. Son-of-a-gun.

'I can see that,' I said swallowing. The flavour was . . . unique.
'But what are they? They're not pretzels.'

June looked at me dubiously. She grabbed a handful of the nasty
little goobers and nibbled away. Without making a face or anything.
'No. They're Twiglets. They're . . . what they are.'

'What is that taste?' I asked, drowning it as best I could with what
was left of my beer.

'*Mar*mite,' she told me. She wore an expression much like the
one I imagine graced Sir Isaac Newton's head after he got conked
by the apple.

'Uh-huh. And Marmite is . . .?'

'Something you have to have grown up with, I suspect. Like
fish-paste. I don't think you're quite ready for it, Marty. Weren't
you going to check your messages?'

Smooth transition, I thought, but I took the hint and didn't push it
any further. I didn't like to think what fish-paste might be. I gave June
the rest of the Twiglets and made for the phone. Even a conversation
with the desk clerk couldn't leave a worse taste in my mouth.

Fortunately, the phone call was a breeze. The message was that
a fax had arrived for me. Five minutes later, a bellboy knocked on
the door and handed me a large brown envelope.

Inside were two pieces of paper. The first was a terse memo from
Mahr. It read:

*The attached will be running on page one of five major newspapers
tomorrow. Further PR efforts suspended indefinitely.*

I glanced at the second sheet. The photograph hadn't repro-
duced very well through the fax machine, but it was clear
enough.

'Oh, Marty,' June said, looking over my shoulder.

The picture showed the scene of the afternoon's riot and had
clearly been taken with a telephoto lens. It must have been snapped
when I stood up on the garbage can to try and look for June
amid the melee. I had one hand raised up in the air, and the
way the lens foreshortened the action, it looked like I had just
struck a police officer on horseback who was falling sideways out

of his saddle. In actuality, he had to have been halfway across the street.

But the camera never lies, does it?

'Shit,' I said.

Some things do taste worse than Twiglets.

EIGHT

As it happens, those hotel mini-bars aren't actually all that mini. There's a lot of filler to wade through – mineral water, juice, other superfluous non-alcoholic beverages – but if you don't mind mixing the contents of your growth-stunted bottles (which I don't) and you're even mildly determined (my middle name) you can assemble a pretty fair drunk out of one of them little suckers.

So I did.

June took off at some point – screw her; more for me – I think roundabout the time I polished off the Crème de Cassis. I don't even have a clue what that is, but it tastes like cough medicine, and I don't mean the good stuff. Robitussen *manqué*. I suspect it's not all that alcoholic, either, but after getting through the various miniatures of gin, rum, vodka, scotch and tequila, it didn't particularly matter. Fortunately they don't stock vanilla extract in mini-bars. Though I sort of remember that I briefly considered calling down to room service for some. I do stuff like that when I'm tanked. And call for hookers. Thank god I passed out before I got the chance. At least I think I passed out; it might have just been sheer stupefaction from watching lawn bowling on the BBC.

I do know that I got a phone call before oblivion beckoned. English telephones have a nasty double ring, a kind of twin short, sharp shock, that jolts you like those electric paddles they use to jump-start hearts. Or so I imagine, never having had either heart surgery or a guest shot on *ER* (though I did once get into a marathon poker game involving both Richard Chamberlain and Chad Everett).

'Yrmmm,' I blathered into the receiver.

'Marty Burns, is that you?'

My agent, Kendall Arlo.

'Hi, Kendall!' I yelled, forgetting for the nonce that the telephone obviates the 6,000-mile distance between London and LA.

'Are you out of your cotton-picking mind?'

'I don't know. D'you mean at this particular moment or in general?'

'I . . . you've been drinking, haven't you? Dog-gone it!'

One of the things I love most about Kendall – I mean a definite second to the big money she negotiated for me for *Burning Bright*, but still worth mentioning – is the way she swears. Or rather, the way she doesn't swear. It's always 'cotton-picking' this and 'dog-gone' that and 'aw, heck'. It's hard to believe that anyone still thinks 'heck' is a useful expletive, but that's Kendall for you. How she maintains her obliviously naive Midwestern wholesomeness amid the sewage, decay and generally vulgar discourse of Hollywood, I don't know. But it works for her, somehow. She's making a mint.

'Drink?' I said. 'Not me, ossifer. You've got me confused with six other guys. Blokes, I mean.'

'Aw, heck, Marty. What in the world are you doing to yourself? You know you promised me that you'd keep away from the hooch.'

'I'm celebrating.'

'And exactly what would that be?'

'The end of an undistinguished career. Sorry, *another* undistinguished career.'

'Oh, Marty, it's not as bad as all that.'

'No?' I asked. 'Then why did you call?'

'I *did* just get off the phone with a VP from Star. They're not too happy, Marty. In fact, they're doggone p-i-s-s-e-d.'

It took me a minute, but even sober, spelling's never been my strong suit. 'So I gather,' I sighed.

'What the heck were you doing at a riot? Did you really hit a policeman?'

'I . . . what do you think, Kendall?'

'Damn it, Marty! Just tell me what's going on.'

Damn it? From Kendall? Maybe this was more serious than I thought. I induced as much instant sobriety as I could.

'It's . . . a long story,' I sighed. 'I didn't hit a cop, *believe* me, I just got caught in an awkward position. Figuratively and literally. It looks a lot worse than it is in the press, too, but you know how that goes. It's like every newspaper here is a supermarket tabloid. Imagine that the *LA Times* was *The National Enquirer*.'

There was silence on the other end of the line. If Kendall didn't pick up on a straight line like that, I knew I must be in trouble.

'How're the network boys there taking it?' I asked.

'Worried, but not frantic. Yet. There waiting to see if anyone here runs with the photos of you. They're saving frantic for that. It's really not very good, Marty. You should have known better.'

'Kendall, haven't you ever been in a situation where you just felt like you had to do the right thing? I mean, where you *knew* what that was and had to do it. Regardless of the consequences.'

'Yeah,' she said tentatively.

'Well, I know it sounds weird, but that's the situation I landed in. I . . . I don't have the energy, or the sobriety, to give you the gruesome details right now, but shit just happened. I didn't mean to get in the middle of this mess – Christ, I'm still not even sure what's going on to tell you the truth – but all I did was try to be a *mensch*. Of course, no good deed goes unpunished. I saw some bad guys and I tried to be a good guy, or so I thought. Maybe I'm just taking this TV action hero thing a little too far.'

'You're not bullshitting me, are you, Marty?' Kendall asked.

I literally gasped.

'Did you say . . .' – I had to clear my throat – '. . . *bullshit*, Kendall?'

'I think you heard me, Martin Burns.'

'No,' I said softly, and I hope sincerely. 'No, Kendall, I am *not* bullshitting you.'

There was a further, but blessedly brief silence from LA. Then: 'Okay, Marty. I believe you. I'll deal with the network here and take the heat from the satellite boys in London. Those stupid accents don't scare me anyway.'

'Are you sure?'

'Absolutely. I take you at your word, Marty. If I ever find out that I can't, you'll have to find another agent.'

'Thank you, Kendall,' I croaked.

'Put away whatever you're drinking and get some sleep, now. We'll talk again later.'

And she hung up.

There was still a splash of crème de cassis rolling around the bottom of the bottle. I raised it to my lips, but thought about what Kendall said. I found the little cap under my pillow, screwed it back on and tossed the bottle in the garbage.

I fell asleep.

*　　*　　*

I woke up once in the night, scared out of my wits and with no idea where I was. As you do sometimes, waking up in a strange place.

I had a vague memory of another dark dream, but I couldn't put anything specific to it. Happily, I was still drunk enough to fall quickly back to sleep.

I didn't remember anything more about it in the morning.

The next day passed uneventfully. The phone rang a lot; I let the messages accumulate at the desk. The television blinked at me, but I just flipped the channel back to bowls. The door got knocked on a few times as well, but I only opened it for the maid. Well, and for the angel of mercy who restocks the mini-bar. I told her to hold the crème de cassis, though. 'Everything in moderation' are the words for my tombstone.

I hadn't planned to go out at all – it's amazing the stuff room service will bring you if you don't care what they charge you for it – but June Hanover called and invited me to a late lunch. I didn't want to go, but I didn't feel like saying no to her either. I should have. It turned out to be stiff and uncomfortable, and by silent agreement we cut it short.

I spent a couple of hours walking around town after lunch. I kept half-expecting that I'd be ambushed by tabloid reporters or photographers on the street, but I reckon that was an overestimation of my notoriety. The only assaults I had to fend off came from the ubiquitous bums and winos wanting spare change. There are just as many of them in London as in LA, though admittedly they're not as well-tanned. Lots more of 'em seem to have dogs, though. Probably make an interesting research topic for a sociology dissertation.

I walked up to Trafalgar Square and ogled Nelson's Column with the rest of the tourists. For some reason – bald ignorance of history and a life wasted in television, I suppose – I had always pictured *Ozzie* Nelson up on top of the big stone phallus. So I was a little disappointed with the statue of the Admiral who brings out the pigeons. And man, are there ever pigeons. The place is filthy with them. Literally. For reasons best known only to the London city fathers, street vendors are licensed to sell bird seed to the tourists to throw at the flying rats. You'd think a country that had experienced one Black Death might have a more parochial perspective on the subject of vermin control, but there you go. (Actually, it all made a worrying kind of sense when I later discovered the proximity of Chinatown to this concrete pigeon farm. No *kung pao* chicken for *this* boy.)

From there, I ventured south toward the Thames. I took the

footbridge across the river at Embankment and gaped at the brilliant view of the London skyline to the east. Actually, London has even less of a skyline than woeful Los Angeles, more like an elevated ground line highlighted by the big dome of St Paul's. It's damn pretty, though, in a quaint, rather than impressive way.

I wandered east for a stretch up the river past a big arts complex. I stopped for a beer at the National Film Theatre cafe and even got asked for an autograph. The request came from an American tourist, but what the hell. He seemed real pleased, so maybe he hadn't been reading the English papers. I wandered inside the theatre complex to find the can and was amazed to spot a poster for a film I had once appeared in tacked-up on their Coming Soon wall. It seemed they were running a 'Forgotten Seventies' series and had unearthed a copy of a bizarre, nudie musical called *Wad*. It was one of the many desperation parts I took after *Salt & Pepper* bit the big one. I didn't actually expose any of my own flesh in it, and thankfully most of my scenes got left on the cutting room floor. You can see me though, as one of a group of horny teens who get spurted over by a giant, singing/lactating breast. In a merciless act of typecasting, the tit belonged to Carol Wayne. Nice lady.

Fortunately, I would be out of London long before the screening date.

I could see the Savoy Hotel across the river, so I found my way up to Waterloo Bridge and wandered back to the north side. I thought about hailing a cab, but early rush hour traffic was already heavy and the hotel didn't look that far away; I decided I'd just hoof it rather than breathe the fumes from the back seat. I managed to get disoriented as I came off the bridge and walked three blocks in the wrong direction before realizing my mistake. By the time I finally walked into the lobby, I was feeling good and tired and ready for a little more liquid refreshment. A delivery guy dropped a bundle of evening papers off at the lobby news stand, so I grabbed a copy off the top of the pile.

All the little hairs on the back of my neck stood on end as I scanned the front page.

NEW VIOLENCE LIGHTS EAST END the headline screamed.

Beneath it was a picture of my bald buddy, Dasra. He'd been killed.

I had the cabby drive around the back streets for a while, but I couldn't find the place. He asked me what I was looking for, but I didn't know the name and there must be a few score Indian restaurants in the East

End, all of which look about the same. Finally, though it was getting dark, I told him to drop me off at Whitechapel High Street.

'This ain't a part of town you want to be wandering about at night, guv,' the driver warned me.

I smiled. I've always wanted to be called 'guv,' ever since I first saw *Mary Poppins*.

'I'm looking for someone,' I told him. 'I'll be fine.'

'If it's a bit of company you're after . . .' he suggested. 'I mean, nothing wrong with a fellow what likes a bit of the dark.'

I pretended not to notice his leer. 'I'm not after anything more exotic than a lamb curry,' I said, and paid the fare.

I tried to get my bearings, determined to try and follow the path Dasra had led as best I could remember. I was smart enough to bring a street map with me with me this time, but I still managed to get completely lost in the space of ten minutes. A couple of times I thought I recognized a building or a landmark and was back on the trail, but then within a block I'd be as lost as I was before. As night set in for real, I still hadn't found the restaurant and not having seen another white face for a while, was starting to feel a little paranoid.

I decided I should just try and head back toward the High Street, where I could catch a cab or public transport. I tried consulting my map, but I couldn't seem to locate the tiny street I was on amidst the tangle of little lines which form the labyrinthine hodgepodge of the East End. The farther I walked, the loster I got.

And the scarier the neighbourhood became.

I stumbled upon a group of Asian teens sitting on parked cars, drinking out of tall cans, and saw them all look up at me as one. I felt the bottom drop out of my stomach (or perhaps the contents of my stomach dropping into my bottom), but while they scowled, they were obviously more interested in their beer than in me. I hurried away before they could change their minds.

As I turned another corner, the already dim streetlights suddenly went out all at the same time. There wasn't another light on anywhere on the street.

'Yikes,' I said out loud. I started retracing my steps, when I saw the glow at the far end of the street. It was so bright I figured it had to be coming from a main drag. I started toward the light, was maybe halfway up the block, when the glow winked out. Just like that.

The darkness was all around me. It seemed impossible; I knew I was on a street smack dab in the heart of London, but I might as well have been dropped into a pit at the bottom of a cavern on a moonless night. Such darkness was simply not possible. Except here I was, standing in it.

'Shit,' I said. A regular Oscar Levant.

When the light slowly came up again, it was like standing on a stage; if there was an audience out there I don't know who they were, but there *I* was in the middle of the action:

There are people everywhere: mobbing the street, hanging out windows, standing on rooftops. They're poor; I can see it in their faces and their clothes. Coarse woollens and stained work shirts, cut in a style sixty years out of date. I puzzle for a moment, then realize the truth: somehow *I'm* sixty years out of date. Their faces are dirty, too, and haggard. They all, even the young ones, look old to me.

And angry.

Lips move, though I can't hear a sound. Somehow that makes it more scary. Spittle flies, fists shake, eyes seethe with fury.

It's a riot. I've been through one recently enough to know.

At the opposite end of the long street – a sign tells me I'm on Cable Street – stand a small cadre of men nattily dressed in black. They wear dark armbands, but I can't make out what's imprinted on them. They all have short-cropped dark hair, and square, dull faces with angry eyes. A few of them yell back at the crowd (they must be nuts), but mostly they look scared. There are police, too; bobbies in their quaint thirties uniforms standing between the furious mob and the men in the black shirts.

I see a stone fly through the air, hurled off a rooftop. It strikes one of the blackshirts on the top of the head. The man crumples to the ground and, as one, the crowd surges forward.

And right through me. Like the ghosts that they are.

The scene vanishes as the darkness around me returns. But this time a small tunnel of light remains. Suddenly, standing a dozen feet in front of me, is the little Asian girl from the convenience store. Her too big T-shirt is smouldering and her long black hair is on fire. I take a step toward her and she reaches out to me, asking me to pick her up, to save her. Her arms, too, are on fire.

Then she's gone.

The light dims, but I can see five figures in black emerging from the rim of the darkness. They have no features, no distinguishing characteristics: living shadows. I flash on the disturbing dreams I've been having. I know I've seen these figures before; I think they live in my unconscious. But as they move toward me, I sense a solidity to them that is unlike the rest of what is around me. I try to take a step back, find that I cannot move.

As the shapes come closer, I feel a coldness waft over me, like a winter wind where no wind blows. I feel my heart beat faster, a pressure in my bladder. The five dark figures reach out to me, but their threatening gestures could not be more different from the little girl's plaintive plea. It is raw menace.

It is death.

'Mr Burns?' a voice said.

The darkness vanished, the five figures with it. I was once more standing on a nondescript East End road, the streetlights all ablaze.

Uma Dharmamitra stood in front of me.

The restaurant, it turned out, was only a couple of blocks away. I could have sworn I'd walked up that street earlier in my wanderings, but I don't how know I could have missed it. Inside, it looked exactly the same as when I'd visited the other afternoon. I mean *exactly*. Not to sound racist or anything, but it seemed like the same people were sitting at the same tables, eating the same meals. Even the same red-headed, hatchet-faced dyke was still there, chowing down on yet another nasty-looking vindaloo. So I wasn't surprised when Uma sat us down at the same corner table, and a waiter dropped a cold Kingfisher in front of me.

The one difference, of course, was that there was no Dasra.

I drained half the beer in one parched gulp, while a waiter poured tea for Uma. She took two delicate sips, then folded her hands over each other on the tacky formica table top.

She stared at me.

'Uh, I suppose I should thank you,' I said.

'What for?'

I studied her, deciding whether or not she knew; whether she could see any of what I had seen on the weirdly dark street.

Whatever in the world that was.

'I got kind of lost out there,' I offered.

'One should know one's way around,' Uma said, and bowed her head slightly. She took another sip of tea, and playing the inscrutable Asian to the hilt, didn't say anything else. There was hardly any conversation in the place, just the sounds of scraping plates and noisy eating.

'So,' I tried, 'how about that Prince Charles? Are those ears zany or what?'

Nothing.

'Listen,' I said, leaning forward. 'I really am grateful for what you did back there. I mean . . .' I wasn't sure what to say, how much to reveal of what I'd just been through. Would she understand, or think I was crazy? 'No kidding,' I told her. 'Best friends for life, autographed picture of Kelsey Grammer, you name it. I . . . did you . . . see anything out there.'

'My vision is excellent. I see many things.'

'How about, like, dudes in black?' I ventured. 'And I don't mean AC/DC.'

Ignoring my question, Uma took another delicate sip from her cup, then pushed it to one side. She laid her hands on the table again – she had tiny, childlike fingers – and leaned forward till our noses were about six inches apart.

'I believe you are here for a reason, Mr Burns,' she said.

'And that is?'

'I am not entirely certain,' she told me. She slumped back in her chair, but continued to stare into my eyes. 'Yet.'

'Did Dasra know?'

'No,' she said. Sorrow crept over her features at the mention of his name. 'Your Dasra was a servant. Though I shall miss him very much. Is he what brought you here tonight?'

'Yeah. I saw the story about his death in the paper. I thought . . .' I didn't know what to say.

'Tell me what you thought, Mr Burns.'

'I don't know. I felt bad. Guilty even. I don't know why, though. I mean, it's not my fault that he's dead. Is it?'

'A baby's yawn,' Uma said.

'Beg pardon?'

'An old Hindi saying. The greatest of storms may be born of a baby's yawn. It means that innocent events may culminate in dire consequences.'

'A butterfly flaps its wings in Tokyo,' I muttered.

'Sorry?'

'You sure that's an ancient Hindi saying?'

Uma shrugged ever so slightly.

'So what happened to Dasra?' I asked.

'Are you certain that you want to know?'

'Of course,' I said. 'That's why I came looking for you.'

'But you have also told me, in no uncertain terms, that you were just passing through these parts. "A stranger," you said.'

'I say a lot of stupid things,' I sighed. 'Occupational hazard.'

'You also said that you'd had enough – how did you put it? – "weird shit" in your life?'

'Like I say, occupational hazard. And the shit seems to find me whether I want it or not. But I'm asking you now and I need to know. What happened? What the hell is going on around here?'

Uma thought for a moment, then nodded at me. Or perhaps at a waiter, because he dropped another beer in front of me, then scampered off.

'Dasra was killed by agents of the Thule.'

'Ultima Thule,' I said. Uma nodded. 'Okay, I'll bite: what *is* Ultima Thule?'

'The end of all things,' Uma said. Like I couldn't have guessed. She read my mind. 'Or so they like to believe.'

'This is some sort of paramilitary organization? Skinheads? Neo-Nazis?'

'That is probably the way the press would describe them, if the press cared enough to report such matters. But the Thule are more than that. They are happy to be thought of – dismissed – as mere skinheads and football hooligans, and they do employ many such individuals in their pursuits. But random violence is only a means to an end. The Thule are of a much darker and more dangerous order than the street thugs who shield them. They have a long history.'

'What kind of history'?

'That depends on who – or perhaps, what – you believe. What do you believe, Mr Burns?'

Uh-oh, I thought, *I've been in this elevator before.*

'That's, um, not one of my favourite questions,' I said.

'In itself, a most informative reply,' Uma said. She offered a wry smile.

'As it happens, questions of belief are a matter I've had cause to . . . confront before. The results weren't entirely pretty. It has to do with the weird shit I was talking about.'

'May I tell you what I believe?' Uma didn't wait for an answer. 'I believe that there is no such thing as "as it happens". I believe that everything that happens occurs for a reason, according to a design. Though such designs are of great intricacy, and we are not generally privileged to see the blueprint, or even understand the purpose.'

I shook my head. 'So what are you saying? You believe in some kind of predestination? That everything is laid out and we have no free will?'

'I would not call it predestination, exactly. We *do* all, for better or worse, choose our own paths. But karma – fate, if you prefer –

prescribes the limits of how and where we may wander. There is free will only in the same way that there is free lunch.'

'Man, if you're not married, I know this Japanese dude you would really hit it off with. You want his number?'

'Humour can be a useful tool, Mr Burns. The Thule, for example, are quite humourless in all regards.'

'Nazis,' I said, doing my best Harrison Ford, 'I hate those guys.'

'But humour can also be a crutch, a disguise. What is it you are afraid of precisely?'

'Let's see. Heights. Depths. Being alone. Being with people. Flying. Walking. Spiders. Oh, yeah, and warm beer.'

Uma stared at me.

'Okay, no more jokes. Though I meant it about the beer.'

The stare went icy.

'Tough room,' I muttered. 'Okay, what am I afraid of?'

We matched stares for a while as I thought about it. Actually, I knew the answer, but felt awkward talking about it. I'd never seriously discussed it with anyone other than Rosa, who'd been through it all with me, and understood in a way I didn't think anyone else ever would or could. Still, thinking about what I'd just seen on that unnaturally dark London street, I gave it a shot.

'I'm afraid of the things that exist that we don't know about. Or pretend not to see. You asked me last time we met about things that I've seen. Well, I've seen that there are worlds, hell, universes maybe, beyond the one that we know. I've seen amazing things: visions of beauty and splendour, colours and wonders that make you just want to cry like a baby. But the price for that beauty is having to see that there's this terrible darkness, too.' – I thought about the dark figures I saw on Cable Street – 'A physical, touchable, very real evil that goes beyond the nastiest and most awful thing that any person has ever done. I think there's a reason why we're not supposed to see these things. I think it's for our own protection, for our own good. And the simple fact of the matter is that, as beautiful as some of it is, the darkness makes me afraid of ever having to see any of it again. Though I think now it's too late to hide.'

Uma smiled at me. 'Clearly, you are ready to face the Thule,' she said. 'As I knew you would be.'

'Ummm, when you say "face the Thule" what do you mean exactly? You still haven't told me who or what these people are.'

'The Thule are known in many ways, have numerous faces . . .'

'My name is legion,' I said.

'Very much so. Are you familiar with the mythology of Thule?'

I shook my head. 'Never heard of it until I saw the graffiti here in London. Sounds sort of like Elmer Fudd cursing. You know: "Wabbit season. Duck season. Oh, Thule".'

'Hmmm,' Uma said, suddenly eyeing me in a very June Hanover sort of way. 'Ultima Thule is a place. At least mythically, it is. Legend has it that it is an island somewhere in the North Sea. "Six days north of Britain", it is said. It is the supposed birthplace of the Germanic races.'

'I don't much care for the connotations of those last two words.'

'With good reason.' Uma nodded. 'Ultima Thule literally means "the end of the world".'

'Wait, I thought it meant "the end of all things".'

'That is how those who call themselves the Thule have come to interpret it. But the original meaning was less threatening. The end of the world was meant in the sense of the limits of known geography. The point of turning back.'

'Here be dragons.'

'Exactly. Thule as a physical locale figures in various Germanic and Nordic myths. Even in certain Celtic legends. The British and the Germans have far more in common than either people cares to acknowledge, you know.'

'Whatever you do, don't mention the war,' I said.

'Yes. Thank you, Mr Fawlty.'

We both smiled.

'The Thule of the here-and-now have culled their name and many of their beliefs from Germanic myth, but their most direct influence is of rather more recent and frightening vintage. Are you familiar with the Order *Templi Orientis*?'

'*Gesundheit*,' I said.

'I take that to mean no.'

I nodded.

'It was one of the many nineteenth-century Theosophist offshoots of the Knights Templars . . .'

'Oh, fuck me,' I groaned.

'Sorry?'

'Why does it always have to be the goddamn Knights Templars? Or if not them, the fucking Freemasons. Every conspiracy, every cult and X-file, every nasty, weird or just plain stupid bit of business for the past five hundred years ends up having something to do the Knights Templars. Why is that?'

'Because they were a nasty bit of business,' Uma said.

Fair enough.

'Actually,' Uma explained, 'the Templars themselves were harmless enough, if a bit addle-minded. It is what they have inspired over the centuries that has been so problematic. The *Templi Orientis* were, themselves, a fairly tame group of Theosophists and would-be kabbalists. Many entirely harmless variations on the Order still exist using that name. Followers of the great fraud Crowley, mostly, and quite pathetic by and large. Like so many of the cults at the turn of the century, the old Order existed largely as an excuse for their members to engage in proscribed sexual practices. Lots of orgies, S&M and so forth.'

'You make it sound like some nineteenth-century Club Med.'

'Hmm. But in turn, they gave rise to sub-orders of a far more malignant variety. Specifically the Order of the New Templars and the Black Order, which formed in Germany at the end of the First World War. And wherein lie the roots of Ultima Thule.'

'So who were these goofballs?'

'The Black Order came together in Munich around 1920, the Order of the New Templars earlier than that. They were devoted in equal measure to experiments in sexual deviancy and to the occult. Heinrich Himmler was a founding member of the Black Order, and there has long been an assumption that Hitler was involved at one time as well. The Thule now choose to believe so in any case.'

'Man,' I said, 'that must have been the happening place to be on a Saturday night in old Bavaria. Adolph and Heinrich and a party of favourites. Bring your own pretzels.'

'Quite. Their activities were not limited to dabbling with the occult, though. Himmler established and recruited members to the Thule Society as part of his duties in the Order. The Thule Society consisted of street thugs who beat and robbed and raped almost at will. They contributed in no small part to the post-war chaos of the Weimar Republic. Not to mention to the coffers of the Black Order.'

'And this is where our Ultima Thule come from?'

'Precisely. The Thule Society was suborned to the SS with Hitler's rise to power in the thirties, and the Black Order itself effectively became the core of the ruling elite of the Third Reich. Much has been written about Hitler's supposed obsession with the supernatural, though I believe most of this to be greatly overstated. Himmler, however, *was* at the centre of Nazi occult interests. It was he who established *Mittelpunkt der Welt* at Wewelsburg Castle.'

'What? Blaupunkt Wee-wee's Burg?'

'*Mittelpunkt der Welt*,' Uma repeated. ' "The centre of the world" is what it means. I believe the name to be a very deliberate, if perhaps unsubtle, reference to Ultima Thule.'

'The *end* of the world.'

'Yes. A sort of half-step along the way, if you will.'

'I think I won't, thank you very much'.

Uma smiled and shrugged. 'In any event, the movement was driven underground with the demise of Nazi Germany, but while fascism has been in abeyance, at least in most of Europe, it never really disappears. The Black Order has returned, in a very real sense, in the form of Ultima Thule. They are rich, they are strong and they are smart. They keep well below ground, reaching out only to stir up trouble where they can. Today it's a riot in East London. Tomorrow it may be an arson attack on a Turkish hostel in Germany.'

'Or perhaps a car bomb at a government building in Oklahoma City.'

Okay, that got my attention. 'Are you saying . . .?'

'I do not know, for certain, Mr Burns. I am just suggesting to you that the Thule's reach is very great and they are very much a growth concern. They don't goose-step through the streets any more, they communicate via computer bulletin boards and have home pages on the World Wide Web. But in the most important ways they remain unchanged from the days of the Black Order: they are filled with hate, they ache for power and they are very much on the move. And they are engaged at a very deep level with the occult.'

'Engaged?'

Uma pursed her lips. 'Perhaps "immersed" would be a more accurate description.'

'Is that why you want me to be involved? Because of . . . what I've been through before?' I thought about it for a minute. 'Because of Shoki?' I tried.

'Who is Shoki?' she asked, but I couldn't tell if she truly didn't know.

'Doesn't matter,' I said.

'And I might point out that it was *you* who came looking for *me* tonight. The choice has been, and remains, entirely yours.'

'I thought there was no free will.'

Uma shrugged.

'I see,' I said.

'Tell me what you see, Mr Burns.'

I sighed. 'I see me stepping into a big old mess all over again, like some boneheaded dufus who won't learn from his mistakes. At least this time it'll be with both eyes open. Well, squinting, anyway. Christ, if Spielberg ever makes a live-action Roadrunner movie, I'm a lead-pipe cinch for the part of Wile E. Coyote.'

'You understand that to stand against the Thule is a difficult and dangerous thing? Dasra's death is the proof, if more were needed. There is not a great deal of time left in which to act. To become involved is to put far more than merely your career at risk.'

'I won't tell my agent.'

'You cannot tell anyone.'

It seemed to me that the whole place had gone quiet, though the same diners seemed to be shovelling the same greasy-looking grub into their mouths. They must have been pretty damn hungry.

'I'm in,' I said. 'I don't think I'd care to see "the end of all things". I'll probably hate myself in the morning – won't that be a change – but maybe there comes a point where you've got to make a stand, believe in *some*thing. Maybe that makes all the difference.'

Uma nodded at me. Or I thought it was at me, until the red-headed bull dyke got up and darted across the room. She had a gun in one hand and a poppadum in the other.

'Time to put yer money where yer mouth is,' she growled, in an Irish accent that was less than lilting.

'This is Siobhan,' Uma told me. 'She will be looking after us.'

NINE

〜

'And what is *that*, exactly?'

'That's called a car. Or have you not seen one before in Los Angeles?' Siobhan said. Her upper lip seemed curled in a perpetual Elvis-like snarl. If all else failed, she'd always find work in Vegas.

'I've never seen one quite that small,' I muttered, walking around the little vehicle. 'You get this from a circus or something? Did the clowns die?'

'It is called a Mini,' Uma said. 'Not terribly comfortable, I grant, but very inconspicuous and extremely economical.'

'I'll spring for gas money if you want to get something . . . roomier. I mean, do you ride *in* it or on *top* of it or what?'

'We can drag you behind by your balls. It's all the same to me,' Siobhan said.

She was really warming up to me, I thought. Starstruck, no doubt.

Uma had formally introduced the coyote-ugly bruiser as Siobhan Smythe. She served as Uma's bodyguard, and I had to admit that I wouldn't have messed with her without a tank or an armoured personnel carrier around me.

'Smythe your real name or just what you use for checking into motels?' I kidded.

'You taking the mickey?' she asked me.

'Excuse me?' I saw Uma's eyes widen and she shook her head at me.

''Cause the last bastard who tried to take the mickey ended up wearing his balls on his forehead. I haven't much use for 'em between the legs, lord knows, but trust me, they're even uglier dooberries when they're planted between yer eyes.'

I was beginning to detect a theme, here.

'Got it,' I said. No more jokes about her name. And I sure as hell wasn't going to take any more mickey out of her, whatever the hell that was. In fact, I wouldn't even mention anyone named Mickey, just to be safe. If the subject of The Monkees came up at any point – and you never know – Davy Jones was my boy through and through.

(By the by, and apropos of virtually nothing at all, I was once supposed to do a guest shot on an episode of *The Monkees* back in my *Salt & Pepper* hey-day. This was when the networks were big on spinning-off their various sit-com kids into singing careers, à la David Cassidy and Bobby Sherman and the Brady brats. I was slotted in to sing a few bars of the latest Boyce and Hart ditty and do that zany Monkee walk, but I got caught trying to cop a feel off this bit of blonde twat who was hanging around the set. It turned out she was only fifteen, and more disastrously, the niece of the producer, with a major crush on mmm-mmm Dolenz. I got booted off the set faster than you could say Daydream Believer, thus ending my recording career before it could even begin. 'For of all sad words of tongue or pen . . .')

The doorman at the Savoy didn't look impressed by the Mini, either. I got the feeling he didn't see too many of them disgorging passengers for the hotel. He looked on with evident dismay as the three of us stood around discussing it, though maybe it was Siobhan he was worried about. God knows what she'd said about *his* balls.

I tried reaching June Hanover before checking out, but she wasn't in the office and all I could get was her machine at home. A man's voice – Terry? – recited the outgoing message. I told the machine that I had decided to head out of town for a few days and enjoy the scenery. Which was sort of true, except for the enjoyment part. I told her I'd catch up with her before I flew out of the country for good. And I thanked her again for her various kindnesses. I should have called my agent, too, but I chickened out. No way I could lie to Kendall, because she always saw right through me. Lying and agents usually go together like love and marriage, especially matrimony Hollywood-style, but then that's what made Kendall special. So I convinced myself that I'd call her in a couple days, after things had shaken out a little.

Not that I had the slightest idea what that might actually entail. Uma had been vague about the plan and what she wanted or expected of me when we spoke in the restaurant the night before. She'd told me that the Thule were trying to recreate Himmler's Black Order right here in England and that their efforts were as much concentrated on building up a supernatural power base as a physical and economic one. Uma's intention was to counter the Thule's occult efforts with a preemptive defensive strike. Kind of a white magic/black magic thing. The first step was to recruit assistance with the supernatural stuff.

'Um, when you say *supernatural*, how do you mean it exactly,' I'd asked.

'It is a simple word, Mr Burns. What is it you do not understand?'

'It's just . . . like I say, I have seen things, some *strange* goddamn things. It's left me pretty open-minded about how the world works. I mean, I used to walk under ladders and open umbrellas in the house and stuff like that with gay abandon. But now that I know there's more to life than either Richard Dawkins or The Amazing Randi can explain, I find I'm a bit more cautious. I sweat a little every time I knock over a salt shaker. And I'm very careful around mirrors.'

'That is a sound way to live. Mirrors may be especially dangerous if broken.'

'Really?' I whispered. 'How come?'

'You could cut yourself on the glass,' Uma said, and broke out into an uncharacteristic cackle. Siobhan thought it was pretty damn witty, too.

'Right,' I said, and waited for the red to fade from my cheeks.

Siobhan drove and I got the shotgun seat by default; I simply refused to squeeze into the back seat of the Mini, despite Siobhan's gentle encouragement ('It's plenty big enough for a tiny bastard like you!'). At five foot eight and three-quarters (every little bit counts) I'm never going to star in the Michael Jordan Story, but there was no way I could sit in back without my knees hooked over my ears. And like the old joke goes: if I could do that, I'd never leave the house.

'Put your damn seat belt on,' Siobhan ordered as we pulled away from the hotel porte-cochere.

I complied quickly. 'I didn't know you cared.'

'Yeah, well, if yer fool head goes through the windshield, it's me that'll be left to clean up, isn't it?'

We drove east, up the Strand, in silence. I gaped at the dome of St Paul's as we cruised past and then some more as we came up on the

Tower. I love Tower Bridge. I know it's actually not that old, but I think it's impressive as hell. Every time I look at it, I can't help but think of those suckers in Arizona who bought London Bridge, not realizing that they weren't getting the really neat one.

'Can we go across it?' I asked.

'What is this, a bloody sightseeing bus?' Siobhan carped. 'Does this car look like it's double-deckered and painted red? Christ, next you'll be after me for a shagging Happy Meal.'

'Hmmmph,' I sulked.

'We can go across the river this way, no?' Uma said.

'It's quicker to take the tunnel.'

'I think we can spare a couple of minutes,' Uma told her.

'Bloody hell. We'll be taking in the Changing of the Guard before you know it. All aboard the tosser express,' Siobhan moaned.

But she turned onto the bridge, so I was happy.

We drove on in silence for a while as we worked our way through the busy, rather grimy streets of south London. The south side of the Thames is clearly the wrong side of the tracks. Siobhan flipped on the radio at one point, but turned it off with a curse when she couldn't find anything she liked.

'Looking for U2?' I said. It was the only Irish band I could think of off the top of my head.

'U-bloody-2? What fucking year were you born?'

I didn't care to say, actually, and decided against any further attempts at small talk. Siobhan started humming a little song to herself, and though I was surprised by how sweet a singing voice she had, I thought it best not to comment on it.

As we turned up the entrance ramp onto a freeway, I thought it was about time to ask exactly where we were going.

'It's a bloody motorway, you git, not a *freeway*,' Siobhan delicately corrected.

'Siobhan,' Uma said with a sigh. The redhead clucked her tongue, but didn't say anything more.

'So?' I prompted again.

'Let me ask you something first,' Uma said. She leaned forward, resting her chin on the back of my seat. 'Why have you asked so few questions until now? You've been remarkably passive, acquiescent perhaps I should say.'

'That surprises you?'

'I am not surprised so much as intrigued. It's not the demeanour I might have expected of a Hollywood personality.'

'Yeah, well, I'm not exactly your standard-issue Malibu type. At least not any more.'

'So you're not even good for a day at the beach, then,' Siobhan sniped, but she couldn't hide a little smile as she peered over at me.

I glanced at her pale skin, white as a dead slug's belly. 'You're hardly a candidate for Miss Redondo Beach,' I said.

'Ah, you've never seen me in a bikini.'

I eyed her up and down and managed, I think, not to make a sour face. Several possible responses came to mind, but I was too scared to say any of them.

'My loss,' I managed.

'That's for sure.'

'Mr Burns?' Uma said.

'Huh?'

'You have not answered my question.'

'Maybe it's time you started calling me "Marty".'

'Thank you, Marty. I am still waiting for an answer, though.'

'I know you are,' I said. To an extent, I was surprised myself at how readily I'd agreed to come along on this little mystery tour. But ever since that first moment when I hurled the bottle at the skinhead in the convenience store, I'd felt a bit like events had moved out of my control, that I was being pulled by an invisible tide down a stream of consequence. It wasn't that I couldn't fight the tide, it was more that, for reasons that weren't clear to me or that I couldn't fully articulate, I didn't *want* to. Those strange, dark dreams were a part of it, too, though I didn't know what part. I just knew that their menace felt very real, very *substantial* to me. Ignoring them, I feared, would be more dangerous than confronting them. Even obliquely. I tried explaining this to Uma.

'Just a feeling,' I told her. I was summarizing. 'Don't you ever run on instinct?'

'*All* the time,' she said with a smile. 'I call it survival mechanism.'

I nodded. 'So where *are* we going?'

'Canterbury,' Uma said.

'Like in the tales?'

'Hmmm? Yes, I suppose so. One might even think of this as a pilgrimage of sorts, as the cathedral is our destination. So to speak. In any event, we must go by way of Ashford. It's not far out of the way and we have to pick someone up there.'

'Another passenger? In *this* car?'

'Pilgrims were not known for their devotion to the creature comforts. And he isn't a large chap from what I understand.'

'From what you understand?'

'I have not actually met him, no. Though I am assured of his skills and abilities. And his devotion to our cause.'

Instinct or not, this was starting to sound just a little half-assed to me. I tried not to let it show in my tone. 'Um, I know what I said and all, but perhaps this would be a good time for you to explain the situation in a *little* more detail. I mean, if that's okay.'

Uma offered me another inscrutable smile, but didn't appear to take any offence. I saw Siobhan roll her eyes a bit, though.

'As I told you last night, the Thule have divided their resources along two paths. In the streets, in places like Tower Hamlets, they recruit physical force among the young and the alienated, like the National Front and the British National Party and many others before them. There is never any shortage of poverty and racial unease in cities like London, leaving many a young fruit ready to be picked. Unlike other fascist organizations, the Thule are careful who they select, however. They are not interested in sheer numbers. At least not right now.'

'Why is that?'

'For the simple reason that they are concentrating their efforts along a second path. The path of the magical. Any white man with a sufficient hatred of blacks or Jews or homosexuals was able to find a home with the old National Front, but the Thule, like Himmler's Black Order before them, regard themselves as rather more elite. They share a devotion, not merely to a fascistic political doctrine, but to a religious and occult philosophy which, by its very nature, decrees an extreme selectivity. The street thugs enlisted to do their bidding are not privy to this hierarchy, nor do they know of the Thule's supernatural agenda. Though a certain indoctrination into the Thule's Odinist belief structure is attempted.'

'Odinist?' I though about that for a second. 'You mean like Thor, Loki, Ragnarok. Those guys?'

'Ah, you are familiar with Germano-Norse mythology, then.'

'The god of thunder, *Might*-y Thorrr!' I sang. I felt myself blushing again.

'There's the musical sensibility of a U2 fan for you,' Siobhan said. 'Ohhh, I'd love to spit-roast that bloody Bono. The Edge, my foot.'

'Ex*cuse* me?' Uma said.

'The Mighty Thor? You know, Stan Lee, Jack Kirby. Marvel comics. No?'

Uma shook her head. She had on another of those June Hanover you're-making-me-nervous looks.

'I don't know a thing about Norse myths,' I admitted. 'Except he had a magic hammer. Thor, I mean.'

'*Mjolnir.*'

'Yeah, that's it! No one else could pick it up, and when he threw it, it came back to him like a boomerang. Really neat. He had to strike it on the ground to turn back into lame old Dr Donald Blake. And he was always fighting with the Hulk. Neither of them ever really won, though, 'cause they were both good guys. He was in *The Avengers*, too. Man, I loved those comics.'

'I do not believe that particular narrative figures in the Thule's belief structure,' Uma said.

'Christ!' Siobhan spat.

'Huh? Oh. Yeah. Sorry. So what's their story then?'

'They are Odinists, but of a particularly corrupt variety. Like the Nazis of the Third Reich, they've pillaged bits and pieces from Germanic and Norse religious belief and adapted them to fit their own needs. Odinism has became fashionable among certain New Age believers – an otherwise harmless bunch, by and large – but the Thule's beliefs are anchored in an especially retrograde variant. Their purpose, I think, has more to do with a loathing for conventional religion, than with any evangelical Odinist zeal. The Thule are almost as virulently anti-Christian as they are anti-Semitic. Essentially, they hate everyone who is not one of them, who does not believe as they do. They have a strong sense of clannishness, a variant of the tribalism which has come so much to the fore in recent years, with little tolerance for those outside their own definition of the clan.'

'The thing I don't quite get – well, *one* of the many things I don't get, I'm writing a book – is why this is all going down *here*. I mean, if these dudes are into all this German and Norse shit, what the fuck are they doing in England? Why aren't they in Germany or Sweden or something?'

'They are,' Uma sighed. 'As I told you, they can be found throughout Europe. But England has proved to be a particularly hospitable environment.'

'That's what I don't understand: this seems like the *last* place that would be hospitable. After all, you whipped these guys' butts fifty years ago. I mean, we did.'

'Out of necessity, yes. And in the dangerous revision written in victor's history, for a greater good. But it must be said that within the English character there is a certain propensity for the fascistic, for rigidity and well-established order. For such an eccentric people, the English harbour a peculiar resentment for that which is different or unique.'

'I wouldn't say that's particularly limited to this country. The French aren't exactly the world's most tolerant people. Christ, they still have an honest to goodness fascist party in Italy, though no one ever seems bothered by the Italians. I think it must be the pizza. And you know that we've got our own charming variety of Nazis in the States, what with the Klan and the militias, all those white supremacist assholes in Montana and Idaho.'

'Of course, a propensity for authoritarianism is not unique to the English, but it is often conveniently forgotten just how reluctant many of the aristocracy were to oppose Hitler before the war. Oswald Mosley and his blackshirts had no small following here . . .'

'Whoa!' I yelled. 'Who?'

'Mosley. He was a prominent British fascist who . . .'

'No, no,' I said. 'What was that about black shirts?'

The vision of the riot I'd seen on the street, the men in the black shirts, came racing back into my head.

'Like Mussolini's followers, Mosley's acolytes took to wearing black shirts as a kind of uniform. Surely you've seen pictures from the time?'

'Of course,' I whispered. My weird vision was starting to make more sense all of a sudden. Not *good* sense, but more sense.

'As I was saying,' Uma went on, 'Mosley found considerable support, particularly among the powerful and moneyed. Even the abdicate, Edward, was a Nazi at heart. That . . . *tendency* or strain remains part of the English character. I see it in the attraction held for people by the so-called nanny state, though it is ironic that a proto-fascist like Margaret Thatcher should have so railed against it.'

'It's not just the English, you know. It runs deep through the blood of all these islands,' Siobhan added. 'Ireland served as a refuelling depot for Nazi submarines during the war. Though it pains me to say it.'

'No way,' I said.

'Sure enough,' Siobhan said. 'Of course, from our point of view the English are still as good as Nazis, right down to their occupying stormtroopers. That's what the Troubles have been all about, eh?'

'I'm not sure I follow.'

'Siobhan was IRA,' Uma said.

'There's no was, whatever Gerry Adams might say to the cameras,' Siobhan said.

'Oh,' I croaked. I cleared my throat. 'Still, you're talking about a tiny minority of people here.'

'Absolutely,' Uma said. 'And I would not live here, work so hard and risk so much to defend this land if I did not love it and its people with all my heart. Nonetheless, the truth remains that the English and the Germans once were and in many ways still are as one people, with deep Nordic roots. It is not by chance that the mythical Thule was said to be located in the British Isles. There are great commonalities to be found in Celtic and Germanic myth and legend.'

'Seems kind of slim,' I suggested.

'Perhaps, but England is full of places of power, many of which remain undisturbed, viable. Few such places survived the two great wars fought on the Continent in this century.'

'Places of power. I assume you ain't talking nuclear power plants.'

'I mean,' Uma said, giving me a very hard look, 'places of magic. Ancient sites which resonate with the power of the land and of the people. Places with an energy, a soul which can be exploited, for dark or light. These are the places we must attempt to make safe before the Thule can usurp them, corrupt them. I believe that they are now ready to do so. Indeed, they may well have begun, so our time is short. Canterbury is host to such a place. There are others.'

'And that's where we're going to go?'

'That is my plan. There are many minor nexuses of power, but there are four essential points, spread across the land. Canterbury is the nearest. There is a second in the West Country – in Cornwall – and another in the far north, among the Orkney islands. If we can get to each of these sites before our enemies, construct glamours of protection, the Thule will be severely hindered in their own efforts.'

'Do the Thule know where these places are?'

'Oh, yes.'

'Then how do we know they won't be there waiting for us?'

'We do not know that at all.'

'Shit,' I said. 'Wait. Canterbury, Cornwall and Orkney; but you said there are four centres of power.'

'Yes I did.'

Nothing more seemed to be forthcoming.

'I see,' I said.

'I know that you do not,' Uma said. 'But you will.'

The Mini's suspension (or lack of it) notwithstanding, the drive down the motorway through Kent was pleasant enough. The countryside was pretty, I suppose, green and gently rolling, but deeply dull. Staring out the window was like looking at a painting by an artist who has the basic skills, but lacks the heart and soul that makes all the difference between mere mimicry and real art. Siobhan kept turning the radio on and off, cursing every time she failed to find anything she wanted to listen to.

After about an hour, Siobhan exited the motorway onto a much smaller road, and then pulled over at a service station to get gas. We all got out to stretch our legs.

'I will pay,' Uma said, heading off toward the little shop. 'Does anyone want anything?'

'I'll take a drink,' Siobhan said as she filled the tank.

'Surprise me,' I said.

Uma rolled her eyes, but nodded and walked off.

'No Twiglets,' I called after her. She didn't respond and I worried that she hadn't heard me.

I studied the prices posted on the big signs, but they didn't make much sense to me. 'I thought gas was supposed to be so much more expensive here,' I said. 'But these prices are great. Only sixty pence a gallon? What's that, less than a dollar?'

Siobhan cocked her head at me. 'Are you really such a dickhead, or is it just part of your Hollywood persona?'

'What?' Here, I'd thought she was starting to like me.

'First of all, it's not "gas", it's petrol. Gas is what you get in your gut when you've had too much lager. And second, it's sixty pence a *litre*, not a gallon. You're in bloody Europe now.'

'Sixty pence a *litre*,' I repeated. 'Let's see, there's two and a half centimetres to an inch and what, four hectares to a rod, so how many litres does it take to make a gallon? Damn, this is the kind of standardized test question I always flunked.'

'There are four and a half litres to the gallon.'

'Four and a half – holy shit! You mean gas costs . . .' – it took me a while to calculate it out while Siobhan watched me shaking her head – '. . . two pound seventy, that's . . . *over four dollars a gallon?*'

'*Petrol* . . . And that's for an imperial gallon. A US gallon is a touch smaller.'

'You're kidding?'

'Why would I want to kid you about something as bloody

stupid as this?' Siobhan removed the nozzle and refitted the gas cap.

'Jeez, like the metric system isn't confusing enough. I thought a gallon was a gallon. Wherever you were.'

'I bet you think a rose is a rose, too. You probably like Sting, too. Tell me true now?'

'Huh? No!' I insisted, knowing when I've been insulted. But I was still marvelling over the price of gas. 'How can anybody here afford to drive?'

'That is the whole idea,' Uma said from behind.

'How do you mean?'

'If the price of petrol is high, then fewer people will drive. Fewer cars, fewer accidents, less pollution.'

'And does it work out that way?'

'There is always a very great chasm between theory and practice. Still, the idea is not unsound.'

'It's obscene,' I said.

'An argument you can take up with our companion-to-be.'

'Huh? Why?'

'We are supposed to meet him at an anti-roads protest. He has, I understand, rather strong beliefs on the subject.'

As we got back into the car, Uma opened up the little bag of goodies she'd bought in the convenience shop. She handed a bottle of Evian to Siobhan, who took a hefty slug, then stuck the bottle between her legs as she turned back onto the road. She pulled out a plastic container of orange juice for herself.

'Didn't you get me anything?' I whined.

'Would it not be a surprise if I had not? Did you not ask to be surprised?'

I crossed my arms and pulled a mopey face. Siobhan shook her head again.

'I did get you something, Marty,' Uma said.

I smiled and turned around. She handed me a small oval item wrapped in tin-foil. Kinder Surprise, the label read.

'Oh, Christ! Indulge the bastard a little more why don't you?'

Ignoring the manifestly jealous Siobhan, I unwrapped the foil, revealing a chocolate egg. Something rattled inside. The surprise, no doubt.

'Neat!' I said. 'Like Crackerjacks.'

Siobhan gunned the gas.

I mean *petrol*, of course.

* * *

The chocolate was so-so, but my prize turned out to be a tiny plastic
. . . well, I don't know what the hell it was. It was a creature of some
sort, half-troll/half-hippopotamus. Or something. The damn thing
was made in Germany, so god knows what they were thinking.

I loved it.

Every so often I'd walk it across the dashboard and have it sing
'Roxanne' to Siobhan. After my third soprano rendition, she said,
'If you don't put that cursed thing away, I'm going to pull over,
drag you out of the car and drive a rusty nail through the back of
your knee with a baseball bat.'

I laughed and pretended that the hippo-troll thought it was funny,
too. I made it hop up and down with high-pitched laughter on the
dashboard.

'Perhaps it would be best if you do put it away now, Marty,' Uma
said. I glanced over my shoulder and saw that she wasn't smiling.

I tossed my prize out the window.

We drove for another twenty minutes before passing a sign marking
the town limits of Ashford. The sign indicated that Ashford was
twinned with a German city whose name I couldn't pronounce.

'That's ominous, huh?' I said.

'Not particularly,' Uma replied.

I wasn't enjoying this trip at all.

Uma pulled out a map and directed Siobhan through the main
part of town and back out the other side. There seemed to be an
awful lot of construction work going on everywhere we looked. The
traffic was stop and go, with the lanes narrowing down every few
hundred yards where they were digging up the streets.

'What a mess,' I said.

'They are in the process of building a new railway station here
for trains passing through the Channel Tunnel. Much of the area
is being rebuilt and the roads rerouted to accommodate it.'

'Is this like a big tourist area?'

'No,' Uma said.

'So what's here?'

'Absolutely nothing. Except a well-connected Member of
Parliament.'

'Ah,' I said. There's a certain comfort to be taken in the knowledge
of the universality of things. Like pork-barrel politics.

Uma told Siobhan to get off the main road just as we reached the
first signs offering directions to the new station. We turned on to a
narrower road, which was covered with mud. Tractors and cranes
and other heavy construction vehicles were parked in a line along

the dirt shoulder. The road widened out – petered out is probably more accurate – into a huge dirt-strewn, largely unpaved bowl of a construction site, surrounded on three sides by high trees. Lots more vehicles were parked willy-nilly around the site, along with a couple of trailers and the usual row of Portaloos.

And about a dozen cop cars.

Police cordons had been strung up all along the perimeter of the site. Two bored-looking officers stood at the end of the road, hailing down anyone who tried to drive through. Behind them a couple of dozen construction workers in hard-hats milled around, drinking coffee and kibitzing with a location crew from the BBC.

Behind them, up in the trees, were the anti-road protesters. They had built a series of small tree-houses in the high branches, linked by swinging cables. I watched in amazement as one of the tree-dwellers whizzed a good ten yards through mid-air via a system of pulleys attached to a harness he wore on his back. It looked dangerous as hell, and I found myself holding my breath until he reached the relative safety of another tree branch.

'What the fuck?' I said.

Siobhan pulled over and parked before the cops could wave us down. We got out of the car and walked onto the construction site. A couple of cops gave us the hairy eyeball, but no one bothered to stop us or ask what we were doing there. I got the feeling that they were used to a lot of people wandering around.

'I am going to see if I can find our companion,' Uma said. 'Perhaps it would be best if you waited here for me.'

I nodded and plopped down on an old tree stump. I expected Siobhan to stay behind as well, but she stuck close to Uma, and they wandered off in the direction of the protesters.

I took a good look around the site. You could see that the whole area must have been wooded until quite recently, but a line of trees had been cut down to extend the road. Part of the area had been paved over already, but most of it was dirt or mud which had hardened in the shape of the tracks of the various machines. Petrified in a million years they'd probably sit in a science museum, though god knows what kind of creature they'd think lived during this time.

I heard a wet noise behind me and saw a guy in a BBC jacket taking a piss against the side of one of the Portaloos. He saw me watching as he shook himself off, and winked at me. I quickly looked the other way, but he wandered over, still zipping himself up.

'Got a light, mate?' A cigarette dangled from his lips.

'No,' I said. 'Wait! Yeah.' I remembered that I'd grabbed a book of Savoy matches and stuffed it in my pocket when I checked out. Just a habit. I tossed him the matches and told him to keep them.

'Cheers,' he said. He lit up. 'Which side you with then?'

'Sorry?'

'Which side? The cunts up in the trees or the cunts what want to cut them down?'

'Um, neither, really.' I was a little put off by his tone.

I could see he was eyeing me up and I was suddenly afraid he would recognize me and go grab the camera crew. The last thing I – or we – needed was more publicity.

'You with ITN?' he asked. 'You look familiar.'

'No. I'm . . . just passing through. I'm here with somebody who's looking for somebody else.'

'Whatever, mate. Just asking.'

'What exactly is going on here?'

He took a long drag on his cigarette. 'Aw, it's a right old mess. Been going on for weeks, now. See, these crusty cunts up in the branches are a bunch of tree fuckers. They don't want *these* cunts . . .' – he gestured at the construction workers with his cigarette – 'to cut the bitches down.'

'Uh-huh,' I said.

'Now, these cunts on the ground are miserable scum. I hate the lot of them. They been sitting around on their arses getting paid for drinking tea day after day.'

'So you're with the protesters.'

'I'm with the Beeb, mate. Your ever lovin' Auntie.'

'No,' I said, 'I mean opinion-wise you side with the, uh, people in the trees.'

'I'm just a bleedin' sound man, ain't I. What do I know? But I'll tell you this, my friend . . .' He leaned forward conspiratorially. I leaned closer to listen. 'They're all a load of fucking cunts.'

With that he put out his cigarette and wandered off.

'Phew!' I sighed. Funny country.

There was a sudden commotion and flurry of activity off to my left. A group of police officers ran off, followed rather more leisurely by the BBC crew. I took a look around for Uma and Siobhan, but couldn't spot them. Lacking anything better to do, I trailed after the action.

One of the protesters, a girl who looked all of about sixteen, was struggling with a couple of guys in hard-hats and day-glo vests. She was shrieking at the top of her lungs and flailing about like a Tasmanian Devil. One of the hard-hats held her under the arms, while the other tried to get a hold of her legs. The girl had purple and orange hair and wore a hoop ring through her nose. Her dirty T-shirt had ridden up her body in the melee, revealing slight, boyish tits and a yellow tattoo of the sun on her pot belly.

Several of the girl's comrades, lurking up in the branches above started screaming along with her. The bunch of them reminded me of nothing so much as a family of braying chimps in a National Geographic documentary. Then the group in the trees started hurling water balloons down at the hard-hats. The balloons dropped like lead weights, and it was only as they exploded on the ground that I realized it was because they were filled with human faeces. One of the balloons hit the target, catching the guy who was fumbling with the girl's legs square atop his helmet, spraying turds all over the trio. The hard-hat let go in disgust and turned away to wipe the shit out of his eyes. The girl just kept on shrieking and fighting, almost breaking free of the other hard-hat who still held her from behind. She managed to shrug one arm free, but the hard-hat reached around and, intentionally or not, I don't know and wouldn't care to guess, grabbed hold of the dangling nose ring. The girl jerked her head to the right, or the man pulled to the left, and the ring came free, a small piece of her nose still attached.

The girl shrieked even louder as a tiny fountain of blood pumped away from the middle of her face. The hard-hat let go of her other arm and stared in amazement for a moment at the ring and nose-fragment still clutched in his hand. He tried to toss it away, but the ring had lodged in his pinky. He shook his hand frantically until he managed to fling it off. I watched it disappear into the tall grass, as the man wiped the girl's blood off onto his vest, with visible disgust.

The police who had dashed over had just been watching all this. They seemed to be put off – understandably, I suppose – by the rain of balloon-o-turds, but a pair of them went scampering after the girl. She was too fast, though, or they were too slow, because she managed to scoot up a rope which had been tossed down from a nearby tree. Man, did she move! She continued shrieking like a banshee, and I could see the blood still pouring down her face, but her buddies in the trees helped pull her up. When she made it safely to one of the little tree-houses, she raised one hand in a gesture of triumph, still clutching her nose with the other, while the protesters cheered wildly and hurled insults and turds down at the police and hard-hats. Then the girl stuck her rear out over the edge of a branch, pulling her trousers down with her free hand. I thought she was just going to moon, but a second later a stream of urine tinkled down on the cops who had given chase. They quickly retreated to a point outside her range of fire.

The protesters in the trees were all jumping up and down and howling or barking in celebration. It further cemented in my mind the image of a pack of chimps, but I couldn't help smiling at the chaos this one small girl had wreaked on the burly hard-hats and ostensibly highly-trained policemen. I didn't know who was right and who was wrong in terms of the underlying protest, but I instinctively found it hard to sympathize with anyone who'd pull the nose off a teenage girl. No matter how bad her toilet habits.

The fun seemed to be over for the moment, so I drifted back toward my tree stump. My buddy from the BBC waltzed past with his crew a minute later. He caught my eye and gave me a big smile. He pointed his thumb back in the direction of the tussle and mouthed something at me.

No prizes for guessing the secret word.

'Marty!'

Uma and Siobhan strolled out of the trees, accompanied by a cross between Dennis Hopper (circa *Easy Rider*, but with a hint of that *Speed* psychopath in the eyes) and the Mayor of Munchkinville. He was a little guy, a shade over five feet tall on a generous ruler, dressed in a rainbow atrocity T-shirt and filthy camouflage trousers. At first I thought he was just a kid because of his height, but the more I studied him the older he looked. He was well-built, for one thing, with thick muscular arms that attested to lifting more than peace signs. He wore his dirty-brown hair in even dirtier, brown dreadlocks, topped by a knit Rasta cap (with matching shoes yet). His scraggly beard was thin enough to see his acne pits through, but just thick enough to catch and retain a variety of crumbs and other unassimilated foreign objects. His upper lip offered something between a real moustache and the residue of chocolate milk. He wore several varieties of earrings, a stud through his nose and one of those eyebrow stick-pin things just like Dasra.

I winced.

He smiled.

His yellow and black teeth put me in mind of rotting bananas. The smell that wafted from him wasn't quite as nice as that, though the faint redolence of marijuana took the edge off what might otherwise have been intolerable. I glanced at Siobhan, who stood conspicuously upwind of him. Judging from her expression, I reckoned that, if nothing else, I was no longer her *least* favourite travelling companion.

'This is Pahoo,' Uma said.

Pahoo put out his hand. Holding my breath, I took it. His palm felt slimy *and* gritty, and he had a grip like a limp carp.

'You'll be riding in the back with him,' Siobhan said with a smirk.

'Swell,' I sighed.

I managed not to gag as my new, best buddy reached around and gave me a hug.

TEN

My plan was to simply refuse to ride in the back of the Mini, to dig my heels in and, if necessary, hold my breath till I turned cobalt blue.

Siobhan got out her baseball bat.

She really did have one in the car. Louisville slugger, George Foster autograph model: an oldie, but a goodie. She didn't have a rusty nail to go with it, but she found a twenty-penny spike amid the construction site debris, and while it gleamed silvery as a new dime, I didn't much fancy the idea of having it driven through the back of my knee.

The rear seat wasn't *so* bad, as it turned out, although it probably helped that Pahoo was pint-sized. I even got over his pungency after a while; of course, we did drive with the windows open. The biggest problem was what to do with his didgeridoo.

'Your what?' I'd been forced to ask as we loaded up his stuff. It looked like a thick, hollowed tree branch, perhaps four and a half feet in length – almost as tall as Pahoo – and tapered slightly at one end. Actually, it eerily reminded me of the Doomsday Machine that munches planets and almost swallows Kirk and Spock in that old episode of *Star Trek*. Pahoo had to get one of his chums to lower it down from his digs in a particularly precarious-looking tree house.

'Me didgeridoo,' he said. As if I'd asked what that two-holed thing he breathes through in the middle of his face was called.

'Does it have warp engines?' I realized *didgeridoo* was a word that I was familiar with, but had never had any specific referent for. Like 'steatopygia'. My little thought choo-choo was running from Rod Laver to Paul Hogan to Olivia

Newton John when I made the connection. 'Tie me Kangaroo Down Sport!'

'What?' Siobhan asked.

'You got it.' Pahoo nodded and smiled.

'Mind me didgeridoo, Lou. Mind me didgeridoo . . .' I sang.

'Not again,' Siobhan said.

'Rolf Harris,' Uma said, nodding. 'I loved that song.'

'Huh? I never heard of Rolf Harris,' I said. 'I remember the song from when I was a kid, though. But I always assumed a didgeridoo was a kind of Australian animal. A long-necked bird or the wild dog with a pouch that ate Meryl Streep's baby or something. Like "platypus duck".'

'No, mate. It's an Aboriginal musical instrument. And it's very beautiful.' And with that he gave us a brief recital.

Beautiful isn't exactly the word I'd have chosen. The noise a didgeridoo makes is rather like blowing across an empty beer bottle, except that you'd need a super-wide mouth to get a sound that low in the bass register. Looking at the damn thing again, I reckoned that there wasn't much more to it than there is to an empty beer bottle (the pleasure of drinking a frosty brewski notwithstanding). I wouldn't exactly call it music that Pahoo extracted from the thing, but after a few bars I recognized, purely from the rhythm, an attempt at 'Tie Me Kangaroo Down Sport'. Whoever the hell Rolf Harris was, it was probably making him spin in his grave. If he was dead.

The thing is, it's a little tough squeezing a four and a half foot didgeridoo into what is essentially a five foot long car. Uma tried to persuade Pahoo to leave it behind with his pals, but it was nothing doing. They argued for a while, and at one point I saw Siobhan start to reach for her Louisville Slugger again, but Uma shook her head at her.

'I need it,' Pahoo said. '*We* need it!' Uma didn't look entirely convinced – I think she thought the thing was an affectation on Pahoo's part – but that settled the issue.

So there we were, whizzing up the road to Canterbury, four in a Mini, the wind at our backs and a didgeridoo strapped to the roof. Depending on our speed, the wind would whistle through the damn thing at just the right angle to evoke a throaty hum. Actually, it sounded rather better than what Pahoo had played. We got a few funny looks from the other motorists, but at least we could travel in confidence that no ship would broadside us in a fog.

We drove through more that's-pretty-say-what-do-we-have-to-eat type scenery. Lots of grazing sheep and fields dotted with tall, thin poles.

'What are those?' I asked.

Uma and Siobhan shrugged, but Pahoo told me: 'Hop poles.'

'They don't make music or anything horrible like that, do they?'

'In a sense, in a natural sense. They use them to grow hops. They train the plants up the poles.'

'Hops? Like for beer?'

'Amen, brother.' Pahoo nodded.

'Wow,' I marvelled. 'It's almost as pretty as a Budweiser ad.'

'Once upon a time this was a major ale producing region. Most of the local breweries are gone now. The hand of multinational corporatism.'

'The *name* of the beast,' I said.

'You think it's funny?' Pahoo asked.

I didn't think anything of it at all. It had just been a line, a bit of snappy patter, amusing road trip repartee. Pahoo looked offended, though. As offended as a smelly little guy can look, anyway.

'Well, it's not like Marx Brothers funny or Robin Williams funny. But, you know, maybe Abbott and Costello funny. Chris Farley funny. No, funnier than Chris Farley. Or is that a tautology?'

I smiled to show I was joshing. Pahoo bared his yellow teeth at me in response.

'That fuck-all, *American* attitude is exactly the problem the whole of the less developed world is up against. It's just that bleeding la-de-da, who gives a toss point of view that causes the death of trees.'

'I beg your pardon?'

'I think you know what I'm saying.'

'Jesus, Mary and Joseph,' Siobhan moaned. She glanced over at Uma. 'Do you *really* want to drive all the way to bloody John O'Groats with this pair?'

Uma didn't say anything, but from the way she sagged in her seat, I could tell she was maybe considering her options. I think she sighed. I probably would have *heard* it, but just then came a particularly resonant bleat from the didgeridoo.

In a field we were passing, a flock of sheep took off in panic away from the car.

I sort of knew how they felt.

I sort of wished I was with them.

Day drained into dusk as we arrived in Canterbury. The first thing you see as you approach the place is the cathedral. Its gothic spires loom over the rest of the town, and the sight of it made me think just how *really* impressive it must have been four or five hundred years ago to flocks of tired pilgrims who'd probably never seen anything grander than a wooden hut or village church. Which I guess was the whole point. It's rather impressive even today, though Canterbury itself struck me as a dreadful little place, deliberately kept small to make the Cathedral look big. A cursory inspection on the drive through revealed an excessive number of candle stores and crappy gift shops of the type designed to separate tourists from their money with maximum efficiency. But for all I knew, the place has been a tourist trap since the days of Chaucer.

Uma sat with a map on her lap and offered direction to Siobhan, who cursed in a steady stream under her breath. Whichever way Uma told her to go led to another street that was closed to traffic or a dead end. For a small town, Canterbury was absurdly difficult to drive around in. After approaching the fifth 'Do not enter' sign down a street not much wider than the car, Siobhan jerked the wheel to the left and pulled up onto the sidewalk. 'For Chrissake,' she hissed and grabbed the map from Uma. Uma started to object, but threw her hands in the air and stared out the side window at a brick wall. An old brick wall. I knew because there was a plaque that said so.

Siobhan mumbled to herself as she studied the map. Pahoo leaned forward at one point to look over her shoulder, but a growl – literally – from Siobhan put him back in his place.

'There's a lot of anger there,' he whispered, nodding to himself.

'Have you considered a career in therapy?' I said.

'Been there, done that.'

I shuddered to think.

'This where we want to go?' Siobhan pointed to a spot on the map. Uma leaned over and nodded.

'Fine,' Siobhan said. She dropped the car back off the sidewalk with a tooth-jarring thud and sped off without further reference to the map. It seemed like we had to drive all around the outskirts of the town to get where we needed to go – I counted four more candle shops – but finally Siobhan pulled into the parking lot behind a small bed and breakfast.

'Get out,' she ordered.

I'd been to a bed-and-breakfast in the States once. For a while back in the late eighties they were all the rage with your turbo yuppy types. B&Bs supposedly offer all the comforts of a hotel with the hominess of . . . well . . . home. Which is what they are. Somebody *else's* home, of course, but gussied up to match moneyed urbanites' expectations of grand country living. Antiques in the rooms, big comfy sofas in the lounge, extravagant yet tiny nouvelle cuisine meals. I prefer Holiday Inns and Ramadas myself. If I want the comforts of home, I'll stay at home; in a hotel I want room service, a big ice bucket and magic fingers in the bed, five minutes for a quarter.

Turns out England's a little different.

'*This* is a bed-and-breakfast?' I asked.

'Umm-hmm,' Uma said with a nod.

The place wasn't a dive, exactly, but I reckoned that the management of the Savoy wouldn't be losing any sleep. Inside, it did indeed look like somebody's home, but a person who didn't have a working vacuum cleaner. There were lots of knick-knacks and snapshots on the walls, and curios and doo-dads on the shelves and other undeniably personal touches, but it struck me less like *home* than, say, *trailer park*.

Siobhan seemed to sense my discomfort. She offered me a smirk. 'We've got reservations.'

'So do I,' I muttered. 'Believe me.'

'Not what a big Hollywood star like yourself is used to, I fancy.'

'I've stayed in worse,' I shrugged. Which was true, just not lately.

Uma found the proprietor and was signing the guest register. The landlady was a squat walrus of a woman with greying brown hair on her head and her upper lip. She smiled at me, but cast a rightly suspicious eye at Pahoo, no doubt catching a waft of his odour and fearing for her sheets. Still, she took Uma's money happily enough and handed over two sets of keys.

'Shall we put away our things?' Uma asked. 'We can have a rest, then get dinner. We will attend to ... business later tonight.'

'I'm bloody knackered,' Siobhan said.

'I suppose it's boys and girls,' I sighed. I glanced at Pahoo and hoped it would be an airy room.

'Unless you want to sleep with me, darling,' Siobhan said with a smile. 'I'll sing you an IRA lullaby.'

'Heh, heh,' I said, swallowing hard.

Uma handed me one of the keys, suppressing a smile. 'I think boys and girls would be for the best,' she said.

'I'm cool,' Pahoo offered.

The rooms were opposite each other on the second floor, which, as

Siobhan kindly pointed out to me, is called the *first* floor in England. No wonder they lost an empire.

'Don't you know any bloody thing at all?' she said.

There were two more numbered doors on our floor and a stairway leading up another flight. There was also a hall toilet, which left a sudden sinking feeling in my stomach.

'These rooms do come with private bathrooms, right?' I asked. Uma had already walked into their room, but Siobhan just looked over her shoulder at me and laughed.

'Fuck,' I said.

As it turned out the room *did* have its own bathroom, if one employed the crudest possible definition of the word. The room itself wasn't too bad, bigger than I expected and quite clean, though with two very single beds arranged twin-style. Pahoo tried to stake out the bed closest to the window, but it was uh-uh, nothing doing. I picked up his didgeridoo, threw it on the other bed and shoved it against the far wall, pushing my own bed up against the wall beneath the window. I opened the window as far as it would go and found a nice little breeze coming through. The window looked out on the street, which hosted several guest houses and B&Bs. There was a small playground-cum-park on the corner, and if I leaned out the window far enough, I could just catch a glimpse of the cathedral spires.

The bathroom, such as it was, had been installed in what had to have been designed as a closet. A stall shower, a tiny sink and a toilet had been squeezed into a space that would normally have been pushed to the brink by a three-piece suit and a shoe tree. Still, it had to be better than sharing the one in the hall. I'm very private about my ablutions.

I kicked my shoes off and lay down on the bed. The pillow was about as comfortable as a sack of golf balls, but the mattress was okay. Pahoo started doing some vaguely yoga-esque exercises on the floor. Every time he bent a certain way, his camouflage pants slipped down his waist, exposing the top of his hairy ass. I turned to face the wall and closed my eyes.

Somehow – tiredness would be the parsimonious explanation – I just fell asleep.

I dreamed that I was in an immense cavern. Dining tables were lined up as far as the eye could see and hundreds of Indian waiters were serving Tandoori chicken to thousands of silent diners. I sat at a table, with Uma on my right and Siobhan on my left. They both silently shovelled food into their mouths in a mechanical fashion. There was no place setting in front of me, so I raised a hand to hail a passing waiter. As I did so, I noticed a swastika emblazoned on my palm. I examined it more closely and saw that the jagged design had been etched into my skin like a tattoo. Embarrassed, I lowered my hand and hid it under the table, but as soon as I did, I could feel something wet against my skin. I bent over and saw Pahoo, naked and on all fours, licking the swastika on my palm with a lizard-like tongue. His eyes had gone all black inside and his tiny penis was stiff and oozing. I pulled my hand away and wiped it off, but I couldn't remove the swastika.

A waiter came over and dropped a plate down in front of me. The only thing on it was a pulsing black cocoon, the size and shape of an avocado. I dug my nails into the soft skin of the thing and it oozed warm blood. I kept peeling away at the skin, digging my fingers through the mushy flesh. The thing cried like a hungry baby as I tore it to bits.

In the middle was a hard stone that glowed red, but was cool to the touch. I held it up to Uma who nodded, but kept on eating. I tapped the stone against my plate, but the plate shattered and flew off the table in pieces. Then I tried banging the stone against the table, but the table broke in the middle, all the dishes sliding down and crashing to the floor. Furious, I threw the stone to the ground, stood on my chair and leapt down on top of it with all the force I could muster.

It cracked like an egg under my weight.

I got down on my hands and knees to inspect the smashed stone and saw that there had been a tiny head inside, but I'd flattened it against the floor. The face was black and round and a bit wrinkled. The eyes glanced up at me and I saw a tear spill out before they closed and it was dead.

I heard deep, throaty breathing and looked up. All the tables, diners, waiters were gone, but the great cavern remained. Lying across from me was Dasra, his bald head split open, a chunk of glistening grey matter poking out. His throat had been slit and, though it didn't bleed, the raspy breathing sound was made by air passing in and out of the cut. The loose, serrated skin at the edge of the wound flapped like broken bird's wings with each laboured breath. I reached out toward him, but his head simply fell off his body. It rolled across the cavern floor, coming to a stop at the feet of five faceless figures in black. They raised their arms to me and . . .

I woke up, but I could still hear Dasra's death rasps. It was Pahoo, sitting naked on the floor, playing his didgeridoo. My unconscious had conjured an eerily accurate representation of his 1/10 scale genitalia. Or maybe it was just the juxtaposition with the didgeridoo.

'Would you please put your pants on?' I said.

He lowered the instrument – I refer to the didgeridoo – and stared down at himself before looking back up at me. 'I am what I am,' he said.

'That's a heavy philosophical position, Popeye, but it don't mean I want to look at your Johnson.'

'You've got a problem with nature, haven't you, mate? You're a fellow what's lost touch with his essence.'

'Me and my essence get along just fine, thank you. We do lunch on alternate Thursdays. I just don't go flashing *my* essence around at strangers.'

Pahoo shook his head at me, but he grabbed his filthy pants off the bed and slipped back into them. As he turned around, I saw that he had a large, incredibly complicated design tattooed on his muscular back. Except it didn't look like any tattoo I'd ever seen. There was no colour, but it had a real quality of depth to it. Almost 3-D.

'What is that supposed to be?' I asked.

'Eh?' He glanced at himself over his shoulder, as if I'd told him he had a bug on his back. 'Celtic rune,' he said. 'I had it branded on.'

A brief image of Chuck Connors flashed into my head, then I realized what he meant. 'Branded? You mean like . . . *branded*? Pokers, hot coals . . . like a cow?'

'They don't use pokers *or* hot coals, mate. It's all done very carefully. There's a very beautiful ritual involved.'

'Fucking hell! You mean to tell me, you sat there and let some lunatic burn that pattern into your skin?'

'I'm going to have another one done on the front. When I get a chance.'

'Jesus Christ. Doesn't it hurt?'

Pahoo sort of shrugged. Or maybe it was a shudder. 'A bit,' he said. 'But there are new levels of power and self-awareness to be experienced on that edge between pain and pleasure. The ritual leaves you feeling detached, spiritual.'

'Delirious might be more accurate,' I said. 'Or stupid.'

'I wouldn't expect your like to understand. You're too distanced from your animus.'

'With friends like you, who needs animus?'

I was rather pleased with this, but Pahoo glowered at me and shook his head.

'So what's the rune supposed to mean?' I asked. Call me a
masochist.

'This particular combination of symbols suggests the essential
unity of Earth and spirit. The big semi-circle represents the totality
of the planet and the winding coils and V-shapes indicate various
elements of nature seeking to combine to form a synthesis. That's
how I read it, at least. There's some what say it's a bit of a fertility
symbol, too.'

'And that would be to help make up for your tiny . . . essence?'

'I'm sure you think you're bleeding hilarious, but that sort of
comment reflects much more poorly on your negative energies than
it does on me. I won't even dignify it with a reply.'

I was about to point out that he already had, but he put on his
shirt and made no move toward the didgeridoo, so I let it go. Let
no man say I'm a slavish victim of my negative energies.

Someone knocked on the door.

'Enter,' I yelled, 'at your own risk.'

Uma stuck her head in, frowning. 'Is everything all right?'

'Peaches and Herb,' I said. 'Just sharing a little boy talk with Mad
Max here.'

'You know, he is a very uptight individual,' Pahoo complained.

Uma tried to smile. 'Perhaps he is just hungry. Shall we see about
dinner?'

'Sounds great,' I said, leaping to my feet. 'As long as we sit in the
no-didgeridooing section.'

I could see Uma straining to maintain the smile. Pahoo continued
to shake his head, but made for the door.

'Negative. Energy,' I heard him mutter. I gestured for Uma to
precede me down the hall. She whispered something, but I didn't
catch it.

'What'd you say?' I asked.

'Nothing,' she replied. 'Just talking to myself.'

I nodded, but I'm pretty sure it was 'heaven help me' that she'd
pleaded.

We strolled through town for a while, arguing about where to eat.
Fortunately, there were at least as many restaurants as candle shops,
though it seemed like every single joint in the goddamn town had
either Chaucer or Marlowe in its name. At first I got all hepped up
because I thought maybe they were big Raymond Chandler fans, but
Uma quickly deflated me. Still, if you ever fancy a Marlowe-burger
or a Chaucer-dog, Canterbury is your place.

Pahoo and Uma were both vegetarians, though Uma said she'd eat seafood. Pahoo, of course, was more dogmatic. Siobhan ate anything. It didn't really surprise me, as I suspect she would have been among the fat and happy survivors of an Andes plane crash. I'm not fussy, at least not until the meal is served and the food turns out to be lousy (assuming someone else has chosen the restaurant).

We walked by a whole host of depressingly touristy looking places, mostly advertising authentic American food. I've never been able to figure that out – who the hell are places like that aimed at? In a tourist town, they must be looking to attract visitors, but why would you go to the trouble of travelling halfway around the world only to eat what you have at home every other day of the year? And who else but Americans would ever order chicken burgers or fajitas in England? Maybe Europeans think of it as a kind of slumming if they can't get into Disneyland, Paris. Or maybe American tourists are dumber than I think. In any case, the places all looked to be doing a booming business, so they must know something I don't. Most people do.

For a nervous minute it looked like we were going to be forced into another Indian meal – Indian restaurants are as prolific in England as burger joints are in the States – but we stumbled across a pleasant-looking pub a ways off the main drag that posted a suitably varied menu. We drew a few odd looks from the locals – imagine, odd looks in a small town pub for a party consisting of a midget crusty, an Indian woman, an Irish dyke and an American TV star – but the staff were friendly enough and the food turned out to be very nice by English standards. (Though Pahoo *nearly* put a damper on things when he made a fuss because they didn't have any wholewheat pasta for his primavera; didn't stop him from practically scraping the finish off his plate when the food arrived, I noticed.) Dinner conversation was a bit spartan, not much more than 'pass the salt', but between the good food and a couple – three genuinely cold pints of Stella Artois, it wasn't a bad meal.

By the time we finished eating and had a another round of drinks – neither Uma nor Siobhan drank any alcohol at all – it was getting on for eleven o'clock and last call. I couldn't quite fathom why the pubs had to close so early and made a remark about it.

'It is a hangover from the First World War,' Uma explained. 'The restrictive hours for public houses were originally instituted as a means of ensuring that workers would get to work on time in the mornings.'

'You have got to be kidding me. That's almost eighty years ago.'

'Yes, but the laws were still in effect when World War Two broke out and the need for social control became even greater.'

'Okay,' I said, 'but that's still fifty years. Hasn't anyone let the news slip that the war is over?'

'It's about class, mate,' Pahoo said. 'Everything that happens or doesn't happen in this poxy country can be explained in terms of class struggle. Haven't you realized that the English can't bear to leave the nineteenth century behind?'

I should have known the little geek would be a Marxist to boot. They never shower. I rolled my eyes and looked at Uma, but she nodded at me with a sad expression.

'I am afraid that is largely true, Marty. If you do not understand the nature of the class system, the depth of its entrenchment in day-to-day life, in everyone's thinking, you will never understand how and why things happen in England.'

I could probably live with that. I kept my mouth shut.

We had strolled back to the central part of town, marked by the remains – or what looked to me like restored remains – of a stone city wall. The pubs were all emptying out and quite a few drunks, mostly teenaged boys, staggered and screamed obscenities at each other on the streets.

'So. Now what?' I asked. It was clear evening, just a goose bump or two on the side of chilly, with one of those juicy moons which you can't quite decide whether or not it's entirely full.

'Now to our work,' Uma said.

We walked along the top of the city wall for a while, heading back toward our B&B. Uma, Pahoo and I waited outside, while Siobhan ran upstairs to her room.

'What's the plan, then?'

'We must begin the first stage of the inoculation process. I will initiate a rite of invocation against the Thule.'

'What, here?' I said.

Siobhan came bounding out the front door. She held a small black case in her large hands. She held it up to Uma and smiled.

'No,' Uma said. 'We must break into Canterbury Cathedral.'

ELEVEN

~

'Canterbury was a Roman settlement,' Uma explained as we walked up the High Street, trying to look like tourists out for a late stroll. 'They called it Durovernum. So historically speaking it has been a place of interest for almost two thousand years.'

Most of the drunks had now disappeared and the street was all but deserted. The only lights I could see came through the windows of an Indian restaurant. At one point a police car drove past, but the cops didn't even glance at us. I think they were just keeping an eye on the shops. I admit I'm not the quickest guy on the uptake, but as we continued our walk, I saw that the cathedral was behind us and we were walking farther away from it. I pointed this out.

'Have you heard that the sky is blue and the sun occasionally rises in the east?' Siobhan asked.

'I know which way we are going, Marty,' Uma said. She went on with her history lesson.

'The cathedral was built on what was formerly the site of a Roman temple. Many Christian churches and cathedrals in Britain were deliberately built on such places, in an attempt to dominate and overcome the established power, physical and spiritual of other, older religions. Not that the Church would ever admit to such a thing.'

'Sort of like Christmas trees and the Easter bunny having pagan origins,' I said.

'Christmas trees, yes. I believe the Easter bunny was invented by a greeting card company.'

'Our Lady of Perpetual Hallmark.'

Uma ignored me.

'Many such sites, like Canterbury Cathedral, are also important markers in the complex ley systems that pre-date even Roman influence, and are sources of pure and potent power throughout the British Isles.'

'Hey, if I'd known I was going to get laid tonight, I'd have put on clean underwear,' I said.

Uma couldn't ignore that. She stopped in her tracks and stared a few meat cleavers at me.

'Sorry, sorry,' I said, holding up my hands. 'Really. I'll be good. What the hell is a ley system?'

'Ley lines exist in both the physical and metaphysical domains,' she told me, starting to walk again. I stopped myself from even letting out a sigh. *Ask a silly question* . . . I thought.

'Ley lines form a kind of . . . grid of supernatural energy that may be drawn upon by those who know how. These energies influence the people who live among them, regardless of whether or not they are aware of or indeed even believe in the existence of the leys.'

'Influence how?'

'In different ways. At the most fundamental level, there is a correspondence between the land's ley energies and the spiritual and psychic health of the people. A spiritual malaise among the populace may cause damage to the leys, but equally a malignancy in the ley system may cause upset, distress, even unrest among those who dwell within its confines. It is just such a malignancy that the Thule would introduce in Britain.'

'And that's what we're going to prevent.'

'With good fortune, yes. But the ley system in Britain is intricate and immense. Ley lines and forces may be found all over the world – they are, for instance, known as Dragon Tracks in China – but for reasons no one really understands, the power of the leys is much greater here than anywhere else. Many, myself included, believe that this concentration of power is a consequence of actions carried out millennia ago by those who populated these Isles in prehistoric times. The ancient Celts seem to have had a particular affinity for leys and similar forms of highly channelled psychic energy. The ley system has grown along with the population over the years, like wrinkles in an old woman's face, though few are aware of this. The Thule are, unfortunately, among those who know it well. But as I have said, their devotion to Celtic lore and ritual is considerable.'

At this point we turned off the High Street and went up a dark, utterly still side road. We walked about three hundred yards, coming to a stop in front of an overgrown lot, closed off by a locked iron gate.

'You said ley lines are physical things, too.'

'Yes,' Uma said. She furtively glanced up and down the street, then nodded to Siobhan. The Irishwoman opened her little black case and pulled out a set of lock picks. She had the gate open in a matter of seconds.

'Handy,' I observed.

'You bet your scrawny arse,' Siobhan said.

We walked inside and Uma slipped the gate closed again behind us. The grass and weeds were waist high and strewn with broken bottles, crushed cans and the odd car battery. The moon and most of the streetlight were blocked out by adjacent buildings making it hard to see, but Uma led the way
as easily as if the lot were bathed in sunlight. We approached a stone wall at the rear, with a low door set in it. It sounded like there was running water on the other side of the wall. Another nod at Siobhan, a fumble with the picks and this door, too, sprang open.

'How are you with pay phones?' I asked her as we ducked under the lintel. Siobhan smiled wickedly.

The door led to a narrow stone path which went along the bank of a small, rushing river lit by the moon. The river, more like a stream really, was a dozen feet across and couldn't have been more than few feet deep. I leaned out a bit and could see where it disappeared back under the High Street in one direction and off into the darkness in the other.

Directly in front of us stood a crumbling stone building topped by a tiny, but delicate minaret. The entire structure was barely twenty feet high.

'This was once an alchemist's tower,' Uma said. I thought 'tower' was a tad extravagant, but perhaps alchemists were little guys. This notion was confirmed when I saw Pahoo gazing up at the minaret with a certain undeniable awe dripping off his face.

Uma nodded at Siobhan again and pick-pick-pick, we were inside.

Whoever owned the place these days was no alchemist. Stacks of toilet paper lined the walls of the tiny building, which consisted of a single room no more than fifteen feet across. I saw a ladder leading up through an open panel in the low ceiling into the minaret. Just out of curiosity I climbed up a couple steps for a gander and wasn't terribly surprised to find the upstairs bit chock-a-block with paper towels.

'If this isn't a sad comment on the state of magic in the modern world, I don't know what is,' I said. I meant it as a joke, but Pahoo nodded in agreement and Uma's expression suggested that she hadn't thought me capable of such profundity. Even Siobhan seemed to find it kind of pithy. I bit my tongue.

Uma was down on her hands and knees feeling around on the floor. Siobhan pulled a penlight out of her bag and ran the beam across the wood planks in front of her.

'It should be . . . got it!' Uma said. She had cleared away a small pyramid of toilet roll and was tugging at a latch set into the floor. Siobhan handed me the flashlight and went over to help. A moment later they had the panel up.

We all gathered around to see what was down there. I waved the penlight around, but it just seemed to be a small cellar full of even more paper products.

'This is it,' Uma said.

'This is what?' I asked.

'The way to the cathedral.'

'Huh!' I said.

Never at a loss for words.

'This tunnel follows precisely along the path of a major ley line,' Uma told me. Siobhan, flashlight in hand, led the way, followed by me and Uma, with Pahoo trailing behind. Pahoo had taken the penlight from me and stopped every so often to study the carvings and engravings in the tunnel wall. The couple I bothered to glance at reminded me of the rune branded into Pahoo's skin.

'How do you know that?' I asked her.

'I can feel it, for one thing. Can't you?'

It was too dark to see if she was poking fun, and I couldn't tell from her voice. I *did* try to feel for it, but there was only a cold draught on the back of my neck. 'No,' I said.

'No matter. One can also trace the physical markers denoting the path of the lines.'

'So the alchemist's tower is a marker? Don't you need two points to form a line?'

'True. One finds many more than two points marking out a major ley line, though. In this case the tower and the Cathedral mark the two necessary points, but this is a very powerful ley and many other landmarks trace it out. If we were to follow the tunnel back in the other direction, it would take us to the heart of a Roman burial mound. The tunnel does not extend much beyond that, but the ley continues for several miles, culminating in the ruins of a Druid altar in the hills. If you continued beyond the Cathedral in this direction, the tunnel would take you to the centre of a Celtic stone circle.'

'And who built this tunnel?'

'It is of Roman vintage, I believe. Though it has served many since that time.'

I stopped in my tracks. I glanced nervously at the ceiling. 'Have any of those it's served been, say, civil engineers?'

'Marty. This tunnel has survived for two thousand years. It is protected by the power of a grand ley. I think it will last the night.'

I started walking again. At one point the tunnel widened out a bit and split into two paths around a large stone column. I pressed my hand against it and found it very cold to the touch.

'What is this?' I asked.

'It is a well,' Uma said. 'It dates, as I understand, to Roman times, though there are tales that its history goes much further back. It is referred to in one tongue as a Well of Souls.'

'Creepy.'

'A bit,' Uma agreed.

I glanced up again. 'So where does it come out?'

'In the sub-basement of Boots,' Uma sighed.

'Boots. That's, like, the big drugstore chain here, right?'

'It is a large chemists, yes.'

'So in the old days to find a ley line you'd start with a cathedral or a stone circle. Today you look for a Wal-Mart.'

'One accepts magic where one finds it,' Uma said. But she didn't sound happy about it.

'How do you *know* all this stuff?' I asked her.

That seemed to stop her, and Uma looked me over curiously. 'Who played Uncle Joe in *Petticoat Junction*?' she asked me.

'Edgar Buchanan,' I said. 'But . . .'

'Who directed *Kiss Me Deadly*?'

'Robert Aldrich. Of course.'

'How do you *know* all this stuff?' she asked.

'It's my . . . it's my business,' I said, nodding.

Uma smiled at me. I felt like the grasshopper who'd finally snatched that damn pebble out of the old master's hand.

We walked another quarter-mile or so before the tunnel began to narrow and slope downward. The ceiling got lower, too, and we all had to hunch a bit. Except Pahoo.

'I'm glad I'm not claustrophobic,' I said. Uma nervously glanced back at me, suggesting that my attempt to whistle past the graveyard of my minor claustrophobia may have been betrayed by my tone of voice.

'It's just a short way from here,' she reassured me. 'We are now under the cathedral grounds. It should be no more than five hundred metres to the entrance to the crypt.'

Five hundred metres was, let's see, there's four and a half litres to the gallon . . .

By the time I figured it out the tunnel had widened out into an oblong chamber, and we were there.

'Can I ask a stupid question?'

'Why stop now?' Siobhan said. Pahoo was just coming out of the narrow bit of tunnel.

'What is it, Marty?'

'Why have we taken this roundabout way to get to here? I mean Raffles, there, seems pretty handy with the lock picks. It can't be that hard to break into a cathedral.'

'You'd be surprised,' Siobhan said.

'It is in fact very well secured, Marty. You must remember that Canterbury Cathedral is the seat of the Church of England. It is politically as well as historically significant. There are regular patrols around the grounds as well as video surveillance. It is potentially a prime target for terrorists.'

'Who'd ever dream of such a dastardly thing?' Siobhan said, and flashed a grin that had no place at all on holy ground.

'This way is much safer,' Uma said. 'And there is a psychic advantage in following the path of the ley. Its energies surround and protect us.'

'And what, nobody else knows about this way in?'

'A few in the Church hierarchy surely do, but they believe no one else does. They have their own interest in the history of the tunnels and the leys, so they leave it be.'

Siobhan set her flashlight down on the ground and aimed it at a large stone door. There was no lock in the door, only a large steel ring set about halfway up. Siobhan started tugging at it, but the thing looked like a bitch. I went over to help her pull.

'Very fucking gracious of you,' she said.

It *was* a bitch. We both worked up a good sweat prying the door open wide enough to squeeze through. The reason why, I saw, was that the door was solid granite and about eighteen inches thick. God knows how it had ever been set there in the first place.

Uma picked up the light and led the way in. Siobhan was right behind her and Pahoo, typically, trailed ten yards behind me.

We walked through another narrow tunnel, though the walls here were unadorned and smooth as a baby's bottom. It was dark, but beyond Uma's flashlight I could see a faint glow radiating from the far end. Hardly enough to read by, not that there was a copy of *The LA Times* handy, but more than enough to stave off any fresh onset of claustrophobia.

The new tunnel brought us out into a very large room, at least thirty yards long and half as wide again, with the ceiling a good twenty feet high. The walls were flawless black stone, with a series of dim lights set close to the ceiling at regular intervals. A stone staircase at the far end of the chamber led, I assumed, up into the cathedral proper. There were no windows and no doors. The tunnel via which we'd entered was the only other point of access.

'What *is* this place?' I asked.

'This is the crypt of Canterbury Cathedral,' Uma said. 'The *true* crypt.'

The floor of the crypt was inlaid with a vast, dizzyingly elaborate pattern of runes. At least, that's what they looked like to me. The patterns were carved into the polished marble and highlighted with a dye or shellac that made them practically glow, even in the chamber's dim light. There were thousands of them, running into and on top of each other, like some lunatic graffiti, but there was also an almost subliminal sense of order to them.

A rectangular tomb stood smack dab in the middle of the crypt. It was about the size of a Cadillac limo and every bit as black and shiny. I had no idea what it was made of – onyx? Obsidian? I'm not sure I even know what obsidian looks like – but anyway its flawless surface gleamed like a dark mirror. Actually, it reminded me of the Vietnam War Memorial in Washington DC, except the tomb bore no inscriptions, and it held even greater power.

It was hard to look away from the tomb and the runes, but I glanced at Pahoo, who was taking it all in with – literally – slack-jawed wonder. Even Siobhan looked impressed. Uma, her face positively orgasmic, stood with her hands held out, palms down, eyes closed. As if the floor radiated something only she could sense.

Except, this time I thought I felt ... *something*, too. A slight tingling and a deep, resounding hum. But perhaps it was just the power of suggestion.

'Who's in there?' I whispered, pointing at the tomb.

Uma slowly opened her eyes. She took a couple of very deep breaths.

'Pendragon,' Pahoo whispered.

Siobhan shook her head. 'Cuchulain,' she said. 'His enemies brought his body across the sea. The Brits have kept him here for the centuries to deny his body its native soil.'

'No,' Uma said. 'There lie the bones of St Thomas à Becket.'

'No,' Siobhan said.

'Can't be,' Pahoo insisted.

Uma just nodded.

'What the *fuck* are you people talking about?' I said a little too loudly. Then I slapped my hand over my mouth. I haven't got a religious bone in my body, but this did *not* seem like an appropriate place to be barking the f-word.

Uma took another deep breath and repeated, 'This is the final resting place of St Thomas à Becket.'

'The guy from the Fred Zinnemann flick? What's it called ... *A Man for All Seasons*?'

The three of them turned and glared at me.

'That's Thomas More, you git,' Siobhan spat.

'Brother, I wouldn't want your karma for all the nose candy in Peru,' Pahoo said.

Uma sort of smiled.

'History records that Thomas à Becket was Archbishop of Canterbury from 1162 to 1170. He was murdered in the cathedral by assassins in the service of Henry II, with whom he had a political quarrel. A series of miracles was then observed and Thomas was canonized. The legend forms the basis of Canterbury's status as a place of pilgrimage. It is to Becket's shrine that the pilgrims in *The Canterbury Tales* are travelling.'

'So what's the big deal about his bones?'

'The story tells us nothing about what was *really* happening,' Uma said.

'Figures,' Pahoo muttered.

'Thomas Becket *was* Archbishop of Canterbury and he *was* murdered by agents of the King.'

'But ...'

'But Becket was, in fact, a dark sorcerer, using the Church to cloak his own evil excursions. This cathedral stands at a nexus of three grand leys. In point of fact, this tomb marks an exact focal point of ley influence. That is why the Romans first built a temple here, why religious and magical forces have so thrived in Canterbury over the centuries. Becket wished to tap into and use those forces for his own ends. He was, in a manner of speaking, allied with the Thule of his day, and his goal was to topple the monarchy and establish a theocracy with himself at the head. Henry's assassins, too, were creatures of magic. They defeated Becket in a magical contest that went on even after Becket's physical extermination. This explains the so-called miracles which were observed. The Church hierarchy moved very swiftly to cover Becket's filthy tracks.'

'And the Church muckety-mucks, the Archbishop and Grand Poobah or whatever, don't they know about this?' I asked.

'Of course they do. They have left the tomb intact, because they fear what is inside. Knowledge of this crypt is held by only a few. There is a false crypt above us for the public, though Becket's remains are supposedly lost. But how would the Church be served by revealing the truth? This place, Becket's tale, is at the heart of the Church of England. The Church won't admit it has gay priests in its ranks; do you expect it to confess that its patron saint was a black magician in league with forces of darkness?'

'I suppose it wouldn't play in Peoria. Or whatever the local equivalent is,' I said. 'And I should care about all this because . . .'

Uma sighed again. 'Because the more things change, the more they remain the same. Just as almost a thousand years ago, Becket tried to use this place to exploit the power of the leys, so now would the Thule. That is why we are here, Marty.'

'And what am I supposed to do?' I asked.

'Nothing, for now. Just watch. This act is mine to conduct. Your moment will come.'

I wasn't sure what she meant, exactly, and I thought that it had a slightly ominous ring, but then lines of power, hidden tunnels and archbishop sorcerers ain't exactly a night at Dodgers Stadium.

Uma took the black case from Siobhan and removed a silver knife with a black handle that matched the stone of Becket's tomb. Pahoo had been down on his haunches, running his fingers along the grooves of the runes in the floor, but he stood up as Uma strode out toward the black tomb.

Uma raised her hand to hold him at bay.

She walked out toward the centre of the chamber, but didn't follow a straight line. She looked down at the runes on the ground as if reading instructions on how to proceed. They led her in a looping circle around the tomb, and she moved with the grace and lightness of a ballerina. The runes came to an end at the edge of a grooved circle at the perimeter of the tomb. Uma performed a little pirouette as she danced off the runes and onto the smooth marble of the inner circle.

As she waltzed across the floor, I thought I could feel an intensification of the tingling feeling I'd felt before. Squatting down, holding my hand out just over the runes, I could feel pressure against my palm, like a slight magnetic field. I flipped my hand over and saw the hair on my knuckles lift ever so slightly off the skin. I glanced up at Siobhan, but she was watching Uma with great intensity. I don't think she liked her charge to be even that far out of her sphere of protection. Especially in so spooky a place.

Uma had knelt down by the side of the tomb. With the knife in her left hand, she reached into her blouse with her right and pulled out a charm that hung on a white gold chain around her neck. I'd noticed it a couple of times during the day, but it looked like your basic New Age crystal type doo-dad, the appeal of which has always eluded me. She separated the charm from the chain.

Then it struck me that it looked very much like the charm Dasra had used to blind the thugs who attacked me.

Uma began chanting in an unfamiliar language I assumed to be Hindi. She twirled the charm between her fingers as she sang, then stood up and turned slow circles around the tomb, never straying out of the inner circle. She made three complete circuits, placing the charm on top of the tomb, square in the middle, when she was done.

Switching the knife to her right hand, she fell back to her knees along one narrow end of the tomb. She started chanting again and with the tip of the knife, scratched a shape into the gleaming black stone. I couldn't make out what she carved, but the high-pitched screech of steel against the stone raised gooseflesh on my arms and likely roused sleeping dogs for miles around. She scooted around to the far side, out of my line of sight, still chanting, and as fresh goosepimples told me, scratched something else into the stone. She repeated the action a third time around the far narrow end, then whirled back into sight in front of us.

At first, I couldn't believe Uma was cutting the shape she was into the cold stone, but the symbol was all too familiar before she even finished it.

Uma was carving perfect little swastikas.

'What the . . .' I started to say, but Siobhan squeezed my bicep and held a finger to her lips, shaking her head. Well, you don't have to do more than cut off my blood supply before I get the message.

Uma finished the last of the swastikas, then stood up, chanting a few final words. She looked back toward the three of us, but I had a feeling she wasn't seeing us. She turned around and raised the knife up above the top of the tomb, bringing it down with all her might against the charm.

In the second before the hard hilt of the knife shattered the charm into a zillion pieces, I thought I saw the crystal pulse with a pale purple glow. I'm sure – well, pretty sure – I could feel a momentary spasm in that magnetic field that set my fillings to vibrating.

Then it was over and Uma was walking back toward us, in a straight line across the runes.

She collapsed just before she reached us. Siobhan only caught her because she's the quickest damn thing I've ever seen on two feet.

Well, the quickest *human* thing.

I had all kinds of questions to ask – why was Uma carving swastikas on St Thomas à Becket's tomb being top of the list – but the time wasn't right for getting answers.

Uma came around within a couple of minutes, but was slow getting to her feet. Nevertheless, she insisted that we get a move on, so we did. Pahoo grabbed the flashlight and led the way out, followed by Uma, supported by Siobhan, and me bringing up the rear. As we made our way back toward the alchemist's tower, I had the uneasy feeling that we were being followed down the tunnel. I kept looking behind me, but there was nothing to be seen in the darkness, and the only sounds were Uma's hard breathing and our feet padding along the ancient stone. When we finally arrived back at the cellar of the minaret, it was the second happiest I've ever been in my life to see a roll of toilet paper.

Uma looked a little better by the time we walked back out onto the High Street. She no longer needed Siobhan's support and even offered a reassuring smile when I raised my eyebrows at her in concern. It was nearly two in the morning when we finally arrived back at the B&B. By the time I climbed the stairs and Pahoo unlocked the door to our room, I felt the accumulated exhaustion of the day overwhelm me. I don't think even my hoity-toity suite at the Savoy could have looked half as welcoming at that moment as my narrow bed in Canterbury. I took a quick leak in the closet/toilet, tossed my clothes on the floor and fell onto the mattress.

Not even the sound of Pahoo taking a particularly noisy dump prevented me from falling all but instantly asleep.

TWELVE

The breakfast half of the B&B service wasn't appreciably better than the bed. I'd slept fitfully, no small thanks to Pahoo's snoring, making for one cranky breakfast boy. Some say I'm not the most pleasant early morning companion at the best of times – both of my ex-wives actually mentioned it in the official divorce documents – but a bad night's sleep on top of our bizarre exploits under the cathedral left me somewhere on the far side of surly.

'Good morning!' Uma chirped as I walked into the dining room. Half-a-dozen small tables were crowded together, all empty but one. Uma had a glass of orange juice in front of her, while Siobhan rammed a nasty looking combination of foodstuffs into her mouth as quickly as she could shovel the glop off her big plate. I detected grey-looking sausage-esque material smothered in egg yolk, and the remnants of what was either a diseased pig's heart or a fried tomato.

'Morning,' I mumbled.

'Did you sleep well?'

'No,' I said.

Uma cocked an eyebrow at me. 'Is everything all right?'

'He snores,' I said. Siobhan laughed, sending a spurt of milk out her nose. 'Where is the garbage pail kid, anyway?'

'Pahoo said he needed to take a walk.'

'I don't suppose he mentioned anything about a shower? A visit to the car wash maybe?'

Uma shook her head. Just then the waitress (actually it was the same woman who'd checked us into the place) came over. She didn't say anything, just put her hand on her hip and looked at me like I was wasting her time.

'Yeah?' I asked.

'Full breakfast or milk and cereal?'

I glanced at the remains on Siobhan's plate. It wasn't pretty. 'That the full breakfast?' I asked.

'Yeah.'

'Milk and cereal, please.'

She pointed at a table in the corner and started to walk off. There was a half-full pitcher of milk, a box of Rice Krispies, a generic brand corn flakes and a stack of chipped bowls.

'Can I have some coffee?' I called after her.

Without even stopping she pointed at a second table along the opposite wall.

'Boy, I hope she ain't expecting a tip,' I said.

'No one in this bloody country does,' Siobhan said. 'That's the whole problem.'

I felt marginally better after my Rice Krispies – snap, crackle, pop! – but four cups of bitter coffee later, I still could have used a nap. No time, though, as Uma insisted we collect our stuff and hit the road. We had to wait another half-hour before Pahoo came shuffling back, oblivious to our impatience. Siobhan berated me for not packing up Pahoo's stuff while we waited, but I wasn't touching any of it. She went up to the room to do it herself, then came back down a minute later.

'I apologize,' she said. I nearly swallowed my tongue with surprise. Siobhan shook her head. 'Perhaps you've got a bit of sense after all.'

Fortunately, Pahoo travels light, so within ten minutes of his return, the bill was paid and we were cruising. I got stuck in back with the little feller again, but he didn't seem quite so pungent. Or maybe, perish the thought, I was getting used to it. I might even have suspected that he'd had a wash, except his hair still looked like something dangling from the rafters of Dracula's castle. He sort of curled himself up into the corner of the car and went back to sleep. He did start to snore again, but blessedly the sound was lost amid the rumble of the Mini's engine and the bellowing of the didgeridoo.

Siobhan stuck to back roads as we headed out of Canterbury. We weren't zipping along, but then I was feeling lazy enough not to mind. With the windows open, the sun streaming in and Pahoo marginally down wind, I got into the rhythm of the trip. Even my surly mood started to evaporate, though it was barely nine-thirty. We'd been on the road for half an hour before it struck me that I didn't know where we were going.

'So what's the story?' I asked.

'We drive to the West Country,' Uma said over her shoulder. She was reading a copy of the morning paper. I can never read in the car without wanting to heave. Even watching her do it made me feel a little bit queasy. 'Cornwall, specifically, a place called Tintagel. It is the site of the second central ley nexus requiring our devotions.'

'More happy ju-ju. Cool. And after that?'

'Scotland, if all proceeds as planned. A place called Dwarfie Stane in the far north. But one step at a time, Marty. This is a delicate business.'

'How far is it to Tintagel?'

Uma looked at Siobhan. 'Three hundred miles?'

Siobhan shrugged. 'Give or take. There's no good direct route via motorway, so it'll likely take us six hours or more in this heap of junk. You still want to stop, yes?'

'Yes. There is no great hurry, so long as we arrive by nightfall. Enjoy the scenery, Marty. This is a very different view of England from that received by most visitors. You are getting a chance to see the real country, the true England.'

'I'm a luck-luck-lucky guy,' I muttered. Uma frowned at me in the rear-view before going back to her paper.

Okay, so maybe I was still feeling a *bit* surly.

I finally managed to doze off in the back seat. The gritty thrum of the little car's loud engine and the vibrations from its lack of suspension were lulling in their way. I only woke up when we came to a stop, and was stunned to realize that I'd been asleep for the better part of two hours. And pleased that there'd been no bad dreams.

'What's going on?' I asked through a yawn. Siobhan and Pahoo were already out of the car, stretching their legs.

'Lunch,' Uma said. She pointed at a pub across the road. The sign featured a surprisingly delicate and detailed drawing of a sad-looking old woman clutching an empty picture frame to her bosom. The place was called The Broken Promise.

'Great,' I said. 'I'll have the heartbreak soup.'

'Country pubs are often very good, Marty. You may be surprised.'

I got out of the car and followed the others across the road. Uma and Pahoo made straight for the rest rooms, so I sidled up next to Siobhan at the bar. I gathered that the bartender wasn't much impressed by the four of us – who would be? – but the only other customer was a toothless old codger in a trench coat babbling to himself in the corner. The innkeeper seemed happy enough with the green of our money. (Actually, it's sort of orange and blue, but you know what I mean.)

I grabbed my pint of Stella Artois and a copy of the menu and picked out a table by the window. Siobhan followed me over, but didn't sit down. She waited until Uma and Pahoo returned before toddling off to the little lesbian's room. She'd ordered tea for Uma and a pint of bitter for Pahoo, drinking mineral water and lemon herself. Pahoo hefted his glass and inspected the liquid.

'Ever drink your own piss?' Pahoo inquired.

I had a hefty mouthful of beer as he said it and consequently executed what, in The Business, is technically known – or so I was once informed by Louis Nye – as a spit take. I managed to turn my head to the side before spraying, missing Uma by a matter of inches, but I caught the window with a veritable shower of beer and saliva. I glanced at the bartender who, of course, had seen the whole thing and glowered furiously at me. I wiped the glass with my napkin, but beer is no substitute for Windex. That's a testimonial. Fortunately, the view wasn't that exciting anyway.

'Thanks a heap,' I said to Pahoo.

'Sorry,' he said, chuckling. Uma struggled to maintain a straight face. Only the bartender and I failed to see the humour.

'What kind of stupid question is that anyway?'

'So you never tried it?' Pahoo asked. I just stared at him. He looked over at Uma who closed her eyes and shook her head. 'Oh, mate, you really should.'

'Should what?' Siobhan asked, sitting herself down.

'Drink your own urine.'

'Done that,' Siobhan said.

'You're kidding.'

'There are some who say it's a source of great natural strength and vitalization. That it has restorative powers. Friends I know swear by it.'

'See,' Pahoo said.

'It didn't do much for me, though. I tried it for a couple of months then got fed up.'

'Oh, that's not long enough,' Pahoo said. 'You got to give it at least six months to feel any effects.'

'Could be. But it's not always easy to explain to people when you're living in close quarters. Not everyone . . .' – she looked at me – '. . . is so open minded about alternative lifestyles. And I have to admit, it's not what you'd call a taste sensation.'

'There's a shocker,' I said. 'Alert the media.'

'It's not as terrible as you likely think. But then Guinness it certainly is not. Or even Murphy's.'

'Does everyone know what they want to eat?' Uma interrupted, mercifully.

'I know what I definitely don't want,' I said. I glanced again at the menu. 'This isn't one of those *good* country pubs, is it?' Uma scowled and shook her head. 'I'll just have fish and chips.'

The others made their selections and Uma went up to the bar to order. I wanted to be gallant and do it myself, but I was too embarrassed to face the bartender. I took a cautious sip of beer, keeping one eye on Pahoo as I swallowed.

Lunch was . . . adequate, in what I was quickly recognizing to be the very modest terms of British cuisine. It's hard to go too far wrong with fish and chips, though I did have a bit of a hard time with my salad. Actually, it was a few stray bits of lettuce with a sliver of onion and a mushy cherry tomato, but I'm not one to complain.

'What salad dressing do you have?' I asked the bartender-cum-waiter.

He stared at me for a minute. 'What do you want?'

'Salad dressing? You know, for the . . . salad?'

'You want salad cream?'

In fact, I didn't have any idea if I wanted salad cream. I looked around at the others, but none would meet my gaze. I should have taken the hint.

'Sure, salad cream sounds fine.' When in Durovernum . . .

The guy disappeared into the back, then returned with a little ramekin full of white stuff. It looked like, well, I didn't like to say.

'This looks like cum,' I said. 'The bastard just went out back and jerked off, didn't he? It's because Pahoo made me spit on his window.'

'You make a god-almighty racket, don't you?' Siobhan said, between forkfuls of shepherd's pie. 'I bet you were an only child.'

'It's just salad cream, Marty,' Uma said. 'Really.'

'What's it made out of?'

'Best not to ask,' Siobhan said. I noted that she didn't put any on her lettuce.

I stuck my fork into the stuff and gingerly dabbed at the tine with my tongue. It tasted like mayonnaise. Really old, really cheap mayonnaise. I shoved it aside.

'Don't like it?'

'I don't think it's been properly refrigerated.'

'You don't need to refrigerate salad cream.'

That didn't encourage me. 'I'll pass. If I want to spend a day with the Hershey squirts, I'll get there the old-fashioned way and drink myself sick.'

I left the salad.

'So how is it you know who played Uncle Joe in *Petticoat Junction*?' I asked Uma.

We were back on the road. Uma had ceded her shotgun seat to Pahoo to ride in back with me. Siobhan wasn't happy about it at first, but as soon as we started moving Pahoo curled up into his ball and went to sleep again. Siobhan sang to herself as she drove.

'I was president of the local Edgar Buchanan fan club. I am particularly fond of his performance in Sam Peckinpah's *Ride the High Country*.' My jaw dropped. 'That is a joke, Marty.'

'You guys don't have a screenplay you're trying to hawk, do you? I mean, this hasn't all been an elaborate ruse to find a producer?'

Uma laughed. She had a kid's laugh, straight from the belly. 'No. No screenplay. Though I did do a degree in film studies at the Polytechnic of Central London. But that was a long time ago, in a very different life.'

'Ever see *R.I.O.T.*?' I asked.

'Crap!' Siobhan barked between choruses of her song.

'Not one of your finest works,' Uma agreed.

'*Chicks 'N' Chevies*?'

'An Alan Smithee film, I believe.'

'All right, Miss Smartypants film student: How about *Bazooka Beach Massacre*?'

'That one I do not know. But perhaps I have been fortunate.'

'Figures. The work you put your heart and soul into as an artist is never appreciated in your time. Though I understand it's a particular favourite on The Titty Channel.'

'You have led rather an interesting life.'

'Ancient Chinese curse. Like mu shu pork.'

'Do you take anything seriously, Marty?'

I took a long, deep breath and let it out. 'Only when I have to. Much safer that way.'

'I wonder,' Uma said.

Siobhan drove on.

'Marty. Wake up.'

'Nyahhh,' I spat, opening my eyes. 'What?'

I'd dozed off again following another stop for piss and petrol –
Ha! Who says you can't teach an old dog new tricks? – but now
Uma was shaking me by the shoulder. Uma and Pahoo had taken
the back seat and though Siobhan fumed and cursed a bit, mostly
an act I think, she agreed to let me ride up front again. I certainly
couldn't be worse company than Pahoo . . . could I?

'Look in front of you,' Siobhan whispered.

We had just crested a slight hill. Directly ahead of us in the valley
below stood Stonehenge.

'Wow,' I said. I meant it, too.

Spinal Tap notwithstanding, Stonehenge is one of those places
that, by it's very name, conjures portentous feelings in everyone.
It's the ultimate icon for the mysterious, the unexplained and the
just plain goofy. It's a link with our pasts, with a part of ourselves
as a species that we will probably never understand. We're talking
number one with a bullet on the list of things that Leonard Nimoy
had to go in search of.

I remember a day on the set of the penultimate film of my first acting
career. It was a no-budget horror flick, a ghost story supposedly set
in England, but shot in and around ye olde Encino. For all that, it
wasn't a bad little project, because though the kid who wrote and
directed it didn't have money enough for decent film stock, he was
a *real* director with honest-to-god talent. Shame he was killed in
a car crash. He'd convinced Peter Cushing to take a small role in
the thing for virtually no money. Cushing was a perfect gentleman,
who put up with all manner of indignity on what passed for the set
without so much as a raised eyebrow of complaint. At least until, on
a sudden whim, the director rewrote the script to include a screwy
reference to Stonehenge.

'No,' Cushing said. 'It may seem a pile of old rocks to you, but
it means rather a great deal more to some of us.'

Seeing the stone circle from the hilltop, I thought I understood.

One of the curious things about the circle is that it actually
looks smaller the closer you get to it. Perhaps it was just the
angle of approach from the road, but as we cruised down
the hill toward Stonehenge, it seemed to become vastly *less*
impressive. The circle sits just off the main road and everybody
who drives past slows to rubber-neck, with a goodly number of

cars turning off onto the side road which provides access to the actual site.

Siobhan drove right past the turn-off.

'Aren't we going to stop?' I asked.

'Why?' Pahoo responded.

'Would you like to stop, Marty?'

I turned around to watch the circle disappear behind us. I flicked a glance at Uma. 'Shouldn't we?'

'There really is no reason. We are going to stop soon, but we will go to a site near Woodhenge.'

'*Wood*henge?' I said, feeling yet again not a little bit like George Burns to Uma's Gracie Allen. 'That sounds like the next best thing, like when you can't get into the movie you want to see. Or like a really pathetic consolation prize on a game show. You know, "some departing pagans receive . . ."'

Uma sighed and looked at me. The stone circle was practically out of sight. 'Stonehenge is a remarkable place,' she told me, 'and if we had more time, I would stop so you could enjoy the wonder of the site.

'But for our present purposes, Stonehenge has no greater value than a roadside cafe.'

'At least you can get a nice cup of tea at a cafe,' Siobhan added.

'I don't understand,' I said. 'Isn't it the holy of pagan holies? I thought we were after, what is it, locuses of supernatural energy. Isn't Stonehenge, like, the *Jurassic Park* of oogy-boogy?'

'Not anymore,' Pahoo snarled.

'I am afraid that is true,' Uma said. 'As I told you in Canterbury there is a connection between the land and the people who live on it. There are those who believe that the depth and strength of the ley system in Britain is a reflection of that connection between the land and the people here. But the connection has been debased at Stonehenge. The circle was once a place of fabulous power, but like a river that is tapped dry, so has the power of Stonehenge and Salisbury Plain been siphoned away over the years by those who have used and abused the site without understanding it. The leys which run through the stone circle are mere trickles now.'

'It's like everything else,' Pahoo said. 'The trees and the mountains and the air and the sea. We ruin it all. We take and take and leave nothing but our shit behind us. It's all going away, mate. And it ain't coming back.'

I rolled my eyes, but managed to hold my tongue. 'And, um, *Wood*henge?' I asked.

'It is not far from here,' Uma said. 'It is, in fact, part of the same ley system that feeds Stonehenge, but as it is less celebrated and known, it has been less damaged. Though it, too, is now a heritage site and thus its power has been diminished, it should still provide us with a fair reading of the larger grid before we get to Cornwall. I would like to try and get the lay of the land – pun very much intended – for any hint of Thule influence.'

Siobhan turned off the main road and sure enough, the sign indicated the way to Woodhenge, though I still felt a little bit like this was an elaborate practical joke. I was sure of it when Siobhan drove right past that turn-off, too.

'Let me guess: we're *actually* going to particle board-henge,' I said.

I thought I heard Uma start to count to herself under her breath, but she said: 'No. However, the main circle is too much of a tourist attraction. There is a long barrow just outside the limits of the official heritage site of which few people are aware.'

Siobhan turned off the already narrow road onto a dirt track that the Mini didn't care for at all. The engine made a fearful noise as the trail led up a pathetically gentle gradient and every lurch through the ruts and gopher holes felt like a kick up the ass with a steel-toed boot. Finally, the 'road' petered out altogether, and there was no choice but to hoof it the rest of the way. Siobhan parked the car, and as Uma got out she pointed to some peculiarly shaped mounds a couple of hundred yards down a rough path.

'I've got to take a piss,' Pahoo said.

'Leave some for the rest of us,' I said to his back. He disappeared into the trees.

Uma had already started down the dirt path, when I noticed Siobhan looking around nervously. I scanned the area, but everything looked okay-fine to me. It was *very* quiet – no traffic noises at all, not even a chirping bird or scampering squirrel – but then, as far as I could tell, we *were* pretty much out in the middle of nowhere. As I followed Uma down the pathway, I spotted a rusty soda can in the brush. I'm sure Pahoo wouldn't agree, but I find something deeply comforting about the sight of spent Coke cans. It's a reassuring token of the global dimensions of American civilization. It would have been far more appropriate if the astronauts had left, say, a case of Coca-Cola on the moon, instead of an American flag. Along with a pair of Levis, maybe. Blue denim, not black. Definitely not that stonewashed bullshit.

Siobhan came up behind me, still looking a little hinky.

'Anything wrong?' I asked.

She shook her head. 'I'm not sure. I've got an itch.'

'With Pahoo in the car, I'm amazed we don't all have one.'

'Not that kind of itch,' she said. I took another look around, but only saw Pahoo returning from nature's call.

'What?' he said, when he saw us looking at him.

'Siobhan's got an itch,' I told him.

Pahoo nodded. 'I hear that.'

They're all nuts, I thought.

The path terminated at the base of the large mound, a dozen feet high and a hundred yards long. The far end of it tapered down and disappeared into a copse of trees in the distance. The near end was marked by three huge, semi-circular stones. Each had a different runic engraving on the face and along the edges. Uma ran her fingers along the grooved lines. In the centre of the middle stone was a tiny swastika.

'What is it?' I asked.

'Sarsen,' Uma said. 'Same as used to build the outer circle at Stonehenge. And there in the centre is a small circle of bluestone.'

'No,' I said, gesturing broadly at the mound, 'I mean: what is *it*?'

'Burial mound,' Pahoo told me. 'For priests and such. At least, judging from the runes. That right?'

Uma nodded at him. 'I believe so. I've not actually visited this locus before. But my understanding is that this mound was a resting place for high priests and maguses. It was probably directly linked with Stonehenge. It certainly shares a ley with it. But these patterns . . . one should not always believe warnings carved in runes.'

'Speak for yourself,' Pahoo said, and made an unfamiliar sign in the air with his fingers.

'So why is there a swastika there? Have the Thule already been here?

'That is a swastika, but it is not the work of the Thule,' Uma said.

I suddenly remembered that Uma had etched swastikas into Becket's tomb in Canterbury during her ritual the night before. I'd meant to ask her about it, but had forgotten. 'I don't understand,' I said.

'The swastika is a very ancient symbol that appears in many different cultures. It can be found in Egyptian, Chinese, even native American iconologies. The word itself is derived from Sanskrit and means well-being, good fortune. It is a rather obvious sun symbol, Marty, can you not see? A token and marker of light.'

'But . . .' I looked at the swastika again. There was something wrong with it. Just like the ones Uma had drawn. It suddenly dawned one. 'It faces the wrong way,' I said. 'The little dangly bits at the end of the arms. They point in the wrong direction.'

Pahoo laughed out loud. Uma chuckled as well.

'No, Marty,' she said. 'This swastika points the *right* way. When the symbol was adopted by the Nazis, it was deliberately reversed, so that arms were bent clockwise. The use of an inverted swastika predates Hitler by several centuries. Reversing the symbol has long been regarded as a means of evoking chaotic forces and dark magic. The Luminous Lodge, who formed the basis of the original Thule Society and the Black Order, promulgated the perverted swastika to the fledgeling Nazis after the First World War.'

I looked at the *good* swastika again, running my fingers over the carving. 'So how old is this place?'

'One cannot be entirely certain, but I would guess two thousand years at least. Not quite so old as Stonehenge itself.'

'These runes are much more recent,' Pahoo said.

'Yes, no more than twelve or thirteen hundred years, I should estimate.'

'Zowie,' I said. Old stuff always impresses me. I think it's a function of being from America, where *nothing* is all that old, and especially Los Angeles, where old is the dirtiest of four-letter words. 'That's a long time to be dead.'

Uma chuckled, then frowned.

'What's the matter?' I said.

She looked at Pahoo, who nodded at her. Uma knelt down and pressed her palms along the base of two of the rocks. I looked around again and realized that Siobhan had wandered off. Which seemed very unlike her.

'Something does not feel right here,' Uma said.

I saw the spray of red explode out of Pahoo's arm even before my mind registered the report of the shot. A second shot went wide of the mark, blowing one of the carved runes into little splinters of sarsen.

Pahoo just stood there, looking at his bleeding arm and blinking without comprehension. I heard a third shot, but was already on the move toward Uma and couldn't tell what, if anything, had been hit. She had ducked down, a bit like an ostrich trying to bury its head, but was still an open target. I scooped her up under one arm and dragged her toward the corner of the burial mound, away from where I *thought* the shots had come. As we reached the edge of the mound, I shoved her around the corner and out of the line of fire. She went down in a pile and I tumbled after her. I thought I heard a fourth shot as I smacked my knee hard against a big rock, but it may have just been my patella.

Uma had landed face down and was trying to get up.

'Keep low,' I whispered.

I couldn't see anyone on our side of the burial mound. The nearest tree line was a good three hundred yards away to my right, and stretching back behind the mound was a vast expanse of open field. If we had to run for it, we were going to be in big trouble. Still on all fours, I cautiously peered out around the edge of the mound.

Pahoo was flat on his back, rocking back and forth with one hand clutching at his injured arm. I saw a dark shape drop down from the branches of a tree twenty yards from the barrow, and I flashed on the figures from my dream and shuddered. Two more gunshots sounded from behind a smaller dirt mound across from the barrow, and though I couldn't see anything, I kissed the dirt again. I started to get up, heard a third shot, and held tight to Mama Earth.

A hand grabbed my ankle and I let out a shriek. I kicked out once before I realized it was Uma. I'd caught her a solid blow to the chest and she tumbled backwards, landing hard against a rock.

'Shit!' I hissed.

I slapped a hand over my mouth – a navy SEAL I'd never be – but the damage had been done. Looking up, I saw a skinhead in dirty khakis approaching Pahoo and the barrow. He held a gun out in front of him. It looked big – an old Colt .45, I think – and very deadly. The skinhead had been moving in on Pahoo, but he turned my way when he heard me yell, and didn't hesitate: three quick shots in a row. Two ricocheted off the stone edge of the barrow, the third ploughed up a streak of grass ahead of me. I scrambled backward and slipped in the dirt, falling down again. The skinhead was coming right at me now, a rictus of delight lighting up his pale, pockmarked face.

He took careful aim this time, bracing the gun with both hands. I saw his right eye squint shut as he prepared to squeeze the trigger.

The shot came from behind him, tearing a fist-sized chunk of flesh out of his right bicep. A second shot caught him full chest, a streak of red leaving a check mark in the air where he fell. The Colt flew out of his hands, going off as it banged against a stone outcrop. The bullet went I know not where.

Siobhan stood behind him, in classic shooter's stance. She broke out of it as he fell and ran toward the skinhead, who was flopping on the ground like a pike, little sprays of blood spurting up like sea foam. Siobhan didn't hesitate for a second: she continued blowing holes in his chest until the flopping stopped.

'Fuuuck,' I whispered.

Siobhan glanced at me, still on hands and knees, spat on the dead skinhead, then walked over.

'You can worship me later,' she said, glaring down. 'Now, we've got to move.'

Siobhan stepped past me to help Uma to her feet. The Indian woman just stared at the bloody skinhead. Siobhan carefully inspected her for damage, but Uma insisted that she was all right. It didn't stop her from leaning on Siobhan as they walked back around to the front of the mound. I noticed bloodstains on Siobhan's clothing, but she didn't seem to be hurt.

'I'm fine, too. Don't worry,' I said. Actually, my knee hurt and I had to limp after them.

Pahoo had managed to get to his feet, though his arm still oozed blood. He was looking at the body sprawled before the big stones like a sacrificial offering. Siobhan tied a strip of cloth around his arm and pulled it tight.

'There's another,' Siobhan said.

'What? Where?' Pahoo panicked.

'Dead,' Siobhan intoned. 'There's another dead. Back over there.'

'You killed him?' I asked.

'No, you damn fool, it was just his time. Of course, I bloody well killed him!'

Siobhan led us around to the second corpse. The first dead man had been pure skinhead: chicken skinned, with a round, bald head, protruding ears and a pug nose. Dressed in khakis, with steel-toed, Herman Munster shoes that looked like they took a month to lace. The second one had a whole different look: a raggedy mop of filthy red hair and a full, thick beard which, even matted with blood, suggested he'd gone for the full English breakfast at *his* B&B. The skinhead had been short and round, but Red Beard was *big*; tall and stocky with a sumo-sized beer belly. He wore black denim jeans and a battered black leather jacket. He looked like a biker to me.

He also had a seriously slit throat. It was the only wound I could see. Taking in the dead man's size, I couldn't imagine how Siobhan did it. But I resolved *I'd* never mess with her – not that I'd planned to.

'Thule?' I asked.

Uma went over to the corpse and very delicately rolled up his sleeve. The man's arms were a mass of swirling red and black tattoos. A big swastika – the *bad* kind – was plastered over each bicep. She tried to take off his shirt, but he was too heavy for her to handle. Siobhan knelt down, cut the shirt open. Red Beard also had a swastika tattooed over his heart. At least, I thought it was a tattoo until I bent down closer to look and saw that, like Pahoo's rune, the swastika had been branded into his flesh. And carved into the skin along each radiating arm were the letters 'O-N-T.'

'*Ordo Novo Templi*,' Uma sighed, before I could ask. She stood up, wiping her hands on her thighs.

'Not the Thule?' I asked.

'Of course it is,' Siobhan hissed. 'You think it's the bloody Girl's Brigade?'

'It is the Thule, Marty,' Uma said. She glanced at Siobhan. 'But how did they find us?'

'I don't know.'

'They grokked to the ceremony in Canterbury,' Pahoo said, nodding. He stood up, still holding his arm, and walked over to take a closer look at the body. 'They know where we're likely to go. They must have tracked us from there.'

'We knew they might be onto us,' Siobhan said. 'It's been a risk all along.'

'It still does not make sense to me,' Uma said.

I saw Siobhan scanning the area of the trees around us. 'You think there's more of them?' I asked.

'There's always more of their kind,' she said. 'But not right here, right now.'

'How can you be so sure?'

'No itch,' she said.

But she was scratching her ass as she said it.

Siobhan led the way back to the car. Pahoo was still wobbly, so Uma and I supported him between us. Siobhan raced ahead and dug a small medical emergency kit out of the back. She sat Pahoo down on the back seat, untied the makeshift tourniquet and gingerly cut away his sleeve to inspect the wound. He groaned as she poured antiseptic over it and dabbed at the wound with gauze.

'It's naught but a graze,' she announced. 'The bullet's passed right on by. I've suffered worse from foreplay.'

You know, I believed her.

Siobhan cleaned and bandaged the wound with an efficiency that bespoke no small experience. She went back to the Mini and reached into the glove compartment. Removing a small plastic vial, she shook a pair of tablets out.

'Here,' she said. 'For the pain. If there is any.'

Pahoo looked at the pills in his hand. 'Codeine?' he asked. Siobhan nodded. He dry swallowed with an audible gulp. '1997,' Pahoo said. 'Good year.' Siobhan winked at him.

Siobhan turned to Uma who was, I thought, being uncharacteristically quiet. She leaned against the side of the car, arms folded, staring blankly into the distance. 'Do you want to do anything in particular about the bodies?' Siobhan asked.

Uma looked up, but she didn't reply. I saw that there were tears in her eyes. Siobhan gave a little shake of her head, then dug through the back of the Mini and came out with a folding shovel. She went back around the side to talk to Pahoo.

'Can you handle a gun?' she asked.

He nodded.

'Shoot anything that moves. I'll bury it later.' She looked at me. 'Come on.'

'Who me?'

'It's high time you made yourself useful for something more than lip. There's graves to be dug.'

A sick feeling in my stomach, I followed her back down the trail.

THIRTEEN

〜

Even the didgeridoo was quiet as we found our way back to the main road and continued toward Cornwall. The tension in the car was as thick as a Jim Carey audience. Siobhan wasn't humming, Pahoo wasn't sleeping, Uma wasn't smiling and I wasn't thinking.

At least, I was trying not to.

Siobhan and I had taken turns digging up a patch of dirt off to the side of the ancient burial mound. Seemed a little ironic, really. We had taken a look at the big stone blocks that sealed the mound, thinking perhaps we could dump the bodies inside, but even if we'd had a sufficiently strong lever to hand, we couldn't possibly have budged the stones. And while I had my doubts about all the mumbo-jumbo that surrounded me, I thought it might not be such a great idea to drop the bodies of a couple of Nazi thugs in with the bones of ancient pagan wizards.

Pahoo was right: my karma was bad enough already.

Siobhan ended up doing most of the digging – fair enough, since she's probably twice as strong as me – and fortunately the ground wasn't too hard. We didn't have the time or energy to dig anything but the shallowest of graves. Still, the physical labour was hardly the worst of it.

'Head or feet?' Siobhan asked, tossing the shovel aside.

'Feet,' I said. No contest.

We went for Red Beard first, since he was nearer. His slick boots went up so high that I couldn't get a good grip on his ankles and had to grab him by the calves, wedging his feet under my arms to lift him. Siobhan grabbed his wrists and hefted his huge upper half off the ground with ease. But as she raised him up, his head lolled back, and the gaping red slash across his throat ripped open a little wider with a sound like swishing corduroy. I was sure his head would just tear right off the remains of his neck, and for a moment I thought I was going to be sick, and lost my grip on his legs.

'Bloody hell!'

'Sorry,' I said, holding a hand up to Siobhan. She shook her head at me, and started dragging the big man by herself across the dirt to his grave.

'Wait,' I sighed. I took a deep breath, got hold of the corpse's feet again. I nodded at Siobhan and with a grunt, I picked him up. I tried not to look down at him as we scrambled the twenty yards to the grave, but even in my peripheral vision that wet red smile of a wound seemed to laugh at me, and for all the strain of our effort, I couldn't seem to catch a decent breath. It wasn't until the body flopped over, landing face down when we dropped it in the grave, that I felt I could swallow clean air again.

I felt a little dizzy and bent over, bracing my hands on my knees. I thought I might faint, but the fuzziness passed. When I stood up, I saw that Siobhan was already fussing with the other body. I jogged over to help her.

The skinhead was much lighter, and the bullet wound in his head less awful to look at, so moving his body was practically a breeze. Still, I was out of breath by the time we tossed the second body in the grave, though Siobhan hadn't even worked up a sweat. She kicked the bodies around until they were more or less neatly aligned at the bottom of the hole. She reached for the shovel, then stopped. She knelt down and grabbed for the bearded man's outstretched hand. She was examining a silver signet ring on his pinky. At first I thought it was emblazoned with a swastika, but it was an elaborate Celtic cross of some kind.

'You're not squeamish are you?' she asked.

I managed not to laugh hysterically. I tried whistling past the graveyard. 'I was in *two* George Romero movies,' I vamped. I crossed two fingers on my right hand and held them up to her. 'Me and Quentin Tarantino are like this.'

'Uh-huh,' she said. And suddenly a butterfly knife was in her hand. With a quick swish, she'd sliced off the dead man's pinky, then pried off the ring using the tip of the blade. She wiped the ring off on the grass, then handed it to me.

'Hold on to it,' she said.

'Why?' I held it in my palm, but kept my hand at a distance from my body. Like that made sense.

'Just put it in your damned pocket.'

'Hrrrrgh,' I gurgled, but I complied.

Siobhan smiled at me as she reached for the shovel. 'Quentin Tarantino's a *pussy* faggot,' she said.

I let her shovel the dirt over the bodies.

'I'm thirsty,' Siobhan announced. We'd been driving for nearly an hour when she turned onto the forecourt of a petrol station and parked the car off to one side. She didn't ask if anyone else wanted anything, just strode off into the little mini-mart. The three of us got out of the car. Uma, who had yet to say a word since we returned from burying the bodies, trundled off to the ladies room. Pahoo held his bandaged arm, flexing and unflexing his fingers.

'Hurt much?'

He shrugged. 'Good codeine. Getting stiff, though.'

'Hmmm,' I said, at a loss for words. What do you say to someone who has just been shot by Nazis? I tried to recall dialogue from old war movies, but could only think of *Von Ryan's Express*, and that was no help at all. Sinatra was badly miscast.

Siobhan came out of the little shop carrying a plastic bag. She pulled out a container of orange juice for herself, drained half of it in a swallow, and tossed the bag at me. She'd bought a half-dozen different drinks and a fistful of candy bars. Also a box of gauze and a tube of disinfectant salve. I fished them out and handed them to Pahoo.

'Need any help?' she asked the little man.

Pahoo shook his head and walked off toward the bathroom, reading the back of the salve container. I was browsing the drinks, trying to choose, when Siobhan apparently read my mind.

'No beer,' she said. 'Sorry.'

I nodded and settled for a sparkling apple thingy. At least it wasn't Snapple. Remarkably, it was cold.

I had devoured most of a Lion Bar when Uma returned to the car, still looking forlorn. I passed her the goody bag, which she poked through unenthusiastically, settling finally on a bottle of sparkling mineral water and a roll of chewy candies.

'How you doing?' I asked.

'I am . . . disturbed.'

'Take a fucking number.'

'Pardon?'

'Join the club,' I said. 'This isn't exactly what I expected.'

'That would be my fault.'

'I didn't say that. I'm not blaming you for anything, Uma. I agreed to come along on this . . . whatever it is. Expedition. And you did warn me. I just . . .' I glanced around and lowered my voice. 'We just killed two people.'

'I *am* aware of that, Marty. My heart is heavy with the responsibility.'

'Don't lose any sleep over that scum,' Siobhan said. 'I won't.'

'Is it really as easy as that?' I asked her. 'Is that what you learned in the IRA?'

'You tell me.'

'Huh? What do you mean?'

'You've killed, too, haven't you? I can smell it on you. And you haven't seemed too bothered up till now.'

In fact, I had killed men before. And other things. Though it had been necessary and I wasn't entirely in possession of my faculties at the time. As I met, or tried to meet, Siobhan's hard gaze, I realized that I had never truly thought about the implications of it, had stored it away in some little mental safe deposit box and hidden the key. It seemed incredible to me now that I had never agonized over it, been racked by nightmares or torn apart with guilt. Out of nowhere, the horror of it washed over me like a great Pacific swell, and I was shooting the narrow tube of my own latent guilt. I felt a total jackass, like I was in one of those dreams where you suddenly realize that you're not wearing any clothes and *that's* why they're all laughing.

I had to sit down on the ground.

'Marty?' Uma said. She knelt down beside me. 'Are you all right? What is it?'

'I don't know.' I felt lightheaded, dizzy. Suddenly nauseous. 'I . . . feel . . . sick.'

I vomited up my apple juice and chocolate bar and a whole colourful mess more on top. I barfed and heaved a steaming mass of stuff that was more than just what I'd eaten. I puked until I was racked by dry heaves and it felt like my diaphragm was tickling my tonsils looking for the emergency exit.

I got it all over my shoes and didn't even care. I fell onto my side, a dribble of vomit spilling down my chin. Uma reached over and wiped it away with a tissue. She stroked my sweaty hair, but I still couldn't look up. I saw another set of feet enter my frame of vision.

'I miss something?' Pahoo said.

'Do you want another drink?'

'No,' I said, nodding my head yes. Uma rolled her eyes and went up to the bar to buy another round: Jack Daniels neat for me, mineral water for her. Siobhan sat by herself at the bar, nursing a pint of Guinness and scaring the bartender. She kept a close eye on the door. Pahoo had opted to take a walk in the woods rather than come inside.

The pub was just up the road from the petrol station – we didn't even have to drive. It was Uma who suggested that perhaps I could do with something a little bit stronger than fizzy apple juice and I readily agreed.

Uma gently placed two glasses down in front of me – she'd added a lager chaser – and slid back down the bench across from me at our corner table. She'd also bought a pack of dry roasted peanuts. She tore the foil open with her teeth, poured a bunch into her palm and tossed the packet on the middle of the table. I picked it up, read the nutritional information, played with the pack, but I didn't want any peanuts. I drained the bourbon in a gulp and slammed the glass against the table top.

'Not a very generous shot,' I said.

'It's pre-measured.'

'What do you mean?'

'You get the same amount of alcohol in every drinking establishment in England. It is very strictly regulated and licensed.'

'You're kidding. What if the bartender wants to give you a little extra?'

'He could,' Uma said. I nodded. 'But they do not.'

'Funny country.'

'*Different* country,' Uma said. 'Or had you not realized? I think, perhaps, you are suffering from being a fish out of water, Marty.'

'Or out of my depth, maybe. Hell, I feel like I've been filleted, grilled and served up with potatoes and broccoli. In an indelicate little sauce.' Uma giggled. 'You seem more like your cheery old self, though.'

'Perhaps I have to be.'

'Because I'm not?'

'No, there is simply no room for any other feelings right now. There is too much to do.'

'Wow. Can you just turn it on and off like that? Where do I buy a switch?'

'I will check to see if I have a spare.' I looked up expecting to see a smile on Uma's face, but there was nothing but concern. 'You do not *have* to go on with us, Marty.'

'You sure?'

Uma started to speak, then hesitated.

'Gotcha,' I said.

'No, you do not *have* to. But I think that you should.'

'Why?' I asked. 'Why me? I don't understand a thing that you're doing. All this ancient Celtic history and New Age bullshit. It really doesn't mean anything to me. I'm risking my career just being with you. Not to mention my life. And maybe your lives by being such a hump. I really don't seem to be helping you much. Not at all, unless you need a designated puker. So what's the point?'

'I believe that you are meant to be here, to be a part of this. I . . . you will not like this, but I *sense* that it is a necessary, an important thing. I believe that you are . . . an attractor.'

'How's that?'

'I think that you are a king of spiritual attractor. A natural, or should I say *un*natural, magnet if you will.'

'For what?'

'For the unusual. The supernatural, if you prefer. I have encountered others like you, but they are few and far between. Dasra was one such, but of limited abilities. It is, in my estimation, a great gift.'

'You're right. I don't like it.'

'Yet you continue to go along. To risk so very much. Why?'

I stopped and thought about for a moment. *Really* thought about it. We're talking studying-your-beer introspection. 'I've been having dreams,' I said.

'Yes?'

'Or visions. Or something, I'm not sure. I have this nasty feeling that I *can't* turn back now. It's still a little vague to me, but I feel like there's something more important at stake here than my career. Not that that's saying much. But, I've become burdened by this sense of . . .'

'What is it, Marty?'

'Darkness,' I said. 'Awful darkness. I don't know if I'm doing any good or not, but I feel like I'm committed; that if I turned back now the darkness would never go away. It would consume me. It feels like this is a kind of test, though I don't know the subject or even what a passing grade is. But I don't think it's a test I can live with failing. Crazy, huh?'

'I would not say that.'

'And there's another thing.'

Uma cocked her head at me. I had to swallow once before I could say the words: 'Good girls go to heaven, bad girls go to London.'

'Excuse me?'

'That's the T-shirt the little girl was wearing.' I glanced up from my almost empty glass. 'In the convenience store that got torched. There was a little girl, a sweet thing who played peek-a-boo with me. I keep seeing her face. She was wearing one of those stupid tourist T-shirts they sell in the West End. But every time I see it, see *her*, my head fills with the smell of burnt meat. How could I live with myself knowing that another baby got burned alive 'cause I wasn't brave enough to do anything? To do . . . what I was meant to do.'

'There is no predestination, Marty. There are energies and channels and endless possibilities, but the future is always an uncharted road.'

'But it's paved on the ruins of the past,' I said. Uma sighed and looked away. I saw Siobhan watching us both. 'Anyway, didn't you know? I have a secret Indian name: Doesn't-sound-too-smart.' I chuckled to myself.

'I do not understand; how is that an Indian name?'

I looked up at Uma, at her lovely brown, *Asian* skin, and started to laugh. 'I mean native American,' I said. 'Sorry, wrong tribe.'

She smiled, but looked no less puzzled. 'I still do not get it.'

'Oh, hell. Neither do I.' I took a long swallow of beer and popped a peanut into my mouth.

'There may well be more death,' Uma said softly.

'How's that?'

'Death. I believe we will encounter more. Perhaps be the cause of it. That is, sadly, the nature of this struggle. As you have seen, our opponents are not possessed of any sense of mercy. We must be of similar constitution.'

'Isn't that where Siobhan comes in?'

'Yes, but it cannot be her burden alone. We are all equally a part of this. We are all of us responsible and not just for our individual actions in this regard. Can you accept that?'

'I think I already have. I think that's why I've got bits of breakfast all over my shoes.'

Uma nodded. 'As I think you must now understand, Siobhan is very . . . capable, though she has a tendency to be headstrong. That is why she was expelled from the IRA.'

'Expelled? From the *IRA*? What do you have to do to get thrown out of the IRA? I mean . . .' The mind boggles. At least mine did.

I glanced again at the Irish woman, saw she was still watching us. I sort of smiled at her in embarrassment, but she remained stone-faced. I felt a shiver run down my back. 'She scares the piss out of me.'

'Yes,' Uma said. 'That is probably for the best.'

'I thought all this Arthurian stuff was bullshit,' I said.

'It is,' Pahoo said. 'But the tourists eat it up. Bloody Americans go for it in a big way.'

'Figures. Probably the same losers who go to those stupid theme restaurants where you watch guys in costumes have fake jousts while you eat chicken with your fingers. And serving wenches.'

Pahoo raised his pierced eyebrow at me.

'I mean they call the waitresses serving wenches. You don't eat them. Unless you're a big tipper, I suppose.'

Cornwall was the first bit of English landscape to impress me. The moors we'd driven through to get to the sea were eerie and otherworldly in their sparseness – very *Hound of the Baskervilles* – and the Cornish coastline is genuinely dramatic. Even more than the visibly old bits of London, the terrain felt very nineteenth century to me in a *Wuthering Heights* kind of way, though having only seen the movie (surprise, surprise), I haven't got a clue where *Wuthering Heights* is set.

Tintagel Castle, or rather the weathered ruin of it, is perched on a particularly impressive bluff overlooking a natural and stormy cove. It's the kind of place that makes you want to strike a pose; just stand up on the heights, hands on hips, one booted foot resting on a hunk of stone, the wind tousling your hair as you stare off into the distance mourning a lost love.

That's what all the other tourists were doing. Except that the balding Americans in their too-low Bermuda shorts and too-high white socks just looked silly. And the fact that their loves weren't lost, but standing ten feet away and snapping photos using the flash in broad daylight took some of the romance out of the place.

'Little bit busy around here isn't it?' I asked. I couldn't help but note the line of customers waiting outside the 'Sword-in-the-Scone' tea room. The town was swarming with tourists which was fair enough, since everything *in* the town was devoted to separating people from their money. Obviously, a common attribute of spiritual Nexi.

'Yes,' Uma sighed.

'Makes me sick,' Pahoo added.

'And you want to do one of your little ritual things here?'

'Not here exactly. But just a short distance away is the ruin of a Celtic monastery. That is the focal point of this ley grid. There is actually nothing special about Tintagel Castle, though English Heritage would not care to admit it. Still, the leys do exert great power here. It *is* a nexus.'

'I thought this is supposed to be, like, Camelot or something.' Siobhan snorted derisively.

'There's no bloody Camelot,' Pahoo told me. 'And this castle was mostly built in the thirteenth century, though there are older ruins on the site. There's an argument whether there's any Arthurian connection to Tintagel.'

'Assuming Arthur existed at all,' Uma said.

'You don't believe?' Pahoo asked.

'I believe in the historical authenticity of a king who inspired, or more likely, commissioned a series of stories. Mallory was a liar and a whore, you know. There were likely several kings and local warlords called Arthur at various times between the fifth and ninth centuries. I am also entirely certain that Cornwall is an extraordinary place of power. Indeed, this region, from here to Salisbury on up to Glastonbury, has no real equal on the planet.'

'Not even Ur?' Pahoo said. 'Jerusalem?'

'Hollywood?' I added.

'Not even,' Uma said, and smiled. 'But for all those fabulous energies, and the not inconsiderable romance of the legends, I remain unconvinced that the power of the place has more than a passing, coincidental connection with a king named Arthur. Though I hear Arthur Askey once lived here.'

'I believe in Pendragon's story. I think the myth's too powerful *not* to be true, in some form,' Pahoo said. 'People still believe in it. And I can *feel* it.'

'People believe in Noah's Ark, too,' I said. 'That's not exactly a compelling basis for zoology, though.'

'Yeah, but Noah's Ark, any biblical story, that kind of thing has the crushing weight of religious dogma attached to it, don't it? There's a huge coercive element propping up that tosh. But there's no coercion behind the Arthurian legends. It's got nothing to support it but the simple truth and power of the story.'

'The desire to believe,' Uma added.

'Romantic hogwash,' Siobhan said. 'Arthur was a wimp, Guinevere was a slag and Lancelot was a faithless prick. And these are the heroes, the legends that English culture, so-called, is built on. Pox on them all.'

'What do you think, Marty?' Uma asked.

'Of Camelot?'

Uma nodded. I glanced past the ruins of the stone parapets, down to the foamy sea crashing on the rocks of Merlin's Cave far below. I felt the palpable history and romance of the place wash over me, the desire to *want* to believe in the grandeur and wonder of the ancient and moving story of love and justice and a magical sword.

'I prefer *Brigadoon*,' I said.

We wandered around the grounds until closing time. I have to admit that I got a kick out of it regardless of the truth behind the stories. I didn't have the guts to say it, but I thought that Siobhan was dead wrong about British mythology. I know that Americans are suckers for all things English and romantic – it's that second bit which excludes warm beer and, sadly, drags in BBC costume dramas – but there *is* a power to the stories. I suspect that like most people my knowledge of Arthurian legend doesn't extend far beyond the Disney-filtered versions that I learned as a kid, but to me the great thing about those stories is that you never outgrow them.

I'd rather chew glass than admit it, but I think maybe Pahoo was right: the stories of Arthur and Guinevere and the Round Table endure, even in their bowdlerized, sanitized way, because they connect with something essential in human nature. Bible stories are boring precisely because they're *so* black and white, so follow-the-numbers; but it seems to me that the tales of Arthur resonate because none of the characters are entirely good or bad. They mean to do the right thing, but they fuck up. Or they intend to do evil and discover that they aren't so nasty after all. Even if the stories aren't remotely true in the historical sense, I don't care. I like them anyway.

And just between the two of us, I've never even seen *Brigadoon*. Wouldn't you just know it: prick a cynic, bleed a romantic.

Pahoo rode up front with Siobhan and directed her around the incredibly narrow country roads – as we scraped wing mirrors with cars coming the other way, I actually felt relieved to be in the tiny Mini – up to a camping site-cum-garbage dump just outside Nowheresville. Three rusted trailers and a dozen or so brightly coloured tents of various sizes were pitched around the site. The ground was muddy in patches, overgrown with weeds and tall grass in others. A pair of decrepit-looking horses grazed what pathetic green they could find. Three big boulders, adorned with graffiti that I now recognized as Celtic runes, formed a circle in the middle of the site. A group of dirty, half-clothed children clambered around them playing tag. I saw a hairy lump of a man sleeping in a tarpaulin that had been suspended between the trunks of two dead trees. His big white belly swelled out of the hammock like a foamy head of root beer. Crouched in his shadow was a topless blonde nursing a naked infant. I instinctively averted my gaze when I saw a spurt of mother's milk dribble down her tit, but it didn't embarrass her – or anyone else, so far as I could tell – in the slightest. A couple of people popped out of their tents at the sound of our car engine; they made Pahoo look like Mr Clean.

'Oh, man, we done landed in *Deliverance II*,' I groaned. 'If I see a kid with a banjo, I am *out* of here.'

'They're Travellers, Marty,' Uma said.

'The new *Star Trek* series?'

'New Age Travellers,' Uma corrected.

'Well, that clears things up,' I said.

'Wanker,' Pahoo muttered. He stepped out of the car while it was still moving. He tiptoed over to the man in the hammock and slapped his naked belly loud enough to frighten a flock of rooks out of the trees. The fat man shot bolt upright, looking mad as hell. He grinned broadly when he saw Pahoo and let out a leonine roar. Rolling off the hammock with surprising grace, he swept the little man up in a big bear hug, until Pahoo's feet dangled off the ground. The woman with the baby got up and took hold of Pahoo as soon as the fat man let him go. She, too, was a good six inches taller than him, and still nursing, but he got her other tit right in the face. The baby started to cry. I couldn't blame it; I don't like to share, either.

Several other Travellers appeared, summoned by the fat man's howl. They were all raggedy looking, dressed like Pahoo in camouflage pants or home-stitched rainbow rags. The men had untrimmed beards and moustaches and several wore dreadlocks. The women also wore their hair long, garishly dyed and woven in with enough beads and trinkets to have bought Manhattan Island six times over. No one in the camp looked older than thirty and I felt like I'd fallen through a time tunnel into 1967. (I once did a guest shot on *Time Tunnel*, by the way, the one where they go back to Pearl Harbor, and James Darren meets himself as a child.) Except that in place of peace signs, this group seemed to emblazon themselves and their possessions with various runes and other equally esoteric symbols. Uma appeared especially intrigued by them.

Pahoo hugged the other crusties – I noted that he went for seconds on the topless broad – and rubbed the no doubt lice-ridden heads of the kids. He glanced back our way, gesturing for us to get out of the car. Uma opened her door, a manufactured ain't-I-happy smile plastered to her puss. She was quickly on the receiving end of an ardent embrace from an especially crusty-looking Traveller. Siobhan opened her door, but seemed reluctant to get out. I hadn't budged an inch.

'Pssst,' I whispered. 'What say you and me go find us a pub somewhere? I'll buy.'

Siobhan shook her head. 'Lord save me from Travellers and tinkers. If even one of these filthy buggers tries to hug me, I'm going to kill 'em all.'

I nodded my encouragement.

I held out as long as I could, fearing the worst. I did everything I could to avoid it, but there comes a time in each man's life when he has to screw up his courage and face his fears. Perhaps it's even the mark of a man.

I had to do number two real bad.

After a surprisingly edible vegetarian chilli dinner, Pahoo whipped out his didgeridoo and, wouldn't you know it, several of the locals had logs of their own. I found myself farting along with the impromptu jam session – I think I carried the better tune – before deciding it was time to face the inevitable. I asked a guy with frizzy hair down to his ass and a yin-yang tattoo on his right cheek the whereabouts of the facilities.

'Gort,' he said.

'Klatu barata niktu,' I replied, taking no chances.

'No, I'm Gort.'

'Well, I'm busting, chief. Where's the toilet at?'

He sort of clucked at me, but gestured off into the bushes. 'Bad karma,' I heard him mutter as I turned away.

It was getting on twilight, and I squinted in hope of spotting a Port-a-potty, but saw nothing but brush. With a sigh, I wandered off, hoping for a plant with big, soft leaves and no aphids.

In fact, I came upon a small dirt path. About fifteen yards into the brush, I ran into the topless woman I'd seen earlier. She was emerging from a rickety wooden outhouse – a crude latrine built above a pit. I could smell the lye.

I only refer to her as the topless woman because I didn't know her name and, well, she was still topless. The baby was cradled in her arms, sucking merrily, and rather noisily, at her tit. If she wasn't careful, the kid was going to end up big as Yaphet Kotto at the end of *Live and Let Die*. I cleared my throat and gurgled 'hi' as we performed a little *pas de deux* along the trail.

'Yer special, ain't ye?' she said.

'Um,' I replied. I couldn't seem to keep my eyes from shooting down to the sight of the suckling kid. It was a boy and older than I first thought. It briefly turned its head to look at me and I saw sharp little teeth in its mouth. Ouch!

'I can feel it,' she said.

I don't wonder, I thought, eying her well-gnawed nipple. I grinned at her, dumbly.

'I can feel it, sure as me skin,' she repeated, and walked back up the trail.

'Da-da-*dum*-da-dum-da-*dum*-dum-dum,' I sang to myself in a banjo twang.

Thankfully there was no reply.

I managed to avoid splinters from the unfinished toilet seat and was pleasantly surprised to find a roll of toilet paper. I thought about stealing some in case I should come across any wood planks that needed planing, but resisted the temptation. I felt a little awkward and exposed out there; since I could see out through the considerable gaps in the wood, I reckoned others could see in. Though why they'd want to, I couldn't imagine. It was getting dark, anyway, and in the end I had to go so bad, nothing else mattered.

Maybe I am sort of special.

The didgeridoo-bees' recital went on for another hour. One crusty dragged out a couple of drums, but it neither added to nor subtracted from my overall musical pleasure. Pahoo sat in a circle with a group of his buddies, laughing and smoking copious amounts of dope. Uma stood with another smaller group of Travellers, listening intently to my buddy Gort. Though I could see she was trying hard, she had a sort of desperate look on her face. But then maybe she needed the toilet, too.

I found Siobhan back by the car, leaning on the hood and keeping an eye on things. As usual. She had a beer in her hand.

'Where'd you get that?' I asked.

'I have a way with people, in case you hadn't noticed. They respond to my Hibernian charms.'

'No fair,' I muttered.

Siobhan handed me the can. It was a bitter and it was warm, but it was alcohol which was the main thing. Sadly, dope and E seemed to be the intoxicants of choice among Pahoo's Traveller friends. I took a big gulp and handed her back the can. 'Thanks.'

'Keep it.' She reached in through the front window and grabbed a fresh one off the seat.

'Charms, indeed,' I said, toasting her.

'It don't mean we're going steady.'

'Damn. Now I'll have to throw away your corsage,' I said, and took another hefty swallow.

Siobhan actually laughed. She toasted me back.

'Wow, you must be drunk,' I said.

'Dream on, TV boy.'

I hauled myself up onto the hood of the Mini, but felt the metal of the hood buckle under my weight. I quickly slid off and leant against the car, next to Siobhan.

'Can I ask you a question?'

'You just did.'

'Hardy-har-har.'

'You can ask,' she said.

'What's the capital of South Dakota?'

Siobhan shot me a look.

'Joke,' I said. 'You know, like an ice-breaker.'

'You're Mortimer and Reeves in one hilarious package.'

'Who?'

'Ask your question.'

'Why are you here?' She turned to look at me again. 'I mean, what's your connection with all this crazy stuff. Granted, *I* couldn't answer that if you asked me, but you just seem . . .'

'What?'

'Out of place. Very out of place. I mean . . .' – I lowered by voice – '. . . were you really kicked out of the IRA?'

'Uma tell you that?' I nodded. 'Let's just say we had a difference of opinion on a matter or three.'

'So how do you go from that to . . . this?' I waved my hand at the Travellers' messy campsite.

'I walked away from the Provisionals because they can no longer see the wood for the trees. They've got a view of the situation that's past its sell-by date, and though in their hearts they know the world has moved on, they can't bring themselves to admit it. When I joined up it was because I thought it was a cause I believed in, a fight worth dying for. Me father spent half his life in a British jail for the same.'

'But that's what I don't get. I admit, the whole Irish thing is over my head – I mean, I don't know who's right or wrong – and no offence, but I don't really care, you know? There's shit a lot closer to home that I don't get either and I can't find time for that. It just seems like . . . if you hate the British so much, right?'

'Let's say I've got a gripe.'

'So why are you doing this? Why are you helping Uma to . . . weave her magic or whatever? Wouldn't it serve your . . . *cause* better to watch it all go to hell?'

'I'm not an anarchist. I know a few who are and I hate them as much as anyone, because they're ignorant and they're selfish. Anarchists are people who despise themselves to the core, but can't face up to their own self-loathing. So they end up turning it on everything and everyone. I half-suspect some of this crowd is like that, which makes me wary of 'em.'

'Plus they smell.'

'That, too,' Siobhan said. 'But sometimes you take your allies where you find them. I walked away from the Troubles not because I gave up on the cause, but because I didn't like what the movement was turning into. I saw a rot creeping in. It's the same rot Uma's fighting in her way. I don't entirely understand it, how Uma can do the things she does, but I know I have to stand with her. If you want to give a name to the rot, and call it Thule, that's fine. But that's just a part of it, if you ask me. The real fight is against those who impose themselves on others regardless of consequence. The Unionists, the Thule . . . it's a many headed beast. I just aim at the biggest heads I can find.'

'Like the wise man said: there's a lot of bastards out there.'

'I take 'em on one at a time, Martin Burns. One at a time.'

We clinked beer cans.

Our expedition set off from the Travellers' camp just before midnight. Pahoo rode in a car with several of his New Age friends. I took shotgun in the Mini with Siobhan at the wheel and Uma in back. Two more carloads of Travellers trailed behind us.

'What now?' I asked, turning around to look at Uma. She was staring out the side window and didn't answer me. 'Hello? Earth to Uma, come in.'

She turned to look at me, but she still didn't respond. She seemed to be somewhere else.

'Houston, I think we have a problem,' I said to Siobhan.

'Uma?' the Irish woman said softly.

'What?' Uma said.

'Are you all right?' Siobhan asked. 'What's wrong?'

'I am not certain. I suddenly had a very odd sense of . . . distortion. I could not quite determine the nature or source of it though.'

'You're probably just missing the sound of that digeridoo,' I said. 'If you'd like, I can belch as we ride along.'

'That will not be necessary. Nice of you to offer, however.'

'What kind of distortion? What do you feel?' Siobhan asked.

'It is gone now. But there was . . . I don't know. An unwelcome presence. It is probably nothing. Just tiredness.'

'You sure we should we go on?'

'We must.'

'So what exactly are we going on to?' I asked again.

'We will enact the second of the rituals. Think of them as inoculations against the Thule. Just as in Canterbury I tapped into the power of the ley grid to shield it against Thule corruption, so we must touch the energies that flow through the earth in this place.'

'And how are you going to do that?'

'Not me. This will be Pahoo's responsibility. Although ley energies are all of a kind, they take on a different character in different locations. Pahoo is far more in touch with the energies here than am I. He has had experience of them, utilized them in the past.'

'And the peanut gallery?'

'Sorry?'

'The Travellers,' I said, pointing in front of and behind us. 'The great unwashed. What's with them?'

'They will be . . . participating in the ritual.'

'You say that with all the enthusiasm of a woman on her way to get root canal treatment.'

'I admit that I am slightly disturbed by the number of persons involved. I do not know them and thus must rely on Pahoo's judgement.'

'Not very encouraging. Not if his dress sense is any indicator.'

'Pahoo insists that their numbers are essential for the Druidic ceremony, and it is not for me to doubt him. The completion of the ritual is the important thing.'

'Druids? You mean like tree worshippers?'

'It is rather more complex than that, Marty. Druidism is a very ancient and highly refined religion, though uncommonly practised in this age. Druids dominated Cornwall in Roman times and were formidable enemies of Rome. Ultimately they were all but wiped

out. The nature and development of the leys in Britain owes much
to the advances of Druid philosophies and magics.'
   'Go figure,' I said. 'You know it's funny.'
   'What's that?'
   'Pahoo.'
   'What about him?'
   'He doesn't look Druish.'
   Siobhan laughed, but Uma wasn't amused. She turned her head
to stare again into the darkness.

Uma, Siobhan and I watched while the crusties organized themselves
for the ceremony on the hillock where the ruins of the Celtic
monastery lay. The rocky bluffs of the Tintagel headland and the
broken walls of the castle loomed no more than half a mile away
and the roar of the crashing surf echoed in the night. The monastery
itself was not fenced off; indeed, what reason? The 'ruins' consisted
of a few irregular, worn stones in the ground and the vague suggestion
that a structure had once stood here. Even in the moonlight, I judged
that there was an impressive view of the sea from the hilltop, but the
place had none of the holy resonance or eerie mystery of the tunnels
and secret crypt beneath Canterbury Cathedral.
   Pahoo's cronies had donned white robes and were gathering in a
circle, with Pahoo, still wearing the same pants and T-shirt, in the
centre. He knelt over a small fire, built in a stone circle. One of
the crusties banged a small drum with a slow, steady rhythm and
another had a little triangle-like instrument which she flicked with
her forefinger every few beats. It wasn't the topless mama, but her
open robe exposed one tiny tit. Uma got closer to the Travellers,
but she didn't enter the circle. Siobhan and I came up behind her.
   The robed Druids began to walk around Pahoo, keeping a steady
distance from each other and maintaining the integrity of the circle.
The ones without instruments all held small sprigs of what looked
like mistletoe to me – though I didn't see any kissing going on
– which they waved first away from, then toward the centre of
the circle with a precision that would have done Busby Berkeley
proud. Pahoo knelt in the centre, in front of a flat slab of stone.
He held a smaller rock in his hand and was tracing runes into the
face of the slab in the ground. He chanted slowly, though every so
often the members of the circle would uniformly bark a response
to something he said. The language was unknown to me, though
it sounded so much like the kind of nonsense thing kids make up to
annoy adults, that for a minute I thought the whole shindig was a

put-on. I glanced at Uma to check, but her sombre expression told me that it was no fooling.

The circle slowed its pace as the chanting grew more fervid. Pahoo would call out a phrase, the drum and triangle would sound, and a member of the circle would neatly slice off a piece of the mistletoe they were carrying. This went on until each sprig had been cut and the movement of the circle came to a complete stop. Then they all knelt down and Pahoo stood up.

'Oh,' I heard Uma whisper.

Pahoo had a grey rabbit in his hand. He held it by the hind legs, upside down, and even in the dim moonlight I could see the creature shivering with fear. With the edge of the stone he'd been using to etch the runes, Pahoo slit the rabbit's throat, then ripped the flesh open all the way up its body. Perhaps it was just the angle, but Pahoo's eyes seemed alight with reflected fire as he cut the animal open. He chanted, and as he opened his mouth I could see strings of saliva between his teeth. For a second I thought he was going to tear a chunk out of the spasming creature with his incisors.

I heard Uma gasp.

Its legs still kicking, the rabbit's innards spilled out, splattering the altar stone. The drum stopped, the triangle stopped, the chanting stopped.

Everything stopped.

I tried to turn my head, but felt like I'd been dropped in a vat of glue. I couldn't move. I tried to just listen, but I couldn't even hear what had been the omnipresent crash of the sea. I felt a cold touch on the back of my neck. It raced down my spine, then my legs.

I heard the crash of the surf again.

The Travellers were all hugging each other and taking off their robes. Three of them had formed a tight circle around Pahoo and held him in a fervid embrace. The dead rabbit lay on the stone at their feet.

A sudden burst of loud music from one of the cars jolted my attention. Two big speakers had been set into the rear of one of the parked hatchbacks and loud, repetitive techno music – house, garage, bungalow, whatever the hell they call the mindless drivel – filled the air. The Travellers started dancing wildly – actually, the word *cavorting* came to mind, though it never had before – among the ruins of the ancient monastery. I couldn't believe it.

Just call me a wallflower.

FOURTEEN

~

We spent what was left of the night at the Travellers' campsite. The happy Druids scraped up a few spare sleeping bags, and though Uma accepted one, they looked flea-ridden to me, so I passed, opting for the back of the Mini. (Siobhan had already called dips on the front.) I don't think I slept more than three hours before a harsh morning sun woke me, but even at that my back and neck were so stiff that it was just as well. Delightful as the camp toilet was, I opted to take a leak in the woods, hoping for nicer once we hit the road.

Neither Uma nor Siobhan had slept any better than me, and by six-thirty we were itching to get a move on. We had to wait another hour for Pahoo to appear; I think he and one of the local babes were making the Crusty with Two Backs.

We packed up the Mini, accepting a dodgy-looking banana bread from the (still) topless woman – was it a religious thing? Maybe I'd have to look into this whole Druid deal – and baby Russ Meyer. Pahoo was quick to tear off a big hunk (of cake) and shove it down his gob, but even though I felt hungry enough to eat a couple of Denny's Grand Slam breakfasts, I gave it the elbow. I was dubious as to what secret ingredients might have been added to the recipe and didn't want to find out the hard way. Uma and Siobhan shared similar reservations. Finally, strapping Pahoo's didgeridoo back on to the Mini's roof, we were ready to go.

The Mini had other ideas.

'Goddammit,' Siobhan yelled, punching the dashboard. Her knowledge of cars didn't extend much beyond hot-wiring them. I don't even know how to do that.

'Starter?' I guessed.

'Oh dear,' Uma said, looking very glum indeed.

'Cars're evil bastards,' was the extent of Pahoo's contribution. He took the banana bread and presumably went back to find his crusty babe.

After another hour we had a more definitive diagnosis of the problem. The fat guy with the Moby Dick belly *did* know his way around an internal combustion engine.

'Head gasket,' he said, shaking his head and wiping his greasy hands on his big stomach. He had that look which anyone who's ever owned a pet lives in dread of; it's the expression on the vet's face that says: I'm sorry, son, but we should put Fluffy to sleep now for his own good.

'Now what do we do?' I asked.

'I could steal something,' Siobhan suggested, a little light in her eyes.

Uma shook her head.

'Something nice,' Siobhan tempted.

Uma wouldn't have it. 'No. Too risky. It would not do to draw attention to ourselves in such a manner.'

'I'm bloody good at it you know,' Siobhan insisted.

But Uma wouldn't hear of it.

'Where we going anyway?' I asked.

'Liverpool,' Uma said. 'There is a companion there we must meet.'

'What?' I asked. 'I thought Scotland was next?'

Uma looked at me and opened her mouth – I was expecting a profanity – but only a sigh came out.

'Okay, whatever. But can't we just take a train or something? You must have the dog here or the local equivalent.'

'The dog?' Siobhan asked.

'You know, Greyhound? The bus?'

Nothing.

'Leave the driving to us . . .' I sang.

'There is the train,' Uma said before Siobhan could belt me. 'But I fear it is more like a snail than a dog.'

In the end, it was Pahoo to the rescue.

'Oh, my god,' I said.

'I bet it drives like a tank,' Siobhan complained. 'Or worse. Christ, will it even go?'

'It will have to do,' Uma sighed. 'Though it is not as inconspicuous as I would prefer.'

It was a VW Microbus. Twenty years old at least, and not looking good for its age. It had been painted over – badly – any number of times. I counted six different colours, including two shades of purple, each uglier than the last. Not that it mattered, because it had all gone to rust. I hadn't seen a Microbus for years, felt sure they'd all gone to German motor heaven, but the mere sight brought back a veritable cascade of memories, circa 1970, largely involving girls who loved dope and didn't wear underwear.

'Man, oh, man, do I remember these babies,' I said. 'There was a time when you could get more tail with one of these things and a nickle bag than with your own TV show.'

Uma and Siobhan both made faces at me.

'It was a long time ago,' I added, blushing.

'Well, don't imagine happy days are here again,' Siobhan said.

'Really, Marty,' Uma chided.

I admit I was embarrassed, but in no small part – and I can only pray that neither of my female companions noticed – because the very sight of the Microbus gave me a bit of a stiffy.

Ah, memories.

The Microbus belonged to one of the Travellers who was willing to trade even-up for the Mini, at least for the time being. Though the engine in the old van was a lot noisier than the car's, we could – small blessing – keep the didgeridoo inside. And even with its ripped-up seats and rust-holes in the floor, it was a lot more comfortable to sit in. As long as you were careful where you put your feet and your ass.

Pahoo sat up front with Siobhan, who would not relinquish the wheel to anyone. We were heading back the same way we had come, until we picked up the motorway that would take us north to Liverpool. Uma sat beside me, arms folded across her chest, looking uncharacteristically glum as we zipped past the eerie Cornish landscape.

'You okay?' I asked.

'Fine, Marty. Just a bit preoccupied.'

'Did it go all right last night? I mean, did the rite do what it was supposed to do?'

'Of course it bloody well did,' Pahoo said from the front. I thought he'd been asleep. 'You think I don't know what I'm fucking doing?'

'I haven't got the slightest *fucking* idea, to be honest. Which is why I asked. But . . .'

'What is it, Marty?' Uma asked.

'You got a problem, mate, then spit it out,' Pahoo said.

'It's just ... did you have to kill the bunny?'

Pahoo turned around to face me. He looked very angry indeed. 'What do you know about it?'

'I just told you, I don't know jack shit.'

He nodded and turned back around.

'But did you have to kill the bunny?'

Pahoo suddenly leapt over the low divide between front and rear.

'Hey,' Siobhan shouted, briefly jerking the Microbus out of lane.

'Listen, mate,' Pahoo said, getting right up in my face. 'It's not for you to tell me my bleeding business. What you know about the land and the spirit couldn't fill a flea's arsehole. I can trace my heritage and bloodline back a thousand bloody years. What I learned, I learned from the ages and mages, understand?'

'Ages and mages. Is that like Dungeons and Dragons?'

'You bloody fool. If I have to slit the throat of a fucking rabbit, you better know it's for good reason. And I ain't explaining what I do to the likes of you.'

'Then perhaps you would explain it to me,' Uma said.

'Eh?'

'I am, of course, familiar with the use of animal sacrifice in the Druidic tradition. Indeed, a boon of the land may only be begged at a price.'

'That's right,' Pahoo said.

'But also as I understand, such cost need not involve loss of life. I, too, was taken aback by your choice of ritual last night. I recognize the place of such a sacrifice, but I question its efficacy given the forces against which we are allied.'

'You saying you disapprove?'

'I am not passing judgement. I am merely voicing a concern. I believe that Marty was disquieted by the ritual and I am pointing out that I share some of that disquiet.'

'Yeah!' I said, though it didn't quite have the killer effect as when you're in grade school.

Pahoo didn't respond right away and I thought I saw real anger flare up in the little man's beady brown eyes. Siobhan must have sensed it, too, because she had one hand off the wheel and was half-looking at Pahoo in anticipation. He took a deep breath and the angry look faded away.

'Sorry,' he said, though he was looking only at Uma. 'I should have told you ahead of time. You're right, the ritual can be done without a living sacrifice, but it's much harder. It requires the harvesting of a whole range of plants and herbs under a new moon. I don't like performing sacrificial rites, none of us do, but we didn't have the time to do it any other way. Time is of the essence, isn't it? Especially with the Thule trailing us.'

'This is true,' Uma croaked.

Pahoo turned his head my way. 'And though I don't enjoy killing things, the local rabbit population is out of control. It's a symptom of a larger imbalance in the ecosystem, but in this case more damage will be done if the population growth goes unchecked. As I had to sacrifice something, it made sense to use a rabbit.'

I nodded, but an image from the night before coalesced in my mind. I saw Pahoo in the middle of the Druids' circle, dying rabbit in hand, his eyes alight with . . . I'm not sure. But I'd be tempted to say glee.

I glanced at Uma, who was also nodding. Pahoo shrugged and climbed back into his shotgun position. Uma unfolded her arms and leaned back in her seat.

But she still didn't look too happy.

It took us about an hour of driving on the back roads – the Microbus was never going to win any checkered flags outside a rust derby – before we saw the signs for the motorway at a town called Exeter. I needed to hit the can, so Siobhan pulled off and we found a roadside cafe to get breakfast. Pahoo announced that he wasn't hungry and wanted to take a walk, so the three of us went inside.

The cafe was a trucker's joint, a cramped little place with tiny plastic tables and benches, run by a small, middle-aged woman who sucked lemons professionally. She looked like she should have tattoos, though none were immediately visible. The menu was a tad limited; I craved pancakes and maple syrup, both apparently unknown in the United Kingdom, but settled for bacon and eggs.

'Beans or chips?' Lemon Lips asked.

'Beans?' I asked.

'Right,' she said and walked away.

'Beans for breakfast?' I asked my companions.

'Of course,' Siobhan said.

'You do not have to eat them, Marty.'

'Maybe I won't.'

I did, of course. Turns out they go pretty good, though the eggs were runny and the bacon fatty and limp. But as you know, I don't like to complain.

I wanted more coffee after the food, though even *I* had learned by now that there are no free refills in England. I started to say something about this practice (it may not have been the first time I'd mentioned it), but Siobhan just rolled her eyes, threw up her hands and went up to the counter to buy another round.

'Works every time,' I chuckled. Uma raised an eyebrow at me.

'So what's going on here, Uma?' I said

'What do you mean?'

'There's something not right. I can feel it. You're walking around like you've got a tack in your shoe. And you've got a look on your face like *you're* the one whose whole life is serving up beans in a greasy-spoon truck stop. What gives?'

Uma sighed. 'I am not sure, exactly. I . . . what do you mean when you say that you can feel that something is not right?'

'He means he's missing his room service at the Savoy Hotel,' Siobhan said. She put two cups down on the table, and went back to get the third, but lemon lips had followed her over with the last coffee.

'That is not what you mean, is it Marty?'

'No,' I said. 'Which isn't to say it's not true.' Siobhan raised her coffee cup to me. 'But it's not what I mean.'

'What is it then?'

'I'm not sure. I . . . you know, as a rule, I'm not a gut-feeling kind of guy. More like: let it stew till it's old and soft and easily digested. Despite tagging along with you on something like a whim. I used to be more impetuous when I was younger and it got me into a lot of trouble.'

'*Bazooka Beach Massacre*,' Siobhan said.

'Thank you, Pauline Kael. I've learned the hard way to try and think things through when I can.'

'So tell me what you are thinking.'

'I think something doesn't feel right,' I said and laughed. 'I admit I'm more than a little at sea about this whole . . . adventure. I mean, I'm still not sure about what we're doing. But even so, it *did* feel sort of right when we started, the thing in Canterbury.'

'And now?' Uma asked.

'Something's out of whack. I hate to sound like a squeamish little kid, but that ceremony last night – the bunny thing – it's sitting in my tummy like bad seafood on a hot day. I just don't know why.'

Uma glanced over at Siobhan. 'Okay, I feel it, too,' Siobhan said.

'Much as I hate to agree with TV lad here. Is there something amiss?'

Uma swirled her coffee and stared into the cup. The cup was stained, but there were no dregs to read. 'I share your feelings. I, too, was disturbed by the ceremony, though I accept Pahoo's rationale for it. As far as I am able to discern the rite was successful and the leys fortified against abuse or appropriation. Like both of you, I cannot pinpoint the source of my disquiet, which in itself creates a further . . . imbalance.'

'What about,' I looked around and lowered my voice, 'what happened at Woodhenge? Is it possible that the Thule are still tracking us?'

Uma deferred to Siobhan.

'Anything is possible. But I don't think that anyone is following us. Not physically, anyway. If they are, they're better than me. And not many are better than me.'

I believed her.

'We are, however, leaving a trail that may be followed,' Uma said.

I frowned, then the little light bulb lit up. 'The rituals,' I said.

'Yes. The Thule are not without their own significant magical resources. They could not help but note the changes we have already induced in the ley grid. Indeed, it is not impossible that they will anticipate our future actions. We need to proceed with alacrity now – and care – lest the Thule get ahead of us. If they have not already.'

'I don't much like the sound of that,' I said.

'Nor I. But I do not know what else to do. Although the ley grid is accessible at many places, there are just the few key nexus points. We have now visited two. It would not be difficult to guess where we will be going next.'

'So what's the plan, then?'

'Our plan,' Uma said, 'is to move quickly.'

'Check,' I yelled at the waitress.

'Bill, Marty. In England, you pay the bill.'

A portentous pronouncement if ever I heard one.

We made better time on the motorway, though we still weren't setting any land speed records in the VW. I'd bought a newspaper when we stopped, not to read, but to plug up the holes in the floorboards. I went for the tabloid that had published the pictures of me from the nudie movie. The front page of that day's copy headlined a story

about a set of brothers in a pop band I'd never heard of, who'd
supposedly taken contracts out on each other's lives. It wasn't an
entirely slow news day, though, because they also found room to
run a big photo of a giggly blonde spilling out of her kid sister's
dress. Who says this isn't the golden age of journalism?

I napped in the back seat, woke up just as we drove past Bristol,
checked out the scenery – which was about as exciting as the
roadside view from your average US Interstate – and went back
to sleep. I didn't wake up again until Siobhan pulled off to refill
on gas – petrol, petrol, *mea culpa* – as we approached the outskirts
of Birmingham which, as the chorus of titters from my companions
informed me, is *not* pronounced like the city in Alabama. Damn
that Randy Newman.

I suggested lunch, but the only place around was one of those
prefab roadside chain restaurants which the others weren't too
enthusiastic about. Given that the logo for the place resembled a
guy sticking his finger down his throat, I figured they knew what
they talking about. Uma went into the little gas station shop and
bought a bunch of pre-packed sandwiches. Siobhan and I both had
eyes for the tarragon chicken salad on whole wheat, but when I saw
that *all* the sandwiches were buttered anyway, I decided to play the
martyr and let her have it. I got dibs on dessert, though, and went
right for the Lion bar. Siobhan gave me the hairy eyeball, but with
traces of tarragon chicken still on her lips, she had no choice but
to grin and bear her Snickers.

Uma had a Turkish Delight. I didn't even like the sound of it, but
de gustibus and all that.

I was back up front with Siobhan, while Pahoo and Uma dozed
in the rear. The landscape, as we hit the road for the last stretch to
Liverpool, lacked the raw drama of Cornwall, but was considerably
more engaging than the boring flats of Kent. It sort of reminded
me of the look of the land in the American northeast and, of
course, I gave myself a mental slap on the forehead for suddenly
recognizing *why* those clever old pilgrims called it *New* England.
Duuuhhh . . .

If you're in a car long enough, the very rhythm of the road begins
to have a kind of hypnotic effect. Siobhan hummed to herself – there
was a big rusty gap and dangly wires in the dash where the radio
should have been – and her tune added to the soporific effect. I'm
sure I didn't doze off, I could feel the bumps and jolts from the VW's
dead shocks and I know my eyes were open, but I drifted into a
semi-conscious state. The road through the windshield turned into

a kind of dark screen on which my sleepy brain projected its own disjointed movie.

I saw the image of the thrown Snapple bottle slipping end over end and exploding across the skinhead's face in the convenience store in London. I saw the burned-out store and the smiling face of the dead little Asian girl in the T-shirt. A boxy van that overtook us on the left became Becket's tomb and a puff of white smoke from its tailpipe formed into the vision of a golden ley line connecting the black sepulchre with the jagged, tempest-tossed ruins of Tintagel Castle. A messy splotch of roadkill jumped up into the air and became the little grey rabbit that Pahoo slit open and sacrificed under the night sky. The ethereal images all swirled into each other across the fuzzy dream screen of the M6 motorway, none really even bothering me – the dread figures in black didn't appear – until I saw the old man standing in the middle of the road.

'Look out!' I yelled.

Siobhan jerked the Microbus onto the hard shoulder, braking hard as she did. Pahoo and Uma were both thrown out of their seats and Siobhan spat a stream of curses. Fortunately there'd been no one close behind us, or it might have resulted in a nasty accident.

'What in Christ's name is wrong with you?' Siobhan snarled.

'Shit,' I said. 'I'm sorry.'

'What were you yelling at?'

'Marty?' Uma said, rubbing the elbow she'd smacked against the side of the bus. Pahoo just squinted at me like a Sergio Leone extra.

'Sorry,' I said again. 'I just . . . I could have sworn I saw someone in the middle of the road. I mean, I couldn't have, but it was very real.'

'You were dreaming, mate,' Pahoo said. 'Maybe you should sit in the back.'

'What exactly did you see, Marty?' Uma asked.

'It's crazy. It's . . . I saw an old black man. In a dress.'

'Couldn't be,' Siobhan said. 'You only see them on the M25.'

'And a hat,' I added, remembering. 'Like a Shriner's thingamajig. What do you call it? A fez.'

'Did it go with the dress?' Siobhan said. 'Was it an ensemble?'

'What did he look like?' Uma asked. She seemed very interested. 'Are you sure it was a dress?'

Closing my eyes, I tried to recreate the image in my mind, but it remained faint. 'It could have been a robe he was wearing. And it wasn't a fez, but it was sort of shaped like that. Like a sand pail.'

'What about his face?'

I shook my head. 'He was black, I'm sure of that, but I can't remember any other details. Look, Pahoo's right: I must have dozed off without realizing it. It had to be a dream.'

'Mmmm,' was all Uma would say.

'I'm really sorry,' I said again to Siobhan. Without thinking, I had touched my hand to her forearm. Her eyes flicked down to my fingers and for just a second I thought I was going to lose them.

'It's a wanker's world,' she said and laughed.

She pulled back onto the road.

We hit Liverpool a little after three o'clock and not a moment too soon. The temperature gauge on the Microbus was rising fast and it was a race to see if we could get where we were going before steam started billowing out of the engine. The heavy afternoon traffic slowed us down, as did the fact that none of us knew the way around the city. Uma was riding up front again and had a big road atlas opened on her lap, while Siobhan cursed all the other drivers.

'Man, oh, man,' I said, eyeing the decayed cityscape. 'And here I thought Gary, Indiana was the ugliest city on Earth.' I rolled down the window, stuck my head out and took a deep breath. 'Nope. Gary wins. At least Liverpool doesn't smell.'

'Wait till we get nearer the river,' Siobhan warned.

Liverpool had the look of a place that's not only past its moment, but that has just plain given up hoping that another moment might ever come again. Cities do have lives, and just like people, you can never entirely write a city off. There's a kind of well-spring of life in every burg, like a beating heart, however faint. As long as there's life, there's hope, as they say. It's just that, to push the metaphor, Liverpool looked like it needed a transplant.

As we drove out of the city centre, the neighbourhoods got worse and worse. Mere urban decay changed before my eyes into raw blight. Much of the town seemed to be one immense, deeply run-down housing estate. Our rusty Microbus was practically a cream puff compared to what was parked on the streets.

'You sure you know where you're going?' I asked.

'I am afraid so,' Uma said.

There weren't a lot of people out walking the streets and none of those I did see were white. The area reminded me of where I'd been attacked in the East End, but if that was an Asian slum, this one was all black. For the first time since I'd been in England, I felt the cold touch of LA race paranoia crawling up my neck.

'This one, I believe,' Uma said, pointing at the road leading to yet another bleak housing estate.

Tebbit Gardens, it was called, though the only green I could see was a pile of rotted shag carpeting spilling from an overturned garbage skip. There was a vandalized security shack at the entrance to the estate, along with the stubby remains of a barrier gate. If there had ever been a guard, his bones must have long since been picked clean by tiny rat teeth. Abandon hope all ye who enter here.

Uma put the atlas away and glanced at a piece of paper she dug out of her purse. She offered hesitant directions to Siobhan who was holding the wheel a little tighter and scanning the terrain with visible concern. Nasty speed bumps – 'sleeping policemen' they call them here, which I found inordinately clever – were set into the road at absurdly short intervals. The VW's meagre suspension didn't like them at all. Me and my sore butt heartily agreed.

'There, I think,' Uma said, pointing at one of the many identical four-storey buildings. A long outdoor balcony ran along each floor, with drying clothes draped over every available inch of rail. There must have been thirty flats on each level, though it seemed like they had to be awfully tiny. I could only think that an extremely sick, misanthropic scumbag would design a building like this. Even for cheap public housing, whoever imagined such a place would be a good idea? But then imagination probably played little part in it.

A group of kids threw rocks at each other out in front of the apartment block and I saw a toddler running madly up and down one of the balconies. I couldn't see an adult around and I prayed that the kid wouldn't tumble off the edge. At least not on top of me. A sign identified the place as 'Morning House,' though 'Tory' had been painted in red over the 'Morning'. Uma glanced at her paper again. 'This is it.'

'This is what?' I asked.

There was no parking lot as such, nor any available spots on the street, though there were lots of signs warning about not parking anywhere. Siobhan simply pulled up as close to the front door as she could. The kids with the rocks stopped assaulting each other as we got out. I had a feeling that they didn't see a lot of white, or even Asian, faces round about these parts. Siobhan walked over to them.

'This is for looking after the vehicle,' she said, and handed a five pound note to the biggest kid. 'If you do a good job, there'll be another when we go.'

The kid took the bill, but had a smirk on his face as he pocketed it.

'If you don't do a good job . . .' Siobhan said. She looked around, then walked over to a boarded-up window on the side of Morning House. She traced an imaginary 'X' on the wood with her finger, then looking straight at the kids, punched her fist right through the inch-thick board.

'Do we have an understanding?' she asked.

There was no trace of smirk left on the big kid's face. I saw his Adam's apple bob up and down as he swallowed.

'Yes, Miss,' he said.

As we walked into the building, Uma leading, I expressed my admiration for Siobhan's technique in dealing with the little thugs.

'But how do you that without hurting your hand?' I asked.

'What makes you think it doesn't hurt?' she replied.

The elevator wasn't working, but otherwise the inside of the apartment block looked a lot better than the outside. I had expected it to be filthy and covered in graffiti, but the walls were spotless and the floors clean enough to eat off. The people who lived here might not be able to control their external environment, but they sure enough looked after their own space.

We walked up to the top floor, emerging from the dim stairwell out onto one of the long balconies. The path was no more than two feet wide – how the hell did anyone get furniture in and out of these places? – and the railings less than three feet high. I glanced down and felt a brief swish of vertigo. I did observe that the gang of kids had barely moved, and that the big one was actually polishing a spot on the VW's front fender with the hem of his T-shirt. On a superficial level I can't say much for Siobhan's interpersonal skills, but there surely is successful method lurking in the depths of her madness.

An array of contrasting smells greeted us as we walked past the row of closed doors. I couldn't put a name to any of them other than to say *spicy*. I felt a little rumble tumble through my tummy. Uma stopped at a door about a third of the way down the row. At first I thought there was something hanging off the door, but as I got up closer I saw that an intricate design had been carved into the wood. This pattern was far less ornate than any of the Celtic runes I'd seen so far, in fact, it looked like a child might have etched it, but though the pattern couldn't have been more different, it still reminded me of the runes a bit because, well, it *radiated* a sense of power. Uma raised her hand to knock, but the door swung open before she could touch the wood.

A small, youthful black woman in a colourful sun dress – it looked like someone had taken a roto-tiller to a peacock and wiped the mess up with the fabric – stood in the doorway. She looked at each of us in turn, then offered the brightest, sunniest, just plain happiest goddamn smile I've ever seen in my life (and I know the former casting director of *Baywatch*). She had perfect white teeth and thick red lips, with a fat tongue to match. She curtsied in an exaggerated manner and beckoned us inside with a sweep of her arm.

'He be waitin',' she said, still smiling.

I nodded to her as I walked on past, and damned if she didn't wink at me. Of course, she did the same to Pahoo, so it's not like it was any big deal.

That spicy smell was thick as flies inside the flat. The ceiling felt awfully low, but perhaps that was because of the brightly coloured streamers which draped down from the corners. More patterns like the one on the door, but in equally vivid colours, graced tapestries hanging on the walls. There was no furniture to speak of, just piles of thick cushions strewn about the carpeted floor, and a few low tables piled high with platters of fruits and nuts. I could see into a kitchen just off the main room, where another young woman, even prettier than the first, was clattering about. She glanced up at one point and smiled.

' 'Allo, my children,' a basso profundo thundered.

I turned around and saw an enormous black man walk into the room and plop himself down onto a sprawl of cushions. The floor shook as he landed.

'Gaaaawd-damn,' I said.

I'd seen him before. Sort of.

It was the man I thought Siobhan was about to run down on the motorway.

Baba Dutty, as the big man called himself, possessed more avuncular hospitality (not to mention body mass) than any dozen Italian maitre 'd's. From the moment we sat down the food and drink didn't stop coming. Damn good eats, too, none of that hippie banana bread shit that Pahoo's yahoos had offered up. We started on plates of fruits and nuts – mango, cassava, green bananas, oranges, limes, almonds, pecans, peanuts and more – worked our way through a series of finger foods on up to a main dish of jerk chicken and red beans with rice nicer than anything I'd ever had *either* side of New Orleans. I washed it all down with lots of Red Stripe lager, though out of respect for Baba Dutty, who insisted after all, I forced down a generous tumbler of spiced rum. I hate rum, but I liked this. I liked *everything*. If Santa Claus was a black man, Baba Dutty was surely his brother.

The conversation had been trivial, if genial, mostly about our drive up, the weather, the quality of the food. As the two young women were clearing away the dishes and bringing out yet more plates of fruit for dessert, and while Baba Dutty was preoccupied with charming Siobhan – ha, good luck, chum! – I leaned over and whispered into Uma's ear.

'So you and the big Baba here are good friends, huh?'

Uma shook her head. 'I have never met him before,' she told me.

'Damn!' I said, looking the place over again. 'What kind of spread must he put out for the folks on his 'A' list?'

The two women who'd been serving us disappeared down the hall, and a third young woman, more drop-dead gorgeous than either of the others, came in and sat down at Baba Dutty's feet. (They had to be size 15s, so there was plenty of room; she could have grown mushrooms in their shade.) She, too, wore a rainbow-splattered dress that would have been hideous on 99 out of 100 women. But she was the one. It rode high on her thighs and low on her chest, revealing acres of flawless brown skin that glistened like glazed caramel. A serpentine silver band crawled up one bicep and a clattery jumble of wooden bracelets dangled from her wrist. Golden motes swam like guppies in her coffee-brown eyes, and zing-zing-zing went my heartstrings when she smiled.

Baba Dutty scooped her up in his tree-trunk of an arm. 'Dis be Alourdes,' Baba Dutty announced. He reached around and gave her ample breast a playful squeeze. 'My number one lady.'

Alourdes slapped his hand and laughed. Then she looked at each of us, smiled and bowed her head. 'You are all welcome,' she said.

Despite my best efforts, my eyes repeatedly drifted lemming-like to the sight of Alourdes' alluring thighs. Her dress was so short, there seemed a perpetual prospect of glimpsing the Statue of Liberty. Hollywood, you'll be shocked to learn, is full of greaseballs whose eyes are blind to anything other than the nearest bit of T&A. I've always hated men whose lives are centred around the act of mental undressing. (Of course, there are a considerable number in town whose lives centre around the act of *physical* undressing, but at least they have the courage of their convictions; though the sentences on those convictions can be harsh.) I realized I had joined their ranks when I saw Uma flash what, for her, had to be a dirty look. I turned and stared at the wall hangings.

'You are a gentleman of taste and discernment, my friend,' Baba Dutty bellowed at me.

'Huh?' I said. I had been stealing another peak at Alourdes' legs from the corner of my eye. Not unlike the corner of Hollywood and Vine.

'Erzulie Freda,' Baba Dutty said, gesturing at one of the tapestries.

'And a happy Hanukkah to you,' I said.

Baba Dutty squinted slightly, but the smile remained on his big round face. 'No, no. De *vévé* on de banner. De mark of Erzulie Freda, de *loa* of sensual love.'

'Very nice,' I said. Actually, it looked like a heart surrounded by stars to me, the kind a not very talented third-grader, with attention deficit disorder, perhaps, might make for his mom on Valentine's day. Nifty colours, though. 'How's that again?'

'Erzulie Freda,' Alourdes said. I forced myself to maintain eye contact – and no other kind – with her. 'She is the *loa* of passionate love.'

'*Loa*,' I said.

'*Loa* are like spirits, Marty,' Uma explained. She was talking to me like *I* was the third-grader. 'In the vodoun system of belief, the *loa* exist in all realms of the natural world. They are the links, the guides between the world of men and the realms beyond.'

'More dan dat,' Baba Dutty said, looking very serious. 'De *loa* guide our actions, structure our lives and our spirits. Dey are de link, yes, between man and god.'

Alourdes nodded along. Pahoo and Uma, too. Only Siobhan looked puzzled by it all.

'Voodoo,' I said.

'*Vodoun*. Baby Dutty is an *houngan*, Marty. A vodoun high priest.'

The fat man dipped his head slightly, closing his eyes in acknowledgement. Alourdes beamed up at him.

I'm always the last to know.

Just after sunset, with a last finger of twilight going under for the third time, we followed Alourdes downstairs. She led us around the back of the building and across an overgrown playground with a rusty old slide and a busted see-saw that was all see and no saw. The kids Siobhan cowed on our arrival had disappeared, but a group of slightly older and harder-looking black teenagers sat along the top of a stone wall, drinking from cans, laughing and smoking dope.

Alourdes had put on a slightly less revealing dress – you had to duck your head an inch or two to see her pudenda – but she was still a sight. The boys stopped to watch her pass, and I saw Siobhan tense up, expecting an encounter. One of the boys said something, his West Indian accent so thick I couldn't make it out, but the meaning was clear from the leer on his face. One of the others shook his head nervously and tugged at his buddy's shirt, but the lech only pushed him away, put two fingers to his lips in a V-shape and flicked his tongue obscenely at Baba Dutty's woman.

Alourdes never broke stride. She half-glanced at the leering teen and made a brief gesture at him. The kid immediately grabbed at his throat, his tongue no longer dangling from his lips so much as protruding. I saw his eyes bulge wide and heard the choking noises that gurgled out of him. He tumbled off the wall, landing hard on his knees, before falling over onto his side.

His companions all ran.

Alourdes continued on to the neighbouring block of flats, stopping in front of the only door that wasn't defaced with graffiti. She opened the door without any key and gestured for us to proceed inside. Uma went in first, followed by Siobhan and then Pahoo. I paused before passing through to glance back at the kid, still rasping on the ground as he rocked back and forth. I looked at Alourdes, who shrugged and then gestured again at the kid as if flicking away a mosquito. The kid sputtered, then loudly inhaled what sounded like a zeppelin's worth of air. He stopped shaking.

Alourdes smiled her killer smile and gestured for me to enter. I smiled back, eyes front, thoughts as clean as virgin snow.

I moved fast.

The room was unlike anything I had ever seen.

Check that. Once, when I first started working on *Salt & Pepper*, we shot in a studio on the old MGM lot. This was just before they tore the whole thing down and turned it into a series of mini-malls or car dealerships. One day when I was supposed to be at the MGM 'school', studying algebra or geography, I hooked off and went wandering. By chance, looking for the ladies' toilet with the notorious peephole, I stumbled into the props warehouse.

Everyone knows that shot at the end of *Citizen Kane*, the one they ripped-off at the end of *Raiders of the Lost Ark*, where you see the immense hall of *chassarie* that marks all that's left of sad Charlie Kane's life.

It had to have been based, maybe even shot, in the MGM props building.

There were hundreds, maybe thousands of lamps. Desk lamps, standing lamps, candelabra, chandeliers of every conceivable size and type. There was furniture: thrones from medieval castles, footstools from eighteenth century French chateaux, kitchen tables from fifties sitcoms, even the busted-up chifferobe that started all the trouble in *To Kill A Mockingbird*. One whole annexe, three floors high and a football field in length, contained nothing but framed pictures. Thousands of them, culled from 2,000 years of would-be, but never-were living room walls.

It was amazing. It was beautiful.

And they burned it all down.

Baba Dutty's temple – his *oufò*, as I later learned it is properly called – reminded me of that wondrous place in miniature.

The room sat in the basement of the building. It was a slightly irregular rectangle, interrupted by a pair of metal support poles painted with vivid, swirling colours and designs and which had small round platforms or stages, no more than a foot high, built around their bases and covered in lace. A series of banners and tapestries, like the ones I'd seen in Baba Dutty's living room, hung along the walls, but the floor was nothing but loosely packed dirt.

The front of the room, what I realized eventually was an altar, was the amazing bit. A series of cantilevered shelves had been built all across the short wall and about halfway down the length of the longer walls. Every usable inch of the shelving, and a good bit of the floor, harboured some manner of tchochke.

There were jars and bottles and containers of every possible size, description and colour. Gallon-sized earthenware jugs painted with bold, dizzy patterns and crystal shot-glasses filled with drops of dark, sticky liquid. Rum and whisky bottles, some full, some empty and stuffed instead with bright flowers, both paper and real. There were sealed Tupperware salad bowls – don't ask me what was inside – and one whole rack with nothing but plastic Head & Shoulders shampoo bottles. Did *loa* have dandruff problems?

Mixed among the glassworks were numerous dolls. Homemade corn husk critters with beans for eyes and pasta shell smiles, and naked, blinded Barbies with safety pins through their plastic titties. Littering the place were beads and rhinestones and enough cubic zirconia to stock a home shopping channel. Bells, big and small, some without clappers. And clappers, some without bells. I saw drums of all sizes and shapes on the altar and on the floor. There were starfish, light bulbs, a stuffed alligator that said Greetings From Asbury Park, NJ, gourds, a broken umbrella, a T-shirt emblazoned with 'Vote Howard the Duck,' a copy of *Life* magazine with a black-and-white picture of the Queen's coronation on the cover, several small flutes, a dozen or more watches (none digital), a Magilla Gorilla pez dispenser . . .

And in the middle of it all, a cross. It was crudely fashioned from wood that looked like it had been salvaged from a shipwreck, painted red and standing about four feet high. Various trinkets and jewels had been fastened to it, and meticulously plaited strands of hemp were suspended from the top and bound about the ends of each arm. Perched at the apex was a battered human skull wearing an extremely stylish pair of RayBans.

Oh yeah, and a Tweety-Pie baseball cap.

I started laughing.

Uma shot me a look, but I couldn't stop. It came from deep in my belly. Or perhaps my unconscious.

'Are you laughing wit' us or at us, my friend?' a voice behind me boomed.

I turned to look at Baba Dutty, fitted out in his priestly mauve robes.

'With you. Definitely with you.' I turned around and gestured at the temple, the incredible array of crazy objects which littered the place. 'This is . . .' – I shook my head, searching for the right word – '. . . great. It's absolutely amazing.'

Baba Dutty came up to me and slapped me on the back. He laughed his big man's laugh.

'You ain't seen no'ting yet,' he promised me.

My eyes had gone so big that you could have pocketed pool balls in the sockets.

Alourdes, legs spread wide, lay on the floor in front of me convulsing like the unholy offspring of Jerry Lee Lewis and Little Richard. Her back was arched like a 'D' as she braced herself with her feet and her shoulders, her head turned awkwardly to support her weight. One hand rubbed furiously at her crotch (clothed, barely), while the other went back and forth from one tit (exposed, totally) to the other. Her tongue flicked out of her open mouth like a viper's as she heaved and moaned, her features screwed up in orgasmic rapture of a kind I've never had the pleasure of being responsible for. My eyes kept returning to her nipples, red as fine claret, big as silver dollars and hard as ball bearings.

'Heh-heh,' I said.

It had started calmly enough. Baba Dutty showed us where to stand, slightly off to the side of the altar, known as the *pedji*, in clear view of the gaudy support pole, which Baba Dutty referred to as the *poteau-mitan*. With a bit of white chalk, he quickly sketched patterns, *vévé*, on the floor around us and told us not to stray outside their limits during the ceremony. Then he left, Alourdes trailing behind him.

'What gives?' I asked Uma.

'Baba Dutty is going to perform a service, in invocation of the *loa*. He was very insistent on our participation.'

'Is this part of what we need to do? To protect the ley grid?'

'Not exactly,' Uma said. 'This is more in the way of a general blessing over our endeavour. Liverpool is not a focal point for the leys. Quite the opposite in fact. The energies here have been poisoned for many years, perhaps beyond salvation.'

'Why's that?'

'Bad karma. Liverpool was the centre of the slave trade for more than a century. It has been nearly two hundred years, but the residual force of that horror remains. It is the reason that Baba Dutty makes his home here.'

Pahoo snorted. 'This stuff gives me the creeps. I don't grok to this African malarkey,' he said. Siobhan didn't say anything, but I saw her studying the various doodads and gewgaws and got the feeling she didn't disagree.

'He's not going to kill a bunny, is he?' I asked. Frankly this set-up didn't strike me as any goofier than Pahoo's Druidic rites. It was a lot more colourful, if nothing else, and definitely featured hotter babes. Uma started to answer me, but was interrupted by the sound of drums.

Alourdes, dressed in a sheer white cotton smock entered the *oufò*, followed by a dozen black women, also in white, but each wearing a kerchief of fire-engine red. Several of them went and picked up drums and bells, the others unfurled small gaily-coloured flags and pennants. Alourdes carried a white banner with a simple *vévé* sketched in black. She flapped it in front of her as if fanning someone who'd fainted. The drummers started beating out a steady rhythm, punctuated by the odd ring of a bell. The procession made one circle of the smaller *poteau-mitan* at the rear of the temple, stopping to chant in French or Haitian or some variant patois, before dancing their way to the larger pole near us. Neither Alourdes, nor any of the other acolytes acknowledged our presence. They circled the big pole three times, chanting, banging drums, waving their flags and following a precisely choreographed parade about the temple. The women with the drums put them down on the small stage at the base of the *poteau-mitan*, and all except Alourdes stepped back to form a circle in front of the altar. Alourdes waved her banner a few more times, chanting in what sounded to me like an odd mixture of French and Latin, before laying the *vévé* down on the ground in front of the little stage. She, too, stepped back into the circle.

Baba Dutty, his satiny purple robe glowing in the candlelight, entered last. I saw that he was wearing a fez-like hat, and I shuddered, remembering my vision on the road. He held out in front of him a wooden rattle – the kind of present you might give to Rosemary's Baby – which he shook in a different a direction every few steps. He, also, chanted in the same odd dialect as Alourdes. At the smaller *poteau-mitan*, Baba Dutty paused and reached into his pocket. He sprinkled what looked like a handful of grain on the small stage. He pulled out a bottle – like the kind from planes or hotel mini-bars – sprinkled a few drops of whatever was inside on the stage and then stood the open bottle in the middle of the grain. He shook his rattle again, then approached the larger *poteau-mitan*.

One of the women handed Baba Dutty two pieces of chalk, one pink, one white. He waved his rattle at her and she went back to her place in the circle. He walked around the pole three times counter-clockwise then put the rattle down and dropped to his knees. With a piece of chalk in each hand he frantically drew *vévés* on the ground. As he drew, two other acolytes came over and placed various objects – open bottles, bits of cake, grain, one of the Barbie dolls – on top of the stage. Then Alourdes approached, holding a live chicken in her hands.

'Oh man, just when you thought it was safe to go back in the temple,' I groaned. Uma elbowed me in the ribs. *Hard.*

Baba Dutty finished off the last of the *vévés* and stood up. He nodded at Alourdes. Holding the chicken under one arm, she took a sip from each of the bottles, then nibbled at a piece of cake, a kernel of grain. Baba Dutty picked up the rattle and pointed it at her. She put the chicken down on the stage. It didn't move at first, then went straight for the grain and started pecking. Before I could even figure out what was happening, a spurt of red spurted up into the air and the chicken's head was off its body.

Turns out chickens *don't* run around very much with their heads cut off.

Everyone in the circle started to chant as Alourdes touched her fingers to the still spouting blood, then to her lips.

'Ugggh,' I groaned.

Alourdes threw the chicken over her shoulder, holding it by the feet. She went first to Baba Dutty, who also tasted its blood. She then walked, her back to the other women, presenting the dead chicken to them. A few tasted the blood, others dabbed it on their fingers and drew crosses on their foreheads. When each had had a go, Alourdes returned to the *poteau-mitan* and held the chicken's corpse up to each corner of the room. She laid it down on the stage and stepped back into the circle.

Uma must have sensed I was about to say something, because her elbow found my ribs again before I could open my mouth. I looked at her and she just put a finger to her lips in a 'shhh' gesture. I glanced at Siobhan and Pahoo, but both were completely absorbed by the ceremony.

Several of the women picked up their drums and started banging away discordantly. Baba Dutty chanted in his patois like a mad Sufi singer, shaking his rattle like Baby Huey on a double speedball. The women swayed back and forth, eyes closed, as the circle moved slowly around the stage. Then Baba Dutty stopped, and one by one the women in the circle quit their gyrations.

Except for Alourdes.

The others pushed Alourdes out of the circle and she tumbled to the ground in front of the *poteau-mitan*. She jerked in heaving spasms, her eyes open wide, revealing nothing but whites. She flopped from her front to her back to her front like a fish on the deck of a trawler, riding a foot or more into the air with each spasm. Instinctively, I stepped toward her, but Uma grabbed my arm and held me back.

The others continued to chant and sing and bang drums, Baba Dutty shook his rattle like the leader of a crazed Bar Mitzvah band as Alourdes fell flat onto her stomach. Slowly, she got to her hands and knees, ass raised high, her cheek still pressed to the ground. She wiggled her ass to and fro in a patently provocative, deeply sexual way. She pulled her skirt up over her hips revealing her bare bottom half. Her hands clawed at the dirt floor as she arched her back and raised her buttocks even higher. With a scream that was equal parts pleasure and pain, she lurched forward as if penetrated from behind. Still on hands and knees, she violently rocked back and forth as if being fucked doggy-style. We're talking German Shepherd. She screamed her passion with each invisible thrust.

Just as quickly, Alourdes shot to her feet. She reached down and grabbed bits of food from the raised stage. She blindly stuffed grain and cake into her mouth, missing with lots of it, barely chewing what did make it between her lips. She swooped up a bottle of clear liquid and poured it into her mouth and mostly down her chin. Even from several feet away, I could smell what must have been 150° proof rum. She reached down again and for a nasty second I thought she was going to pick up the chicken carcass and try and stuff that into her mouth, too, but then her whole body jerked around in another direction.

She turned to face our little group. Still jerking and shaking like a Tourette's patient, she spasmed her way across the floor, right up to the boundary formed by the *vévés* Baba Dutty had sketched on the ground. Her eyes remained half-rolled up in her head, but for a second they unrolled and she stared straight at me.

Except I don't think it was her.

Her eyes rolled back up like a window-shade, and that's when she fell again to the ground on her back and started rubbing at her cunt through the thin white fabric of her dress. With claw-like hands she tore away what remained of the top half of the dress, revealing fully the plentiful brown mounds of her perfect breasts. Her nipples were almost as hard as I was.

Then she just stopped.

I felt a perverse desire to applaud or stuff a fiver in her garter, but I managed to suppress it. Alourdes just lay there, eyes shut, breathing hard. She was still half-naked, but she didn't look sexy to me anymore, just . . . vulnerable. I wanted to cover her up and took a half-step toward her when Uma again grabbed my arm. I meant to step back, I really did.

But I couldn't.

My legs seemed to move of their own accord. I was aware of having no control over them as my right foot passed over the line of the *vévé* and onto the temple floor. I felt a jolt of electricity as my foot made contact with the ground. It shot up my calf and thigh, raising every hair on my leg as it went. I felt Uma let go of my arm – I think maybe she got a shock – and was aware of turning my head to look at her. Her eyes had gone wide with concern and fear. I didn't much care for the look, though I suspected I wore one to match. I'm sure I tried to shake my head at her as if to say 'I don't know what's happening here, help!' But I don't think I succeeded.

I felt my left leg cross over the *vévé* border, and as it did, just before it touched the dirt on the floor of the *oufò* proper with another shock of current, I flashed back to a ceremony in a different sort of temple, when the spirit of Shoki, the great Japanese warrior, had entered me.

Then it all went black.

When I opened my eyes again, I found myself sprawled across the fluffy cushions in Baba Dutty's living room. Uma held my hand and looked concerned, Siobhan let out a big sigh.

'What the fuck is going on?' I croaked.

Baba Dutty's enormous head bobbed into view. He had a devilish smile on his face as he scratched thoughtfully under his chin. He had taken off his robes, now wore an 'I love Bob Marley' T-shirt. He pointed one of those Kielbasa-sized fingers at a spot between my eyes.

'So, it be you,' he said, nodding. 'It be you.'

Who the hell was he expecting, Danny Bonaduce?

FIFTEEN

'I feel like I've been hit by a truck,' I said.
  ' 'Ave you been?'
  'What?'
  ' 'It by a truck,' Baba Dutty said.
  I thought about it, though it wasn't an especially difficult question.
'No,' I admitted.
  Baba Dutty grunted.
  'But I imagine that this is what it must feel like,' I explained.
  'I don't t'ink so.'
  'You don't?'
  He shook his head.
  '*You* ever been hit by a truck?' I asked.
  'Oh, yeah,' Baba Dutty said, nodding.
  Well, he had me there. Teach me to crack wise.
  'And I also been t'rough *danse-loa*, been chosen and mounted
as *cheval*. Many, many times. De truck it not nearly so bad.' He
looked thoughtful for a moment, scratching under his chin again,
then added: 'It were a small truck, t'ough.'
  After I'd come around and saw that nothing was broken, bleeding
or missing, Baba Dutty explained what had happened to me in the
oufò. '*Loa* come and take over your body. Just like they do for
Alourdes. Dat is de purpose of de ceremony, don't you see.'
  'I don't think I do. Might have been nice if you had warned me
ahead of time.'
  Baba Dutty flicked a glance at Uma, who sat across from me sipping
a cup of tea. 'Dat's why I draw the *vévé*. It should 'ave protect you.'

Uma put her tea down and leaned forward. 'The patterns Baba Dutty drew on the ground should have, oh, hidden us from the *loa*. Made us invisible to them. During the ceremony, the *loa* choose an initiate whom they will mount. That is to say, who they will possess and through whom they can act and make physical their presence.'

'And you do this all the time?' I asked. 'Like instead of renting videos?'

Baba Dutty nodded in a does-the-pope-shit-in-the-woods way. 'Wit'out *loa* to protect us, to guide us, our lives would drift like old wood in de sea. Dey point to de right path t'rough life.'

'So these *loa* are like gods or something, yeah?'

'T'ere is only one *Gran Maître*. Only god be god,' Baba Dutty said. '*Loa* are *loa*.'

'Vodoun is a monotheistic religion, Marty. The *loa* are, forgive me, Baba Dutty, the *loa* are more analogous to angels in Christian belief.' She looked dubiously at the big black man. 'It is a weak analogy, though.'

'*Loa* are not angels. *Loa* are *loa*,' he repeated.

I thought back, trying to remember what happened after I stepped out of the protection offered by the *vévé*, but it was just a big black space. 'So what happens exactly when the *loa* possess you?'

'You saw *loa* mount Alourdes,' Baba Dutty shrugged. I remembered the way she had gone down and all fours, looking like she was being entered from behind. I instinctively clenched my buttocks. 'Dat was Maîtresse Erzulie.'

'Erzulie?'

'Erzulie is the *loa* who is the embodiment of sensual love,' Uma told me.

Made sense. I mean, as much as any of this could.

'And so what, Erzulie . . . mounted me, too?' I asked.

Uma and Baba Dutty exchanged another look. A lesser man might have started to feel paranoid.

'No,' he said. 'You were *cheval* to Maître Carrefour, keeper of de gate between worlds.' That had a too familiar ring to it. 'Carrefour is husband to Erzulie, don't you see.'

'I see,' I said, though really I didn't. 'So Carrefour came down to look for his car keys, have a word with the missus, what?'

'More 'n a word,' Siobhan muttered, then coughed. She'd been so quiet I hadn't even noticed she was in the room.

'Why? What happened?' I forced a weak smile, suddenly feeling

like a drunk trying to find out exactly what kind of fool he made
of himself at the office Christmas party.

Uma and Siobhan were conspicuously looking the other way, but
Baba Dutty was fearless. He held up the fat index finger of his right
hand. He raised his left hand and formed a perfect circle with his
thumb and other index finger. He pushed his right finger into the
circle and quickly rammed it in and out several times in the only
symbol more universally recognized than the Coca-Cola sign.

I felt the blood drain not just out of my face, but down my torso,
past my guts and right into my ass. I went white as a Klan rally.

'What are you saying? That we . . . that I had sex with Alourdes?'
I whispered.

Baba Dutty smiled and shrugged. 'Maître Carrefour exercise his
conjugal rights. Shit 'appens.'

I was having trouble breathing. '*I had sex with Alourdes?*' I
said again.

'It had no'ting to do wit' you, nor wit' Alourdes. It were de will
of de *loa.*'

'I had sex with Alourdes?' I practically screamed, then I lowered
my voice. 'In front of everybody?'

'Marty . . .' Uma said, but she had no thought to finish and was
finding it hard to look my way.

Siobhan, bless her tiny dyke terrorist heart, dangled a sprig
of comfort at me. 'It didn't last very long,' she said, then
coughed again.

Well, I felt *so* much better.

Baba Dutty asked me to take a walk with him. I still felt kind of
rough, not to mention mortified, but something told me that it
might be a good idea. We left the others in the care of Baba Dutty's
'ladies'. There were enough of them to staff an escort service and I
wondered what the neighbours made of Baba Dutty's set-up. Given
the way Alourdes dealt with the snotty teenager, I reckoned there
weren't a lot of complaints.

It was getting on for midnight as we wandered out of the flat.
Baba Dutty set a leisurely pace as we strolled around the dimly-lit,
overgrown grounds of the council estate. There was nary a soul
to be seen and almost all the windows of the hundreds of flats
in the dozen or more buildings we went past were dark. In any
other circumstances I would have been paranoid to the point of
scared-shiftless to be out in such a place. With Baba Dutty at my
side, I didn't even feel the need to glance over my shoulder.

'You 'ave been *cheval* before, yes?' Baba Dutty asked.

I thought again about the time I was possessed by the spirit of Shoki. 'Yes,' I said, 'but it wasn't for a *loa* and it wasn't, well, it wasn't quite the same.'

'*Loa* 'ave dere ways. Dey show demselves in different faces to different people, don't you see. But dey still be *loa*.'

'How did you know?' I asked.

'Hah?'

'About me. That I'd been, um, *cheval*? How could you tell that?'

Baba Dutty let out a brief bark of his thunderous laugh. I expected lights to snap on in the nearby flats. 'You marked boy! Don't you know dat?'

I didn't much like the sound of that. 'What do you mean "marked"?'

Baba Dutty stopped in his tracks. He put his hands on his hips and took a look around. I followed his gaze, but there wasn't much to see.

'You see dere?' he said, pointing at a nearby bus stop. The glass had all been knocked out of the little shelter, the plastic seats busted up and the timetable defaced with graffiti. 'What you see?'

'A bus stop?'

'You asking or telling?'

'It's a bus stop,' I said.

''Ow you know dat?'

'It's, well . . .' I pointed at it then sort of threw up my hands and shrugged. 'It's . . . a bus stop. I mean, it's not a very nice one, but it's got the . . . thing and the, you know and . . .' I should have been a poet.

'Yah?' he coaxed.

I let out an exasperated sigh. 'Well, there's a goddamn sign, isn't there? It says "bus stop".'

'Dat's what you got, boy. You got a big fucking sign over you head. I tell you: you can't read dat sign, you don't know dat's a bus stop. You can't read de sign, you don't know dat you been marked. Me, I can read since I'm a baby boy. Dat's what make me *houngan*.'

I tried to look up over my head. If there was a sign there, I'd have bet it flashed 'SUCKER' in big neon letters. I couldn't see a thing, of course.

'So what does it mean? Marked for what?' I asked.

'I t'ink you a kind of window, a doorway. Maître Carrefour he

mount you when he not even called. Dat's what surprise me so.
For *loa* to come wit'out invocation, not even the *vévé*, it a very
unusual t'ing. Carrefour, he come because he 'ave to, don't you
see. He trying to tell you somet'ing. Tell to us all.'

'But tell me what? What's the message?'

'Maybe not for me to say. But you special, boy. I keep my eye
on you.'

I thought he was being a bit obtuse, but then I'd yet to meet a
holy man of any stripe who didn't talk in fortune cookies, especially
when he didn't really know what he was talking about. 'Uma said
something to me,' I said, thinking out loud as much as making
conversation.

'Yah?'

'She said . . . she thought that I was maybe a kind of magnet
or something. A focal point, she said, for . . . energies. I didn't
know what she meant, to tell you the truth, but I wonder if that
has something to do with it.'

'Could be. Dis Uma, she know t'ings.'

'But what does it all mean?' I pleaded. 'I assume that you're part
of this crusade against the Thule, right? I mean, that's why Uma
brought us here, isn't it?'

Baba Dutty's eyes widened and he looked all around us at the
mere mention of Thule. 'We all looking at de same evil.'

'But what's your stake in it? How does your . . .' I was about
to say mumbo-jumbo, but caught myself –' . . . magic fit in with
Uma's. Or Pahoo's. You guys make for an odd family portrait.'

Baba Dutty held up the back of his right hand to me. He touched
the skin with his left finger. 'Dis 'ere my stake,' he said. He bent
down and picked up a handful of soil from the ground. 'And dis.
Dis was a cursed place for people like me, Liverpool. You know
dat millions of Africans was condemned to misery and deat' from
dis place.'

'Actually, I didn't know until earlier today. Not the kind of thing
the tourist board mentions, you know.'

'An empire dey built on de spoils of my people. On de
pain of their lives. You can call it ignorance, you can call
it apat'y, but the hist'ry is dere to be read and remembered.
The T'ule, dey would rewrite de hist'ry, don't you see. De
T'ule would build a whole new empire on de backs of slaves.
Many of d'ose slaves would be black, like me sure enough.
But many more would be brown, like Miss Uma Dharmamitra.
And so many, too, would be as pale even as your Miss Smyt'e,

t'ough I admit I 'ave never before seen anyone quite so pale
as dat.'

We both laughed.

'So de family portrait is not so very strange, I t'ink. The picture de
T'ule would paint, would be much 'arder to set your eyes upon.'

'And you think that Uma's right, that I have a part to play in the
fight against them?'

'I be certain of it. You got a job to do yet, boy. Dat is surely de
reason for why Maître Carrefour take you for *cheval*.'

'I suppose.' I sighed thinking about what had happened, what
I didn't actually *remember* happening. 'Still, I wish he had just
faxed,' I said.

The others were eating (again) when we got back to the flat. Despite
living in a run-down housing estate, Baba Dutty clearly wasn't one
to pass up a nosh. I reckoned that the *houngan* business had its
rewards.

I wandered down the hall to use the toilet. The door was locked,
but just as I was about to go back down the hall, it opened in front
of me and Alourdes came out, still adjusting her skirt. This one
almost hid some of her thighs, not that it should have mattered at
that point.

' 'Allo,' she said and smiled.

'!'

She gave me a little pat on the belly as she squeezed by, and was
halfway up the hall before I found my voice.

'Wait,' I said.

She turned around, still smiling, and looking like a million dollars.
Hell, ten million. Christ, this was weird.

'I, um, I feel like I should, you know . . . since we . . . I mean, I
usually at least buy breakfast the next morning.'

Alourdes walked back up the hall and stood very close to me. She
took my hand in hers and looked up into my eyes. 'What happens
during the *danse-loa* is the will of the *loa*. We are all their vessels
on earth. We trust in them and in their wisdom. I remember no
more of what happened than do you. I take joy in being *cheval* for
Erzulie. What happened can only be for the greater good.'

She raised my hand to her lips and gave me a gentle kiss. Then
she walked down the hall with the kind of grace that klutzes like
me can only dream about. I felt a little better, but I also felt kind
of sad. I wanted her more than ever, but here I'd already had her
and forgotten her.

Goddamn *loa.*

I felt sure that there was a moral to be learned here somewhere, but fucked three times to France if I could figure out what it was.

We crashed at Baba Dutty's place that night. Uma and Siobhan got a room to themselves, while Pahoo and I made do with the pillows on the living room floor. Wonder of wonders, Pahoo availed himself of Baba Dutty's shower before going to sleep, though he was still wearing the same raggedy clothes. He started snoring almost as soon as he put his head down and I had to resist the temptation to smother him with one of the fluffy cushions. After a while I managed to nod off.

I didn't sleep well. Tired as I was, I had one of those nights when you feel like you haven't slept at all, but then the nasty light of morning arrives to tell you that you have. I had a sense of lots of bad dreams, though despite flashes of images and hints of sour emotion, I could only remember the details of one.

I was standing in a deep pit, white flames all around. Sweat poured out of me as the heat grew intense. In a circle above me stood the five figures in black, as faceless and menacing as ever.

'Choose,' a cold voice commanded.

I looked down and saw tiny figures perched in the palm of each hand, like the humunculi from *Bride of Frankenstein*. In my right hand sat June Hanover and Kendall my agent; In my left, Uma and Siobhan.

'Choose!' the voice screeched again.

I didn't want to. To close either fist would be to kill those I held.

The flames grew hotter, the black figures loomed larger. I knew I was out of time.

'CHOOSE!'

I woke with a start.

Alourdes came out, wearing only a thin robe (what, I wondered, did she do in cold weather?), to start preparing breakfast. The sight of her jolted a brief memory of an earlier, highly pornographic dream, but even that little spark faded as soon as she disappeared out of my sight into the kitchen.

Baba Dutty soon came down the hall nodding his good mornings, followed a few minutes later by Uma and Siobhan. Baba Dutty wore a pair of lime green slacks and a tweed sports jacket over a salmon pink shirt. I had to look the other way. Alourdes and one of the other Baba-ettes served up the food. I stuck with coffee and a bit of vaguely fruit-like cake, but the others tucked in like vultures on St Carrion's Day. Baba Dutty, I wasn't surprised to see, had seconds and thirds of just about everything. He wasn't the most polite of eaters – he chewed with his mouth open and grunted as he ate – but you could just see the pleasure in his face with every morsel that he swallowed. Usually, sloppy eaters make me a little sick, but here was a man who enjoyed his food so much that it became kind of infectious. I found myself wolfing down a plate of fried green bananas when I was sure that I wasn't even hungry. Damned if I didn't top it off with a couple of beignets, too. And half a cassava melon.

Baba Dutty leant back in his chair when he was done and rubbed his enormous belly. He let out an explosive belch (the neighbours must have thought the Concorde was flying overhead), then smiled broadly. Reaching into his jacket, he pulled out a cigar and rolled it between his fingers, then ran it under his nose. He bit off the end and spat it onto his plate. Patting at his pockets looking for a light, Baba Dutty suddenly remembered that he wasn't alone this morning.

'Smoke?' he asked, pulling a couple more stogies from his pocket.

Uma respectfully declined, while Pahoo looked appalled. Siobhan went for it though, so I figured what the hell.

In LA, the only people who are worse pariahs than smokers are those without cars. It doesn't much bother me since cigarettes are about the only vice to which I haven't fallen prey, but I've never minded a nice cigar. There's just something about them – yeah, yeah, I know: phallic symbolism and all that; well, fuck Uncle Sigmund. Broderick Crawford turned me on to the pleasures of cigars back when we both did guest shots on an episode of *Longstreet*. I might even have got hooked on them, but I was always sort of afraid I'd end up with his voice. Or worse, his stomach.

Baba Dutty lit me up. I took a puff, let it out, looked at the cigar. Puffed again.

'Wow,' I said. Siobhan seemed to be enjoying hers, too.

Baba Dutty laughed.

'What are these?' I asked.

'Cubanos.'

'But they're illegal. How do you get them?'

Everyone at the table looked at me oddly. Siobhan shook her head at me between exquisite puffs.

'What?' I said.

'You in England, boy. Cuban cigars not illegal here. What's a matter wit' you?'

'We've not nearly enough time to explore that subject,' Siobhan said.

'No,' Uma said, 'we really should be going.'

But Baba Dutty wouldn't budge until our cigars were just ashen memories. Alourdes had to bring more food, too, because it took us forty-five minutes to reach the bitter, sweet end. Not a bad life, this *houngan* gig.

'So, what's the agenda for today?' I asked, when we finally got up from the table.

'I am afraid we have another rather long drive ahead of us,' Uma said. She glanced over at Siobhan who merely shrugged her indifference. I think she was still off in Cuban cigar-land.

'Dwarfie Stane?' Pahoo asked.

'It is the logical place to go,' Uma said, nodding. 'It is what I had planned. Baba Dutty?'

The big black man scratched his chin. 'I t'ink so. T'ough I don't fancy de trip, me.'

'You mentioned that before, Dwarfie Stane. Sounds like something an incontinent midget leaves on the sheets,' I said.

'It is a place, Marty,' Uma said. 'It is in the very far north of Scotland, in the Orkney Islands. On Hoy. Orkney, it is said, is the site of the mythical Ultima Thule. Though I have my doubts. What it most definitely is, though, is a vital spiritual nexus. Dwarfie Stane is an ancient tomb and temple, and a place of enormous power.'

'Unpredictable, t'ough. Difficult to manage.'

'But worth the chance, don't you think?'

Baba Dutty nodded. 'We take my car,' he said.

'Now this is a set of wheels,' I said. I gave Baba Dutty a big thumbs-up. 'Where in the world did you get it?'

'Dis my baby,' he smiled.

Baba Dutty's car was a huge, American Ford LTD. It was least fifteen years old, canary yellow and absolutely immaculate. It was a dinosaur, the last of a breed of gas guzzler that post-industrial economics had cruelly consigned to the dustbin of history. Tragic, really.

'V–8?' I asked.

Baba Dutty just waved his hand at me dismissively. Of course it was a V–8; is water wet?

'Beautiful,' I mused as I ran my hand along the perfect finish.

'I bet this bad boy scares the ever-loving shit out of Mini drivers.'

We loaded our stuff in the trunk – even with the didgeridoo, there was enough room left over for a small travelling circus – and stashed a stuffed-to-the-brim picnic cooler on the floor in back. I should have figured Baba Dutty for a snacker. Siobhan got in the right front door, forgetting that the car was left-hand drive. She started to slide over, but Baba Dutty held up a finger.

'No one drive de boat, but me,' he said. Siobhan started to scowl and I got ready to duck, but then Baba Dutty added with a wink: 'Not even you, pretty miss.'

Son of a gun, it worked. Siobhan nodded and took shotgun.

Which only goes to prove that flattery can, indeed, get you absolutely anywhere.

Studying Baba Dutty's road atlas, I made it a depressing 700-plus miles to John O'Groats, the northernmost bit of the Scottish mainland. From there it would be a boat ride across to Hoy.

We never made it out of town.

As it turned out, we were lucky that the Thule made their move when they did. Perhaps they were overanxious or overconfident. Maybe they figured it would be easier to take their shot on the wrong side of the Liverpool tracks, where cops are few and far between. Maybe they just didn't give a shit.

We had barely pulled out of the confines of the housing estate and onto the surface streets of town when they came roaring up beside us on the right. It was a white Ford Transit van – stolen, I assume – with a logo for Caravia & Son Software stencilled on the side.

'Go!' Siobhan yelled at Baba Dutty, before I even knew what was happening. He reacted fast, flooring it, but not quite fast enough. The van's panel door flew open and inside squatted two balaclava-clad figures with machine pistols in their hands. They opened fire immediately.

I hunched over as the bullets blew the glass out of the driver's side windows. The interior was peppered with a thousand tiny shards, but incredibly none of them cut me. I felt Baba Dutty swerve and bounce the LTD off a couple of parked cars to our left, then gun the engine for all it was worth. I could hear horns blaring and brakes squealing, and a very loud crash off to our right. I didn't hear any more bullets and hazarded a look up.

The van had been forced to slip in behind us as the street ahead narrowed. Baba Dutty was driving like a man possessed – figuratively speaking; I think – with blood streaming down the side of his neck. He seemed to have pretty good control of the car, though, so I guessed, or prayed, that he'd only been cut by the glass and not actually shot. Siobhan had produced a gun and was in the process of rolling down her window. I glanced over at Uma, who had hunkered down as I had. Her hair was full of bits of glass, but she, too, was looking up and didn't seem to be hurt. Pahoo had curled himself into a little ball on the floor. He wasn't moving, but I didn't see any blood.

Baba Dutty had to slow down as we came up on a large roundabout. The van took advantage and ploughed into us from behind. Siobhan, who had crawled halfway out the window, nearly went flying. I had to lean over and grab her by the leg to keep her from tumbling out of the car. More gunshots came from behind. I heard the crack of the back windscreen and the whump-whump-whump of bullets tearing up the beautiful fabric of the seats in front of me. I let go of Siobhan and hunkered down again.

Baba Dutty had to swerve around the car in front that was patiently waiting to edge onto the roundabout. Baba Dutty didn't hesitate again, just pulled right out into traffic, evoking a chorus of bellowing horns and screaming tyres. I heard more crashes off to the side, but the LTD kept going. There was another spurt of gunfire, but this time it came from in front. I looked up again.

Siobhan was hanging out the window firing at the van that still dogged our tracks. I couldn't tell if she hit the target.

Baba Dutty went three-quarters of the way around then feinted a turn off to the left before jerking the wheel to the right and slamming the LTD up over the concrete kerb and onto the grass verge in the middle of the roundabout. He cut directly across the diameter of the circle, jumping back off onto the road on the opposite side.

The van had gone for his feint, then broke hard to make the correction. Cars slammed into each other at all points on the roundabout, including a tiny Fiat that folded like an accordion against our rear fender. The impact sent the LTD into a fishtail, but Baba Dutty handled the skid like a stunt driver. He made for the nearest radial off the roundabout.

Behind us, I saw the white van follow our tracks up onto the grass verge. The truck jumped about a foot into the air as it hopped the kerb and sort of wobbled as it landed on the grass, but still it kept on coming. Baba Dutty had made it across the lanes of the roundabout and was turning off onto the side street when another chorus of gunshots rang out and I felt at least one of our rear tyres go to Michelin heaven.

Baba Dutty was good, but he lost control of the car with the blow-out. The LTD careened left, then right across the central divider and into the oncoming traffic. I saw Baba Dutty make a final desperate jerk at the wheel as a McDonald's truck loomed in front of us, then I shut my eyes.

I heard the explosion, then I felt the impact.

The explosion came from the van blowing up behind us. I was too busy cowering, but Siobhan saw it all and later told me that even as Baba Dutty managed to avoid collision with the looming truck – he couldn't miss the lamppost on the sidewalk, which explained the impact – the van took another leap as it came off the grass and back onto the roundabout. But that wobble I had seen on its first landing must have been a busted axle, because the second landing wasn't anywhere near as neat. In fact, the van flipped right over onto its side and skidded cleanly across the roundabout.

Its impact with the McDonalds truck wasn't anywhere near as neat.

Flames billowed out of both vehicles as I turned around to look. The van was engulfed by fire, as was the back half of the truck. We all watched for a few seconds, inhaling the scent of Big Macs a-frying, but no one emerged from either vehicle.

'Dat what it like to be 'it by a truck,' Baba Dutty said, nodding. Bloody pedant!

'We've got to move,' Siobhan yelled. She was already out of the car, gun in hand held down at her side.

'Is anyone hurt?' Uma asked.

Pahoo uncurled from his foetal position. He'd suffered a few cuts after all and looked kind of dazed, but still moved with alacrity. I felt a twinge in my back – a lick of whiplash, I suspect – but I, too, got out of the car fast. I pulled Uma out behind me.

Baba Dutty was a bloody mess. He'd taken a full blast of window glass, but incredibly hadn't been shot. He held one hand against his neck to staunch a still spurting cut, but seemed more distressed by the state of his LTD than anything else. There wasn't a piece of it that hadn't suffered damage.

'You can't get d'ese parts no more,' he said, shaking his head.

'We've got to bloody *move*,' Siobhan said. She grabbed one of the bags from out of the trunk of the car.

The roundabout and the adjacent streets had become a parking lot. The scream of police sirens could be heard and people were still running from the site of the burning wrecks and agonizing over the damage to their cars. I realized that we were only about twenty yards away from the fire and that the McDonald's truck might still blow. No telling how much gas was in its tank.

Trying to look inconspicuous – it wasn't too hard in all that chaos, despite Baba Dutty's bloodied, high voltage rags – Siobhan, shielding Uma under one arm, led us across the street and down the block. Surely witnesses would finger the LTD, which would eventually be traced to Baba Dutty, but there was no time to worry about that now. We had to be elsewhere when the cops arrived and started asking questions.

We turned a corner and had walked about a block and a half through the run-down neighbourhood, far enough to put the accident scene completely out of sight, when Baba Dutty suddenly went down.

One second he was standing beside me, the next he was on the dirty sidewalk, a fountain of blood spurting from a big hole in the middle of his middle.

Two seconds and three shots later, Siobhan went down as well.

Pahoo just stood there looking confused, but I leapt at Uma, tackling her to the ground and rolling in the direction of the nearest doorway. I heard a scream from across the street, then another series of gunshots. A window shattered above me and I saw bricks in the building I was rolling toward burst into shards just to my left. There was a brief pause in which I could hear the gurgle of Baba Dutty's blood as it poured out onto the hard concrete. Pahoo had tumbled down beside him.

I looked up and saw two dark figures moving quickly up the street toward us. One held a rifle with a sniper's scope, the other a semi-automatic pistol. A car came down the street and briefly slowed at the sight of the carnage, which proved a big mistake. The man with the pistol fired off a stream of shots through the driver's side window. The car scraped two parked cars before slamming to a stop.

The two assassins turned back our way, but they'd made their mistake. Siobhan was on her feet. I don't know where they had been secreted, but she now held a gun in each hand and was running full tilt at the shooters. She was screaming at the top of her lungs, firing both guns as she ran.

The crazy dyke was ambidextrous.

The sniper went down right away. I saw him get hit in the belly, then two more to the groin, capped by an ugly kill shot to the throat. His rifle went flying up in the air as he fell.

His partner kept his cool and started shooting back, running straight at Siobhan as he fired. I saw the Irishwoman take a bullet in her left thigh, but it barely slowed her. The gun in her left hand was empty and she tossed it, but she continued firing with her right. She took another bullet to the torso, but it just spun her around before she was back on her vector, emptying her clip.

It was a fucking massacre of one.

The Thule killer took a series of hits smack dab in the chest. I saw waves of blood geyser out of his front and back. His inertia kept him going for a couple of paces, but by then Siobhan had zeroed in on him. His left eye went with one shot, his teeth with a second, the entire top of his skull with the next three.

Siobhan popped another clip into her gun and continued shooting at what, by then, had to be a corpse. When the second clip was spent, she started kicking at him. I saw her foot sink deep into the mush that had been the killer's head before I had to look away.

'Marty.' Uma's voice was faint. I looked down and realized I was still lying on top of her. I was practically smothering her.

'Are you all right?' I asked, rolling off.

She nodded and took a deep breath. 'Baba Dutty,' she moaned.

Pahoo had risen to his knees, looking dazed. I think he was checking himself for bullet-holes and couldn't believe that were weren't any. Uma lurched over to Baba Dutty's side.

The *houngan* was still breathing, but I didn't think he would be for long. He didn't look as bad as the dude Siobhan had mashed, but there was a gaping hole in his chest, and though I don't like to dwell on it, I thought I could see no doubt vital organs poking through the gap. He had taken a second hit to his big belly and was blood-soaked to his toes.

'Oh no,' Uma cried. She ever so gently touched the back of her hand to his dark cheek.

Baba Dutty's eyes fluttered open. He breathed in fractured, white-noise rasps. With blood still gurgling out of him, it could only be a matter of seconds.

'Maa . . . maaa . . .' he croaked. I couldn't believe he was even *attempting* to speak. Uma leant over, taking hold of his hand, and pressed her ear to his lips. I could see her straining to understand what he was trying to say.

'Marty,' she said, looking up. 'I think he wants you.'

I got down on my knees beside him. I took a quick look around

– Christ, surely the cops would be here any minute – then dropped my head next to his.

'Baba Dutty,' I whispered.

'Maa . . . maaaa.'

'It's me, It's Marty,' I said, but I couldn't tell if he understood. He blinked and I didn't think his eyes would open again. But they did. His pink tongue flopped out of his mouth and flicked at his lips. He turned his head and looked me straight in the eye.

'*Maa-maître Ca-arref-efour*,' he said.

'What?'

I don't know where he found the strength, but he jerked his hand out of Uma's grasp and reached toward me. He pressed his palm to my forehead. I could feel the sweat and blood, the coldness that would soon possess him entirely.

'*Maître Carrefour*,' he gasped.

His hand stiffened against me for a second and I felt very cold. I felt his death.

He was gone.

SIXTEEN

~

'Penny for your thoughts,' I said to Uma.

'I do not think they would be worth even that much right now.'

She sat across from me on the Intercity train, nervously drumming her fingers against the dirty window. The train's motor thrummed beneath us, but though departure time had passed fifteen minutes earlier, there was no sign of any movement. Pahoo sat beside me, arms folded, his eyes moving back and forth from the view of the platform through the window to the narrow aisle that ran the length of the car. I detected a slight twitch in his left eyelid.

The seat beside Uma was vacant. Siobhan should have been sitting there, spitting insults at me. The emptiness practically screamed its presence.

'She'll turn up in London,' I said, looking at my watch for the hundredth time. 'She knew that's what she'd most likely have to do. It's only a few hours and her, you know, problems may have needed a lot of attention.'

'I know,' Uma said.

'I thought she seemed okay when we left her. Didn't you?' I asked Pahoo.

The little guy gave me a dirty look before grudgingly nodding. 'I suppose.'

Thanks a lot, pal, I thought. Uma drummed a faster beat, tango to salsa.

'I mean, these friends of hers will know what to do, right? They'll have a doctor or whatever?'

'I am concerned that they may not be entirely happy to see her,'

Uma said. 'She . . . left the movement in a somewhat acrimonious manner.'

'But surely they'll help her out under the circumstances. She said herself that you're never *really* out.'

Uma sort of nodded. We sat there in silence for another five minutes before the train finally lurched to a start. It moved a few yards up the platform, stopped, then jerked back into motion. It did that three more times before pulling out of the station for real. The sudden movements set my back to aching again.

'I suppose it'll be a quiet trip back to London, anyway,' I said. 'We can hum U2 tunes all the way.'

'Not a chance, tosspot,' a less-than-lilting Irish voice said from behind.

Looking like death warmed over by a wonky microwave oven, Siobhan plopped down in the empty seat. She grinned as she laid her hand on top of Uma's.

'I think it's time we talked about danger pay,' she said.

Neither Uma nor I wanted to leave Baba Dutty's bloody body on the sidewalk like that, but we didn't have any choice. Siobhan came limping back over. The wound in her thigh was messy, but she'd been lucky: the shot to her side had just grazed her and the first bullet, which caught her left bicep, had passed right on through. It wasn't even bleeding anymore. She looked like hell, though.

'Get up,' she yelled.

I didn't have to be told twice, but Uma was lost in another world as she stared down at Baba Dutty, still cradling his head. His blood was all over her.

'Move, bitch!' Siobhan shrieked.

Uma looked up at her, a confused expression on her face that seemed to say: *there's really no call for that sort of language.* I could hear sirens again and a small group of locals gathered at the far end of the street, keeping a safe distance, but watching us intently.

'We'd better skate,' Pahoo said. Miraculously, like Uma, he hadn't suffered a scratch.

'Come on,' Siobhan said, and she yanked Uma up by the arm.

Pahoo led the way to the nearest corner, away from the crowd of witnesses. We must have made quite a sight, what with Siobhan limping and bleeding from her multiple gunshot wounds, Uma half-dazed and fairly covered in Baba Dutty's blood (unbeknownst to me at the time, I had a big smear of it across my forehead, as well) and tiny, filthy Pahoo taking point, still wearing his sixties-reject clothes.

It was a miracle that we got away.

Bullet-holes and all, Siobhan hot-wired the first likely car she came across. She was in no shape to drive, but insisted on doing it anyway. None of us were about to argue. After what happened with Baba Dutty driving, I don't think Enzo Ferrari himself could have pried the wheel from her hands.

She put a suitable distance between us and the scene of our various crimes. We found a public garage at a shopping centre on the outskirts of town and pulled into a dark corner. It was only as we were all sitting there in silence, comprehending to ourselves all that had happened that I paid attention to the smell. I realized I had been smelling it since we got into the car, but I simply couldn't find the mental resources to devote to thinking about it. I suddenly recognized it for what it was.

The car reeked of blood.

'We can't go on like this,' I said.

'Sherlock fucking Holmes,' Siobhan barked.

'Easy,' Uma said. She raised her hand to offer the bodyguard a comforting touch, but realized in mid-gesture that she was about to stroke an entrance-wound. She put her hand back in her lap. 'Take it easy, now. We need to think.'

Uma appeared to have recovered her composure, which I found incredibly reassuring.

'We've got to drive out of here,' Pahoo said. 'Just get the fuck out of Liverpool.'

'No,' Uma said. 'Not in this car. For all we know, the theft has already been reported. It is too big a chance. And Siobhan needs medical attention.'

'I'll be fine,' Siobhan said, not very convincingly.

'Do not be absurd. Obviously, though, we cannot go to a hospital.'

'We could go back to the voodoo palace,' Pahoo suggested.

'The law'll be there all too soon,' Siobhan said.

'Not only that,' I pointed out. 'The Thule must have known we were there. They had to have followed us out of the estate to set up that ambush. They've been a step ahead of us . . . since Canterbury, I think. Though I don't understand how.'

'I agree,' Uma said.

'Oh, fuck-shit-fuck,' Siobhan said. She was clutching at her leg. 'There's only one thing to do.'

Since Pahoo was the only one not covered in blood and grue, we sent him out to do the shopping. He came back with sweat pants and shirts for the three of us; not very stylish, but eminently practical given the circumstances. He also bought antiseptic and bandages to tide Siobhan over for a little while, and paper towels and a bottle of water so that Uma and I could clean ourselves up enough to be seen in public. Though Siobhan limped badly as we abandoned the car, we'd managed to staunch the immediate flow of blood from her wounds. I offered to let her lean on me as she walked, but she only laughed. 'Not even if they'd blown my bloody leg off.'

She made the call from a public phone in the shopping centre. She dialled the number and said one word. She nodded her head and hung up. Then she dialled a second number.

Her IRA comrades agreed to help out her out, but we couldn't be with her when she met up with them. Siobhan was looking paler and weaker by the minute, and Uma didn't want to leave her on her own, but Siobhan just said no, adding grimly 'These are people you *don't* fuck with.'

We left her at a bus stop, having agreed to try and meet at the Liverpool train station later on. If she couldn't make it there, then she'd catch up with us at Uma's Indian restaurant in London . . . whenever. Siobhan didn't even look back at us as she got on the arriving bus. Through the window I saw her walk up the aisle, but all the seats were taken. I watched as she leaned over a guy with slicked-back hair and a leather jacket. She whispered in his ear and he jumped out of the seat and up the aisle so fast, he might have sat on a rat. Siobhan took the seat. The bus pulled out.

'I think she'll be fine,' I said to the others.

We didn't talk much during the trip back to London. The railroad car simply wasn't private enough to talk about anything important, but as much as anything I think we were all of us just too stunned by everything that had happened. Siobhan confirmed that she felt all right, though she admitted that much of that feeling may have been attributable to the truly estimable amounts of drugs she had been administered. Her IRA friends had found a doctor to clean up her various injuries. Even the leg wound proved not to be too severe, though Siobhan visibly winced every time she moved it – so the drugs couldn't have been that terrific – and she limped badly the one time she walked down the aisle to use the toilet.

Pahoo and Siobhan dozed for part of the journey, but Uma and I stared out the window at the dull scenery that went whizzing past.

Uma, I thought, had visibly aged in the past twenty-four hours, her glowing copper skin was dull, and her fine, chiselled cheeks were looking drawn. She caught me staring at her.

'What is it?' she asked. 'What?'

I simply shook my head and tried to look sorry. There was nothing I could say.

No matter how I twisted and squirmed, I couldn't seem to find a comfortable position in my seat. The jolt in the car crash had definitely done something unpleasant to my neck and upper back, and I had a headache that just wouldn't quit. I'd cadged a codeine tablet from Siobhan before she fell asleep, but even that failed to dull the pain which pulsed back and forth across my temples like cuts from a honed pendulum. Though I've never been prone to motion sickness, the rickety-rack rhythm of the train started me feeling queasy. I thought I was going to heave at one point and had to run to the toilet at the end of the car, but I hate barfing (well, who doesn't?) and managed to hold it down. I did take a squat, which made my tummy feel a little better, but as I was washing my hands in the tiny sink I felt an ice pick penetrate the right side of my head. The stab of pain started in my temple and ran straight back through the middle of my skull. It was so strong that I had to grab hold of the edge of the basin to avoid falling to the floor. Just as I thought it had passed, a second bolt of pain detonated in my left temple. This one shot across my forehead to a point behind my eyes. I did go down to my knees with this second attack, but then it, too, passed. I got back to my feet and stood there for a second, wary of further spasms, thinking: stroke. But to my relief there was nothing more, and the headache that I'd had even began to fade. I washed my face with cold water and went back to my seat.

I still felt a bit out of it, but the rest of the train trip passed without incident.

The four of us sat around a corner table in Uma's Indian restaurant near Whitechapel. Siobhan took a seat facing the door, but she had to sit kind of sideways and prop her bad leg up on an empty chair. She was looking even paler than before, if such a thing was possible, and a bar of Procol Harum played in my head. The same crowd seemed to fill the place – so far as I could tell there was never an empty table – and the same bored waiter plonked a cold Kingfisher down in front of me unbidden. He also left plates of hors d'oeuvres and poppadums and chutney, all of which was most welcome.

'Do you want to try to get back up to Dwarfie Stane?'

Pahoo asked. His mouth was full of onion bhaji at the time. It wasn't pretty.

'No,' Uma said. 'Not without Baba Dutty.'

'Poor Alourdes,' I said. 'And the others. Man, did we ever leave them in the shit. The cops must be swarming all over that place.'

'Alourdes can look after herself,' Uma said. 'She is practically *mambo*. A fully fledged priestess,' Uma added before I could crack wise. 'She will have known the moment that Baba Dutty died.'

I didn't ask.

'Couldn't we get her to perform the rite at Dwarfie Stane?' Pahoo said.

'I think not. No. She is *practically mambo*. She does not have Baba Dutty's abilities or knowledge. Nor do I, for that matter. I am sure that Alourdes would agree to take Dwarfie Stane on, but it would be out of pride and I could not allow it. I would not take it on myself.'

'I could help,' Pahoo offered.

'Have you experience of the northern leys?'

'Not really.'

'Then it would be insufficient. You know that already.'

Pahoo looked insulted.

'What's the big deal?' I asked.

Uma looked at me with great weariness. I think she was beginning to feel sorry she'd ever hooked up with me. Most women seem to end up thinking that. I'd love to do something about it, but I haven't a clue what.

'Do you perform Shakespeare, Marty?'

I started to laugh.

'Something is funny?'

'Me do Shakespeare? I suppose I could play Yorick, though typecasting never works, but that's about it.'

'Why is that?'

'I'm a TV actor, you know? Sit-coms and private eyes are one thing, but . . . I can't even stand *reading* Shakespeare much less try to perform the lines.'

'I am . . .' – Uma searched the air – 'Joanna Lumley.'

'Er?' I said.

'Pahoo is . . .'

'. . . Vic Reeves,' he said, smiling. Uma's eyebrows went up, but she nodded. I could see where she was going.

'Baba Dutty was Ralph Richardson. Laurence Olivier. John Gielgud.'

'And Dwarfie Stane is Hamlet,' I said.

'You understand exactly. Though perhaps Macbeth might better complete the thought.'

'So if we can't complete the ritual up there, what happens? I thought we had to reach the last nexus, protect the ley grid before the Thule can do their nasty business to it.'

'I feel now that it is too late for that. I believe the Thule have been anticipating our moves. The fact that they found us again in Liverpool suggests to me that they would be waiting at Dwarfie Stane as well. That avenue is closed.'

'So what happens?' I asked. 'That's it, they win? Baba Dutty died for nothing?'

'No. They do not win. At least not as of yet. Given our actions at Canterbury and Tintagel, Dwarfie Stane leaves us at a stalemate for the time being.'

'I get the feeling that you don't play to tie in this game,' I said.

'No. It remains to be won or lost.'

'So what should we do?' Pahoo asked.

Uma took a deep breath, but she didn't say anything. She glanced over at Siobhan, who looked like a punch-drunk boxer.

'We may have to seek out our King Lear,' Uma said.

I heard Pahoo start to ask her what that meant. I was about to echo his puzzlement when pain exploded through my head. I remember seeing a pattern of falling stars and clutching my temples between my hands. I think I may have screamed.

I was unconscious before I landed face-first in the mulligatawny.

'What's that smell?' I asked.

'Soup,' Uma said. 'Quite nice soup, though not to bathe in. I cleaned it off your face with a wash cloth, but I am afraid bits are still lodged in your hair.'

Which is how I learned that I'd passed out into the mulligatawny. Second question: 'Where are we?'

'Not far from the restaurant. This is my home.'

I was lying on a very comfy couch in a crowded little room. Two walls were lined floor to ceiling with shelves, bursting with books, papers and folders. Several small, brightly coloured prints depicting figures from Hindu mythology dotted another wall, while the fourth was dominated by a large, ornate tapestry showing a confrontation between that nasty-looking, multi-armed Indian bitch with the knives and the dude with the elephant head. The hand-sewn shawl that had been draped over me was also decorated with the image of the queen of hand-jobs.

'Can you sit up?'

Good question, I thought. I tried it, managed to do it in only two goes. Pin a rose on me.

'Zowie,' I said.

'Sorry?'

'I feel like I've been hit by a . . .' I caught myself this time: you can only fool a Firefly twice. 'I don't feel so good. What time is it? How long have I been out?'

'It is just past three in the morning. You have been unconscious for nearly four hours.'

'Goddamn.'

'Do you remember what happened?'

'I remember sitting in the restaurant, talking about what we were going to do, then I just remember the pain. Like a little stick of dynamite going off in the middle of my head. I felt a flash of it earlier, when we were on the train . . .'

'You did not say anything.'

'It came and went. And since Siobhan wasn't moaning with three bullet holes in her, I didn't think a little headache was worth mentioning. I think maybe it's from the car crash. I thought I caught a touch of whiplash when we got hit from behind, but maybe it's worse than I thought.'

'Hmmm,' Uma said. 'How do you feel now?'

Another good question. I sat up a little straighter and stretched, slowly twisting my neck back and forth. 'The headache seems to be gone,' I said. 'My neck's still a little stiff though. And I've got to pee real bad.'

Uma pointed the way to the bathroom. It was tiny, like the rest of the flat, but hospital clean. Little charms and knick-knacks dangled from the shelves and another tiny print of the guy with the elephant ears hung above the towel rack. I did my business and washed up a little, getting as much of the curry soup out of my hair as I could without actually shampooing it.

Uma had a cup of tea waiting for me, along with a plate of biscuits.

'I know you prefer beer, but under the circumstances . . .'

'Thanks,' I said. The tea was just right. I nibbled at the biscuits though I wasn't hungry. (Chocolate biscuits are sort of like Mt Everest: you have to have them because they're there.)

'Do you remember anything from while you were asleep?' Uma asked. 'Any dreams?'

I was about to say no, that there was only the deep darkness, but I suddenly had a flash: a wisp of a vision came to me in that way that dreams creep up on your waking life.

'I . . . I think there was something to do with Baba Dutty, but it's vague.'

'Can you remember anything specifically?'

Uma seemed extremely interested. I closed my eyes and tried to recapture the image. 'I can sort of see him. He's dressed like in the vodoun temple, the *oufò*, in his fancy robes and stupid hat and all, but . . .' The memory kept squirting out of my mental grasp. 'No, I can't get anything more.'

'Try hard,' Uma insisted.

I closed my eyes again, and for a second I had a flash of the pain that knocked me out before. I held my hand against my forehead and felt Uma come over and grab me around the shoulders, but I didn't open my eyes. In the lightning flash that came with the pain, I saw Baba Dutty again. His big, ebony face loomed large in my mind's eye and I saw his lips move as he whispered something at me. Then he was gone and the dark figures that had been haunting my dreams took his place and the blackness returned.

I started to slump, would have pulled another mulligatawny had Uma not been there to brace me. The dizziness passed as quickly as it came, and I opened my eyes.

'Are you all right, Marty?'

'*Mangé ginen*,' I said.

'What?'

'*Mangé ginen*.'

'What is it? What does that mean?'

'I haven't got the slightest fucking idea,' I told her.

'Where are the others?' I asked when Uma came back into the room with a fresh pot of tea. And a beer, god bless her.

'Siobhan is sleeping.'

'No shit? I didn't think she ever let you out of her sight.'

'Siobhan is very loyal. But she was also very tired. And there is little danger here.'

'And Pahoo? I mean speaking of little dangers.'

Uma tittered her little girl's laugh. 'He has opted to find accommodation elsewhere tonight. I got the rather distinct impression that he has a lady friend in town with whom he preferred to spend his evening.'

'Goddamn! That smelly little bastard gets more tail than Brad Pitt.'

'He does seem to have his admirers, I grant you.'

'But you're not one of them.'

'No,' Uma said, making a fish face. 'He's not really my type. I prefer someone . . .'

'Taller? Cleaner? With his own TV series?' I waggled my eyebrows at her, just teasing. Mostly.

Uma gave me one of those 'oh, you kid' looks that your maiden aunt gives you when you say something vaguely suggestive. She still seemed to be thinking about my question though.

'Darker,' she finally said.

Fair enough. I took the hint. 'So what's with John Merrick there,' I said, nodding at the wall hanging.

'Pardon?'

'The elephant man. You've got him all over the place.'

'Ganesh. He is the god of wisdom and of writing, and is lord of the Ganas.'

'*Gonifs?*'

'Ganas. They are minor deities who punish wrongdoers and those who go back on their word.'

'Definitely not on the side of agents then.'

'That tapestry was a gift from . . . well . . .'

'Someone darker?'

Uma blushed. 'Yes. It does not depict an actual scene from legend, but was made specifically for me.'

'Let me guess, the babe with the hands and the hostility issues is supposed to be Siobhan.'

'That is Kali, the destroyer, goddess of death. She annihilates all that she sees, for nothing is eternal.'

'So it *is* Siobhan,' I said.

'Ganesh signifies knowledge, learning, rationality. He is, mythically speaking, no match for Kali's savage fury, but intellectually he is her opposite. Kali, however, is but one aspect of the *Jaganmata*, the earth mother. Kali is her dark face. Her other face is that of 'the bright one', the consort of Shiva. The *Devi-Uma.*'

'No shit?' I said.

'No shit, Marty.'

'So you're named for a goddess?' Uma dipped her head. 'Figures:

I'm named after an Ernest Borgnine character. So Uma and Kali are the same?'

'Not the same. They are different aspects of the *Devi*, the goddess. Bright and dark. Torn between the pursuit and destruction of knowledge, of the wisdom personified by Ganesh. That is how I read the tapestry, at any rate.'

'You're a complicated lady. You know, I don't think you'd like LA.'

'I have never been there.'

'Well, if you do go, definitely make the scene as Kali. Works for Sandra Bullock.'

'You are a very odd fellow, Martin Burns. I honestly do not know what to make of you.'

'I'll have them send you a videotape of the autopsy.'

'And when might we look forward to that?' a certain Irish tenor inquired.

Siobhan stood in the doorway, wearing a badly wrinkled, bright pink bathrobe that I had to believe belonged to Uma; it was unimaginable that Siobhan could ever have bought it herself. She looked like a wad of chewed bubble gum.

'Could be any time now, darling, so best get your licks in while you can.'

'I prefer licking other things,' she said, plopping herself down with a grunt.

'Who doesn't?' I asked. I didn't need a clock to tell it was a giddy hour indeed. 'What are you doing up anyway?'

'You bloody Yanks make more noise than a drum and fife corps,' she complained.

'Sorry,' I said, meaning it.

Siobhan waved it off. 'I'd have likely woken up anyway. I couldn't really get meself comfortable.'

'How's the leg?'

'How's the head?'

Got it. She wouldn't moan if I didn't. Uma poured her a cup of tea.

'Is the little stinker still out shagging?' Siobhan asked. Uma nodded. 'Would you ever believe it?'

'So am I right? Does nobody like Pahoo?'

'It is not so much a matter of like or dislike,' Uma said, playing the diplomat.

'I don't like him,' Siobhan said. I nodded encouragement.

'You are entitled to think as you will, and I agree that he is a difficult personality, but he is a necessary part of what we hope to achieve.'

'But why?' Uma gave me a look of exasperation, but I held up a hand. 'I'm not being nasty. Okay, I'm not *just* being nasty. But what's made him so necessary? Couldn't someone else have played Elmer Fudd at Tintagel?'

'What have you noticed about us, Marty?'

'How do you mean?'

'I mean, has anything in particular struck you about the characteristics of this little . . . fellowship?'

'You mean other than the fact that I stand out like a spare prick at a . . .'

I looked at Siobhan. Then at Uma. The light bulb lit.

'It's quite the little rainbow coalition you've assembled here,' I said. I had thought about it before, when we wandered into those lily-white country pubs out in the sticks. And chatting with Baba Dutty. 'I suppose that's not by accident.'

'There are those who say nothing happens by accident.'

'I know, but sometimes a cigar is just a cigar. No offence,' I said to Siobhan. She shrugged.

'Marty,' Uma said, 'part of the Thule's strength comes from their invisibility, their ability to hide in the cracks, to thrive in places where they are seen but not noticed. It is in those dark places that their forces are mustered, their malignancy given room to fester without hindrance.

'Those like us, with brown or black skin, with desires and feelings which do not accord with those socially sanctioned, with proclivities and beliefs and practices which are considered eccentric – or worse – for us there are no interstices, no gaps in which to hide. Nor should we feel compelled to do so. For hiding is no protection from the Thule; sooner or later they would come for us all, individually.'

' "We must all hang together, or assuredly we shall all hang separately." '

'Precisely. We must join together against the likes of the Thule in public, as you have done, but we must also mount that same struggle in the dark places. Together our voices are louder than any one of us; just so, together our knowledge, our power, is greater than any one of us.'

'So where does a white European male like me fit into all this?' I asked.

'Like we haven't all asked ourselves that question three hundred and forty-seven times,' Siobhan said.

I looked at Uma. She didn't reply, but she had a frighteningly knowing look on her face. I picked up my beer, but it was empty.

Bad omen, I thought.

Siobhan dry-swallowed a few more painkillers before going back to bed. I washed up the plates and saucers while Uma dug a pair of extra pillows out of the closet. She stuck her head in the kitchen to say goodnight, but I wouldn't allow her the easy getaway.

'What is it you aren't telling me?' I asked her.

She emitted a little groan. 'I am *very* tired, Marty.'

We stared at each other for a little while; she did seem to have aged three years in the three nights we'd been away. 'Okay,' I said, turning back to the sink.

Uma just stood there.

'I thought you were tired?'

'I think I am already asleep.'

'So go to bed.'

I struggled to get the tea stains out of an old mug using a filthy sponge and cold water. Uma hadn't moved.

'What is it that you want to know, Marty?'

I turned off the tap, looked around for a towel, ended up wiping my hands on the front of my shirt. Uma shook her head and retrieved a dish towel from one of the drawers. It was too late, but I used it to be polite. I tossed it on the counter.

'What does *"mangé ginen"* mean? You know, don't you?'

'I looked it up.'

'And . . .'

'And it refers to a vodoun rite. It is the ceremony in which invocations and offerings are made to the spirits of the dead. Sacrifices.'

'You're not talking bunny rabbits here, are you?'

'I am not certain.'

'What does it have to do with me? Why did I dream it?'

'I cannot say.'

'Cannot?'

'I am not sure, Marty, and I would not care to speculate right now. Surely you know the saying that a little knowledge is a dangerous thing.'

'Yeah,' I said, 'and absolute power corrupts absolutely.'

'What are you accusing me of?'

I let out a long sigh and shook my head. 'Nothing. Nothing at all. I guess . . . we're both pretty tired.'

Uma nodded. She didn't go, though.

'What are you planning? Something nasty's going to happen tomorrow, isn't it? I feel it.'

'There is a person whom we must seek out. An individual of exceptional power.'

'Powerful enough to stop the Thule? Even without going to Dwarfie Stane?'

'I believe so, yes.'

'So why didn't we just go look for this dude right from the get-go?' I asked.

'Because . . .' Uma had that look I've seen on the faces of exasperated parents confronted with four-year-olds who must know why dogs have four legs, and how come the roof is up and the floor is down and people ride in a hole in the ground. 'There is very great risk entailed in even seeking this person out. And even should we locate him, help may not be forthcoming.'

'Doesn't sound too promising.'

'I make no promises whatsoever.'

'Ask me no questions, I'll tell you no lies,' I muttered.

We both went to bed and to sleep.

SEVENTEEN

~

Pahoo came scratching at the door like a mangy old Tom at eight the next morning. He didn't look like he'd had a lot of sleep, but then he wasn't complaining about it. Miraculously, he was wearing a different pair of pants which could pass for clean on a cloudy day. He, or someone, had even combed the crumbs out of his beard. Must have been quite the night.

Siobhan shambled out of her room looking like ... well, like someone who'd been shot three times the day before. She heavily favoured her bad leg as she limped into the kitchen to pour herself a cup of coffee. She did a double take when she saw Pahoo – I think she'd actually named the objects in his beard and had become attached to one or two of them – but she didn't say anything. Pahoo, in turn, seemed stunned by the sight of Siobhan in a pink bathrobe, but he possessed a strong enough self-preservation instinct not to pass comment.

'Uma still in bed?' Siobhan asked.

'She's gone,' I said.

'What?' Siobhan and Pahoo barked in stereo.

I handed Siobhan a note which I'd found on the coffee table. Pahoo read it over her shoulder. All that it said was that Uma had to find a friend and would be back as soon as she could. We were all supposed to wait for her at the flat.

'Why didn't you wake me up, you fucking arsehole?' Siobhan screamed.

'Whoa! Attitude check, babe,' I said. 'I didn't hear her go out. I slept right on through.'

'Bloody jackass! You should have come to get me as soon as you found the note.'

'Well, that was all of fifteen minutes ago. And you're the goddamn bodyguard. What's the big deal, anyway? Uma can take care of herself.'

Siobhan scrunched up the note and bounced it off my face. 'Hellfire,' she said and limped back to her room.

Pahoo was looking at me, shaking his head.

'Uh-uh, lover boy,' I said, wagging a finger at him. 'I'm *afraid* of her, but you I don't take jack-shit from.'

Like Clark Kent in a phone booth, Siobhan was suddenly back and dressed. She had a gun in her hand and checked the clip. She tucked it into a holster at the small of her back and loosely draped her shirt over it. She moved fast with a barely a trace of the limp.

'You stay here. If Uma shows, keep her here till I get back. No matter what.'

'Where are you . . .' I started to say, but the door slammed and she was gone.

'Shit,' I muttered.

'Anything to eat?' Pahoo asked.

I glowered at him, but some people are just glower-proof. I went back to the living room to have a think. Something I definitely do not do enough of in this life.

Pahoo and I kept out of each other's way as much as possible in a tiny apartment. He stuck to the kitchen for a while, then wandered into a bedroom for a nap. I figured I'd flip on the TV, but there wasn't one in the living room! That led me to have serious doubts as to the whole quality of Uma's character, and worse, left me with nothing to do. I briefly considered giving June Hanover a call, but I didn't know what I would say to her. I know I *should* have given my agent a call – she was probably getting a little frantic – but I couldn't summon up the energy for it. Better to wait and see how things shook out with this mysterious Grand Poobah that Uma hoped to find.

I spent the morning browsing through the mini-library in Uma's living room. A lot of the books were in other languages – there were many in Hindi (I suppose it could have been Urdu, I wouldn't know) and quite a few in French and Latin, of all things – but lots of them were in English, though of a distinctly olde variety. She had a whole series of shelves devoted to philosophy texts and several more to seriously dry reading on theology. But one entire bookcase held volumes on mysticism, mythology and occult practices. I half-expected to find a human skin-bound copy of the *Necronomicon* – or at least an Arkham House edition of *The Lurker at the Threshold* – but while disappointed in both those regards, I did find several volumes on the subject of *vodoun* and African religion. I got so involved in one of them that I never even heard the front door open. Good thing I never made my living as a private eye.

Uma came into the room, Siobhan right behind her. Siobhan still looked a little mad.

'It is only me,' Uma said. People always say that when they come in, though I've never understood why. Until then.

'Yeah,' I said, looking up from the book. 'But am *I* only *me*?'

I wanted to talk to Uma in private, but Siobhan made it clear that she wasn't about to allow her charge out of her sight again. Pahoo had gone for another one of his walks, though beyond the dog turds on the sidewalks, it didn't seem like there was a whole lot of nature for him to commune with in the East End.

Uma wouldn't do anything else until she had a cup of tea. I said no to a beer – they call it tough love – and watched Uma fuss. She didn't use tea bags, but brewed a pot fresh using loose tea. Seemed like a lot of effort for so little reward, but Uma whistled while she worked, so I reckon it was one of those *process* things people are always talking about that I never understand. She got the biscuit tin out of a cupboard and put it on table. *Now* she was talking my language.

'What do you think happened to Baba Dutty?' I asked her, when she finally sat down with her tea.

'What do you think?'

'I asked you first,' I said.

'I am rubber, you are glue . . .' Uma said, shrugging.

I thought of a couple more schoolyard ripostes, filed them back away. 'I think maybe he's in here,' I said, tapping the side of my head.

'That's a tight squeeze,' Siobhan said.

Uma nibbled her biscuit and stared into her cup.

'Uma?'

'You have been reading,' she said.

'I have.'

'And what have you learned?'

'Not much. But then I've always been a lousy student. I did find your books on voodoo, though. I mean *vodoun*. And there's all this stuff about . . .' – I pulled the scrap of paper I'd been making notes on out of my pocket – '. . . *ti-bon-ange*. You know what that means?'

'I am familiar with the phrase.'

'And you already knew what *mangé ginen* meant, too, didn't you? You know a lot of strange shit.'

'Yes.'

'So why didn't you tell me before?'

'I did not want to alarm you without good reason. I am still not certain that there is any cause for . . . concern.'

'What are you two on about, then?' Siobhan asked.

'It's Baba Dutty,' I told her. 'He's inside me somewhere. Or his soul, his *ti-bon-ange*, is. That's what Uma suspects, anyway. Isn't it?'

Uma nodded. 'Baba Dutty was an *houngan* of exceptional power. He was not only *houngan*, he was *bokor*. Do you understand what that means?'

I shook my head.

'An *houngan* is essentially a priest, albeit one who is also a kind of white magician. The *bokor* is more like what we might call a sorcerer, venturing into the blacker *vodoun* arts, with a particular ability to manipulate the souls of the living and the dead. It is very rare for one man to be both *houngan* and *bokor*. But then Baba Dutty was a rare individual.'

'And *mangé ginen*? The words from my dream? It's a reference to ritual sacrifice, right?'

'It is not so much a sacrifice as an offering to the dead. An appeal to the spirit of the departed to return and engage once more in human affairs.'

'What does that mean?' I asked.

Uma shook her head. 'I am still not certain. I believe it is possible that Baba Dutty projected a piece of himself inside of you. Perhaps it was just chance, you were the one who held him when he died, but I suspect it was by design. I believe it has to do with your part in our endeavour.'

'But what part? What do I do? I mean, I know this sounds goofy as all get out, but I've been . . . *possessed* before. I've shared the consciousness of another . . . force. Don't look at me like that, Siobhan.'

'Like what?' she smirked.

'What I'm saying is, it didn't feel like this. Not at all. In fact, I don't feel much of anything right now, just a vague sense that something isn't quite right, you know? Just a hint of annoyance. Like I've forgotten my mother's birthday.'

'Have you ever been touched by the *ti-bon-ange* of a *bokor* and *houngan* before?' Uma asked.

'Not to the best of my recollection.'

Uma threw up her hands and shrugged her shoulders. I'd never been hit by a truck before, either. I took her point.

'Maybe it's just the inner you trying to break out of that godawful exterior,' Siobhan suggested. 'Maybe it's your feminine side bursting out. Or your masculine.'

I made a face at her.

'Whatever it is has got to be better than what we've seen so far,' she added.

'So what do I about this?' I asked Uma.

'I would say there is nothing *to* do for now. Try to remember any more dreams you might have. We will just have to see what develops.'

'Terrific.'

'We may be able to find answers later this evening.'

'Why? What are we doing? Where did you go this morning?'

'I went in search of our . . . King Lear. The one who might still be able to assist us in completing the task at hand.'

'You found him?'

'We shall see,' she said. And would add nothing more.

We were about ready to leave without him, when Pahoo finally returned.

'Shit is definitely happening,' he reported.

'What do you mean?' Uma asked.

'The Thule are making waves. I met up with a group of Tinkers . . .'

'Aw, Christ!' Siobhan moaned.

'Tinkers?' I asked.

'Irish scum,' Siobhan said. I think she would have spat but for Uma's nice carpet.

'They're fellow Travellers,' Pahoo explained. 'And they told me that weird emanations are coming from the London Stone. And from King's Cross.'

'There is nothing special about King's Cross,' Uma said. 'Unless you are looking for prostitutes.' For some reason she glanced at me just then. 'Boudicca's bones do not rest there, you know.'

'What?' I said.

'Believe what you like,' Pahoo said, ignoring me. 'But I went up to Parliament Hill and killed a vole. There are powerful vibrations in the grid. Things are very definitely happening.'

'You killed a vole?' I asked.

'Perhaps we should go to Spitalfields,' Uma said. She looked uncertainly at Siobhan.

'Just stopped by there,' Pahoo said. 'Nothing at all, not even a trace of activity. I couldn't do much under the circumstances, but I would have sensed it in the air if the Thule were at work.'

'Hello?' I tried. 'Anybody home? Marty Burns here, anyone listening?'

'Please, Marty,' Uma said. I could see she was trying to decide what to do. 'Has anyone listened to the news today?'

We all stared at each other.

Uma hurried toward one of the bedrooms and we all followed like baby chicks. She found the remote, flipped on the television (she was okay after all; what a relief) and punched up the twenty-four-hour news on teletext. The service provided little more than headlines, but sure enough there was a local story about fresh 'disturbances' in Tower Hamlets. At least my name didn't figure in them this time.

'You may be right. I fear that things have begun,' Uma said. She turned off the TV.

'What do we do?' I asked.

'We had best get underway.'

We made our way across town in an old, brown Ford Sierra, about as bland and boring a car as has ever been designed. I don't know whose it was or where it came from – I knew better than to ask – and naturally Siobhan automatically took her place behind the wheel. The traffic was murder, and I could hear her grunt a little every time she had to depress the clutch pedal, so her leg must have hurt like the devil. It didn't slow her down, though, and she took the crowded, narrow London streets like Michael Schumacher.

'So who is this guy we're going to see?' I asked.

'I do not have the actual name, only an address and a contact. This particular individual and I have been aware of each other's existence and efforts, but we have never met. The negotiations to arrange even this visit have been . . . complex.'

'You sure you know what you're doing? That we can trust these people?' Pahoo asked.

'As certain as I can be under the circumstances. Are you at all versed in kabbalistic lore?'

Pahoo shook his head. 'I've heard stories, and know enough

not to fuck around with it. Those old Jews are too bloody scary for me.'

'Say what?' I said, thinking of the rune branded in Pahoo's chest.

'That is wise,' Uma told him. 'I have studied a bit myself, but unfortunately I have never fully mastered Hebrew and most of the translations, even the Latin, are worthless. My knowledge therefore is almost entirely second-hand and largely unreliable.'

'Hebrew?' I said.

'Are you familiar with kabbalah, Marty?'

'It's one of those words that sort of floats loosely around in my head. Like "duodenum". Kaballah's like Jewish voodoo, right?'

'Your analogy is not a bad one. There are, in fact, several commonalities in intriguing regards. Too peculiar to be coincidental, I believe.'

'Let me guess; next stop on the rainbow coalition, multicult tour: Temple Beth-Shalom.'

'We will not be going to an actual synagogue, but the person we seek is undoubtedly Jewish. A kabbalist wizard, you might say, though I don't imagine that the *tzaddik* would much care for that particular description.'

'*Tzaddik?*'

'It means "righteous man",' Uma explained.

'A *mensch*, you mean,' I said. Pahoo turned and gave me a funny look. 'What?'

Pahoo just shook his head.

'*Tzaddik* may refer to a kind of exalted rabbi. Though it has another, rather more complex connotation, as well,' Uma added, but she didn't explain.

We drove through the middle of town and back out on the northwest side. The traffic didn't subside much, although the neighbourhood took on a more overtly suburban and wealthier look. We drove past Hampstead, which echoed bits of Santa Monica, but without the ocean, and on through to Golder's Green. Uma pulled out her street map and provided directions for Siobhan. We passed several synagogues, the first I'd actually noticed in London, and lots of other markers – butchers, bagel joints, Chinese restaurants – of what was obviously a substantial Jewish community. It reminded me of the Fairfax district in LA, but a little more upscale. Actually, its upper-middle-class sterility reminded me of American suburbia more than anyplace I had yet seen in England.

'Here, I believe,' Uma said, pointing to a medium-sized, detached house, identical to a dozen others, in the middle of a quiet street. Siobhan pulled up in front. We all got out.

'Are you *sure* this is right?' Pahoo asked again.

'This is the address I was given,' Uma told him. Siobhan was taking a hard look up and down the street, sniffing at the air like a retriever. 'Anything wrong?' Uma asked her.

Siobhan grunted noncommittally.

'You haven't got one of your itches, have you?' I asked. I looked around nervously.

'No,' she said. 'No itches. Just the usual pain in the arse. But I'm almost used to you.'

'Hardy-har-har,' the lord of the bon mot replied.

I followed the others up a neat little pathway to the front door. We passed a spiffy red Rover parked in the driveway in front of the garage, and I noted a sticker for an American university pasted inside the rear window. On the opposite side there was a tiny Israeli flag and sitting on the rear bench was a child safety seat. With Siobhan by her side, still looking a little hinky, Uma rang the bell. A *mezuzah* was affixed to the doorpost on the right side.

There was a loud clatter from inside followed by a shrill 'Dammit!' There was more heavy construction noise from behind the door – road graders would have been my first guess – and the four of us managed to exchange a single look. Uma rang the bell again and a muffled 'I'm coming already, for heaven's sake' was heard from within.

The woman who opened the door was even smaller than Pahoo. She wore baggy blue jeans, white Nike trainers and a black sweatshirt with Bugs Bunny peering over the Warner Brothers logo on the front. She had short-cropped, dyed black hair with tiny puffs of grey sprinkled about like sugar on a cruller. The grey dots extended to her bushy black eyebrows. She had fat little cheeks, with a large brown mole on the left side trailing three rather lengthy hairs, and a bit of a moustache, too, in that post-menopausal lady way. I would have guessed her age at close to seventy, though certainly not aloud and to her face. For she had eyes as bright and piercing as arc lamps, and they took in each of our faces in turn.

'Uma?' the old lady asked.

'Yes. You are Mrs Stein?'

'Lily,' she said, and held out her hand. Uma shook it lightly. 'So nice you could stop by. Please, come in.'

Uma walked through the doorway.

'You must be Siobhan,' Lily Stein said, in what was very definitely an American accent. She held out her hand again. Siobhan shook it more firmly. 'Such a muscular girl. And that complexion. Lovely. We must talk skin care.'

'Pleasure,' Siobhan said. And I couldn't be sure, but I'd have bet she was actually blushing. I liked this Lily.

'You must be Pahoo,' she said, taking the little man's hand in her even tinier one. She went on before he could answer. 'Where do you get a name like that? Pahoo? I never heard of it before. Still, I've got a cousin, would you believe she named her little girl Ariel? This is what happens when you live in Syosset, believe me. Ariel. What is she, a television set? *Meshuga*!'

Pahoo just nodded and followed Siobhan inside.

'Martin Burns,' she said, eyeing me up and down. 'A genuine pleasure it is to have such a lovely star in my home. I remember you yet from *Salt & Pepper*. Oh, my daughter – she's a doctor now you know, her own practice – she had such a crush on you. With the pictures and the magazines, oy, she used to make us crazy. And such a wonderful new show you have. Maybe a little too much with the car chases and the *shiksas* with the plastic boobies, but *very* entertaining.'

'Thanks,' I said with a confused smile. 'Call me Marty. Hi.'

I took her hand. Her skin was warm and soft and as she gave my fingers just the gentlest of squeezes before letting go to gesture me inside, I felt a little jolt in my temple where I'd been getting the headaches. It quickly passed and I went inside.

The others stood together in the hallway, looking nervous and awkward as a group of relatives visiting their matronly aunt in a nursing home. Even Uma.

'What, are you standing?' Lily said. 'Go on into the living room and have a seat.'

They quickly followed her instructions. Lily took my arm and escorted me down the hall behind them.

'You're American,' I said.

'Sure. Why not?'

I didn't know how to answer that. Why not, indeed?

The others stood in the middle of the large living room. The decor was . . . innovative. The carpeting was a thick orange shag, just shy of machete-hacking length. There was nothing wrong with any of the furniture in the room – in fact, it proved very comfortable to sit in – but no two pieces quite matched, much as the colour of the walls didn't quite go with the carpet. There were two massive, glass-fronted bookcases stuffed to overflowing with leather-bound volumes, and a big-screen TV along one wall. The opposite wall featured French doors leading out to a patio and rear garden. The room had tchotchkes galore, along with several dozen framed photographs of people whom I took to be members of the Stein family. Prominent among the knick-knacks was a series of tiny figurines, made out of heavy grey clay and formed into roughly human shapes. They were very crude, but suggested an existential angst that I found deeply affecting. Naturally, they didn't fit in at all with anything else in the place. I picked one up to examine it more closely.

'You like, Martin? I make those myself,' Lily said. She seemed very proud.

'They're . . . very powerful,' I said. The little man in my hands appeared to be screaming with torment, though his round head didn't actually have a face as such. It was a bit eerie.

'Have a seat,' Lily ordered. We sat down almost as one, Uma and Siobhan on the sofa, Pahoo and me in oversized comfy chairs. Mine had a little button set into a panel on the side. I pushed it and the chair began to hum and vibrate.

'Nice, huh?' Lily asked, nodding the correct answer. 'I have a little sciatica.'

'It's great,' I said, fumbling for the off-switch.

'I'm just going to get for everyone a little snack,' Lily said and she was gone.

The four of us sat there, looking ill at ease. Siobhan kept her eyes peeled out the window, while Uma ran her gaze over the shelves of books. Pahoo struggled not to get absorbed into the mass of chair he was sitting in – he looked like a bug caught in a Venus fly trap – and I tried to keep track of my feet in the dense thicket of shag carpet.

'You *sure* this is the right place?' Pahoo asked yet again. Uma nodded, but she looked uncertain.

After a few minutes, Lily came in carrying a big silver tray with cups and saucers, a teapot and a cafetiere. She put it down on the coffee table in front of the table and said to Siobhan: 'Be a darling and pour, yes?'

Siobhan nodded. Lily scampered back out to the kitchen.

Pahoo took coffee, Lily and Siobhan had tea. I wasn't thirsty. Lily came in carrying a second, smaller salver with an array of biscuits and small pastries. Siobhan gestured at the tea tray and Lily said, 'Tea, please, sweetie, with a thimbleful of milk, two sugars. That's a dear.'

Lily sat down on the sofa between Uma and Siobhan, then noticed that I didn't have a cup in my hand.

'Coffee, Martin? Tea?'

'It's Marty, please. Nothing, thank you.'

'I've got juice in the kitchen. Orange? Apple?'

'No, I'm fine.'

'Coke?'

'Thanks, no,' I said again, grinning like an idiot.

'Mineral water? Plain or sparkling.'

'Really. I'm not thirsty right now. Maybe later.'

Lily made a face and shrugged as if to say *whoever heard of such a thing?*

'You'll have a snack though, Martin,' she said. It wasn't a question.

'Absolutely,' I said, and grabbed a *ruggalah* off the tray, along with a napkin. I shoved it in my mouth quickly.

'Mury ood,' I said, spitting crumbs.

And it was. The pastries were seriously yummy and we all lavished praise on Lily when she confessed to having baked the chocolate and walnut *ruggalah* herself. There was a round of exceedingly vacuous small talk as we munched, before we got down to the business at hand.

'So,' Lily said when everyone had eaten their fill, 'what are we going to do about these Nazi cocksuckers?'

Uma explained to Lily about our little road trip, up to and including the events of Baba Dutty's murder. She spared no detail, not hesitating to report on the Thule thugs Siobhan had killed at Woodhenge and in Liverpool. She didn't mention the injuries Siobhan herself had suffered at the Thule's hands, but as she spoke Lily stared intently at Siobhan and said, 'You poor, brave darling.'

I don't think she was referring only to the physical wounds, either.

Uma told the old woman about my episodes of headaches and blackout, and about the odd dreams of Baba Dutty that I'd reported. I hadn't mentioned, even to Uma, specifically about the dark figures in my dreams, and was too embarrassed to raise the subject now. Lily turned to look at me while Uma spoke and her eyes felt like heat lamps on my cheeks. I tried to meet her gaze, but couldn't do it. The look on her face was intense but unreadable. There was a long, uncomfortable silence when Uma finally finished her story.

'So what is it you're proposing, darling?' Lily finally asked. 'What is it you're looking for here?'

'You do not already know?'

'What, I know lots of things. I know to how make a nice split-pea soup. I can name every stop on the Piccadilly Line. Believe it or not, I can change the oil filter in that Rover parked out front, I shouldn't have to pay those *gonif* mechanics. But now I'm asking you what exactly *you're* looking for.'

Lily was perched in the edge of her chair, and had spoken with a smile on her face and a bit of a twinkle in her eye, but underneath her words I could sense a seriousness which I didn't fully understand. Uma felt it, too, I knew, because she thought long and hard before answering, and there was no mirth to be found in her visage.

'We seek the *tzaddik*,' Uma said. 'One of the thirty-six.'

Lily nodded, as if a magic word had been spoken, and leaned back into her chair. 'And if you found this *tzaddik*, if I could point you to the *lamed vavnik*, what then?'

Uma took a deep breath. 'I still have in mind to complete the process of ritual that we have begun. I believe it can be done here, in London. At Spitalfields. I have heard the tales of what happened there sixty years ago, how a great *tzaddik* routed the dark forces gathered by Crowley and Mosley at the Battle of Cable Street. There are those who say it marked a hidden turning point in the war that was to come. I would do the same again, while another such war is still only a fear. I had thought we could do it ourselves, but without Baba Dutty's assistance, the circle is unfinished. I would ask the *tzaddik* to square the circle before it is too late.'

'I see,' Lily said. She looked like she was trying to decide whether to have the fish or the chicken, though the pot roast sounded nice. 'What do you know of the *lamed vavnik*?' she asked.

'I am not entirely familiar with that term. You speak of the thirty-six?'

Lily nodded, just slightly.

'I know of the kabbalistic legend: that at any time, in every era, there are thirty-six righteous men whose merits support the world. There are only ever thirty-six and it is they who invoke the presence and benevolence of God. They are invisible and anonymous, but like the leys beneath the ground, all depends on their well-being. And I am led to understand that a *tzaddik*, one of the thirty-six, may be found in London.'

There was a hint of question in Uma's last words, but Lily didn't respond to it. 'And you?' Lily said, pointing at Pahoo.

'I've never heard of any of this before. I'm strictly power of the earth. I don't mess with you lot.'

Lily frowned, but went on to Siobhan. 'You?'

'I do what Uma tells me. I don't pretend to understand, but I accept. I do as I'm asked, so long as I think it's right. Uma's never given me reason to doubt her.'

Lily nodded. 'And you, Martin?'

'Me what?'

'What do you know of the *lamed vavnik*?'

'Man, I feel like I am in the wrong movie theatre. Like I paid to see the new John Woo flick, and here I am watching a Bulgarian art film with no subtitles. Like I keep telling Uma, I've been through some strange shit, but I don't know *what* the hell you're talking about here. *Lamed vavnik* could be noodle pudding for all I know.'

Lily laughed. 'Fair enough. I appreciate your honesty, Martin.' She squinted her eyes at me. 'You are Jewish, yes?'

I never know how to answer that question. 'Not really,' I said apologetically. 'I mean culturally, sort of, but not practising. I had a dreidle once, if that counts.'

'Your mother?'

'Her mom was Jewish.'

'You are bar-mitzvah?'

'No,' I said. 'Only on TV.'

She tsk-tsked me. 'Circumcised?'

The others were all watching me, Siobhan with an evil grin, and I felt myself blush. 'Ummm, yeah.'

'Good,' Lily said. I felt like I'd been given a lollipop by the doctor for being such a brave boy.

'Will you take us to the *tzaddik* then?' Pahoo asked. He shifted in his chair again, seeming particularly uncomfortable.

Lily didn't answer him, but turned back to Uma. 'Do you know the price of confronting the *lamed vavnik*?'

'I do not. But I am willing to pay whatever is asked of me. I can do no more.'

'That's very nice, sweetie, but *you* don't pay the price.'

'I do not understand, Lily.'

'I know you don't,' Lily sighed. 'The price would be paid by the *tzaddik*, by the *lamed vavnik*. The *lamed vavnik* walks alone in the world, hidden, as you say. The price of revelation can only be death.'

'Oh,' Uma squeaked.

'This is not to say that the *lamed vavnik* would not pay this price if it were the right thing to do. For what other reason would the *lamed vavnik* exist?'

'I do not believe I could ask that price of anyone,' Uma said.

'The decision's not yours to make now, darling.' Lily's bright eyes grew dark and her voice took on a power and authority which had not been manifest before.

'What you call the ley grid, I call the fifth *sefirot*: *gevurah*, which if you translate, means something like 'power'. It is about *gevurah* that the great struggle with the *sitra achra*, those of the other side, takes place. The struggle has gone on since the Name was first spoken and the universe carved out of chaos. It will go on until the Name is erased and forgotten; which is to say that the struggle is eternal. The *sitra achra* are the darkness, they exist only to separate humanity from the *shekhinah*, from the light of pure being. They suck like leeches on the light, drawing their existence from it. Without dark, of course, there is no light. The *sitra achra* exist within the *sefirot*, the divine structures of harmony, but are also a necessary limitation to it. The *lamed vavnik* ensures that they do not drink too much of the light and leave the world only in darkness.'

'I understand,' Uma said. Which left her three up on me. 'You speak of the *bodhisattva*, of *karuna*.'

'Yes, darling. All is the same in a good heart. A samosa is just a spicy knish, after all, and a dosa a big blintz.'

'So, the Thule are what? Chicken saag?' I asked.

'The Thule are another manifestation of the *sitra achra*,' Lily said. 'They know it, but they'd never admit it. They think they're special. They've cloaked themselves in all manner of nonsense – Odinism, yet! – but they're bargain basement theosophists at heart. Blavatsky, Crowley, they were a bunch of losers who wouldn't know their *tuchis* from the tetragrammaton. Most of these miserable anti-Semites don't even know that their whole belief system was swiped from Kabbalah. Unfortunately, the fact that they're ignorant doesn't make them any less dangerous. The Thule may be pathetic tools of the *sitra achra*, but a hammer in a child's hand can still destroy the most beautiful sculpture.'

'You will help us then?' Uma asked.

'I will help you.'

'When can we see the *tzaddik*?' Pahoo asked.

Lily looked at him and smiled. Uma turned and I saw tears in her eyes. I caught on at that moment – I think Siobhan did, too – and I knew why Uma was crying. We all stared at Pahoo.

'What?' he asked, defensively.

'Sweetie-pie,' Lily said with a chuckle, 'you're looking at the *tzaddik*. If you weren't such a masculinist pig, you'd see that *I'm* the *lamed vavnik*.'

'Noooo,' Pahoo said, getting out of his chair. He glanced at each of us in turn until he saw that it was true. He started to laugh. It was a chuckle that slowly consumed him, until he could barely stand up. He had to brace himself against the back of the chair. I felt a drop of acid bubble out of my stomach.

'Something funny, darling?' Lily asked.

Pahoo waved her off. He walked over to the window and waved his hand a couple of times. Seconds later glass shattered and wood splintered. A group of three men, dressed in black, with balaclavas and Uzis burst into the room through the french doors. Siobhan was on her feet and moving, her gun already in her hand, but two more black-clad figures had entered from another part of the house and were already on top of her. One rammed the butt of his rifle full-force into her gut, doubling her over, and the other quickly set to pistol-whipping her across the back of the head until she was unconscious. The rest of us had yet to even move.

Pahoo walked over to the prone Siobhan and gave her a gratuitous kick to the groin. 'Paddy cunt. I've been dying to do this dyke for days. Gonna fuck her first, though, so she knows what she's been missing.'

He walked around the sofa and up to Lily's chair. He leaned down and raised her head up by the chin. 'The *lamed vavnik*. The great kabbalist magus.' He shook his head as if still in disbelief. 'You stupid kike whore. I am going to butcher you like the pig you are and eat your liver with a big glass of milk.'

Lily spat in his face. Pahoo laughed, wiped away the spittle, then drew back and punched her in the face as hard as he could. I heard her nose break.

'Bring on the cattle cars,' he said.

EIGHTEEN

Pahoo and the Thule goons bound my wrists together with duct tape. They didn't bother with Uma or Lily, but they took extra care with Siobhan, securing her legs and using handcuffs on her as well. Even so, as soon she started to come around from the beating, Pahoo kicked her in the head one more time, and she passed out again. The side of her head looked like a rotten eggplant. A rotten, *bleeding* eggplant.

'You did not have to do that,' Uma said to him.

'No,' Pahoo agreed, 'but it was fun.'

'I told you I never liked him,' I said. 'He stank from the start, literally, and then he killed the bunny.'

'Christ,' Pahoo said, 'what is it with you and the bloody rabbit? We're going to do far worse to you lot, mate, so I'd start worrying about other things.'

'I should have paid greater attention, Marty,' Uma said. 'I did suspect something was amiss, but I could not discern what it was. I did not see this at all.'

'That's because at the end of the day, you're still just a fucking wog, and not half as smart as any white man.'

'I'm a white man,' I said, not proudly.

'Yeah, but you're half-yid ain't you? And a bloody actor to boot. By the way, your show is crap.'

'I've always thought that all critics are Nazis. I hadn't realized that all Nazis are critics, too. But then I've never been any good at syllogism.'

'We're not Nazis,' Pahoo snarled.

'Oh, sorry. Say, is that a swastika in your pocket or are you just happy to see me?'

'You've got a cheek, haven't you? We'll see if you still got it when your belly's slit and you're watching your guts unwind.'

'So you don't call yourself a Nazi, darling?' Lily said. They were the first words she'd spoken since Pahoo had struck her. She clutched at her swollen nose, blood staining the sleeves of her sweatshirt, the flesh under her eyes already turning purple.

'I sympathize, of course, but I don't strictly identify,' Pahoo said. 'The Thule are a breed purer than the Nazis were, closer to our Norse roots. Hitler and Himmler turned their backs on Wodan, on the Thule and the Black Order. They got distracted from without, forgot the basis of their power and what they should have aspired to. *We* haven't abandoned the purity of the earth spirit for the artificial heat of technology.'

'Oh, Christ,' I said. I hadn't meant to.

'I've got no problem with wogs and such. In their place. I don't like them, but I've got no problem. As long as that place ain't here.'

'What about Jews?' I asked.

'*Everybody* hates the Jews,' Pahoo said. Ask a stupid question . . .

'The world is fire and ice,' Pahoo went on, 'that's the fundamental truth. And these Isles, Ultima Thule itself, are at the heart of the ice. We are ice people, that's been proven, written in nature and in history. Your kind . . .' – he pointed at Uma and sneered – '. . . are born of fire. You claim you care about the power of the leys, of the soil, but you won't accept the truth that your very presence here contaminates them, defiles and demeans them. The land of ice, the people of the ice, cannot be pure while your kind remains. We stand for purity. We are of ice. Our forefathers grew strong in ice and snow. Ice is the natural heritage of Nordic men.'

'You're a cold motherfucker, I'll give you that,' I said. 'Where do you get this stuff?'

'Hoerbiger,' Lily said, shaking her head.

Pahoo looked at her with surprise. 'Smart Jew,' he said, nodding.

'Who?' Uma asked.

'Hans Hoerbiger,' Lily said. 'He is the founding father of *Welteislehre*: the doctrine of cosmic ice. Pseudo-scientific bullshit of the silliest kind. It's a pathetic corruption of Norse myth and Icelandic *eddas*, Ymir and the Frost Giants and all that, with a little Wagner and *Nibelungen* thrown in for the soundtrack. Hoerbiger was very big with the Nazis in the post-Weimar days, in part because of how *Welteislehre* meshed with Teutonic myth, but also because it contained within it a complete rejection of contemporary science. *Jewish* science, as they saw it. The more things change . . .'

'You would say that,' Pahoo said. 'But you can't, you won't, begin to understand.'

'The pathetic thing,' Lily continued, 'the truly ironic thing, which I'm sure our little *Nazi* darling here doesn't even know, is that there's a whole contemporary school of *black* racists who make almost the exact same argument for why Africans are inherently superior to Europeans. But bullshit is bullshit, and a Nazi is a Nazi. Whatever you choose to call yourself.'

Pahoo walked over and sat down on the side of Lily's chair. He leaned over, slipping his arm around her shoulders, and gave her a hard kiss on the lips. When she tried to push him away, he reached up and pressed his thumb into her broken nose until she cried out. He stuck his tongue in her mouth when she did.

'I'm your death, *darling*,' he said. 'That's all you need to know.'

It was just after ten o'clock when Pahoo sent one of his thugs to move Lily's Rover and fetch a black van which they backed into the garage.

'The time has come,' Pahoo announced.

'Where are you taking us?' Uma asked.

'Home sweet home, Uma my darling. Spitalfields. You'll get to play your part in a ritual there after all. But not quite the way you planned. Now that we've got the *tzaddik*, we've got something much better than bunnies to sacrifice tonight.'

'Don't suppose you could just drop me at the Savoy,' I muttered.

'I need to use the toilet,' Lily said.

'Piss your knickers, kike.'

Two of the Thule rather indelicately dragged the still unconscious Siobhan through the house and threw her into the back of the van. She groaned as they bounced her around, but she was out of it. They bound Uma and Lily's hands, and prodded the three of us at gunpoint to follow Siobhan into the vehicle. A driver and one guard rode up front, while Pahoo and the other two stayed in back with us. Pahoo gave Siobhan another spiteful little kick as he climbed in, but she didn't stir. Her head had swollen from the beating and had gone all lopsided.

The driver set a nice easy pace as we pulled out of the driveway and cruised through the quiet, suburban streets of North London. There were no windows in back. From my place on the floor I could just barely see out the windshield enough to count the streetlights as they went by. At one point I heard a police siren, saw the flashing lights and felt a spark of hope rise, but as the van pulled over to the kerb, the cop car whizzed on by and the spark sputtered.

A few minutes later, the van came to a thudding halt as we hit something in the middle of the road.

I got thrown over onto my side, smacking my head against the raised wheel well. Uma landed on top of me and one of the Thule guards tumbled down on top of her. I heard Pahoo yell 'Fuck,' but as bottom man in the dog-pile I couldn't see what was going on. There was a loud crash as the windshield of the van shattered, followed by a piercing scream. Then I heard gun shots.

'Get off me, you cunt,' Pahoo yelled, disentangling himself from Lily and the other guard – I wasn't sure which of them he was talking to. Then there were three more shots from up front. I heard another window break and a second anguished scream.

The Thule goon who'd fallen on top of Uma scrambled to his feet, and Uma rolled off me. The guard rushed in a crouch toward the front of the van which, I saw, was now empty. As he stuck his head out over the front seat, gun at the ready, a thick, black shadow reached out from the side and grabbed him by the scruff of the neck. He squeezed off a few shots, but they went through the roof of the van. A second later he was yanked out of sight.

His scream was cut off by a crunching sound. Breaking bones was my guess.

Pahoo was on his knees above Lily. He held her around the neck from behind, her chin resting atop the crook of his elbow. The last of the thugs was just recovering his Uzi.

'Kill them all,' Pahoo said. 'Right now.'

The guard checked his gun, then hesitated a moment as he looked back and forth between Uma and me. He made his decision, pointing the barrel at my chest, bracing the gun with his other hand.

Wrong decision.

Uma, hands still bound behind her, pivoted on her ass, rolled onto her side and kicked out with her left leg. The gun went flying out of the goon's hand before he even knew what had happened. Uma flipped herself over twice, pivoted again and struck out with her right leg, catching the Thule pig under the chin, snapping his head back and into the side of the van. Screaming like a bloody demon as she did it, Uma tucked her legs, rolled again and barrelled into the stunned guard's stomach head-first. The bastard let out a baby's whimper, before doubling over. But as soon as he did, Uma flexed her legs, raised her shoulder and drove it as hard as she could into the middle of his face. It had to have hurt her, too, but this time as the back of his head smashed into the van, he collapsed and didn't get up again.

It had gone quiet outside. There was so sign of the Thule guards or whoever it was that had ambushed them. Uma looked dazed – I'd yet to even move – but she spun around to face Pahoo. He looked scared and very small now, even for him, but the thick muscles in his little arm were bunched tight as he applied pressure to Lily's throat. She tried to shake free, but with her hands bound, she could only gasp for air. Her eyes bulged wide with terror.

'Back off, Uma, or I'll kill her,' Pahoo warned.

Uma froze on her knees. I shifted slightly and saw Pahoo's grip tighten around Lily's neck. Lily gagged. 'Don't be stupid, you bloody cunt,' he said to me. 'You're not really a hero, you only play one on TV.'

It was a stand-off. Lily's tongue was hanging out of her mouth and she was issuing death-rattle wheezes. Wherever the hell we were, surely someone had heard the godawful racket from the struggle. It couldn't continue for much longer.

It didn't.

A grey fist burst through the wall of the van. Just tore right on through as if the steel panel was paper. The fist opened, grabbed a ... *fistful* of Pahoo's greasy dreadlocks and pulled.

Pahoo's head made contact with the wall in much the same way that tennis balls make contact with a pro's racket strings: *pulverized* is the word.

Pahoo let go of Lily. I remember reading once about sucking chest wounds, and I imagine the sound they make is much like Lily's desperate gasp for breath. Uma immediately rolled to her side but, still bound, there was little she could do.

Incredibly, Pahoo's skull hadn't been crushed and he started back to his knees. It was a bad choice, for as he did so, the fist returned by way of a new hole in the van wall, about two feet from the first. A second hand appeared beside it. There was, I realized later, the nightmare shriek of metal being physically torn asunder, and then the side of the van simply wasn't there.

Standing in the gap, out there in the night where the wild things most definitely do grow, was . . . a creature. I don't know what else to call it.

It was human-shaped, with two arms, two legs, one very round head, standing a good six and a half feet tall. But it had no eyes and only a slight bulge where its nose should have been. There was a coin slit of a mouth that neither frowned nor smiled. Either expression would have been difficult, though, since the thing had no lips. The creature seemed to absorb what dim light there was, but its . . . skin? . . . was a mottled grey, lumpy and coarse. The proportions of it weren't quite right, as if it had been sculpted by a blind alien artist trying to approximate human form from verbal description. It looked like . . .

Like one of the those odd little sculptures that littered Lily's living room.

'*Golem*,' Uma whispered. There was awe in her face.

Pahoo, who looked like he should have little cartoon birds flying around his head, looked at her and blinked. Then he turned around.

Sometimes, on really bad nights, I still hear his screams.

The golem reached into the van and took hold of Pahoo with its malformed hands. It grabbed him by the shoulders and pulled the little Nazi out into the night. I crawled forward and saw – luck? fate? design? – that the van had come to a stop in the middle of a fairly run-down street in an industrial district. It seemed an unlikely place to encounter any passers-by.

Pahoo kicked out at the golem, but though the blows struck home, the creature didn't feel them. At one point, Pahoo connected with a powerful kick to the golem's groin. But the golem, which stood unclothed, was as sexless as it was featureless. In any event, the kick evoked no visible reaction.

Unless you want to count tearing off Pahoo's right arm as a reaction. Some would, but I think the timing was purely coincidental.

Pahoo screeched in agony as a fountain of blood whooshed out of his ragged shoulder socket. The golem held the arm for a moment then tossed it to one side. Inasmuch as the creature didn't have any eyes, I couldn't figure out how it could see what it was doing (of course, I couldn't figure out how it existed at all, but why ask why?), still, it must have had some sense of visual aesthetics and/or bilateral symmetry, for a moment later it removed Pahoo's other arm.

I can't honestly say that Pahoo's wailing got any worse. But then I don't think it could have. The golem dropped him and he landed hard. He rolled and spasmed along the street, blood spurting out of him as if he were a weird, Damien Hirst museum piece. ('The Arms Trade' was my mental title-card for the work.) The golem just stood there, holding Pahoo's severed arm by the pinky.

Lily managed to crawl over beside me. Uma, slack-jawed, hadn't moved. Lily raised herself up and looked out through the hole in the van.

'Oh, my God,' she croaked. She raised her hand and gestured at the golem. Ignoring Pahoo, writhing and shrieking on the ground, it walked over to the van. I held my breath as it approached, marvelling at the very existence of such a thing. It did not, in fact, have skin as such, but was moulded entirely out of dirt and clay. As it reached up to lift Lily out of the van, I could see how roughly formed its fingers were – like Homer Simpson's. I glanced down and saw that its feet were toeless blocks of solid clay.

The golem picked Lily up and put her down on the sidewalk with surprising gentleness. Her knees buckled slightly as she touched ground, and the golem was quick to offer a supporting touch to her back.

Lily staggered over to where Pahoo lay on the ground in a thick pool of blood, the golem heeling behind her like an obedient pup. Pahoo had stopped jerking and bucking, but he continued to cry and moan. Lily knelt down beside him, careful not to tread in the expanding circle of his blood. He turned his head toward her, but I don't know if he really saw anything at that point.

'*Chazza*,' she said.

She spat in his face again.

Lily stood up and took a step back. The golem walked around her and picked the little man up by the throat with one massive, malformed hand. Pahoo was shivering now, though whether from fear or shock, I couldn't say. The golem raised his other hand and covered Pahoo's eyes with its blocky fingers.

It squeezed its hand into a fist, crushing Pahoo's throat. If Pahoo made another sound as he died, only the golem – if it had ears – could hear it.

Lily looked up the street at the sound of a car engine. Whoever it was fortunately – for them – didn't come our way. Lily walked back to the van, the golem again trailing a step behind her. The very sight of the thing scared me down to my Odor-eaters.

'We'd better go,' Lily said. 'There's not a lot of time and very much to do.'

NINETEEN

～

The windshield had been smashed, half the side panel ripped away and there were bullet holes in the roof, but we had no choice other than to drive the black van to Uma's place in the East End. The other Thule goons hadn't been as lovingly dismembered as had Pahoo, but they were all extremely and thoroughly dead. We left the bodies in the street in an area called Tottenham where, Lily informed me, 'no one will even notice', and kept to side streets as much as we could. If a cop stopped us, we were going to have a hell of a time explaining what we were doing. Not to mention the oversized, overcooked Pillsbury Doughboy in the back.

Siobhan had finally come around, but she could barely sit up, much less drive. Uma didn't drive and I didn't fancy the wrong side of the road, so Lily took the wheel and followed Uma's directions. The flow of blood from the cuts in Siobhan's head had finally been staunched, but her eyes were blurry and I guessed that she was seriously concussed. Her eyelids kept drooping down, so Uma and I took turns talking to her, or at her, to try and keep her awake. I thought I'd remembered from an old TV movie I once appeared in that it was important not to let a person with concussion go to sleep. Siobhan seemed to recognize Uma well enough and was intermittently lucid as Uma explained what had transpired, but she kept referring to me as 'Bono,' and blew raspberries at me.

Even while talking to Siobhan, I found it hard to take my eyes off the golem. Lily had gestured it into the van where it lay down on the floor. She had stuck her fingers into its tiny mouth and removed a small piece of parchment, stuffing it in her pocket. The golem had gone all stiff as soon as she'd removed the paper and it hadn't moved a muscle – did it have muscles? – since. Still, it was a hell of a thing. Uma kept glancing at it, too.

'This has been wondrous to behold,' she said.

'Have you ever seen one before?'

'Seamus?' Siobhan asked, squinting at the now lifeless hulk.

'No,' Uma said, patting her bodyguard's hand. 'I have, of course, read of such creatures, but I never imagined that I would be so privileged as to encounter one. Such a being as this could only be raised by the *lamed vavnik*. I am not certain, Marty, that you understand the power, the incredible strength that such a creation represents. It is far beyond anything I have ever known.'

'I'm sure I don't understand,' I sighed. 'But then you could fill an ocean, a *big* ocean, with the volume of things I don't understand.'

Uma nodded, which I didn't find comforting.

'I guess Pahoo understands, though,' I said with a dry chuckle.

'Yes,' Uma said. She didn't laugh.

'It's not your fault.'

'No?' she asked.

'Scumbag,' Siobhan spat. Presumably she meant Pahoo, but her eyes had gone watery again, so it wasn't clear. I gave her the benefit of the doubt.

'Amen,' I said. 'You think you should have known who . . . what he was, don't you?'

'I feel a fool, Marty. I *am* rather a fool. It was my task to ensure that our mission succeeded. But I did not sense Pahoo's true nature and that failure may well have doomed us all. It certainly doomed poor Baba Dutty. And the rite at Tintagel was surely tainted by Pahoo's dark practices; even *you* sensed that.'

'*Me?*'

Uma nodded. 'You have several times referred to the rabbit that was sacrificed. That was not right.'

'I was half-joking about the bunny, Uma. I mean, Baba Dutty killed a chicken in the *oufò*, too.'

'Yes, but I . . . expected that. The sacrificial offerings to the *loa* are a necessary, intrinsic element in *vodoun* practice. Druidic sacrifices are not. I was disturbed by it, but I did not pursue my disquiet. I suppose the attack on Pahoo at Woodhenge had convinced me of his trustworthiness.'

'It was all a set-up, wasn't it?' I said, thinking back on events. 'The ambush was intended to make Pahoo look good. Those scumbags who shot at us must have aimed not to seriously hurt him. I'll bet

they didn't know they were going to end up dead, though. It took
guts to sit there and get shot, I'll give the little dickwad that, but I
suspect Pahoo didn't tell his skinhead buddies about Siobhan.'

'Sunday, bloody Sunday,' Siobhan sang at mention of her name.

'I am sure he did not. I see now that from the start the Thule's plan
was to manipulate us into uncovering the identity of the *tzaddik*. As
did I, they surely heard rumours of the presence of a *lamed vavnik*.
They would not have found Lily on their own, and they could never
be certain to succeed in poisoning the leys and effecting their occult
designs while a *lamed vavnik* dwelt in the land. And I handed her
over to them.'

'Fortunately, she's a bit of a handful,' I said, looking again at the
lifeless golem. 'So what now?'

Uma shook her head. 'I relinquish my position of leadership. I
have brought death and caused death to those who trusted me. I
will do so no more.'

'Bollocks!' Siobhan said, addressing no one, and everyone, in
particular.

I didn't have anything to add.

In a world of walking golems, body-possessing *loa* and power-crazed
Nazi druids, an uneventful drive through nighttime London may not
seem like much, but stepping out of that battered black van in the
dark alley behind Uma's Indian restaurant felt like nothing short of
a miracle. Uma was quick to leap out of the van and I saw why: a
half-dozen very tough-looking Asian youths appeared as if by magic
– you should pardon the expression – all around us in the alley. They
bowed their heads when they saw Uma and vanished back into the
shadows.

'Goddamn,' I muttered to myself.

Siobhan was able to get to her feet, but grudgingly accepted a
helping hand down out of the van. Though she tottered on her
land legs, she wouldn't countenance any further assistance and
wobbled her way inside the restaurant's back door, holding the
side of her head as if it might fall off at any second. Lily got out
on the driver's side and walked around to where Uma and I were
standing. We were still staring at the golem.

'Will anyone disturb things back here?' Lily asked.

Uma looked off into the darkness and shook her head. 'No
chance.'

'I figured. So I'll leave it then.'

'Is that safe?' I asked.

'It can't go anyplace without this,' she said, and held up the scrap of parchment I'd seen her remove from the creature's mouth.

'What is it?' I whispered.

'The name of God, honey.'

I nodded, knowingly. *Not with a ten-foot pole* I thought.

We followed Siobhan through the dark kitchen and inside the restaurant, which for once was deserted. Siobhan had pulled two tables together and lay sprawled across them on her back, eyes closed.

'Hey!' I yelled. 'I don't think you should go to sleep.'

'I'm not sleeping, tosser,' she slurred. 'Just resting my eyes.'

'I will keep an eye on her,' Uma said, in a voice that bespoke the agony of defeat. She went into the kitchen and came back out with a bunch of wet towels. She sat down beside the Irish woman and began cleaning up the mess on the side of her head. I saw Siobhan wince several times and she moaned once, but it meant she was, at least, still conscious.

'Any chance of drink?' I asked.

Uma pointed at a big glass-doored refrigerator by the entrance to the kitchen, filled with bottles of Kingfisher.

'Heaven, I'm in heaven,' I started to sing. It elicited another moan from Siobhan. 'Anyone else?'

'I'd like tea,' Lily said. Uma nodded, looking pathetic.

I went into the kitchen, grabbed a beer on the way, and drained half of it before I did anything else. I saw a big industrial sized hot water dispenser, but couldn't figure out how to turn the damn thing on. In the end I boiled the water in a saucepan on the stove and rooted around until I found a stash of tea bags. I poured a cup for Siobhan just in case.

'What, no milk?' Lily said when I put the tea in front of her.

I found a container of milk in a one of the kitchen fridges and brought it out with me, grabbing another Kingfisher along the way.

'Anything else?' I asked, handing Lily the milk.

'Sugar?'

The sugar bowls were stacked on a shelf in the corner. I went and got one and put it down in front of her.

She poured her thimble's worth of milk into her tea along with two heaping spoonfuls of sugar. She stirred it for a while, then took a long, loud slurp.

'Lovely cup of tea, darling,' she said.

I sat down across from her and swigged my beer from the bottle.

'How's the shnoz?' I asked her.

Lily put her tea down, reached up and gently touched the bridge of her nose. She winced slightly with the effort. 'It hurts.'

'I'd guess it's busted.'

'What are you, a doctor now? Never mind. We've got bigger things to worry.' Lily glanced over at Uma and Siobhan, who was sitting up again. 'You want to join us, darlings? Or have you had enough?'

Uma shot Lily one of the dirtiest looks I've ever seen, but she didn't say anything. She stood up, sending her chair over backward in the process and stalked off into the bathroom.

'A rough time that one's having,' Lily confided to me. 'Very bad.'

With no small effort, Siobhan heaved herself off the table and lurched across the restaurant, practically falling down into a chair at our table.

'Nice to see you among the living again, honey.'

'You call this living?' Siobhan said.

'Just ask Pahoo,' I said.

'Heh. Sorry I missed that. I'd loved to have seen the little fucker's arms come off.'

'It's not good to speak so,' Lily said.

'Not good? It was your monster that tore him into crusty bits, wasn't it?'

'Yes,' Lily said softly.

'How did you do that?' I asked. 'Where the hell did the . . . golem come from?'

'The golem is . . . what it is. It is formed from the earth and empowered by the name of God. As the one who gave it shape, it responds to me in . . . well, it's hard to explain. You can think of it as something like my *familiar*. Though even if I commanded, there are things it simply will not do.'

'Why not?' I said.

'Because it *is* empowered by the name of God.'

'I don't get it,' I said. 'Why doesn't it . . .'

'Listen!' Lily yelled, losing patience. 'It took a lifetime of devotion, decades of studying the *Heikhalot* to understand the *masseh bereshit* sufficiently to make a golem. When you've done the same, then you can question.'

As Lily picked up her teacup I saw that her hands were shaking. Maybe what the thing did to Pahoo took *her* by surprise, too. I was afraid to say anything else at all.

'It's you,' Siobhan said, waving her blood-encrusted towel at me. 'You drive everyone bloody mad, don't you?'

I shook my head and held up my hands in surrender. I felt guilty as hell without actually knowing what for. Fortunately, Uma returned from the ladies' room just then and we all looked at her. She walked across the room, shoulders slumped, to a point about halfway between our table and the door to the kitchen, and stopped. She looked at us, then over in the direction of the back door. I don't know exactly what she was thinking, but it was clear she was making a decision.

She stood there for a good thirty seconds. Then she stood up straighter, strode purposefully to our table and sat down. She looked at Lily expectantly.

'Thank you, darling. It's not easy, I know.'

Uma merely bowed her head.

'And you, sweetie,' Lily said to me, 'I'm sorry I snapped at you. It wasn't called for. But it's been a very long night.'

'Forget it,' I said.

Lily patted my hand. 'I'm afraid it's not over yet. There's some nasty business still to do.'

It was eerie.

I've lived in cities all my life, been out on the streets – sometimes literally – at every hour of the day and night. I was in New York once during a surprise blizzard in the middle of March. I remember walking out of my hotel at about three in the morning, and for the first time ever seeing the city at a total standstill, without so much as a single yellow taxi moving on the silent streets.

There may not have been any snow, but the East End was even quieter than that this night.

'Where are the people?' I whispered. 'Did you do something? Or the Thule?'

'What am I,' Lily asked, 'a magician?'

I just stared at her.

'Yeah, okay. But I mean, how could I do this?'

There wasn't a soul to be seen as we walked past the shuttered shops and dark windows on Commercial Street; not a person, not a car, not even a horny tomcat looking for a little late night pussy. If not for the changing traffic lights, I might have believed that time itself had closed its eyes and was holding its breath, waiting for what was going to happen.

'I believe it is magic,' Uma said. 'At least of a sort. I think there are moments when even the least spiritually inclined can sense events of import, much as they intuitively sense the leys. Perhaps they do not know what it is they feel, certainly most do not, could not, understand. But they feel it nonetheless. They stay in. They go to sleep. They sit in the darkness or toss in their beds and wait, and hope that the moment will pass.'

'They sound a hell of a lot smarter than us,' I muttered.

'Quite likely,' Uma said.

'Amen,' Siobhan added. Unsteady and hurting though she was, her head bandaged with a torn-up waiter's apron still smelling of curry, she had insisted on coming along. Uma tried to talk her out of it, but I think we were all glad she was there. Courtesy of Uma's young friends in the dark, Siobhan was armed to the teeth.

'What about the golem?' I asked.

'It's with us,' Lily said, and would say no more. I had watched her put the little scrap of parchment back into the creature's mouth before we left. The golem had instantly come to life, its stiff body loosening like a patch of dried dirt in a rain shower. It moved like a shadow as it leapt down out of the back of the van. Lily had briefly touched her fingertips to its forehead, then the golem simply merged into the greater darkness of the night.

It made not a sound as it went.

As we came around a small bend in the road, Christ Church, Spitalfields, its weird, white steeple reflecting the bright moonlight, appeared like a toothy phantom. Without a word being said, we all stopped and stared up at it. The church was practically a beacon in the night. The longer I looked at it, the more it seemed to glow. I closed my eyes, then rubbed them with my palms, but when I looked again the light seemed even brighter still.

'Is it me?' I said.

'Who else would you bloody well be?'

'It *is* you, Martin. It's all of us. And those already below.'

'I believe that it has begun. The Thule are here.'

'Swell,' I said. 'Game on.'

'Not *in* the church,' Lily had explained in the restaurant, '*under* the church.'

'Like in the basement?'

'It is called the crypt, Marty. As in Canterbury.'

'Whatever,' I said.

'It's under the crypt, too,' Lily said. 'It's under everything. The Christians in the Middle Ages used it as a plague pit, because they didn't understand, feared the energies that flow from the site. This has been a place of power for many thousands of years, long before the city was even known as London. Before Trinovantum or Troia Nova. The Romans built a temple on the site and buried their honoured dead in its sanctified soil. A thousand years before that, the Druids danced their *meshuga* circles and shed blood in praise of *their* gods. It wouldn't surprise me if the first humans to walk the earth of these islands prayed and sacrificed and buried *their* children here. It is a *very* ancient place.'

'And the Thule know this,' I said.

'Oh, yes. The catacombs and passageways that lie beneath Spitalfields cross the heart of the land's magic. It is from this spot that what Uma calls the ley grid, what I would call the flesh of the *sefirot* on earth, emanates. It is the focal point of all mystical energies in Britain. That's why the Thule will be there, poisoning the well if they can.'

'Zowie!' I said.

'You bet your ass, darling.'

As we walked past the church, I craned my neck to take in the looming white steeple and felt a wave of electricity wash over me. I felt a vibration deep in my bones like a series of little earthquakes, and imagined my marrow bubbling within. I had another flash of pain through the back of my head, and thought for a second as if I might fall over, but it passed quickly, taking the electric current with it.

Flashing, in my mind's myopic eye, were the figures of darkness. An involuntary shudder went through me.

Lily led the way across the deserted street and up the block, past Spitalfields Market. We turned the corner and wound our way down a series of narrow rows. Lily stopped in front of a new-ish building and pressed the doorbell. I couldn't tell for sure, but glancing back at the church to get my bearings, I thought I remembered that this was very near the site of the final Jack the Ripper murder. We hadn't done a photo op here because Mahr had complained that the modern architecture ruined the atmosphere. He should have been with us at that moment, because I felt creeped-out as all get up.

The deep silence was finally broken by the sound of deadbolts turning. The door opened, revealing a small woman, dressed to the nines for a hot night at Club Taliban: she was covered in a sheet of black from head to toe. Even her eyes were covered, with only a small screened slit in the headpiece to see out of. Actually, I can only

assume it was a *she* underneath; for all I know it was Jimmy Hoffa
or one of a troupe of Russian dancing bears. No actual body shape
could be discerned through that mass of black cloth and whoever
was hanging out under there didn't say a word. She just looked us
over, bowed her head at Lily and beckoned us inside.

Lily led the way down a carpeted hall. I heard the deadbolts shoot
closed again behind us, but when I turned around the little figure in
black had already disappeared. Siobhan glanced over her shoulder
as well, and shrugged at me when I raised a questioning eyebrow.
She did, however, now hold a beretta 9mm pistol in her hand. We
passed a series of doors which opened into largely empty rooms.
One held a few scattered boxes, another a bunch of folding chairs
formed into a loose circle, but there was no sign that anyone lived
here. Nothing hung on the walls, no TVs or comfy chairs. Not even
an old newspaper or candy wrapper screwed up in the corner. There
was certainly no one else around.

Lily opened a door at the end of the hall revealing a steep staircase
leading down. She flicked a little timer switch on the wall lighting
a series of dim bulbs in the ceiling. She led the way down without
saying a word. Uma followed behind her, then me, with Siobhan
bringing up the rear.

Lily yanked at a dangling cord as soon she reached bottom – a
good thing, because the lights on the stairs clicked off a second or
two later – turning on another weak ceiling light which failed to
even chase the shadows from the corners of the basement. Probably
just as well, because the bits that were visible were filthy. The grey
concrete floor was thick with grime and if you *could* see into the
corners, I suspected you might find not just dust bunnies, but dust
wolverines. Whatever she might have been, the woman in the black
hijab clearly wasn't the cleaning lady.

Set into the wall, just visible at the far end of the large basement,
was a wooden door. Dangling from a nail in the wall beside the
door hung a long, thin key. The door had no knob, but it did
have a lock.

'Well, that's great security,' I said. 'Imagine trying to explain this
set-up to the insurance adjustor after a burglary.'

Lily turned and smiled at me. 'Would you like to do the
honours?'

'Okey-doke,' I said, and stepped in front of her to grab the key.
My fingers had barely touched the metal when I yanked my hand
away in pain.

'Motherfucker!' I yelled. Touching the key was like sticking your hand in a pot of boiling water. I glanced at my fingers, saw tiny blisters bubbling across the tips. The smell of burnt flesh lingered in the air. 'Goddamn.'

'Don't be such a wise-ass next time,' Lily said. Uma shook her head at me.

Lily slipped the key off the nail, no problem. No burned fingers, no sizzling skin, no blisters. She turned the key in the lock and opened the door, gesturing for us to go ahead of her. Siobhan went in front of Uma and I trailed behind. I was careful not to even brush against the door as I passed through. Lily went last, closing the door and locking it again. She hung the key back on a nail that dangled on this side of the wall.

'Problem?' she said, watching me stare at the key.

I shook my head. 'Damn good security,' I told her.

Lily nodded and squeezed past to lead the way forward.

The passageway had a wooden slat floor, but the walls had been cut from rough stone. The way was lit by dim yellow bulbs in metal mesh lamps set at regular intervals. It had been a warm evening on the streets above, but there was a serious chill below. I could feel a slight but constant draught blowing across my neck which set me a little on edge. Okay, a little *more* on edge.

'Who pays the electricity bills?' I asked after we'd walked a ways in silence.

'What?'

'These lights. They're electric right? No hocus-pocus or anything.'

'No hocus-pocus,' Lily agreed.

'So who pays the electric? I mean, somebody has to, don't they? The electricity company can't be sending out a bill addressed to "the spooky broad in black". So who pays?'

Lily took hold of my arm. 'Darling. What difference does it make? Don't you think there are maybe better things to worry about right now?'

'I suppose,' I muttered. But I still would have liked to know.

The tunnel sloped downward as we went along, occasionally getting slightly narrower or wider. We passed a series of conduits marked 'British Gas', so I reckoned we were actually in a service tunnel and that they paid the bills. I didn't comment on it, though.

The passage ended at a steel, spiral staircase with steps wide enough for only one person at a time to descend. A metal grate blocked access going down, and there was a big red DANGER sign welded to the grate. It wasn't locked though, so Lily tugged it open and started down without a moment's hesitation.

'That sign there to keep people away?' I asked.

'Um-hmmm.'

'So it's not really dangerous.'

'I didn't say that.'

The steps were thin and steep, and we took our time going down. We passed a couple of extended platforms at lower levels, but continued to descend until there was no place left to go. There was another steel grate at the very bottom, but this one didn't open at Lily's touch. She tried rattling it, but it was secure. We had to perform an intricate little dance number on the narrow staircase, until Siobhan managed to wriggle down to the front. She pushed at the door a couple of times, then ploughed into it with her shoulder. It bent a bit, but didn't open. She made the rest of us climb back up a ways, then bracing herself against the handrail, launched a massive mule-kick directly against the lock.

The door snapped open.

The only lights at the bottom were those dangling from the edge of the spiral stairs. They cast a circle of illumination for a distance of ten yards, but beyond that was purest black. For all you could see, there might have been a brick wall out there, or a silent army. I started feeling creeped-out again, but then I caught the glint of a dented old Coke can lying under the very last of the metal steps. *God bless America*, I thought.

'Darling?' Lily said. Siobhan had already removed the flashlights from the bag she been carrying over her shoulder. She handed one to Lily and kept the other for herself. Lily flipped hers on – it was far more powerful than the stair lights had been – revealing a wide passageway ahead. The ground was hard-packed soil, the walls sharp edges of rough-hewn rock. Siobhan ran her flashlight beam up along the ceiling and across the sides of the passage. There was nothing to be seen or heard.

'You'd think there'd be rats and stuff down here,' I said.

'No. The rats know better,' Lily said. Then she led the way on.

Very reassuring.

The passage wasn't especially steep, but it led us inexorably farther down. The air grew cooler as we went and the intensity of the draught that blew through the tunnel became stronger. It also changed direction, and now blew directly in our faces. By the time the passageway levelled out and widened enough that the flashlight beams could no longer pick out the walls, it was like standing on a subway platform with a train bearing down on the station at full speed. The eerie thing about that wind, though, was that it didn't make a sound.

Lily led the way around an elbow bend and then up a slight grade where rough steps had been chiselled into the path, which narrowed once again. In the brief illumination of the dancing flashlight beams, I saw that markings were carved into the walls here. At first I thought they were runes, but they had a different aspect from the ones I'd seen. I saw words carved into the stone, as well, in what looked to me like a gibberish hybrid of Latin and Hebrew. There were markings which may have been words, but in an alphabet unlike any I'd ever come across. At one point, I reached out and touched my finger to one of the carvings, then drew it back just as fast.

The walls felt as cold as the key to the door had been hot.

The corridor took another snakey turn so sharp that Lily, though she was only three or four yards in front of me, briefly disappeared from my sight. Like a puppy that's wandered ahead of its master, I glanced back over my shoulder at Siobhan for reassurance. When I saw the look on her face – that same itchy expression she'd had before the Thule ambush at Woodhenge – I wished I hadn't.

Coming out the other side of the dogleg, I saw that the path sloped up and then down again, with a source of light spilling out ahead of us that illuminated the little bump in the road. Uma leaned over Lily's shoulder as the older woman said something in her ear. Lily turned off her flashlight and handed it to Uma. Against the bright backlight, I saw her go up the path, then dip down out of sight on the downhill side. Uma waited behind.

'What gives?' I asked as Siobhan and I came up beside her.

'She said to wait.'

'What for?'

'Just do as you're told,' Siobhan snapped at me.

A few seconds later, Lily's silhouette reappeared atop the crest and waved us on. As we followed on up the path, the light from ahead grew brighter. Uma handed the flashlight to Siobhan, who stuffed it back in her bag along with the one she'd been carrying. There was no need for them here.

As the path led back down, I saw the frame of a large doorway through which the light and the cold wind cascaded. Lily stood in the doorway, arms extended outward. As we came up behind her, I found I couldn't look straight ahead for the brightness of the glare. Lily turned around to face us and I swear she'd picked up a bit of a tan from the light. Her rosy fat cheeks made her look like a cherubic Florida grandmother.

'Come,' she said. And stepped into the light.

We were immersed in it as we stepped though the doorway, though I couldn't figure out where the light actually came from. I had to squint and hold my hand up to my forehead to see anything at all, but I could tell that we'd passed into an enormous underground chamber. The light was everywhere, surrounding us like an electrified fog. We left brief trails of darkness in it as we moved, like writing with your finger on frosted glass. And there was a low, constant humming noise in here, as if the same note was struck in several different octaves, echoed and held. I found it an oddly comforting sound.

Lily shielded her eyes with the crook of her elbow. 'The glasses,' she said, over her shoulder. Her voice was all but lost in the hum.

Siobhan reached into her bag of tricks and pulled out four pairs of sunglasses. Lily took a pair of round, John Lennon shades, while Uma and Siobhan put on very stylish Wayfarers. I ended up with a pair of sub-Roy Orbison dime store specials. I almost voiced a gripe – Uma looked totally cool in hers – but decided this wasn't a good time.

Even with the sunglasses it was tough not to squint, but at least I could make out more of the space we were in. It was, indeed, enormous; though hard to see the roof, I estimated it to be sixty feet high. The chamber had to be a couple of hundred feet across, and generally round in shape as near as I could tell. What I hadn't been able to discern before putting the shades on were the large stones which were set in the ground in the middle of the chamber and in rows a few feet out from the walls at various points. The stones were of varying height and shape: some three times human size, others no bigger than a shoe box. They reminded me a little bit of the dolmens at Stonehenge, but these stones were more refined, more manifestly *sculpted* and precise. If they were arranged in a pattern, I couldn't discern what the nature of it was from where we stood, but there was a strong sense of regularity about the positions.

And the stones appeared to be a part of the light. You had to stare at one very carefully in order to pick it out. I couldn't tell if the material of the stone absorbed the ambient light or was the actual source of it.

'What is this place?' I asked Lily. The light practically swallowed my words, insinuating itself as a palpable presence in my open mouth.

'It is old beyond memory. It's the fountain of hope. This is the heart of London, the heart of Britain,' she yelled in response. It came out as a whisper. 'It is one of the hearts of the world.'

Well, that explained it then.

'Is it safe?' I asked.

Lily turned around, and despite the intensity of the glare, lowered her glasses and stared at me through a squint.

I got the message.

'I have dreamed of this place,' Uma said. She was looking all around, head turning slow circles, her mouth gaping wide with wonder and glee. 'But I thought it was heaven.'

'Maybe it is, darling,' Lily said. 'But it's gonna go straight to hell if we don't get started.'

Uma nodded, but seemed reluctant to move. Lily took the bag from Siobhan and rifled through it. She removed from it a silver rod, perhaps six inches long, with delicate etchings engraved in the handle which culminated in a tiny hand, with a single, sharp pointing finger jutting from the end.

'Mene, mene tekel upharsin,' I said. I remembered the biblical words from an episode of *Night Gallery*.

Lily looked up at me. 'That's a funny thing to say. You want I should write it on the wall with the *yad*?' She held up the silver pointer.

'I don't know why I said it. I suppose this feels like the lion's den.'

'But you know the words were written on Belshazzar's wall, not in the den of lions. And Daniel had an angel to protect him.'

'Sunday school was a lot of years ago,' I said. Not to mention *Night Gallery*. 'And we've got Siobhan.'

Lily shrugged. Then she walked out toward the middle of the great chamber and squatted down on the ground. Using the pointer, the *yad*, she began drawing patterns in the dirt. I took another look around and realized that the stones were indeed set into a rough pattern: a kind of series of bridged quincunxes. Lily traced lines connecting the pillars that formed the centre of each quincunx. Uma stood, arms crossed over her chest, silently monitoring.

The sound was what first alerted me.

The humming noise had grown louder, taking on new resonance as Lily worked. The sound came from all around us and, I found myself thinking, from *within* as well. I've heard the expression 'music of the spheres' over the years, and I know it's supposed to refer to the perfect sound ostensibly made by the very movements of the universe, but I can't imagine that if such music exists, it could sound any more lovely than what I heard in that great chamber beneath London.

Until a discordant note crept in.

I thought the key being struck – where? by what? – was merely shifting. It added an even greater richness at first, which as great artists have always known, the slightest flaw in perfection always does. The note initially sounded like a low-pitched counter-hum to the larger harmony. But then a second off-note was struck. And a third. And suddenly the soothing, paradisiacal hum raised goosebumps on my arms.

The light changed, too; Lily's doodles with the *yad* had not added any more intensity to the light, but adjusted the focus of it, providing a kind of crystalline clarity to my vision. Every line and plane took on greater sharpness and definition. It felt a bit like when you look through another person's glasses, but without the accompanying dizziness. It was, I found myself musing, the way the world had always been meant to be seen.

But that clarity began to fade. The light remained bright, but became occluded, opaque. I thought perhaps that this, too, was in my imagination at first, but when I waved my hand in front of me, the trails of darkness appeared and did not disperse quite so quickly. And Uma and Lily were getting harder to see as the light grew denser. I glanced at Siobhan, who was already moving toward the others. I followed her, careful not to step on any of the lines in the ground Lily had drawn.

If stepping on a sidewalk crack breaks your mother's back, I dreaded to think what treading on one of these babies might lead to.

Lily stopped her work, and both she and Uma looked all around the chamber. The *yad* in her hand was pointing toward the roof. I glanced up and saw long tendrils of darkness swimming like black eels in the thickening light above us. Siobhan had her gun in her hand, and even with her shades on, I recognized the 'itchy' look on her face. Lily said something I couldn't hear, then quickly dropped to the ground and traced more patterns in the dirt.

That's when the little kids appeared.

A dozen of them, all about three feet tall.

I don't know how they got there; the light had grown so heavy that they could have come from anywhere, even the passageway by which we had entered. And for all I knew there were a hundred other such portals into the chamber. All I know is that in the middle of the night, in that bizarre chamber under the East End of London with its magical light and wondrous song – at the heart of the world, if Lily was to be believed (and who was I to doubt her?) – we were surrounded by a circle of children, as if on some very weird kindergarten outing.

Children wearing black robes and droopy black hats.

Children carrying sharp little knives and glinting pick-axes.

Children with long red beards.

Children who, a moment of logic and clarity revealed, were not children at all, but stunted, dwarflike creatures.

'*Alfar*,' Lily whispered.

Snow White's little buddies smiled as one. They had sharp teeth which glinted bright as their deadly honed tools.

'Kill them,' Lily yelled.

They came at us.

TWENTY

Siobhan began shooting as soon as Lily yelled: a flurry of rounds point-blank into the nearest of the dwarves. The thing lost hold of its axe as the impact sent it hurtling backwards. The creature's features were pulped into a chopped blob of dark grue, its pointy teeth showering to the ground like silver snowflakes. Whatever these little bastards were, they could be hurt, though the dwarf's spurting blood sizzled when it touched the floor of the chamber. The dwarf flailed about on the ground, boiling black fluids pumping from its ruined face. The damn thing didn't want to die.

Siobhan blew away two more of the midget monsters, who screamed like hungry babies when they got hit. One of them lay still on the ground, but the other charged straight at Siobhan, waving its knife in front of it. Siobhan kicked out at it, but the dwarf-thing buried the blade in the back of her right calf. Siobhan let out a scream as she fell over backwards, but still managed to press the barrel of the gun to the dwarf's back and empty her clip.

The dwarf was virtually cut in half when she was done.

I only had time to catch a glimpse of Uma fending off another group of the creatures around Lily, who continued sketching in the ground with her pointer, when one of the dwarves came running toward me. Its face was lined with thick ridges and there were . . . *things* . . . wriggling around in its beard. The shiny pick-axe in its hand definitely had my attention, but it was hard to look away from its black, bird-like eyes. It swiped at me, using the edge of the blade like a scythe and only a well-timed leap straight up into the air, saved me losing a foot.

The dwarf had run under and past, but pivoted like a second-baseman turning a double play and came back at me. Another pair of dwarves approached from behind and I quickly looked for a rock or anything else that might serve as a weapon.

Nothing.

Five shots rang out from the side and one of the pair of dwarves went down under the hail of Siobhan's bullets. The unstoppable Irishwoman, dragging her injured leg behind her, was already heading back in Uma's direction.

The two remaining dwarves came at me from opposite sides, ignoring their injured buddy and grinning their horrid, pointy-toothed grins. I tensed the muscles in my legs preparing to jump again, figuring my height was my only real advantage in the fight.

The dwarves raised their blades, then froze.

The hum, which had degenerated into a shrill and almost painful cacophony, again took on a warm, harmonious lilt. The light brightened and cleared a bit, forcing the dwarves to cringe and shield their eyes. I hazarded a glance away from my diminutive foes and saw that all the dwarves were cowering where they stood. Not a moment too soon, either, as three of the little fuckers were advancing on Uma, who'd fallen, bloody, to the ground beside Lily, who was holding off a pick-wielding dwarf with the point of the *yad*. Siobhan had locked her sights on one of the attacking dwarves, but she, too, started looking around her.

The ground rumbled slightly – 2.8 on the Richter: trust a native Angelino – and for just a second the hum achieved its perfect harmonic. It soon went sour again, though it retained more of its harmony, only to be drowned out by a harsh, painful sound, as of the flesh of a great beast being torn.

The ground which Lily had been marking started to roil and bubble. The dirt rose up from the floor in a slow-motion geyser, forming a huge mound. Chunks of soil flaked off the mound, as if an invisible sculptor was having at it with a chisel, until all that was left was the shape of a man.

While the dwarves stood stunned, Lily scrambled to her feet and touched her finger to the forehead of the man-shaped mound.

With a liquid scream like waves crashing against a rocky shore, the golem came to life.

As soon the golem moved, so did the dwarves. The light in the chamber flickered, as did the hum which intermittently sounded as smooth as Stan Getz and as harsh as Ornette Coleman. Whatever sensitivities the great chamber held must have been confused by the presence of two such massively contradictory forces.

The golem swept into action against the dwarves presenting the immediate threat to Lily and Uma. It snatched the nearest one up in its massive hands and simply mashed it into a ball, like crumpling a sheet of paper, before throwing the remains aside. The other dwarves, including the two stalking me, turned and ran toward the golem in a concerted attack. The golem picked up two more of the little sacks of shit, wound itself up and like a hammer-thrower at the Olympics, launched the suckers into flight. I followed the arc of one as it flew high into the air before coming to an abrupt face-first stop against a stone wall. I didn't see the other, but I heard it land with a sickening crunch.

'Short people got *no reason* to live,' I found myself singing. The chamber, I thought, hummed along.

Two more of the creatures had come in low – not that they had much choice – and were chopping away at the golem's lower half with their axes. Chunks of golem . . . flesh? . . . were coming off under their blows. The golem swatted one away so hard that its spine snapped, its upper torso twisted almost all the way around, but the second scored a deep cut in the back of the golem's knee, sending the inhuman thing sprawling. The dwarf quickly ran up to bury its blade in the golem's head when Uma came out of nowhere like a streak, with both feet flying. She caught the dwarf broadside and sent it tumbling away from the golem. Uma landed on her pride with rather a thud, knocking the wind out of her. Another dwarf came running up, blade in hand, but a well-aimed shot to the gut from Siobhan, apparently the last in her clip, diverted the knife from its target. The dwarf quickly got to its feet, but it was too late. The golem had reformed itself – its leg looked perfect again – and clapped its hands to the dwarf's head. The golem jerked its arms and the little creature was just a pair of shoulders.

There were only three of the midget monsters left now and they were slowly circling the golem, feinting at it, but I didn't believe they had a chance. Siobhan was slapping a fresh clip into her gun, and both Uma and Lily were back on their feet. Lily stood in the midst of the large pattern she had drawn, eyes closed, lips moving, swaying slightly as she spoke, as I remembered seeing old men in synagogues do when they prayed. The light grew ever clearer, the chamber's hum ever stronger and sweeter, and I strongly sensed that the ritual of protection was almost complete.

The head shot that took Lily out put Lee Harvey Oswald (or whoever it was on the grassy knoll) to shame.

Uma screamed as the *tzaddik's* brains literally erupted out of the hole in her head. The light dimmed again and the homophonous hum became the bitter squeal of a Bernard Herrmann violin chorus.

A line of five dark figures emerged into the flickering light, and I froze as the nightmare vision that had been haunting me – the dark image from my dreams – became real before me. They were only men after all, I realized after a minute, but I saw the outlines of the weapons in their hands and started moving. I heard shots ring out, the sound of the bullets pinging close off ancient stone, but I never stopped. Siobhan was half on her feet and I scooped her up as I ran along, propelling us over to the pillar of rock behind which Uma had dragged Lily. Siobhan pushed me away as we got there, swivelling around, gun held out before her.

The dark figures – the Thule, of course – had stepped back into the increasingly murky and opaque light.

The golem continued to be circled by its tiny assailants. One or more of the Thule tried shooting at the golem, but though he was on target the lead had no impact on a creature made of earth and clay. Siobhan fired a couple of rounds in the Thules' direction, but it was impossible to draw a bead on them or to learn if her aim was true.

Stalemate.

Uma leaned over Lily, who still held the silver *yad* clutched tightly in her hand. Incredibly, the *lamed vavnik* wasn't dead, but the hole in her head and the sea of blood in which she lay indicated that she would be in a matter of minutes, if not seconds.

'What do we do?' I asked.

Uma just shook her head. Tears streamed down her face as she clutched Lily's pale hand between her own.

'Come out and die quickly,' a scratchy voice called across the chamber. 'The Jew is dead. The monster dies with her. If you make us wait, you will suffer for it.'

'Eat me, you Nazi cunts,' Siobhan replied. She fired off another shot as an exclamation point.

'Shit,' I said. 'Will the golem die with her?'

Uma just continued to shake her head. I don't know if she didn't know, wouldn't say or was simply shocked beyond caring. I glanced out at the golem, still parrying with the evil dwarves, and suddenly it did look frailer to me. I thought I could see little bits of clay flaking off its body.

'Martin,' a thin voice croaked.

Sometimes the dead won't die: with bits of her brain visible in her dyed hair, Lily's brown eyes fluttered open. Blood cascaded out from between her desiccated lips and from her broken nose. I should have been thrilled or amazed or incredulous.

'What do we do?' I shrieked in panic. Uma had stopped crying, her face gone slack with astonishment. She continued to clutch Lily's hand.

'Darling,' she squeaked, and with her other hand, and what I can only imagine was the most monumental of human – or whatever she was – efforts, Lily raised up her other hand, still holding the smaller hand of the *yad*. Her lips opened and a sound of unholy pain escaped from her throat, along with another bubble of brackish blood. She lifted the *yad* up and touched it to a point in the middle of my forehead.

I felt the electric bolt like a blow from a jackhammer. It sent me tumbling, literally, ass-backward. My vision exploded into a field of purest white light. I felt my heart stop, the blood freeze in my veins. I tasted something charred on the back of my tongue and I smelled . . .

I smelled a field of lilies.

I raised my head and saw Uma gaping at me, mouth hanging open. She still held tight to Lily's now lifeless hand. I crawled back over to them and looked at the *tzaddik*. Her eyes were shut, the blood no longer pumping from her wounds. Despite the horrendous injuries done to her, she looked remarkably peaceful.

The *yad* had burned and gone black in her hand.

I pressed two fingers to my lips and then touched them to hers.

'They're bound to come for us any minute now,' Siobhan warned.

I saw that the golem was still alive, but had fallen to its knees. The dwarves were hacking away at it, piece by piece. It feebly swatted at them, but it was clearly running out of time.

As were we.

'Baba Dutty,' I said.

Uma continued to gape at me.

'Baba Dutty,' I said again.

'He is dead,' Uma told me. And two plus two equals four.

'I know,' I said. I tapped the side of my head. 'But he's also in here.'

'Well, let him out,' Uma yelled.

'I don't know how.'

'How do you know he is in there?'

'I just *know*,' I told her. 'I think he needs a . . . ceremony.'

'Fucking hell!' Uma said. It was the first profanity I'd ever heard her use.

'If you're going to do something, it'd better be fast,' Siobhan yelled. I saw the line of dark figures coming toward us in the distance. Siobhan squeezed off two more ineffectual shots.

'The stone,' Uma cried, staring up the weird pillar.

And I saw it, too, It wasn't decorated or consecrated as the one in Baba Dutty's *oufò* had been, but it looked exactly like a *poteau-mitan*, right down to the little platform at the base of the pillar.

'What do we do?' I asked.

'I'm not sure,' Uma said. She was looking all around her as if the answer might be written somewhere.

'Ladies . . .' Siobhan hissed.

'An offering,' Uma yelled, slapping her palm against her forehead.

'What? What do we offer?'

Siobhan was starting to fire regularly now. How many bullets did she have left?

'I don't know,' Uma cried. 'Something rare, precious. Gold or silver, perhaps.'

Uma had a gold ring on her right hand. She tried to take it off, but it wouldn't budge. 'It's bloody stuck!'

I grabbed her hand and twisted the ring. I pulled until she screamed.

No go.

'Last clip,' Siobhan yelled. She started shooting again.

'Do the coins here have any silver in them?' I asked, slapping at my pockets.

'I don't think so.'

There was another object in my pocket. Something round. I'd been carrying it with my loose change for days, stuffing it into my trouser pocket every morning without even thinking about it.

The signet ring Siobhan had sliced off the dead Thule's hand. I held it up in front of Uma's face.

'Yes!' she shrieked.

I threw myself at the base of the pillar. I didn't have a clue what I was doing. I closed my eyes and pictured Baba Dutty's big black face. I imagined myself back in the *oufò*, rutting with Alourdes.

I slapped the ring down on the base of the would-be *poteau-mitan*.

That now way-too-familiar bolt of pain rocketed through the back of my head. I was starting to feel as lit up as a pinball machine flashing TILT.

Baba Dutty's bellowing belly-laugh escaped through my lips.

'Mother of god,' I heard Siobhan say.

I stood up, hands perched on either side of the stone pillar. Words escaped my lips without my knowing even what they meant:

'*Papa Legba ouvri baye-a pou mwen. Pou mwen pase. Le ma tounen, ma salyie loa yo.*'

Another thunderous crack echoed through the chamber, like a rending of the earth itself. I felt my body start to jerk and spasm as the crackle of mad electricity sizzled up and down my spine. I'd been through this once before, though, and recognized the *danse-loa* for what it was. I felt the presence enter me like hot cocoa filling a mug. I was once again *cheval*. But not, I sensed, for Maître Carrefour this time. Unlike the mounting in the Liverpool *oufò*, I maintained a sense of my own identity and awareness.

This was a much greater *loa* coming through.

I stepped back from the *poteau-mitan* and looked down on Uma. She bowed her head and looked away.

'Vishnu,' I heard her say. And I knew that was my name. Though from somewhere I heard Baba Dutty laugh, for to him my name was Samedi.

And from someplace else – though it could only have been a place deep within myself – I heard another voice; it was an old woman's voice and she called me by a different name yet.

'*Uriel*,' she said. 'Darling.'

And this name, too, belonged to me.

The golem, which lay on its back, savaged by the evil dwarves known to the Norse as the *Alfar*, suddenly rose up. The dwarves looked puzzled for a moment, then looked past the golem at me.

'Hot enough for you?' I cackled.

They ran.

I strode out into the middle of the complex pattern which the *lamed vavnik* had etched into the ground of the great chamber at London's heart. I spoke in a mixed babble of words that I had no possible means to understand: Hindi, Hebrew, a slave's corrupted French. I swayed and twirled and danced as I spoke, and with each word the light around me grew brighter and crisper, the humming music of the spheres more perfect, more exact until the notes formed a name, and that name was the fabric of pure being.

Guns were fired from the distance, but the bullets burned and melted in mid-air. The light gathered around me, swirling and billowing, all trace of darkness banished in its blinding embrace. The golem strode past me, gathering Uma and Siobhan in its arms, shielding them within the fierce embrace of its all-encompassing and inhuman grasp.

The light grew brighter still, till nothing could be seen through its dazzle. A vortex of incandescence spun around me, shooting off waves of power that burned away all evil before it. There were screams from the corners of the chamber, but they were quickly doused by the purity of the light. The hum achieved the limits of unisonance: a perfect, implacable, unsustainable harmony.

And then it was gone.

I stood there, basking in the afterglow for a time I couldn't measure. There were voices in my head, but they were drifting, fading. I thought I heard Lily and Baba Dutty share a laugh, but that too faded like a dream in the morning light.

'Marty?' Uma said. She approached me warily, Siobhan a half-step behind. They both looked awe-struck. The golem stood where they left it, *golem*-like.

'Yeah,' I said. 'It's only me.'

'Bloody hell,' Uma said, unable to restrain a blistering smile.

'Maybe you're not such a wanker after all, Martin Burns,' Siobhan said.

High praise, indeed.

There was no trace of the murderous midgets or their Thule masters in the chamber. Uma pointed out a row of dark lines in the floor and suggested that might be their remains, but there was no way of knowing for sure.

'It does not really matter,' Uma said. 'This lot may be dead, but there are more out there.'

'Well, that's a cheery note,' I said.

'That is simply the way it is. There are *always* more of them.'

'Yeah, but *this* is safe now, right?' I waved at the bright, humming chamber.

'Yes,' Uma said. I let out a big sigh. 'For now.'

I'll take a win where I can steal it.

'What about the old woman?' Siobhan asked. 'Do we take her body with us?'

'No,' I said. Uma looked a little surprised. 'This is the place for her. It's where she should rest.'

'How do we get out of here without her?'

'It knows the way,' I said, pointing at the golem. 'Don't you?'

The golem, which hadn't moved since letting Uma and Siobhan go, now came forward. It walked past us toward a doorway opposite the one through which we'd entered.

'Good boy, Fido,' I said.

The golem, of course, had no face, couldn't roll its eyes at me or curl its lip. It did turn its head as it went by though, and I got the message.

Its name was *not* Fido.

We walked in silence through the narrow tunnels that led ever upward. The golem set a quick pace and though we'd bandaged Siobhan's leg as best we could, it wasn't easy keeping up. At times it seemed like we were going in circles, but the corridors were so featureless and samey that it was difficult to be sure.

We had no choice but to trust the golem.

After a while, the old stone tunnels gave way to more obviously modern ones. The walls became concrete, electric lights flickered dimly above and the mark of British Gas was once more to be seen. The golem marched on, oblivious to it all.

It led us up a small staircase which culminated in a solid brick wall. You could sort of see the outline of where a doorway must once have been, but it had been bricked over decades, if not centuries before. There was no getting through without dynamite.

I cleared my throat at the golem. It ignored me.

It punched its massive arm through a foot of solid brick. It kept punching until there was a gap big enough for us to crawl through.

Then it stepped back out of the way.

'Fourth floor,' I said. 'Plastic basilicas, women's lingerie, wet dreams and other picture postcards. All out.'

Uma hauled herself up and through the hole in the wall. She put a hand out to help Siobhan climb through after her. The Irishwoman had a hard time, but issued not a word of complaint. I started to follow her through, taking Uma's arm, but I stopped with one leg dangling on either side of the gap.

'Marty?' Uma said.

'Something I gotta do,' I told her.

I went back into the tunnel and down two steps to where the golem waited. I reached up and stuck my fingers into its slit of a mouth. I removed the tiny fragment of parchment.

The golem crumbled in front of my eyes. It was standing there, then it was gone.

I stared at the dry dust, already drifting away down the steps. 'Thank you, darling,' someone said.

It was dark on the other side of the hole in the wall. That was because, we soon discovered, we were standing in a broom closet. Uma opened the door, and we stepped out into the crypt of Christ Church, Spitalfields. We knew that because there was a big sign draped across the wall, along with a list of the social services provided therein. An old black man sat at a table in the middle of the room, reading a newspaper and handrolling a cigarette. He all but jumped out of his socks when he saw us.

'Where'd you lot come from?' he demanded.

I walked up to him and put my hand on his shoulder. 'Brother,' I told him, 'there are some things you just don't want to know.'

TWENTY-ONE

'Where did you get that brilliant tan?' June Hanover asked. She wore a green power suit, but the way the colour reflected off her skin made her look kind of nauseous.

'Torquay,' I said. 'It's the English Riviera, you know.'

She cast a quizzical glance at me.

'Joke – I saw it on a tourist brochure. Actually, I hopped over to Cannes for a few days. Titty beaches and all that.'

She nodded. Obviously, if a bit sadly, that seemed to mesh with her image of me.

'Well, you look great,' she said, mustering a smile.

'Thanks.'

In fact, I did look pretty sensational, though the closest I'd been to the south of France was a slight frog in my throat. Still, I needed a cover story. That astonishing light that manifested during the final ritual beneath Spitalfields had left my skin with a deep golden glow that had yet to fade two days after the fact. No one back home would possibly believe I'd been in England for a couple of weeks. Of course, if I *did* return pasty-faced there'd only be rumours in the trades that I'd been drying out in rehab. LA's a no-win kind of town.

After emerging from the crypt of Christ Church, the three of us had managed to drag ourselves back to Uma's flat without further incident. No cops, no Thule thugs waiting for us on the street, no more evil midgets.

Just the glorious East End of London.

The gash in Siobhan's leg wasn't pretty, and it certainly could have taken a dozen or more stitches, but she would have none of it. Uma cleaned the wound and bandaged it up under Siobhan's supervision. The Irishwoman popped a handful of codeine and went to bed. Uma and I chatted for a little while, but exhaustion overcame us both quickly enough.

We fell asleep leaning against each other on Uma's living room sofa.

Both women were gone when I woke up just after noon. Uma'd left a note saying she'd be back later in the day, but I didn't feel like waiting. I was dying for a long hot shower, but there was only a bathtub in Uma's flat. I splashed water on my face, had the half-a-glass of orange juice that was left in the fridge, and let myself out.

I walked out into a lovely summer's day full of bright sunshine, a high blue sky and 72 degrees in the shade. Might have been imported straight from southern California.

Just for the hell of it, I wandered over to Uma's Indian restaurant. I found it no problem and opened the door. The place was packed as usual, but everybody in the place froze in mid-gesture and stared at me with unwelcome glances. Uma's corner table was empty and there was no sign of Siobhan. I thought for sure the waiters would recognize me, but they, too, stared at me with unease.

'Heh-heh,' I said. 'You know, I think maybe I'm in the mood for Chinese.'

I beat a hasty retreat.

Straight back to the waiting arms of the Savoy. I checked in, claimed the bags I'd left in storage before beginning my mystical adventures, then went up to my suite and immediately stripped off and had an hour-long, hot (well, *English*-hot) shower. I reacquainted myself with my old friend the mini-bar. I napped, watched a semi-dirty movie on the pay-per-view (it *was* Sean Young – score another point for the boy!) and had me a big old room service dinner.

I fell asleep watching sheepdog trials on the BBC.

'You look different, Marty,' June said.

I'd called her earlier that morning and arranged to meet her in the lobby. I thought it would be best to get the skinny from June before raising my head the rest of the way above The Business parapets.

'I'm probably just goggle-eyed from staring at all those topless mademoiselles on the beach. Oooh-la-la!'

'No, I don't think that's it. You must have done something else in France.'

'Now that you mention it . . .' I whispered conspiratorially – June leaned in closer – '. . . I did defeat the forces of evil and make the world safe for democracy.'

'Oh, you,' she said, huffing in mock exasperation. 'Just tell me: what was her name?'

'Who?'

'This so-called "force of evil".'

'I'm sure I don't know what you're talking about,' I said. But I smiled and winked at her in that patented Marty Burns, PI way, that only took forty-seven takes to get right for *Burning Bright's* opening credits.

'Fine. Be that way.'

I waved down a waiter and ordered a couple of coffees, even though this was all going on *my* tab.

'So what's the word from Doggy Island? Does Mahr still spit three times and make the evil eye at mention of my name?'

June put her hand on my arm. 'Not at all, Marty. Haven't you seen the numbers?'

I shook my head and looked puzzled.

'Didn't you even talk to your agent?' she asked, incredulous.

'No. When I lay low, I go as low as you can go. Limbo Marty Burns they call me. *Believe* me, I haven't seen or heard a thing about the show since I last spoke with you.'

'Oh, Marty. What kind of star are you?'

'Ursula Minor. So what's the story?'

'I would have brought the numbers to show you, if I'd realized. Marty, the ratings are terrific. You're on the A-list again, and all is most definitely forgiven. *Burning Bright* came in at number four on the Star charts last week and number two this week.'

'No shit,' I said. I broke out in a big smile. 'What's number one?'

'Snooker,' June said. 'Of course.'

I laughed and laughed.

'Hey, babe.'

I had to wipe my eyes, and then when I saw the fellow, wipe them again.

A tall, thin, very *European*-looking dude, dressed all in black leather, with too-close-cropped blonde hair smiled down at us. He bent down and gave June Hanover a kiss/tonsilectomy which she returned with equal fervour.

He wore a tiny nose ring and *two* of those nasty eyebrow pins.

'Hullo,' he said to me straightening up.

'Hey,' I said, trying to hide my wince.

'Marty, this is Terry. My . . .'

'Friend,' I prompted.

'Yes,' she said, looking oddly at me.

'Wows!' Terry gasped. He reached down for an item on the coffee table in front of us. 'This is perfect,' he marvelled.

It was an old bit of orange peel which had gone a bit crimson around the edge. Oxidation, I reckon.

'This is what I have been seeking,' he said.

'Huh?'

'Terry makes things,' June explained. 'Boxes, mostly. He's an artist. *Time Out* called his last event "indefatigable".'

Was that a good thing? I acted impressed to be safe. Terry tried on a Ron Howard aw-shucks looks, but the needles in his eyebrows spoiled it.

'This is like a wound,' he said, holding up the orange peel. 'A bloody wound.'

'Nice,' I said. It didn't look a damned thing like a bloody wound. I should know.

But he looked so happy, I didn't have the heart to tell him.

June wanted to take me back to Canary Wharf for more PR nonsense, but I made excuses. I gave her a hug, then she and Terry went off, his hand squeezing her ass like a little rubber ball as they left the Savoy. Go figure.

Feeling a little more confident about my status, I bit the bullet and called my agent, who had become more than a little crazed wondering where I was. Kendall even said 'hell' and 'damn' a couple of times, so I knew she was really upset. (And I was a little worried that maybe Hollywood was finally starting to get to her.) I managed to calm her down, though, and she confirmed what June had told me: *Burning Bright* was a UK hit and my boyish (if thinning) hair was still looking fair. Kendall expressed concern about my admittedly curious behaviour, but she was mollified by a cross-my-heart-and-hope- to-die promise that, first-class willing, I would be on a plane back to LA the following day at the latest.

I wandered out of the Savoy and hailed a cab.

'Where to, guv?'

'Commercial Street,' I said. 'Spitalfields.'

I got out in front of Christ Church and gaped up at the looming steeple. I shook my head, wondering if there was another building in the world as remarkable, both above *and* below. I remembered, then, Lily saying that this was only 'one of the hearts of the world', and reckoned that there probably was.

I took a leisurely stroll around the neighbourhood. I thought about stopping in for a quick pint at the nearby pub, but half-feared King might still be in there pontificating. I walked around the grim streets behind the church, but they didn't seem quite so gloomy to me as before. I turned up Brick Lane, following the route of the protest march, past the big mosque bustling with little Asian men in white robes and skull caps, the countless Balti houses and kebaberies. I wandered all the way up to the north end of the street, where a couple of bagel joints stood opposite the Indian restaurants. The contrast had struck me as odd before, but now I nodded my approval.

I walked all the way back to Whitechapel High Street and across, wending my way towards Uma's Indian restaurant. I opened the door – it was, needless to say, packed – but no one gave me a second glance. Uma was sitting in the corner with Siobhan, a tea service on the table between them. I sat down in the empty chair and the waiter immediately put a Kingfisher down in front of me, then toddled off.

'What do you recommend?' I asked, smiling.

'Get a real job,' Siobhan snarled.

'Believe me, I'm thinking about it,' I said.

'How are you feeling, Marty?' Uma asked.

'Pretty damn good, I'm surprised to say. Things are . . . good. Definitely good.'

'I am pleased to hear that.'

'How are you feeling?' I said to Siobhan.

'Fit as a fiddle and ready for love.'

'I'll bet that's a sight.'

'You'll never know,' she said. She flashed me a grin worthy of any evil dwarf.

'Are you leaving us, Marty?'

'Tomorrow,' I said. 'Hollywood beckons. Like Gregory Peck strapped to the back of the whale.'

They both looked at me oddly.

'I've got to get a life outside of the movies,' I muttered. 'So what about you two? What are you going to do?'

'There is still much to be done,' Uma said. 'There are many fights yet to be fought. Eternal vigilance is the price of liberty. So the Buddha says.'

'I thought that was Thomas Jefferson.'

Uma shrugged.

'I know it ain't Gerry Adams,' I added.

'Watch it, wanker,' Siobhan said.

'And the Thule?' I asked.

'They are still out there. They always were, they always will be.'

'That's a bit of a sour note,' I said.

'We succeeded in our task, which was no small thing. We have dealt them a blow, but they will return. Those we destroyed will be replaced by others. There are no limits, sadly, on hate.'

'And you'll keep fighting them?'

Uma gestured with her head: half-nod, half-shrug.

'How will you manage without me?'

'I think we might just find a way,' Siobhan said.

'The Thule are organized in cells,' Uma said. 'We have eliminated a particularly powerful group and word will get out. But others will come to replace them.'

'Fortunately,' Siobhan said, 'I do have just a bit of experience with organizations that work in cells.'

'I'll bet you do.'

We sat there for a while sipping our tea and beer.

'Are you looking forward to getting back to Los Angeles?' Uma asked me.

It was an exit question if ever I've heard one, but I thought about it for a minute. 'You know, I am,' I said.

And it was true. Shooting on the new season of *Burning Bright* would start in a few weeks and I realized how much I was looking forward to it.

It's taken me almost forty years of living in the City of Angels to get there, but I think I've finally gone native.

I looked up at Uma, and there was a whole laundry list of questions on the tip of my tongue, begging to be asked. I saw her eyes widen at me and the corners of her lips lift up in a slightly wry smile.

I didn't ask a one of them.

I got up and gave Uma a big hug and a wet kiss on the lips. I turned to Siobhan and saw a look of raw terror in her eyes. I knew there was a good chance that she was carrying a gun, but I took the risk.

I gave her a hug and ran out of the restaurant.

I got to the airport early, as I always do. It's a terrible and stupid compulsion, because once I arrive, I sit there nervously waiting for my boarding call. What's *really* stupid is that I get to the airport early, but then board the plane as late as I can, even though first-class passengers always get to go on first if they want. I just don't like sitting and waiting on the plane. Of course, I don't like sitting in the *airport* and waiting, either, but then neurotic compulsions have an illogic all their own, and aren't meant to be argued with.

I was having a beer in the bar. I could have gone into the special lounge reserved for first-class customers, but the people who drink in those places are exceptionally creepy. Marty Burns, Man of the People, prefers drinking with the proles.

They'd announced my plane, but were still boarding aisles 23–30, so I ordered another half-pint of Stella. Two Brits in cheap blue suits sat next to me at the bar, drinking warm beer and slapping each other's back a lot as drunks are wont to do. They'd been a bit loud, but I simply ignored them, concentrating my attention on the amber delights of Belgium's finest brewery (under licence). I hadn't noticed the Asian gentleman who came in.

'Fucking Paki,' I heard one of the blue suits say.

His pal nodded. 'Bloody everywhere. Fuckers.'

The Asian man had to have heard them, but he ignored it. He paid for his Coca-Cola and thanked the bartender politely. He sat down at a little table away from the bar.

I planned to ignore the bastards, too. They were boarding the last rows on my flight, so I picked my change off the bar and dropped it in my pocket. My hand brushed against something already in there and I pulled out the little piece of parchment that I'd removed from the mouth of the golem.

Written on it was a single word in Hebrew.

'I remember when this was still a white man's country,' blue suit number two said. 'A little less dark is what this country needs.'

I looked again at the word on the parchment. I put it back in my pocket.

Then I hauled off and slugged the racist pig as hard as I could hit. He fell off his barstool and hit the ground with a thud. His buddy cowered when I turned to face him.

'A little bloody tolerance is what we *all* need,' I said.

I saw the bartender reach for the telephone.

I heard the final boarding call for my flight.

I hazarded a quick glance at the Asian dude with the Coke. He raised his glass to me and smiled broadly. I nodded back at him and ran.

I made the plane just in time.

AFTERWORD &
ACKNOWLEDGEMENTS

I've taken the usual author's liberties in this novel, with everything from bits of London geography, to the no doubt sacred rites, beliefs and mythologies of several religions and cultures. But good golly, that's why they call it fiction.

Nevertheless, I have tried not to wander *too* far afield in most regards, and want to acknowledge a few sources which provided useful information:

One cannot write about the East End, and Christ Church, Spitalfields, in particular, without acknowledging the often astonishing work of Iain Sinclair, the poet laureate of mysterious London. Those interested in reading Sinclair's observations about Nicholas Hawksmoor's (literally) fabulous churches are directed to *Lud Heat & Suicide Bridge*. I came to Sinclair by way of Alan Moore and Eddie Campbell's remarkable *From Hell*, a brilliant retelling of the story of the Whitechapel murders in comic book form. I have no idea if Moore's version of events bears even the faintest relation to the truth, but the quality of art and storytelling is uniformly brilliant and everyone really should buy it. Those intrigued by Hawksmoor may also want to check out Peter Ackroyd's somewhat elliptical novel, and Kerry Downes' scholarly study of the architect and his works, both of which are entitled *Hawksmoor*. *Architectural Design Profile #22* is a study of Christ Church, Spitalfields, edited by Colin Amery, John Martin Robinson and Gavin Stamp. Good luck finding a copy.

Two excellent reference books which proved helpful are *The London Encyclopaedia*, a treasure edited by Ben Weinreb & Christopher Hibbert; and *Dictionary of Jewish Lore and Legend* by Alan Unterman. All errors and distortions of fact in the novel (deliberate or otherwise) are, of course, entirely attributable to me.

I also have to thank several people for their kind contributions toward the completion of this book: Louis Schechter for his support; Gordon Van Gelder for his editorial advice and exceptionally good nature (not to mention the lyrics to *H. R. Pufnstuff*); and, of course, Mr Stephen Jones.

Thanks most of all to Jane . . . for everything else. Yet again!